Star Wolf
A Shattered Galaxy Novel
by
David G. Johnson

To Chris,
Keep the faith.

David Johnson

25th 3:1

Cover artwork by Elsbro (https://www.fiverr.com/elsbro)

Cover design courtesy of Mary C. Findley

Dedication

To God and His Son, Jesus Christ, without whom nothing in my life would be possible.

To my daughter, Ariel, and my wife, Amy, who put up with a moody curmudgeon, always struggling to find time to write. Without you, none of this would have come to fruition. Thank you for supporting and enabling my dreams.

To the members of my author group, Iron Sharpening Iron, you are a constant source of strength and support. Your input was invaluable.

Finally, to one of my greatest fans, Ben B., for following me out of Fantasy and into Outer Space.

Acknowledgments

This section is always the hardest. There are so many to thank, and so many opportunities to inadvertently forget someone. Thanks to my cover artist, Elsbro (the link to his Fiverr.com page is below). Thanks to Mary Findley, the fantastic designer who took Elsbro's artwork and made it into a brilliant cover as well as doing my print and ebook formatting.

Thanks to my editor, Anna Lindsay (author page linked below), who, even when I hit some slowdowns, didn't give up on encouraging me to finish and whose work made this book much better thanks to her input. Thanks to my ISI groupmate Cindy who kept herding me off Facebook and back into my writing desk. Thanks to Dr. Knight, who consulted on some medical details. Thanks to my beta readers, Jim, Sherry, and Kessie (whose Amazon author page links are below) for helping me work out a few kinks.

Last but not least thanks to the fans and readers who have supported my other books and who were clamoring for more. I pray that this new and futuristic setting, with an expanded imagining of a universe in which our Lord tarries on His return until a time when mankind reaches the stars, is one which you will find thoroughly entertaining, edifying, and satisfying. Without all of you, none of this would be possible.

Elsbro—cover artwork: https://www.fiverr.com/elsbro

Mary Findley—cover design: https://elkjerkyforthesoul.wordpress.com/image-displays/

Anna Lindsay—author/editor: https://smile.amazon.com/Anna-Lindsay/e/B00O8EGKQ2

Jim Dempsey—author/beta-reader: https://smile.amazon.com/Parenting-Unchained-Overcoming-Deceptions-Christian-ebook/dp/B00MAHBUQO

Sherry Chamblee—author/beta-reader:
https://smile.amazon.com/Sherry-Chamblee/e/B00BA06RJ2
K.M. Carroll—author/beta-reader:

https://smile.amazon.com/K.-M.-Carroll/e/B00H2WIUN8

Table of Contents

Foreword

For those of you familiar with my writing, this brief foreword will be no surprise. For those of you for whom Star Wolf is the first of my works you have encountered, I promise to keep this foreword brief so you may continue on to the story.

I try to let everyone know right up front that I am a Christian author. I personally hold a Christian worldview, and all of my novels are necessarily written from this worldview, as I have no other worldview from which to write.

That being said, however, I endeavor in all my works to primarily write an entertaining story. I write *for* my readers, not *at* them. This is not in any way a sermon wrapped in a story. I know many Christian works are, unfortunately, which has left many non-Christian readers with an understandable skepticism toward works by known Christian authors.

I am happy to report that I have fans and solid reviewers who have enjoyed my work without sharing my worldview. I write as a long-time fan of fantasy and science fiction, who happens to be a Christian. There are definitely Christian themes in my works, but I strive, with every novel, to make them intrinsic to the story, endemic to the situation as they might naturally arise in the lives of characters, some of whom are people of faith.

I also do my best to steer away from the "Christians are good guys, non-Christians are bad guys" trope that permeates so much "Christian fiction". I build complex characters and hence one can find honor, nobility, and heroism, or, just as in real life, treachery, misguided zeal, and base behavior, both in those who label themselves Christians and in those who do not.

Christians are far from perfect, and non-Christians are not all bad. You will find contained in this novel a balance of characters on both sides of the faith-fence to love and to loathe. If I managed paint my characters as complex, flawed, and unpredictable as real people are, I have done my job.

It is also important that my readers understand it is not necessary to share my worldview to enjoy my stories. My novels are written to be great adventure stories. However, in the afterword of each novel, I do take the time to share my own testimony of how I came to faith, and what faith in Christ means to me. For those not interested in delving deeper into that aspect of the author, I assure you that you will miss nothing of pertinence to the story itself by skipping the afterword. It is included solely for the benefit of those who may be curious about what I believe and why.

Without further ado, we now move into our adventure. I hope you will have as much fun reading this story as I have had writing it. If so, leaving a review on Amazon or Goodreads is always a helpful way to show appreciation. I do not ask that anyone necessarily leave a positive review, only an honest one. Those are always welcome, ideally *after actually reading the book*, of course.

KNOWN GALAXY – ACCORDING TO MAN

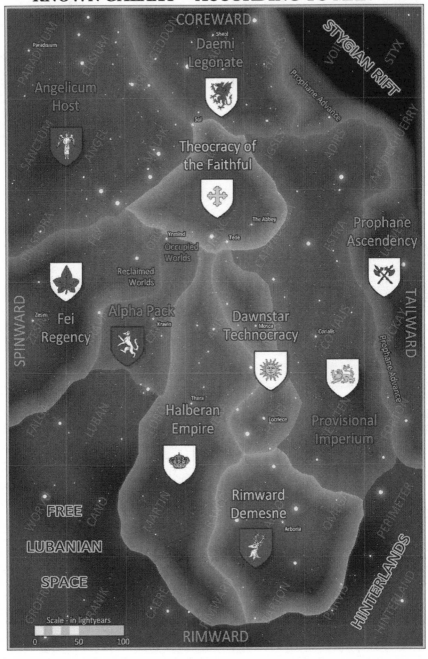

FACTION ALLIANCE CHART

SHATTERED GALAXY FACTIONS
NON-HUMANS

Prophane Ascendency   Daemi Legonate   Angelicum Host   Fei Regency   Alpha Pack

HUMANITI

The Imperium   *The Faithful*   *The New Empire*

Provisional Imperium Dawnstar Technocracy Theocracy of the   Halberan Empire Rimward Demesne
(High Archon Zarsus)   (Tubal)   Faithful (Enoch)   (Seth)   (Phoebe)

One – Freedom Flight

Sharp cracks punctuated John Salzmann's rage-filled bellows and his wife Elena's shrieks of agony. The tortured couple, backs bared and bleeding, hung from shackles that bound their wrists and denied them even the comfort of collapse. John yanked futilely at his chains and roared in frustration, his fury focused on the rotund, balding, pock-faced inquisitor whose whip continued to alternate between his two targets.

John barely recognized his own voice, much less the unbearable wail coming from his beloved Elena. He had never heard her scream in pain before. It was a sound he wished never to hear again. Yet the hard and passionless face of their tormentor remained utterly indifferent to the woes of his victims. It was not the way of the Faithful, but John could not repress his inward desire to repay tenfold every stroke the inquisitor administered to his beloved Elena.

The smell of blood and fear filled the chamber. Hanging in agony, skin shredded, face twisted in rage, John bore little resemblance to the athletic, carefree, towheaded youth he had been when he first met Elena. Yet, even after their years together on Tede, even after all the suffering they had endured in this prison, Elena's long chestnut hair and large brown eyes appeared as beautiful to John as they had the day they met. He prayed the Lion of Judah would come and whisk her away to anywhere far from the horror of this place. The bloody patchwork pattern on her skin bore witness that the inquisitor had been working diligently at his task for quite some time.

"You Faithful beat all I've ever seen," said the torturer. "You're all meek as lambs, yet tough as iron. I've had battle-hardened soldiers break quicker than this."

Just then, the door from the prisoner corridor opened, and a single, silvery-gray furred Lubanian in guard's uniform entered. The very sight of a man-sized wolf, dressed in human clothes and walking about on hind legs, was enough to distract

John from his inquisitor-inflicted agony. The guard's lupine snout protruded from beneath the visor of his tac-helmet. There were several Lubanian guards at this prison, but John still found the sight of them disturbing.

On John and Elena's homeworld of Tede, aliens were never permitted outside the starport. Aliens were common enough on the core world where John had studied medicine and done his residency, but he had rarely interacted with them. His focus was on treating humans, the only specialty he would need on Tede.

Humaniti had discovered a handful of major and thousands of minor alien species during their exploration of space, but Lubanians were one of the most commonly encountered aliens on human worlds, especially along the spinward borders of Humaniti space.

The new arrival took up a position near the door. The alien guard seemed to be staring at him, but who knew for certain what those wolfish eyes were doing beneath the tac helmet's shaded visor. The other two human guards ignored the newcomer completely, and the jailor paid him no more than a passing glance before returning to his monologue. The torturer growled in John's ear, grabbing a handful of bloodied blonde hair and yanking John's head back to guarantee full attention.

"Perhaps it is time for a new tactic. I've interrogated enough of you Faithful to know you'll never betray your friends to save yourself. You wouldn't even if I peeled every inch of skin from your bones as an encouragement.

"However," the jailor whispered into John's ear. "I've never had the pleasure of interrogating a husband and wife together before. If you won't save yourself..."

"No!" John shrieked.

John swung his head to the side, trying with what little strength he retained to bash his skull into the inquisitor's face. The torturer was too quick and evaded John's feeble effort with a brief chuckle.

"Here is my proposal," the jailor continued. "Whichever of you tells me where to find the hidden Brothers of the Lion monastery on the Tede system's mainworld, will end their spouse's torment."

After a brief pause, and having received no response from either John or Elena, the jailor growled, "Bah! Have it your way."

The leathery slither of the whip cut through the air as the jailor drew it back in preparation of resuming his work.

"Wait!" John called out.

13

"John, no!" objected Elena.

"Shut up, witch!" replied the jailor. "Out with it, man. I won't stay my hand for long."

The inquisitor emphasized the point by cracking the whip in the air, causing the couple, who had learned the pain that normally accompanied that sound, to flinch and shudder.

"Do you swear by all you hold sacred that her torture is done if I tell you where to find the monastery?"

John tried to bluff, as though he were in some position to force the jailor to keep his word. John was an accomplished gambler, but this time he was holding a busted hand with no choice but to bet into a losing pot.

"Not another lash will fall," the fat torturer assured him with a smug smile. "In truth, I have no interest in you sheepish, Faithful devotees. Those Brothers of the Lion, however, are another matter altogether. They have become an intolerable nuisance to my employers. Now stop stalling or your wife will know the full range of pain I can deliver."

"John, you can't!" Elena said, tears filling her eyes. "Don't do this!"

"I must," he answered.

Had Elena ever sounded so desperate? There was no reason to believe the inquisitor would keep his word, but refusing to cooperate guaranteed their torment would continue. If there was even the remotest chance of sparing Elena, John had to try.

"I was supposed to protect you, Elena. I failed. I can at least end your pain."

"This won't save us," Elena pleaded.

John knew what she meant. What he was about to do was risky, even if the inquisitor kept his word. At best, this would buy them a week or two. If they couldn't find a way to escape before then, John's gamble would only have made things worse. Still, at this point he was out of options.

"The Lion of Judah will look after His own, my love, but He entrusted me to look after you."

"Very touching," the inquisitor said, cutting a new lash across Elena's back, eliciting a pain-filled scream. "But you are wasting my time with this sentimental backwash. Speak quickly before I change my mind."

"Their secret monastery is in the hills to the east of Elucia City."

"Oh, John!"

Resignation filled Elena's voice as she sagged in her shackles. John felt as though he had delivered another

14

punishing lash to his wife's back with his very attempt to spare her. All defiance had fled from her battered form. It was too late to back out now. John had made his bet and had to play out the hand.

"They are in an underground cave complex," John continued. "There are cave entrances on the south-facing hillsides that lead to the hidden monastery deep inside the hills."

"See?" the inquisitor said, walking back into John and Elena's view and setting the whip on a table. "Was that so hard?"

John sighed. It looked like the gamble worked. They were safe from the whip, for now.

"Now, to fulfil my promise."

The inquisitor grinned and locked eyes with John as he drew a knife from his belt. Grabbing a handful of Elena's hair and raising her head, he slit her throat with practiced smoothness.

Elena quietly gurgled, looking at John with pleading eyes as her lifeblood poured from her.

"No!" John screamed in a voice wracked with impotent rage. "You lying demon!"

"Don't you dare impugn my honor, knee-bender."

"You gave your word!"

"And I kept it! Her torture is over, just like I said," the inquisitor replied through a twisted smirk. "However, if we don't find those monks where you said they'd be, then yours hasn't even begun."

He turned to the Lubanian guard near the door.

"You."

"Yes sir?" the Lubanian replied, snapping to attention.

"Return him to his cell. We're done talking today. I fear I have offended this man's tender sensibilities. In truth," the inquisitor's sadistic smile widened, "I hope he lied. It will give me the opportunity to set a new galactic record for how slowly I kill him."

The Lubanian nodded crisply and moved toward John. The torturer then turned toward one of the human guards.

"And you."

"Yeah?" the guard replied, still leaning slightly against the wall and not granting the jailor the same respect that the Lubanian had.

"Go immediately to the comms room. Broadcast to the System Express jumper waiting in orbit that the Brothers of the Lion are holed up east of Elucia city in the hills. Have them

15

jump immediately to rendezvous with the strike fleet waiting at Hececcrir. Maybe we can finally root out the Brothers of the Lion operations in this subsector once and for all."

The human guard gave a half-nod and slipped out the door opposite the one through which the Lubanian had entered.

The hairy, lupine humanoid detached John's shackled hands from the hooks suspending him, and grabbed him roughly by the nape of his neck. Lubanians were much stronger than humans. The wolf-alien's one-handed grip was more than enough to keep John upright, even on wobbly, weakened legs, while eliminating any hope of an escape.

They barreled through the door into the corridor leading to the prisoner quarters, leaving the other human guard behind with the inquisitor. The callous torturer paid no further heed to John, having busied himself with cleaning and sorting the pain-inducing tools of his trade.

*****

As soon as he and his prisoner were clear of the torture chamber, Molon released his tight grip on the battered human's neck. The Lubanian dropped his left hand to a more supporting position around the human's waist, preventing him from hitting the floor. Draping the man's right arm around his own furry neck, he addressed the human.

"Sorry about the rough handling," Molon said to the weary and bloodied prisoner. "It had to look convincing. Can you walk?"

The human scrunched his face.

"Huh, what?"

The puzzled prisoner squinted at Molon. Molon sighed in frustration. Humans weren't exactly the quickest sophonts in the galaxy. They always seemed to need everything spelled out for them, but right now, there was no time to coddle a sluggish human intellect.

"You do speak Humaniti Common, right?"

John's head bobbled a weak nod.

"So, answer the question, can you walk?"

"B-but," the man stammered, "you're a Technocracy dog-soldier. Why help me?"

Molon gritted his teeth and fought the urge to bite something, namely the dim-witted, rude prisoner hanging from his neck. He took a deep breath. This man was a hermit-worlder. He had likely never seen a non-human sophont up close before. Some hermitages even refused to teach that non-human sophonts existed. Distinguishing Lubanian sub-races was way outside this human's experience, so Molon couldn't

16

fault him for it. Didn't make it any less offensive, though.

"Look, pal, dossier says you're a doctor, that right?"

"Yes," the human prisoner replied.

"I'm a Lupus Lubanian. Lupus. Wolf, not dog. Basic biology, remember?"

"Yes," the man nodded.

"Great," Molon said mustering patience he knew he possessed in short supply. "One more dog crack outta you and you can find your own way home, got it?"

"Sorry," the human mumbled, still clearly trying to get a grip on the situation.

"Null sweat. Now, you wanna stand here gabbin' or get out of here alive?"

"Uh," the man answered, "let's get out alive."

"Excellent choice. Now, for the last time, can you walk?"

"I doubt it," the prisoner replied with a shake of his head.

"Figures... Here," Molon said, fishing a black capsule out of one of the uniform's pockets and offering it to the man. "Take this."

"What is it?" The man raised an eyebrow.

Maybe he should just deck this uncooperative dimwit right here. No payday was worth this much grief. Carrying an unconscious body might be faster and less frustrating than playing twenty questions in the middle of a rescue attempt. Instead, Molon dug deep and drew up one more cupful of patience.

"An adrenocap," Molon explained. "Crush it between your teeth and swallow. It'll help you walk."

The man paused briefly, peering warily at Molon as if he were still unsure if he was being helped or murdered. After a last, wary gaze, the human bit into the capsule and swallowed.

"Who are you?" the prisoner asked, as he shuddered and contorted his face at the bitter taste of the adrenocap.

"I'm Captain Molon Hawkins, you are Dr. John Salzmann, and that's all the questions we have time for on today's episode of *Stump the Chump*. If you want to see tomorrow's episode, stop talking and start moving."

"But," John's face fell. "Elena."

John sagged, dissolving into tears as he put his full weight on Molon's neck. Molon was concerned the man might have damage to his lungs the way he was laboring to breathe. This was not the time or place for a counseling session.

"Focus!" Molon growled, shaking John a bit. "She's dead, and if you don't pull it together, we'll both be joining her."

"I understand," John replied, his voice taking on a clinical, detached tone. Blinking back tears John straightened a little and asked, "What now?"

"When that capsule kicks in, it will feel like a cattle prod up your backside. Your eyes will wanna pop outta your skull."

"I'm a physician," John said. "That pill didn't look like any brand of adrenocap I've ever seen."

"Merc budget, Doc. We don't buy retail. Trust me, that black beauty will get you on your feet again, quick."

"I know what an adrenocap does," John answered with a defensive tone. "I've just never personally taken one."

"Well," Molon smirked. "You are in for a real treat."

"I can't wait," John replied with a shake of his head.

"Anyway, once it kicks in, we have eight, maybe ten, minutes before you crash...hard. If we aren't back to the STS by then, we're dead."

"That's reassuring."

"Sorry, Doc. I'm good, but I can't fight our way out and carry you at the same time."

Ignoring the guard-issue blaster pistol holstered at his side, Molon reached under his uniform jacket and drew from his rear waistband a .45 caliber automag. He quickly fumbled through another pocket, pulled out a suppressor, and screwed it onto the end of the barrel. Just then, John's eyes bugged out wildly. Molon felt the prisoner stand up on his own, taking all the weight off Molon's shoulder.

"There's your wakeup call. Time to go."

Molon dashed down the corridor with John stumble-running barefoot closely behind. They took a few turns before coming to a security door. Pausing briefly, Molon swiped a key card through the electronic lock, and the sound of releasing locks greeted his ears. No alarms sounded. So far, so good.

Molon and John rushed through the doorway into a small room beyond. At a table sat two uniformed guards, a Lupus Lubanian and a human, playing cards. Their curious looks went slack as Molon sent a single, silenced shot into the forehead of each guard without breaking stride. John stood staring at the two dead guards.

"You wanna sing a hymn?" Molon growled.

John shook his head.

"Then keep up."

Molon took off down the corridor with John following behind. The corridors beyond the guardroom were not the rough-hewn stone passageways of the prison area, but smoothly carved and nicely painted halls. Electric lights artfully embedded in the ceilings replaced the bare, dangling bulbs of the dungeon area. The pair of refugees made several more turns before stopping at a large metal door, quite out of place in the otherwise modernized area of the complex. Above it was a sign that read:

HANGAR: AUTHORIZED PERSONNEL ONLY.

"How you holding up?" Molon asked as the human swayed a bit on his feet.

"The adrenocap rush is starting to wear off, but I'm okay for now."

John managed a weak smile. Molon scowled as he checked his chronometer. Six minutes. The adrenocap shouldn't be wearing off this quickly, but given how badly John had been beaten, it could have been worse. Still, time was running out.

"Hold it together for a couple more minutes, and we are home free. I'm sorry, John, but I gotta grab your neck again."

"Whatever it takes," John said through a slack-faced smile.

The human had courage. He might be a little slow on the uptake, but given what Molon had witnessed in the torture room and thus far on their flight toward freedom, John was no coward.

"When I give the signal, you start raving like a maniac. We sell this story or we never see the other side of this door."

John nodded, and Molon once again grabbed him with his left hand behind the neck with a much gentler grip than before. Angling his body, he put John between the automag in his right hand and the viewing hatch in the metal door. Molon kicked the door with a booted foot.

"Open up," he growled at the slideable viewing panel in the door. "Inquisitor wants this prisoner moved."

The metal panel slid open, and a pair of Lubanian eyes peered out through the yellow visor of a tac-helmet.

"I didn't get any notice about a prisoner move," the door guard grumbled. His eyes narrowed. "Where are your orders?"

"You want orders?" Molon growled in response. "I got orders, but I ain't dropping this rabbit to fish them out for you."

Molon squeezed John's neck slightly, signaling it was show time.

"Yeah, show him your stinking orders, dog-boy," John exclaimed, twitching and squirming. "Then we can all howl at the moon together! Bwahahaha! Owwwooooo!"

John added a few barks to the end of the howl for emphasis. Molon could see enough of the guard to note he was a Lupus Lubanian like Molon. Annoying as it was, John got bonus points for the whole dog-boy comment. That was sure to get a rise out of the Lupus door guard.

Molon feigned a pained look as the door guard growled through the viewing panel. The question was, was the guard's reaction rooted in annoyance at the racial slur, or suspicion of Molon's empty-handed excuse? Molon gave him another nudge toward annoyance.

"Look, bub," Molon said, rotating his wrist and turning John's back to the door to show the bloody welts from the whip. "You see what they already did to him? And he's still bouncing off the walls. This pale is either crazy or amped, I tell ya."

John snarled on queue. Molon was impressed that the severely beaten human even managed to work up enough spittle to look like he was drooling with madness, or perhaps even rabid.

"You want me to turn him loose and fish out the orders, null sweat. Then, once you've seen 'em, I'll watch the door and *you* catch this rabbit again. Crazy pale killed six guards before I caught him the first time. No fur off my muzzle either way."

Indecision filled the eyes looking through the peephole, but the Lubanian didn't give any indication of opening the door. This wasn't working. Time for a course adjustment.

"I've got another idea," Molon continued. "Open up. You hold my rabbit, I fish out your papers. Then neither of us has to chase an amped, psycho pale through the compound. Whadda you say, bub?"

The eye panel slid closed. Molon and John waited for what seemed like an eternity before hearing the welcome sound of a metal bar being drawn back on the other side of the door. The heavy portal creaked open, and Molon propelled John through.

As the Lubanian guard scrambled to catch the stumbling prisoner, Molon placed the automag beneath the guard's chin and fired a round up through his skull. The guard collapsed in a heap as John wobbled, trying to remain on his feet. No one else was manning the door, so Molon quickly closed and bolted it behind them.

"Do you intend to murder everyone we meet?" John asked.

"Probably."

"Can't you just render them unconscious or something instead?"

"I'll take it under advisement. How are you holding up?"

"Fading fast." John shook his head, breathing hard and steadying himself with a hand on Molon's shoulder.

"Dig deep a little longer, Doc. Nothing but shuttle techs between us and the STS now."

"You planning to murder them too?"

"Nah, we'll need them to cut the STS loose."

"Thank the Lion."

"You can try," Molon replied, "but I don't think He's listening."

Molon tucked the automag away in his rear waistband again, suppressor still attached. He walked John down the short flight of stairs and through the door into the main hangar area. John became increasingly dependent on Molon to support more of his weight with each step. Time was up.

Two "surface-to-space" shuttles were docked in the hangar, Molon's at the far end and a shiny new Dawnstar STS nearer the door from the guardroom. As the escapees walked past, Molon attached a small ball of clay with an embedded timer to the underside of the Dawnstar STS. He pushed a button on the device and the counter began a ten-minute countdown. Pity he couldn't take this STS. It was a brand new Sleekline model 3700, with loads of bells and whistles his fifteen-year-old Atmostar 70 lacked. What a waste.

"You grease monkeys finish refueling my STS yet?" Molon growled in a commanding tone at two techs busy attending the far shuttle.

"Yes, sir! Refueled and ready," the lead tech answered with a salute and a nervous twitch in his voice. They detached the fueling hose and began clearing the area.

"Do I look like an officer, you worthless puke?"

"Um..." the tech quivered his response.

"Don't call me sir," Molon snarled, interrupting the tech before he could fully respond. "I work for a living."

Molon used his muzzle to gesture at the sergeant's stripes on his uniform sleeve. The techs had obviously been low-ranking enlisted. They looked nervous, not anxious to further agitate an armed Lubanian non-com; just the effect Molon wanted.

"Get set to launch, boss wants this one topside in a hurry."

The hangar techs scrambled to disconnect the battery recharging lines and release Molon's STS for launch. Without another word or even a glance at the ground crew, he carried John's nearly limp body up the ramp and into the shuttle by the nape of his neck. The adrenocap was spent.

Molon dropped John into one of the two passenger seats of the four-seater personal STS. John's head lolled as he fumbled to buckle himself into the seat with the last shreds of his fading adrenaline boost. Molon had no time to help. He had to leave the human to his own devices.

Pulling his automag from his rear waistband and dumping it into a netted pocket attached to a bulkhead, he hit the controls to close the hatch. Settling into the pilot's seat, he flipped the controls activating the engines and the shuttle's communication system. Molon punched the ground control channel into the comms and keyed the mic.

"Control, this is STS niner eight six one seven three requesting clearance to depart."

"*Roger,*" came the reply through the comm system. "*You are cleared for departure niner eight six one seven three. Have a good flight.*"

Freedom rang through the air — the familiar clang of magnetic moorings releasing their hold on the STS. The antigrav-systems lifted the STS clear of the hangar deck. Molon nudged the controls and began edging the shuttle toward the gaping cave mouth linking the hangar to the world outside.

No sooner had the shuttle gone airborne than red lights began flashing throughout the hangar. A klaxon rang echoing throughout the hangar as well as across the comms. Molon's HUD flashed the message: *Clearance revoked, return to dock and power down.*

"*STS niner eight six one seven three,*" came a voice across the communications panel. "*An emergency alarm has been activated. I am revoking your clearance until we determine the nature of the emergency. Please return to the hangar deck and await further instructions.*"

"... —rry control... —mission... —peat... —tions," Molon affected his best communication difficulties impression, keying and unkeying the mic along with garbling his voice. Then he switched off the local comms channel completely. So much for a smooth getaway.

Glancing at the synchronized timer on his left wrist, there was only a minute and a half left before the other shuttle blew; surely not enough time to get a flight capable pilot to the hangar, find his little surprise, and launch pursuit. The techs certainly weren't going to chase him, and he had stalled long enough. He punched up full forward on the thruster controls and jetted toward the exit of the hangar cave. If this backwater dirtball prison colony had force shielding installed at the exit, this flight was going to be short and would end in fiery glory.

Molon sighed with relief as the STS exited the hangar cave mouth without crashing into an energy barrier and bursting into flames. So far, so good. Pulling the shuttle into a steep climb, he focused the aft cameras on the cave entrance receding in the distance below.

Hopefully this backwater prison colony did not have an actual Atmospheric Defense Force with a ready intercept squadron capable of reaching him before he could rendezvous with *Star Wolf* waiting in orbit. He set the autopilot coordinates for where *Star Wolf* was supposed to be. A wolfish grin crept across his face as he watched the bright flash on the aft camera display monitor. A fireball erupted from the cave entrance far below as the explosives he had attached to the other STS detonated. No sign of pursuit showed on the radar, but he knew they might not be out of the woods yet.

"You see, Dr. Salzmann," Molon said, spinning his seat around to face his passenger.

John Salzmann was slumped in his chair, unconscious in a post-adrenal crash. Fortunately, he had managed to get his seatbelt buckled before losing consciousness, or Molon would be picking the hermit-worlder up off the deck.

"That's just as well. You've been through one heck of an ordeal, Doc. At least if we get jumped by System Defense forces before we can dock with *Star Wolf* and make the jump into voidspace, you get to die peacefully in your sleep. That's more than I can say for the rest of us."

Two – On Course for Tede

Molon opened the hatch of the four-man STS, unbuckled his passenger's seat harness, and slung the still-sleeping Dr. John Salzmann over his left shoulder. As he exited into *Star Wolf*'s shuttle bay, Molon spotted the familiar face of Senior Chief Darius 'Monkey' Monk, chief of *Star Wolf*'s deck crew. The deck chief, dressed in beige coveralls, came bounding toward Molon with his usual energy and verve. The olive-skinned human was short and stocky, with vaguely simian features. The sleeves of his jumper were rolled up to the elbow, revealing a thick mat of black hair covering his forearms.

"Welcome back, Cap," the deck chief greeted him, with an enthusiastic grin and a sloppy salute.

"Thanks, Monkey," Molon replied, reflexively returning the salute. "Senior chief, give this bird a good once-over," Molon said, motioning his head toward the STS, "and a bug sweep. She was out of my sight for over an hour, no telling what surprises Dawnstar's techs might have left behind."

"Aye, sir."

"Oh, and reinstall the hidden meson cannon, would you?"

"Sure thing, Cap. Thought you wuz crazy havin' me take it out inna first place."

"Couldn't risk their deckies finding a high TL weapon on what was supposed to be a civvy STS. Still, flying unarmed was like showing up naked to a royal ball."

This drew a chuckle from the deck chief.

"On it, Cap. Nut'n else?"

"Yeah, there is. Set up a new transponder code, and repaint the hull numbers to match. I left a mess planetside. Dawnstar's men will be scouring the sector and every known voidspace entry point for this one."

"Whaddaya think I am, Cap, some kinda boot just outta trainin' camp? Stirrin' up trouble's what you do. Hidin' your mess is what I do," Monkey said, thumbing his chest.

"You're right, Monkey. First things first, though. Get that

smug eyesore of a grinning sunburst decal off my hull. My brain hurts just looking at it."

"Aye, Cap. Tubal sure picked an obnoxious emblem for Dawnstar's sigil, huh? Spineless weasel, maybe he's compensatin' for somethin'."

Molon laughed, nodding in agreement, and headed for the exit. The deck chief let out a sharp whistle, and two more beige-clad deck hands jumped up to help him see to the maintenance of the STS.

Molon made his way from *Star Wolf's* shuttle bay to the starboard elevator, punching the button for the bridge deck. He lugged John's unconscious form down the short hallway and into the cramped medic station, having to duck to get himself and John through the tight portal. A muscled, dyed-blond corpsman, Madrick 'Patch' Kakuma, snapped a sharp salute and stood rigidly at attention.

"Captain on deck!" Patch said to no one in particular, since he was the only other person present.

"At ease, Patch," Molon said, laying John down on one of the small examination bunks and returning a half-hearted salute. "You are not with the Imperial Marines anymore, corpsman. I know you are new here, but ease up a bit on the military protocol. It gives me the twitches."

Kakuma could not help himself. Trained as an elite commando and recipient of the coveted Special Assault Reconnaissance Corpsman accreditation, Patch was hardwired military. Rare circumstances and solid conscience had brought him out of the Provisional Imperium Marines and into service aboard *Star Wolf*. They were lucky to have him.

"Sorry, sir," Patch replied, relaxing visibly and blushing slightly at the good-natured reprimand. "Force of habit."

"A good habit to break."

"Aye, sir. Civvy casualty?"

"Yeah, he's out from an adrenocap crash, but they worked him over pretty good. Give him a thorough once-over. What I witnessed looked superficial, from a shock-whip mostly, but no telling what they did to him before I got there."

"Yes, sir," Patch said, shaking his head as he began to examine John's injuries. "Looks like this guy's back went through a cheese grater."

"He definitely got dealt. Didn't exactly give his face a free pass either. Do what you can. We need him up and functional by the morning."

"Aye, skipper. You want me to scan for sub-cute trackers too?"

"Not a bad idea. I doubt they had any plans on him leaving alive, but better safe than sorry."

"Aye, sir. If you want to interrogate him now, I can slip him some stims to counter the adreno-crash."

"Nah, he's not a prisoner, he's our mission. Let him rest. He's gonna have enough to process when he wakes up. Have him up and at the command officers meeting in the morning. We have a lot to discuss."

"Aye, sir. I'm off duty at 0200, but I will pass the word on to my relief."

"Thanks, Patch," Molon said as he ducked out of the med station.

Upon arriving at the starboard bridge entrance, Molon tapped his security code into the access panel. The portal opened, and he strode confidently onto *Star Wolf*'s bridge. All eyes turned to see who had entered. Ensign Zach Zarizzo, a crack pilot and one of the newest additions to the *Star Wolf* crew, jumped up from the helm station and snapped to attention as soon as he spotted Molon. None of the other bridge officers followed suit.

"Captain on the bridge!" announced the eager young officer.

"At ease, Z-Man," Molon answered using the helmsman's call sign rather than his name.

Call signs had become the customary address aboard *Star Wolf,* for everyone besides the captain anyway. Few knew or used Molon's call sign, 'Lobo', save for his XO and long-time partner, Jane 'Twitch' Richardson. Even Twitch normally reserved it for occasions when she *really* wanted to get his attention. If Twitch called him Lobo, he was about to get an earful about something. Thinking about his XO, he noted her conspicuous absence from the bridge.

"We're at status amber, where is Twitch?" Molon asked no one in particular, more wondering aloud than actually inquiring.

Z-Man sank wordlessly into his seat at the helm, deferring the answer to his superior officers.

"Well, O fearless leader," began a beautiful dark-haired, gray-skinned woman, who had just evacuated the captain's chair.

Lieutenant Commander Yasu 'Voide' Matsumura, was Molon's chief of security and third in *Star Wolf*'s chain of command, right behind Twitch and himself.

"I saw you were coming in clean," Voide continued through a sly smile. "So, I called for Z-Man to relieve her. She had only been on duty for sixteen straight hours, but you know how anemic those humans can be, right?"

"Oh," Molon said, flashing his security chief a quizzical look. "Was I gone that long?"

"Yeah," Voide answered, with a playful double-blink of her bright yellow eyes. "If you had been gone much longer, I was thinking I would have to come and rescue you myself."

"Hah, rescue me, in what, our slow, clunky, unarmed cargo STS? That'd have been a hoot!"

"Who needs a ship?" Voide replied.

Voide was alluding to the ability of her race, the Prophane, to personally enter voidspace, briefly, without need for ships or life-support — effectively a short-distance *teleport*. Molon cocked his head to one side.

"The hundred sixty klicks from orbit to ground would be a bit much for even a Prophane jump-trooper, much less an untrained Pariah, don't you think?"

"For you, Molon," she winked, "I'd have given it a shot."

This drew a laugh from the Lubanian captain. He raised an eyebrow and drew his top lip back revealing a single canine, his best version of a wolfish smirk, while relaxing his ears into a playful semi-droop.

"You bucking for a bonus or something, Voide?"

"Why, you offering one?"

"You *might* risk your life pushing your ability to kill me if I crossed you, but to save me? Not a chance."

Voide gave Molon a playful raising and lowering of her eyebrows.

Voide was a good and loyal officer. She was also, however, what could be best described as a high-functioning sociopath with a playfully sarcastic wit. She was Prophane, after all, and stable, predictable behavior wasn't exactly in her DNA.

"So, did you solve the conundrum of our missing pair-of-docs?" Voide punned. "Are we getting paid?"

"I rescued one," Molon frowned. "Dr. Elena Salzmann didn't make it. We'll go over everything in the morning briefing. For now, let's get back to Tede, best speed. Z-Man, have you got us a course?"

"Well, sir," answered the young helmsman, "I can retrace the rabbit trail route we discovered from Hatacks. Then we hit the mapped voidspace jump route from Hatacks to Tede. Barring any misjumps or running into any Dawnstar SysDef en route, I put us back in the Tede system in just under three days."

"Lion's breath, son," Molon said, fighting his frustration at

Z-Man's verbosity, "we'd be halfway there by now if you were flying instead of talking. A simple yes would have sufficed."

"Sorry, sir."

"Null sweat, son. Just set up the jump and get us into voidspace ASAP."

"Aye, sir," Z-Man responded, blushing slightly at the captain's rebuke as he worked the helm controls.

"Everyone look sharp," Molon continued in a voice loud enough to address the entire bridge crew. "Prison Colony Ratuen may have gotten a System Express jumper out to Hececcrir before I toasted the place."

"I didn't spot anything leaving the system, captain," replied Lieutenant Junior Grade Jerry "Hoot" Barundi, currently manning the bridge sensor station. "It's possible something might have gotten out of the system without me spotting it, but I doubt it."

"That's good news, but Hececcrir is Tubal Halberan's main star base in this subsector. It hosts a huge Dawnstar shipyard. If the message did get out, there could be half a dozen Dawnstar ships dropping in on Tede within a week."

"Aye, captain," the young helmsman responded. "Already en route. We'll reach the rabbit trail voidspace entry point in just under two hours."

Molon turned to the waifish female operating the communications station. Her powder-blue skin, bluish-green hair and slightly pointed ears showed she was a Fei; a race known for their incredible terraforming skills and mild telepathic abilities.

"Mel,"

"Yes, Molon?" Lieutenant Imeldria "Mel" Sarum, *Star Wolf*'s senior communications officer answered in a sweetly quiet voice, turning her shining emerald-colored eyes toward him.

Mel had the habit of addressing almost everyone informally. If Mel didn't call someone by their first name, it meant she either didn't trust them or had another reason to keep her distance. Molon wasn't sure if this had more to do with Fei customary address or her empathic tendencies, but the verbal intimacy was somehow comforting.

"Queue up a broadband blast to transmit as soon as we hit Tede space. Message: 'the doctor is in'. Set it to repeat hourly until we get a response."

"I shall comply," Mel replied. "Is this to be the signal for our contact?"

"It is. Then we wait. The contract stipulates that our

patron will contact us to arrange swapping the rescuees for the payment."

"Should I also send a message to the government on Tede to warn them of the possible attack from Hececcrir?" Mel said, demonstrating the empathy for which her race was known.

"We will leave that up to the good doctor, since he's the one that tipped Tubal's people where to attack. I'll let him square that with the system feds. As far as we know, our deal isn't with the Tede government. Contract was set for an anonymous drop."

Voide was shaking her head.

"Something you want to get off your chest, Voide?" Molon asked, already guessing the answer.

"You really believe whoever the patron is on this contract will pay off for half the cargo?" asked Voide, as if Dr. Salzmann were nothing more than a container of canned goods.

"They'd better," answered Molon. "This crate is due for maintenance, and we're low on missiles after that scuffle with those pirate raiders last month. I hate flying light, but it is what it is."

"Remind me, Molon, when was the last time we had an antsy patron pay in full for us delivering half the job?" Voide asked, not bothering to suppress her frown.

"Yeah, yeah, I know," Molon answered, biting back a growl.

Voide's assessment was likely dead on. Still, he didn't appreciate having it delivered in her needlessly snarky tone.

"But Tede is controlled by the Theocracy of the Faithful," Molon continued. "If Enoch and the TotF are behind this job, maybe we'll catch a break."

"Uh-huh," Voide scrunched up her face. "And if poop was platinum we'd all be rich. You really think by-the-book knee-benders are hiring merc crews on the sly to pull rescue missions?"

"Maybe," Molon answered, trying to sound convincing, more for his own benefit than Voide's. "Do you always have to be such a cynic?"

"It's a survival skill," she grinned.

"I'll bet," Molon answered.

"Besides," Voide said, refusing to let the matter drop. "That contract payment was hefty. We were lucky to snag it as fast as we did."

"And?" Molon growled, wondering where this was heading.

"And, there is no way a bunch of pew-warmers put up that

kind of stake for us to go mess up some routine kidnapping."

"Voide..." Molon squinted and shook his head, hoping the pleading tone in his voice would end the increasingly depressing exchange; it didn't.

"People get snatched off border worlds all the time, and the ransom they ask isn't a quarter of what this contract is paying."

"What's your point?" Molon growled.

"The point is, there is something bigger going on here."

Molon fixed his gaze on her and gritted his teeth. Most of his crew withered and found someplace else to be when he locked that look onto them. Voide, however, just smiled defiantly back at him as though his angry glare were no more than a playful wink.

"Just a warm ball of sunshine, ain't you, Voide?"

"I do my best."

"Keep it up and I might have to make you morale officer."

"I thought I was."

Molon could not hold back a laugh at that thought. He let out a half bark, half yip that startled the young helmsman, Z-Man, half out of his chair.

"Anyway," Molon added, shaking his head. "Dr. Salzmann might have more insights in the morning. If the Theocracy contracted the rescue, those religious types aren't as unforgiving or likely to stiff us as most patrons."

"Oh yeah?" Voide scoffed. "Don't bet your payday on that."

"Unfortunately," Molon replied, "that's all we've got left to bet."

Three – Search for Reason

The casual chatter in *Star Wolf*'s conference room halted as the door slid open. Dr. John Salzmann stood, pale-faced and stunned, in the doorway. The bob-tailed, gray-furred Lubanian corpsman who had escorted him saluted the other Lubanian present, who was seated near the far end of the table. John recognized the seated, silvery-gray-furred Lubanian as Molon Hawkins, the one who had rescued him from the Dawnstar detention center. John's bob-tailed escort nudged John into the conference room, and withdrew.

The sight before John's eyes was so bewildering it stunned him into temporary paralysis. There, sitting around a conference room table, in addition to the Lubanian who had rescued him from the prison, were four other individuals, only one of whom looked completely human.

Next to the only empty seat at the table was a human woman with salt-and-pepper-laced, close-cut ginger hair. She had long, slender limbs, and despite her age she had a toned and fit musculature, topped by an aesthetically unremarkable yet elegant, almost regal face. John would not describe her as beautiful, yet she bore a comeliness stemming from the whole of her appearance being more striking than the mere sum of her parts. He noted she had an implanted data jack in the back of her neck at the base of her skull. He had seen similar implants during his residency on a core world. They were used to interface the human mind directly to some type of mechanical or computer systems.

Next to her sat a huge, hulking brute that looked almost human in a misshapen, twisted sort of way. The bald, mocha-skinned man would be nearly two meters tall if he stood, and must have weighed close to a hundred-sixty-five kilos. His physical bulk, deformed facial features, and large lump above his left shoulder reminded John of the old Terran story of Quasimodo. The man had huge, thick-fingered hands, but anchored to his wrists and fingers like strange wire-frame gloves were two mechanical glove-hands. The mechanical fingers were much more elegant and dexterous looking than his actual appendages. The man flashed a disturbing smile, showing several missing teeth and a deformed jaw with a pronounced underbite.

Sitting next to Molon was an attractive, athletically-muscled female alien with dark gray skin and shining yellow eyes. Her features looked human enough, but her skin tone and eyes marked her definitively as something else. Slightly elongated upper canine teeth also gave her a feral, vampiric quality. Her smile resembled more a predator noting that dinner had just arrived than any type of welcoming gesture.

The last being at the table, sitting next to the dark gray alien female, was another alien female, stunningly beautiful, with powder-blue skin. She seemed about average in height, from what he could tell with her sitting down, but her limbs, neck, and fingers were long and waifishly thin. She had short, blue-green hair in a bob-cut, which left her slightly pointed ears exposed. Deep, captivating, emerald eyes for a brief moment seized John and almost made him forget why he was standing there. Finally, he broke free from his daze, turning to address the human-looking woman.

"Are we the only humans on this ship?"

"Hey!" the dark-skinned man with the mechanical hands bellowed. "What do I look like, some kind of trained gorilla?"

Suddenly John called to mind his wife Elena's research on malmorphsy, a genetic mutation wrought on many races by a bioweapon developed by the Daemi.

"Oh, I'm sorry, you poor man," John said in a slightly patronizing tone, momentarily forgetting everyone else in the room. "You suffer from malmorphsy. I didn't recognize the symptoms at first. That was really my wife's area of study. Please accept my apologies."

"Now, hold on a sec, Doc Fancy Pants," the man answered, his warped smile now replaced with a scowl. "I'm a malmorph, but I wouldn't say I *suffer* from anything. I got more good than harm out of the deal, so save your pity for those that need it, hermit-worlder."

"Okay, everybody settle down," Molon interjected. "Dr. Salzmann, please take a seat next to Commander Richardson," Molon said, pointing to the empty chair next to the human woman.

John hesitated for a moment before sliding warily into the open seat. In a room full of aliens, the seat next to a human looked like the best spot.

"Everyone please be aware," Molon explained, "Dr.

Salzmann comes from a Faithful-controlled hermit-world, so I doubt he's seen this many non-human sophonts in one place before. Cut him some slack while he adjusts."

The crew turned generally unsympathetic eyes toward John, save for the powder-blue skinned woman. He could almost sense a comforting empathy from her that outweighed the heavy stares from the other officers.

"To answer your question, John," Molon continued, "most members of *Star Wolf's* crew are human. The command officers just happen to show a disproportionate percentage of other sophonts. Let me introduce you to my officers.

"Beside you is executive officer and chief helmsman, Commander Jane Richardson," Molon said, nodding toward the human female at the table.

"Twitch," she said, nodding to John.

"Yes," Molon continued, "most crewman have call signs they prefer to their formal names. Commander Richardson's is Twitch.

"The large fellow you have already managed to annoy is Lieutenant Commander Malik Dubronski, my chief engineer."

"Call me Dub," said the malmorph engineer. "That is unless you prefer *freakishly deformed mutant,* but that's a mouthful."

John feared open animosity directed at him for his initial reaction to Dub's appearance. Years of reading faces across a card table, however, told him the smiles from the others around the table indicated that Dub was only razzing him.

"Yeah, it is," John answered, trusting his gambling instincts had led him to read the situation correctly. "But maybe I will save the deformed mutant thing for formal occasions."

Dub's twisted smile gave John hope that there might be a kindred spirit resting in the malmorph's heart. It appeared that his bungled first impression had not completely ruined his chance at a positive relationship with the malmorph chief engineer.

"This gray-skinned ball of danger on my right is Lieutenant Commander Yasu Matsumura, my security chief, call sign Voide. She served with Galactic Security. Voide is a Prophane Pariah."

"A Prophane?" John gasped, his mind racing at the implications of what Molon had just said about his security officer. "Humaniti has been at war with the Prophane since before the Shattering. I thought Prophane died in captivity? How do you have a Prophane in your crew, much less one that

33

served with GalSec?"

"I guess," Molon explained, "as deep as Tede is in Faithful territory, and so far from the tailward border of Humaniti space, you ain't up on all the details of the Prophane, so I'll lay it out for you.

"Adult Prophane prisoners die in captivity within a week. They have some type of self-poisoning ability. Scientists still haven't quite figured out if it is natural or technological. Pariahs are Prophane who were captured as children. Below a certain age, Prophane either haven't developed or haven't been taught how to trigger this suicide reaction."

"But aren't their loyalties divided?" John asked.

"You know," Voide interjected, baring her elongated canines threateningly. "I'm sitting right here. You got a question, pale, ask it, but don't just keep discussing me like I'm a lab experiment?"

John flushed while Molon laughed.

"I'm sorry, ma'am," John said, turning to address Voide directly. "I don't mean to question your loyalties. I have just never heard of a Prophane serving on a non-Prophane ship before."

"Null sweat, John," Molon answered. "Voide, if he is going to be kicking around here for the next week, we might as well clue him in on what he needs to know to be comfortable."

"Fine, then," Voide snapped. "You want a briefing, pale, here it is. A Pariah is a Prophane separated from the Ascendency as a child and raised apart from them. Prophane hate Pariahs more than any other race, which is saying a lot. As for divided loyalties, let's just say that if we encountered a Prophane ship, and they found out I was on board *Star Wolf*, they would ignore every other target, sacrificing every last Prophane ship in their attack force if that is what it took to reach and kill me. Destroying Pariahs takes precedence over everything else."

"Wow," John replied.

"Yeah, wow. So don't worry, pale. Double-agent really isn't a viable career option, but thanks for asking." Voide's face morphed into a feral grin. "Still, there is good news."

"Good news," John answered cautiously. This woman scared him.

"Yeah, I only eat human children on special occasions."

"Okay, enough," Molon said, placing a hand on Voide's shoulder. "Let's all take a deep breath and get back to the introductions. By the way, John, she was joking."

"Molon is right," Voide added, flashing her elongated

canines in John's direction. "I actually eat them at least twice a week."

"Knock it off, Voide," Molon snapped.

John tried to affect a good-natured smile, but he doubted even his best poker-face was capable of hiding his trepidation. He would not be on the security chief's friend list anytime soon. Trying to put this behind him, he took mental note that he would need to be a bit more diplomatic around the aliens...um, non-human sophonts, from here on out.

"And the lovely blue vision beside Voide," Molon continued with his introductions, "is my communications officer, Lieutenant Imeldria Sarum, call sign Mel. She is Fei, formerly with the Wyldefey, the Fei Regency's terraforming division."

"I heard the Fei have allied with the Theocracy of the Faithful," said John, trying to form a positive impression with at least one of Molon's bridge officers.

"The Fei have no desire for conflict with anyone," Mel answered, a troubled frown gracing her lovely face.

He'd missed the mark again.

"Out of necessity," Mel continued, "and an unwillingness to face the Lubanian Alpha Pack as well as New Empire forces under Seth Halberan alone, the Regency determined that allying with Patriarch Enoch Halberan of the Theocracy of the Faithful, and the Angelicum Host, was our best hope for survival."

John saw a compassion in her eyes even though the thought of picking sides in an unwanted and unprovoked war was clearly distasteful to her. John more than understood. His own world of Tede had no desire to take part in any conflict. Its unfortunate position—in Theocracy space but adjacent to both Dawnstar and the Provisional Imperium borders—left it vulnerable to ongoing border conflicts.

"Now that introductions are out of the way," Molon said, glancing at a datapad in front of him, "let's discuss the situation concerning our new guest first. Then he can be excused, and we can move on to regular ship's business."

"What situation would that be exactly?" John inquired. It seemed everyone knew a good deal more about what he was doing here than he did.

"We were hired to bust you outta that Dawnstar prison colony in the Ratuen system," Molon answered.

"Dawnstar?" John asked. "What would Dawnstar want with us?"

"I don't know why you were taken, John. Only that we

were hired to facilitate a jailbreak."

"Hired? By whom?"

"Actually, we were hoping you might tell us that," added Voide, with an accusatory tone.

"I don't know anything," John replied.

"Obviously," snapped Voide.

"That is to say," John corrected, furrowing his brow at the security chief, determined not to let her jibes unsettle him, "My corporation's board of directors would be the most likely candidate. But I have no idea how they knew where or by whom we were taken."

"*Your* corporation?" Voide inquired, her yellow eyes lighting up even brighter.

John mentally kicked himself for his carelessness as he wrestled with exactly how much to reveal. Molon and his crew had extracted him from the detention camp, but who was to say they were not pirates? If they truly knew how much John was worth, they might end up trying to ransom him themselves. Once again, his trusting nature and loose lips had landed him in an awkward situation. He would have to be more careful.

"Well, it was my parents' corporation actually. I have very little to do with it. It is a small pharmaceuticals company on Tede. Generally any allocation of credits beyond picking up a meal check requires a consensus of the board. Perhaps it was the Tede government that hired you."

"Doubtful," Molon replied. "Unless you're tied to the Tede government."

"No," John quickly responded, gazing down at the deck. "But if you took the job, don't you know who you are working for?"

"It was an anonymous contract," answered Molon.

"Anonymous contract?" John asked. "Then how do you know you are really getting paid?"

Molon's furrowed brow and slight snarl was what John imagined frustration would look like on the face of a wolf.

"It was a secured contract, with the credits in escrow. If I report we were unable to complete the job, they revert back to the depositor. If the depositor acknowledges completion, the credits are released to me. The payment's secure; we just don't know who the depositor is."

"I wish I had an answer for you," John said, shaking his head and wracking his brain but coming up with nothing. "I truly have no idea."

"Hmm," Molon said, scratching the fur on his chin. "Why

don't we start with why you were taken, and reason it out from there? Do you have any idea why Dawnstar would want to kidnap you and your wife?"

Suddenly a wave of grief hit John like a tsunami. He struggled to breathe against the tightness in his chest. In all the confusion of finding himself on a ship led by aliens, he had nearly forgotten the terrible fate that had befallen Elena. They had killed her, right before his eyes. But why? John felt tears welling up in his eyes as he fought to blink them back.

"John," Molon said with a strange and awkward compassion in his lupine voice. "I know what happened to your wife was terrible. I wish I could have prevented it."

John felt heat rush to his face. Through gritted teeth he spun toward Molon, his eyes boring a hole in the middle of the Lubanian captain.

"You could have!"

"No, John, I—"

"You had a blaster on your side. I saw you drop other guards with a single shot. You could have taken out the two guards and the jailor before they even drew their weapons. But you stood there and watched her die!"

"John, let me explain."

"Explain what?" John fumed.

"Did you notice I didn't use the blaster pistol at all during our escape?" Molon pleaded. "I used my automag, *after* I attached a suppressor to silence the shots."

"So what?" John said, clenching his fists and raising his voice at Molon. "If you can shoot a slug thrower, you can fire a blaster."

"John, that facility may have looked like a hole in a hill, but it was a Dawnstar detention center."

"And?" John said, doing his best to follow Molon's explanation while holding his anger and frustration in check.

Molon rubbed the back of his neck and took a deep breath. He turned to John with soft eyes, not the sharp frustration John had seen during the rescue. This calmed John a bit as he listed to the Lubanian captain, grasping for understanding.

"Dawnstar, pre-Shattering," Molon explained, "was the primary megacorporation responsible for defense R&D for the Empire. That facility was lined with blast detectors. Any energy discharge would have set off every alarm in the compound. If I'd used a blaster, we'd both be dead."

John heard all that Molon said, but it was not yet pushing through his blanket of emotions to register on his conscious mind.

"John," Molon continued in a calm voice. "We we were hired to rescue both of you. I had every reason to get your wife out safely, but there was nothing I could do. Had I gone for my automag in the interrogation chamber, I'd have been dead before I got a shot off."

John felt the rage in him subside a little as rationality slowly took control of his mind, allowing him to reason through Molon's words.

"Why not come in with your gun ready, like you did at the guard station?"

Molon shook his head.

"Couldn't. I'd already been through the guard station on my way in. I knew what to expect. I had no idea what was beyond the interrogation chamber door."

"You must have known something," John argued desperately. "You had a guard uniform and everything."

While Molon's voice remained calm, John could tell his patience with the barrage of questions was wearing thin. Maybe this Lubanian captain really had done all he could. Maybe there had been no way to get Elena out safely.

"I took out a Lubanian guard on the perimeter of the compound. I swiped his uniform and flew into the shuttle bay. I chatted up some guards and found out where they were holding you two as quickly as I could, but by the time I arrived you were already spilling your guts about the Brothers of the Lion's hidden monastery location. The inquisitor was on Elena before I could do anything."

Suddenly John felt an unnatural calm flow over him. Moments before he had been furious at Molon for not doing more to save Elena, but now all he felt was peace. Then the blue-skinned Fei, Mel, spoke to him in a voice as soothing as a summer breeze. Her voice had an eerie, ethereal quality, almost as though he were hearing her with both his ears and his mind at the same time.

"John, I know your heart is full of pain, but you must believe Molon. If he says there was nothing he could do, that is the truth. He has risked his life for every officer in this room. He would have given his own life if it could have saved you and Elena."

John could not explain his sudden change of heart, but he found himself unable to doubt anything Mel had just told him. He was filled with a complete and unshakable trust for Molon Hawkins and the *Star Wolf* crew. Something was not right about this, but to save his life he could not figure what it was, nor did he have any inclination to try. John turned and addressed the captain with a steady placidity in his voice.

"I'm sorry, Captain Hawkins. I am sure you did your best, and I am grateful to you for helping me escape. Now, what was it you wanted to know again?"

The Lubanian captain shot a fierce look in the direction of his Fei coms officer.

"We will talk later, Mel."

"I am certain," she replied with a subdued smile.

"Anyway, John," Molon said, returning his gaze to John. "What would Dawnstar want with you and Elena?"

John thought through their history searching his memory for any link. Only one thought came to mind.

"Elena used to work for Dawnstar."

"Really?" Voide interjected. "That's too convenient for coincidence."

"I agree," John added, rubbing the back of his neck. "But that was pre-Shattering."

"Did they have a facility on Tede?" Molon asked.

"No. She didn't work for them directly. They were funding her research into a cure for malmorphsy. She would send them results from her testing."

"A cure?" Dub asked, understandably interested.

"Yes," John continued. "Elena had focused on curing malmorphsy in human subjects but Dawnstar wanted her to focus her efforts primarily on aliens."

"Watch it, pale," Voide snapped.

"Um, sorry, non-human sophonts," John felt his face flush. He was going to have to break that habit. "Since there are only humans living in the Tede system, they would bring her DNA samples from out-system malmorphs."

"Did she provide them with what they were looking for?" Molon asked.

"I think the research was going well, but after the Shattering, we were on the wrong side of some imaginary line, so the funding and genetic samples stopped coming."

"What happened with her research after that?" asked Dub, the malmorph engineer, sitting forward in his chair.

"As I said, we have many human malmorphs on Tede. Elena was elated to continue her work with a renewed focus on her human patients. To my knowledge, in the eight years since the Shattering, no one from Dawnstar has tried to contact her at all."

"It's thin," said Molon, "but that's got to be the link."

"But it makes no sense," John objected, shaking his head vigorously.

39

"Why not?" Molon asked.

"Because," John said, "the inquisitor never asked Elena anything about her research."

Molon's ears drooped and his brow furrowed. Silence overtook the room for a brief moment as the impact of John's comment sank in. Molon turned and glared intensely at John.

"Then what did he ask about?"

"The Brothers of the Lion and their base on Tede," John replied, glancing about at nothing in particular as his voice wavered. "If Dawnstar wanted Elena's research, why didn't they just ask for it? She would have gladly shared her data. There was no reason to kill her!"

Molon scowled and scratched his cheek as he shook his head.

"You're right. Makes no sense, but maybe once we meet the patron who hired us, maybe they can shed some light."

"So you are returning me to Tede, then?" John still wasn't sure he was out of danger, but everything about Molon's story seemed to add up.

"Of course. In the meantime, we currently have no full-time physician on board, so you can use the stateroom next to the infirmary. Can you find your way back there?"

"Yes, I believe so."

"Good. That will be your cabin until we reach Tede."

"How long is the journey to Tede, captain?"

"Two more days. Until then, take it easy. Check in with the corpsman on duty in the infirmary. He can show you the galley, facilities, and how to reach me if you need anything."

"Thank you, Captain Hawkins. I am truly grateful for all you have done."

John said his goodbyes around the table and left to retrace his steps to the infirmary. There was a lot to think about between here and Tede, but if the *Star Wolf* crew were pirates, they were as nice a bunch of pirates as one could hope for.

Four – Dead Ends

The door chime sounded. John Salzmann glanced up from the datapad filled with the *Star Wolf*'s collected medical journals, which he had been studying. There was precious little data on xenobiology back on Tede, so he had passed most of the last two days reviewing the biology of known non-human sophont races.

"Yes?" he called out.

The door slid open at his acknowledgement, and a young ensign stuck his head in the doorway to John's stateroom.

"Doc, captain said to let you know we should drop out of voidspace into the Tede system very soon. He'd like you to join him on the bridge."

"Thank you, ensign. I will be right there."

The young man nodded and withdrew, letting the door close behind him. John was home again, or was about to be at least. Home. What did that mean anymore?

With Elena gone, what was left for him on Tede? A corporation he didn't care about beyond the lifestyle it provided and the altruistic opportunities it opened? Corporate life didn't suit him, but living out his days as a wealthy dilettante in the same casual manner in which he had frittered away most of his life would be an empty shell without Elena. She had been the anchor of reason keeping him from drifting away completely on a sea of whimsy.

Where was his life supposed to go from here? Before he tackled that question, he needed to unravel the mystery of his unknown benefactor. Who could have known Dawnstar forces had taken them? Who had the wherewithal to hire mercenaries the caliber of *Star Wolf*'s crew to mount a rescue? John had questions in abundance. Answers were in short supply.

As he entered the bridge, the first shift crewmen were at their stations. Twitch was at the helm, with some form of glowing remote interface plugged into the data jack on the back of her neck. A green light pulsing in uneven flashes from the end of the wireless interface showed she was jacked into one of

41

the ship's systems.

Mel was on comms, and Voide was at the security station. Dub was seated at the engineering station, though this was the first time that John had ever seen the malmorph chief engineer man the bridge station. Young officers John didn't recognize sat at the astrogation and sensor stations, while Molon occupied his central position in the captain's chair.

"Glad you could join us, John," Molon greeted. "Sorry I don't have a seat to offer you, but I figured you might want to be on the bridge when we hit system."

"I appreciate it, captain," John said with a nod as he took a position standing near the captain's chair.

"If there is anyone in Tede you want to contact, Mel can help you connect as soon as we clear voidspace."

"Actually," John said, rubbing his chin, "with a few calls maybe I can help discover the identity of your mystery employer."

"That'd be nice," Voide interjected. "Getting paid sooner rather than later is always good."

On the viewscreen, the swirling colors John had been told were indicative of travel through voidspace began to shimmer and align as though a kaleidoscopic sea were suddenly being poured down a distant, rectangular drain. John felt his stomach lurch, and he thought he might be ill at any moment.

"Stomach doing flips, Doc?" Molon inquired reading John's discomfort on his face.

John nodded, taking a tight grip onto the back of the captain's chair to steady himself.

"You'll get used to it. Going into voidspace is like a whisper. Coming out is more like a drunken, nausea-filled shout. Ensign Reese, get Doc a sick-bag."

The young ensign manning the astrogation station reached below the station panels and pulled out a yellow bag with a self-sealing top. He sprinted over to John and handed him the bag.

"Thank you, ensign," John said with a weak smile.

"No problem, Doc. Don't worry, almost everyone pops their first time coming out of voidspace. Nothing to be embarrassed about."

John nodded but did not answer, deciding that keeping his mouth tightly closed and his mind focused on controlling his stomach required his full attention. He had slept through the emergence back at Hatacks, so this was his first time coming out of voidspace while awake.

Most of John's space travel previously had been on small

ships traveling between the inhabited colonies around the Tede system. He had never traveled between distant star systems while conscious before. There was something to be said for the cryo-suspension used during passages when booked in low berths. That's how he had traveled as a medical student to the core system of Sarren where he had attended medical school and done his residency.

Furthermore, despite his wealth and position, Salzmann Pharmaceuticals didn't splurge on expensive high berth passages, not even for executives, so his interstellar business trips since inheriting his family company had always been in frozen sleep booked in a low berth.

He did, however, have extensive experience drinking far too much for a single evening and facing the reality of a full schedule the next day. Holding his insides inside wasn't a completely new challenge. Who knew his younger days of drunken debauchery would serve at least one positive purpose? Still, he was glad to have the sick bag close at hand just in case.

As John watched the swirling colors of voidspace on the view screen, he marveled at this wonder mankind had discovered over three centuries ago. Another dimension, where space could be folded and distance as man knew it was irrelevant. The invention of the first voidspace drive, the VS1, had allowed man to slip through voidspace and fold two distant points together, emerging at the other end as smoothly as a trip around the solar system.

The first voidspace jump had only traversed two light years, but it had done it in less than a day. Technology and experience had made incredibly complex folding calculations possible; yielding routes that connected massive distances and allowed hundreds of light years to be traversed in mere weeks or months instead of millennia.

As John watched the chaotic swirl of colors begin to form a more and more orderly pattern, arranging themselves into more organized lines. Finally, the tiny black rectangle filled with stars grew closer and larger by the second. With a final lurch that almost, but not quite, freed his lunch from its captivity, they transitioned into normal space.

Suddenly John felt perfectly well again. The nausea dissipated almost instantly as the colorful display on the front viewscreens transitioned into a more familiar diorama of the stars and constellations of the Tede system.

Tede was a binary star system consisting of an orange dwarf star called Tede Alpha and its far companion, an orange sub-dwarf named Tede Beta. The system had a few satellite worlds, and one habitable planet around the main star that took the system name from the stars. Tede was a small world, with a gravity roughly half that of the human homeworld of Earth.

"Good job, Doc," the young ensign Reese said. "You got some stamina to hold it together your first transition."

John nodded, not sure that merely refraining from puking was an accomplishment to be particularly proud of.

"Recognize your home, John?" asked Captain Hawkins as the Tede mainworld loomed closer on the viewscreens.

"Tede may be a hermit-world, captain," John said, trying to rein in his growing annoyance at being treated like some ground-hugger. "But we have five inhabited bodies within our system. I have been to all of them save the restricted military research and development station on Tede Alpha's outermost planet, Tenis. This is not my first time in space."

"Sorry, Doc," Molon said with a grin. "We don't exactly bump into hermit-worlders every day. I guess we've some preconceptions of our own to break."

"Coming into comm range of Tede mainworld now, Molon," Mel commented. "I have released the queued message as requested."

"Thanks, Mel. So, Doc, who do you want to call while we wait?"

John made his way to stand beside the blue-skinned comms officer at her station. The smell of her as he drew near whisked his breath away. Mel gave off the scent of a meadow filled with wildflowers, yet he realized this was not completely an olfactory sensation. It was almost like he could feel her presence pushing this sensation into his soul.

"John?" Mel asked.

This near total stranger addressed him familiarly rather than formally. Somehow it felt right. It was as if he and Mel had been friends for years, even though they had only met days ago.

"Are you alright, John?" Mel inquired.

John suddenly realized he had just been standing silently beside the communications officer. He looked away to hide the flush he felt rising in his face. John was unsure if he had been standing there soaking in Mel's presence for ten seconds or ten minutes.

"I'm sorry," he covered, "I was just thinking."

John punched in the communication codes for Ben Perry's office in Elucia City. Mel patched the call through. A bookish female appeared on the viewscreen.

44

"High Governor Perry's office, how may I assist you?"

"Hi Maggie, it's me," John said, stepping to the center of the bridge to stand beside Captain Hawkins. "Is Ben in? I need to speak with him."

"Oh, Dr. Salzmann, my goodness," Maggie replied, her eyes turning glassy. "We heard you had disappeared. Yes, just a moment, I will get High Governor Perry for you right away."

The familiar logo of Tede's central government replaced Maggie's face on the viewscreen as she held the call, to be replaced less than a minute later by the balding, bespectacled face of Ben Perry, the top bureaucrat in Tede's central government.

"John, thank the Lion of Judah, you're alive! There were crazy reports that you had disappeared."

"A bit worse for wear, Ben, but definitely alive. Do I have you to thank for that?"

Ben Perry's brow furrowed.

"Beg pardon?"

John nodded, smiling at his friend to try and convey he hadn't completely lost his mind.

"It appears someone placed an anonymous contract on the System Express network for mercenaries to affect our rescue. I thought you might have been behind that."

Ben Perry flushed a bit as he shook his head.

"John, you know I would have. I would do anything in the world for you, but we had no idea what had happened to you. When I heard you were missing, I put the Elucia City security forces on full alert, and we scoured the city. Reports came in that some had seen assault ships landing directly on the surface and outside the starport without clearance or authority."

"Couldn't SysSec identify the ships?"

"No. SysSec never even detected their approach."

"How is that possible, Ben? We have monitoring stations near all the voidspace entry points into the system."

"Well," the High Governor said, rubbing his hands together. "The security stations reported some anomalous readings, but we had no clear visuals or even reliable eyewitness reports about whom the ships belonged to. SysSec suspects they were running signal scramblers. When we couldn't locate you, I sent a System Express shuttle to Haven reporting the incident and requesting guidance and assistance, but word hasn't returned yet from the capital. I wish I could take credit, John, but it wasn't me."

"Well if it wasn't you, and you are still waiting on word

45

back from Haven, then chances are it isn't the Theocracy either."

"Not likely," Ben laughed. "Patriarch Halberan is a good man doing the best he can in an impossible situation. Nevertheless, everyone knows he hasn't got the ships, even with help from the Angelicum and Fei forces, to secure all of the border worlds. Tede just isn't a priority system. We're neither strategically nor materially important. We've known for a long time that we're on our own out here. Whoever hired your mercenaries, Lion bless them, it certainly wasn't anyone from the Theocracy."

"I see," John said, rubbing his chin. "Well, Ben, I need to make a few more calls —"

"Actually, High Governor Perry," Molon interrupted, "if I might ask an indulgence?"

John had no idea what Molon was up to, but his socialite experience took over as he gracefully recovered from the unexpected interruption.

"Oh, Ben, please excuse my oversight. This fine gentleman is Captain Molon Hawkins, the person responsible for my rescue."

It was clear from the unsettled look on High Governor Perry's face that he was no more comfortable with non-human sophonts than John had been when he first arrived on *Star Wolf*. Fortunately, politicians thrived on navigating uncomfortable situations.

"Um, certainly...captain. It is nice to meet you. We are grateful for your efforts. What can I do for you?"

"I would like to request clearance for my ship to maintain a high orbit over Elucia City while we wait for contact from the patron who issued the contract to rescue Dr. Salzmann. Additionally, *Star Wolf* isn't rigged for terrestrial landing, but I may need to dispatch an STS to your starport in order to meet with the patron and return John to Tede. If you would clear us for that, I would be very grateful."

Ben Perry began fidgeting with his fingers and shuffling some papers on his desk.

"Um, yes, about that..."

"Ben, come on," John urged, guessing the reason for High Governor Perry's hesitation. "These are the good guys. What is the problem?"

"John, you know aliens are not allowed outside the starport. I can grant clearance for orbit, and I can clear an STS for landing, but understand that any aliens who land at the starport will not be permitted to leave the secure zone."

46

John flashed Molon a sympathetic look, cringing inwardly at the commonly used term, *alien,* that was considered impolite by non-human sophonts. Still, on Tede, a humans-only hermit-world with extremely limited non-human interaction, that was the commonly-used term.

"I'm sorry, captain," John said, turning to Molon. "Even Ben can't change the law."

"No worries," Molon replied with a gracious smile. "We're not here to cause trouble, just to pick up a paycheck, resupply and leave. We will play by the rules."

"Thank you for your understanding, captain," High Governor Perry said, mopping at his brow with a handkerchief.

"Ok, then Ben. Just have them send the clearance codes to this comm ID. I will be in touch when I can and fill you in on everything that happened."

"Not a problem, John. You will probably need to wait until tomorrow morning, reference my time, to get all the appropriate clearances logged."

"That will be fine, Ben," John said. He snapped his fingers, catching Ben's attention before they dropped the connection.

"Oh, Ben, I almost forgot. You might want to send an alert out to the Retar SysSec base. There is a possibility that Provisional Imperium or Dawnstar forces may try to launch an assault on the old monastery caves."

A smile crossed the face of the administrator.

"Really? That would prove interesting."

"Yeah, but Retar should be ready in case something goes awry and some survive the assault."

"I appreciate the heads up on that, John. I will pass the word. It really is good to see you alive. You and Elena please do drop by as soon as you get settled."

John's smile faded. He struggled to steady himself as his breath caught once again in his chest.

"Ben... Elena didn't make it."

A long silence followed John's statement. Ben Perry's head fell forward into his palms for a brief moment before he looked up again.

"I'm so sorry, John. We will pray for you."

John could hear the sincerity in Ben's voice. Not everyone had openly embraced his and Elena's marriage. Ben, however, had always been a true friend and had never been anything but supportive.

"Thanks, Ben," John replied, blinking back the water welling up in his eyes. "She is in the Lion's hands now."

Ben gave a final nod before the viewscreen went blank,

and a respectful silence encapsulated the bridge. After a few moments, Molon spoke up.

"About that monastery, don't you want to put a call through to those monks?" There was a stern, almost accusatory tone in Molon's voice. "I mean, you put Tubal's forces onto them. You might want to warn them."

"Don't worry, captain," John replied with a broad grin. "I would never betray followers of the Lion of Judah. The Brothers of the Lion abandoned those caves six months ago after some rumors hit that they might be hunted even onto Tede. They left the caves thoroughly booby-trapped, however, so anyone pursuing them there would believe they met strong resistance from the Brothers. Wherever their new base is, it isn't here."

Molon flashed a wolfish grin.

"So you lied to the inquisitor?"

"I equivocated," John replied.

"That was a heck of a gamble. What did you expect to happen when the Dawnstar forces discovered the deception?"

John's grin faded. He rubbed the back of his neck and shook his head slightly as he responded.

"At that point all I could think about was stopping Elena's pain. I hoped this gambit would, at least temporarily. The Brothers of the Lion rigging the caves would bear out my story that they at least had been there. It was the best thing I could think of at that moment to buy us some time while I thought of a way to get us out of there."

"That was incredibly brave and thoughtful," Mel said, sending another strange wash of positive feelings running through John's body.

"And incredibly risky," Voide added. "If they investigated the caves and found out they had been abandoned for months, you would have brought a world of pain down on both of you."

John felt the anger welling up inside at the accusation, pushing past the waves of calm emanating from Mel. Voide seemed to have the uncanny ability to push his buttons like no one else. He wanted to let the provocations go, but he just couldn't seem to rein in his tongue where Voide was concerned.

"Maybe you have the ability to coldly calculate all the angles while you and the person you care most about in the world are being tortured, but we humans are frailer than that I suppose."

"Enough," growled Molon, glaring at Voide. "It was a smart and gutsy play, John. I might have done the same thing."

John's shoulders sagged as he clenched his fists.

"Not smart enough. The son of a pig killed her anyway."

"You can't blame yourself for that. He would've killed Elena no matter what you did. That's on him, not you."

"Thank you, captain," John said, closing his eyes and taking a deep breath before continuing. "You may be right, but that doesn't make it any easier."

"I do have a question though," Molon added.

John shifted uneasily on his feet wondering what was coming next. He liked the captain, but this topic of conversation, in the open environment of the bridge, was straining John's self-control. He tossed a silent prayer heavenward that a subject change was imminent.

"What is it, captain," he asked, choking back the trepidation at the question.

"The governor mentioned Haven. I thoroughly reviewed this part of the Orenc sector before we arrived but that is not a system I am familiar with."

"Oh," John answered, sighing with relief that Molon was not going to probe the events on Ratuen any further. "The home base of the Theocracy of the Faithful is in Orenc subsector C, around a star system called Hiped. The nickname for it within the Theocracy is *Haven*."

"Ah, I see," Molon replied, nodding. "Well, do you have anyone else you wanna call while we wait?"

John knew who his next called needed to go to, but something deep inside him still cautioned about fully trusting the *Star Wolf* crew. If they had any idea what he was worth, the temptation to hold him for ransom would be almost overwhelming. So far, Captain Hawkins had dealt squarely, but John's gambling instincts were screaming for him not to show his cards just yet.

Still, there was little other choice at this point. He needed Molon's cooperation to get back to the surface. John sent another silent prayer heavenward that his faith in his rescuers would prove true. Then he turned to answer Molon.

"Yes. I need to call my corporation's headquarters."

"Your parents' corporation, you mean," Voide said with slyness in her voice that let John know in no uncertain terms his cover story in the briefing room had fooled no one.

"No, my corporation," John admitted. "It was my parents' but I inherited it. If neither Ben nor the Theocracy was behind the rescue, Salzmann Pharmaceuticals is the only other idea I have for who it could have been."

John gave Mel the communication codes, and she patched

the call through. A thin male in a full business suit popped onto the screen.

"Salzmann Pharmaceuticals, how may I direct your call?"

John once again stepped into the center of the bridge and addressed the operator.

"This is John Salzmann. I need to speak to Chairman Biggs."

The young man fidgeted briefly before clearing his throat to reply and affecting a smile.

"I'm sorry sir, Chairman Biggs is in an emergency meeting of the board of directors and has left explicit instructions that he not be disturbed. Can I put you through to his assistant? I am certain he will return your call as soon as he is out of the meeting."

"Young man," John said, in a commanding tone none on the bridge had heard from the normally amiable doctor. "Did you not hear me? This is John Salzmann, President and CEO of the company that, for the moment at least, issues your pay vouchers. I'm glad the board is in session, as it will give me a chance to speak to all of them. Please, patch me through to the board room now."

The young man swallowed visibly and moved a shaky hand toward the comm controls at his desk.

"Just a moment, Dr. Salzmann. I will see what I can do about patching you into the board room. Please hold."

"You do that."

The Salzmann Pharmaceuticals logo popped on screen, and pleasant, indistinct music piped through the bridge speakers.

"Wow, pale," said Voide, "you do have a backbone hidden deep in there. You should let it out more often."

John laughed, not certain if Voide's comment was an actual compliment or just sarcasm, but he chose to take it as the former.

"Yeah," John replied. "I am the terror of interns and entry level clerks everywhere."

The nervous youth reappeared, even more rattled than before. His hands shook and his voice wavered his response.

"Dr. Salzmann, Chairman Biggs says he will be happy to call you as soon as the meeting is concluded if you would leave your comm codes with me."

"Son," John continued, his voice taking on a steely sternness, "patch me into that board room comm system right now or so help me your great, great grandchildren won't be able to find work on Tede. Do I make myself clear?"

"Yes, but Chairman Biggs—"

"Reports to me."

"Y-yes sir. Patching you in right away sir."

Moments later the image of a room full of stuffed suits filled the screen, with a heavy-set man in a gray pin-striped suit yelling at the rest of the room.

"Now it is imperative we take this action immediately before it is too late—"

Awareness that the comm system had been activated suddenly came over the boardroom. The heavy-set man turned and flashed a fake smile in John's direction.

"John, we are so glad you could make it for this meeting. We heard rumors you were off planet."

John fought the instinct to retch at Biggs' sycophantic overtures. The guy was a weasel, but he had one of the best financial and business minds on Tede.

"Yes, Bill. I am so glad you immediately and willingly took my call."

John fought back a smirk as Biggs flushed like a card player caught bluffing his last chips into a losing pot.

"Of course, John," Chairman Bill Biggs said with a smarmy tone in his voice. "You are always welcome here."

"Thanks, Bill. It is comforting to know I am welcome to drop in on board meetings for *my* company."

"Of course, John," Biggs said as he flushed a deeper red and busied his hands checking something on his datapad. "So what can we do for you?"

"Maybe nothing. Given your statement about the rumors of me being off planet, I take it you were not aware that Elena and I had been kidnapped?"

The fat man fidgeted, and several exchanged glances from the others present in the boardroom spoke volumes.

"Kidnapped? Oh, goodness no," Biggs said, fumbling with his fingers before wringing his hands. "We had no idea."

"So," John said, a steely tone entering his voice as he glowered at the chairman thorugh the comm system. "You didn't think it strange that I was suddenly out of touch for weeks?"

"Well, John," Biggs said, clearing his throat and reaching for a glass of water. After a large gulp, he continued. "There might have been some whispered scuttlebutt to that effect, but who believes these kinds of things. I mean people being snatched off hermit-worlds isn't a common occurrence, you know. Most hermit-worlders can't pay much of a ransom."

"Good to know you were skeptical," John pressed. "So

51

what did you think happened to us, Bill?"

"Well, John," Biggs laughed nervously, "you are quite the gambler. We thought you might have taken Elena and gone chasing some card game somewhere, who knows. It is not our place to judge you."

"That's comforting," John replied and silently stared at Biggs, waiting for the stout man to continue.

"Still," Biggs said, finally breaking the nervous silence, "in the best interest of the company, we thought it best to call an emergency meeting to discuss all possibilities."

"Doubtless those possibilities involve the disposition of my voting shares should I fail to turn up in a reasonable time?" John asked.

Sweat beaded on Bill Bigg's forehead. A few more sideways glances told John his guess was right on the money.

"Among so many other things, yes, John, that was one item on the agenda. Fortunately, you are fine, and we can table that discussion for another time."

"Don't worry, I will relieve you of that burden. Larry," John said addressing Lawrence Filburne, Salzmann Pharmaceuticals' chief legal counsel.

"Yes John," Filburne answered.

"Get in touch with Saul Peterson, my personal attorney, today. He has in his possession a folder labeled Sigma Initiative. Work with him through everything needed to implement this plan right away."

"Yes sir," Filburne answered.

"Uh, John," Biggs interjected, "what exactly is this Sigma Initiative? Shouldn't you discuss the details with the board before enacting a new policy?"

John flashed the heavy-set chairman a condescending smile. John had put off this showdown for too long. It was sad that it took such a violent and tragic set of circumstances for him finally to pull the trigger on this.

"You are right, Bill. So, while I have you all here, let me lay it out for you. Last year I set up a trust of investors called the Sigma Seven. The Sigma Initiative contains all the paperwork to ensure, in the event of my death or extended absence, that voting control of my shares will default to this Sigma Seven trust."

Biggs was clearly flustered, and a number of other board members looked as if they were on the verge of coming out of their seats.

"Who are these people?" Biggs objected. "You can't just turn voting control over to strangers. They haven't been vetted by the board. This is highly irregular."

"Nevertheless, Larry will work through everything with Saul and will verify that everything is legal and proper. The board won't need to worry about the disposition of my voting shares in the future."

"But, John!" Biggs said, his voice rising to a semi-shriek and the nervous perspiration on his face changing to a deep crimson flush of frustration.

"No need to thank me, Bill, I am happy to take one more worry off your already busy plate. Now you can move on to all the other items on your agenda. I will leave you to it. Keep up the good work, everyone."

John nodded to Mel who cut the connection before Biggs could voice another objection.

"Well, that was fun," John said flashing a smile toward Molon. "Unfortunately it appears my company wasn't behind the rescue attempt either, although I wouldn't necessarily rule them out of being involved in me going missing in the first place."

"Seriously?" Molon asked, his ears twitching forward and a lupine scowl crawling over his features.

"No, not really," John sighed. "Biggs might have the motive and desire to act directly against me, but the guy has all the spine and fortitude of seaweed."

"Well," Molon replied, shaking his head, "unless you have any other ideas about the possible identity of our patron, there isn't much else to do but wait."

"Actually captain," John answered rubbing his chin as his head buzzed with an idea, "there is."

Molon raised an eyebrow and waited for John to elaborate.

"I'd like to go back to my house and take a look around, maybe pick up a few things. If I won't be free to leave until the contract is settled, at least I can grab a bit of home while I wait."

"That should be fine," Molon nodded.

"Captain?" Twitch interrupted.

"What's up, Twitch?" Molon answered.

"We need to make a supply run. We may not be able to restock armaments here on this hermit-world, but quite a few supplies we need should be available."

"Good call. Assemble a resupply detail: humans only as you might need to venture outside the secure starport area to get the supplies we need."

"Voide," he said, turning to his security chief. "It looks like we're going dirtside. Prep for an undercover infil-exfil op, and

53

meet us in the shuttle bay 0800 Elucia City local time. You'll be escorting John to his house and back."

"Undercover?" Voide asked.

"Yeah. We don't know for sure locals weren't involved in the Salzmanns getting snatched, so I don't want him exposed any longer than necessary, and I sure don't want him going anywhere unescorted. I'll wait in the starport for our patron to call."

"Aye, sir," Voide acknowledged.

"Mel," Molon continued, turning to his comms officer. "As soon as you get any response to our message, patch it through the cargo STS to my personal communicator."

"Yes, Molon."

"I hope you understand, Doc," Molon continued, returning his gaze to John. "I don't want you out of sight until everything is settled with this mystery patron. Like it or not, you are our living pay voucher for this one."

"I understand," John replied, wondering if he would become a captive if the mysterious patron didn't respond.

John's stomach churned as he wrestled with how to broach the next subject wracking his mind without appearing to undermine the captain's authority. He had no desire to make a nuisance of himself, but he couldn't reconcile Molon's promise to abide by Tede's anti-alien laws with the just-uttered instruction to the Prophane Pariah security chief to escort him home.

"Um, no offense, captain," John interrupted, lowering his voice so that hopefully only Molon might hear, "but have you forgotten Ben's cautioning regarding Tede law?"

"What do you mean?" Molon asked.

"Well, captain," John paused, trying to figure the least-offensive way to proceed. "The starport authorities will never let Voide out of the secure zone. You might need to arrange a human escort, if you insist an escort is necessary."

Voide's hearing had to be more sensitive than John gave her credit for. She flashed John a feral grin.

"What's the matter, pale? You don't like my company?"

John didn't want to honestly answer that question. He wasn't crazy about the idea of being alone with the Pariah, but fortunately he had another answer that was equally true.

"It's not about that. The law says no non-human sophonts outside the starport secure area."

"Don't worry, pale," Voide replied. "It won't be a problem."
*****
The door chime to Molon's quarters sounded.

54

"Come."

Twitch strode in, headed straight for the cabinet where Molon kept his best brandy, and poured herself a double before dropping onto his couch.

"Make yourself at home," Molon quipped.

"Don't I always?"

"True," Molon replied. "Still, a full glass right off the bat? Usually we have to argue for half an hour before you work up to a full glass."

"You want one?" Twitch asked. "This is going to be a double-sized convo."

"Sure, thanks," Molon replied.

"Well, help yourself," Twitch said without budging off the couch. "It's top notch stuff."

Molon grinned at his XO before getting up, walking over to the cabinet, and pouring a full glass of his own. If Twitch said booze was going to help whatever she came to talk about, he believed her.

"Thanks for sharing my booze," Molon said with a grin. "That's very generous of me."

"Anytime," Twitch answered, taking a deep draught of her glass. "Your booze is my booze."

"You know," Molon said with a shake of his head, "on any other ship, this would be considered rank insubordination."

"Good thing I'm not on another ship," Twitch replied with a smile.

"Or serving a different captain on this one," Molon quipped.

"I think you know better," Twitch replied, her tone growing suddenly serious. "If *Star Wolf* had a different captain, I wouldn't be here."

"Should I be comforted or worried?" Molon asked, raising an eyebrow.

"Bit of both, actually."

Molon and Twitch had been together for a long time. Being around her was like slipping into a comfortable pair of shoes that had been broken in long ago and now just fit like a second skin. She had been his first partner in the Scouts. They had been to remote regions, mapping new worlds and exploring new systems. They had been undercover together, and had saved each other's behinds more times than he could count.

They had always been a great team. Molon was the brawn and Twitch was the brains. His job was getting them into messes, and hers had been getting them out of it. He handled

55

the grunt work, and Twitch handled the paperwork. Their old CO in the Scouts had said he had never seen a more perfect pair. Molon trusted Twitch more than he trusted himself.

"So, I'm guessing you didn't just drop by to drink up all my brandy and chit-chat, eh?"

"Nope," Twitch replied.

Molon waited, but Twitch just took another drink.

"So am I supposed to guess, or are you going to tell me what the problem is?"

"You are, Lobo, as always."

Uh oh. Twitch used his call sign. That was never good news.

"What'd I do now?"

"Same thing you always do. You've set up what should have been a routine away mission to turn into a real Charlie Foxtrot."

Charlie Foxtrot -- phonetic code for the letters C and F. Military personnel used to use the phonetic alphabet to make sure their communications were not misunderstood. Not unlike Twitch, telling him in no uncertain terms that she thought his call was a total cluster-frack.

"Well, I don't see it, so enlighten me."

"That's the problem," Twitch said, suddenly shifting her relaxed posture into a straight-backed stiffness. "You never see it. You have an absolute blind spot when it comes to your crew. How many traitors, turncoats, or spies have we had in the four years we've been on *Star Wolf*?"

"I dunno," Molon said rubbing the fur on the back of his neck. "Half a dozen or so."

"Fourteen," Twitch answered.

"Fourteen?" Molon raised an eyebrow. "That many?"

"Yeah. And how many of those turnabouts did you see coming, Lobo?"

Molon took a deep draught of his brandy and rose to get a refill. He knew the answer. It went without saying.

"That's right," Twitch pressed. "None. Because the honorable Molon Hawkins thinks everyone else in the universe plays it just as straight as he does. Join his crew and you can tie a grenade to his tail. He'll never suspect a thing."

"Aw, come on now Twitch. Some of those guys were pros. Who could have spotted them?"

"Me. In fact, of the eleven you let me meet before you hired them, I warned you against each one. Did you listen? No."

Molon slumped back into his desk chair and cocked his

head at his XO.

"And if I'd listened to you, we wouldn't have half the crew we are running with now. In fact, I recall you said we shouldn't take on Mel and Voide."

"Mel is damaged, Molon," Twitch said getting up to refill her own glass. "She's going to crack under pressure, you just wait."

"Come on, Twitch, give the kid a break. What she went through on Tetoyl at the hands of that Alpha Pack governor Dragk would have broken most people. She's stronger than you give her credit for."

"She's cracked, Molon," Twitch said, dropping heavily back onto the couch. "And the minute you put any pressure on her, she'll shatter."

"You're wrong on this one, Twitch," Molon said, shaking his head emphatically. "She's been with us almost a year now and we've been through plenty of scrapes. Mel ain't cracked yet."

Twitch laughed. "She's a comms jockey, Molon. I'm not talking about patching through messages; I'm talking about really coming under fire."

"She'll be fine," Molon said through gritted teeth. "But since Mel isn't on the away mission in the morning, I'm guessing she is not the focus of this hypothetical Charlie Foxtrot."

"No, that would be your other darling, our resident psychopath."

"Voide?" Molon asked with a shrug, sensing the direction this conversation was heading.

"Do you have another psychopath in the crew you haven't told me about?" Twitch said, raising an eyebrow.

"Voide's battle-tested. So what am I missing?" Molon was almost afraid to ask. When Twitch got like this, she wasn't likely to back down easily.

"She resents authority and restriction. Heck, she only obeys you because you let her do whatever she pleases almost without exception."

"That's a load of bull," Molon growled, half under his breath. "Besides, she's not on a diplomatic mission tomorrow. She's doing a straightforward undercover infil/exfil. She won't be talking to anyone but the Doc, most likely."

Twitch harrumphed and set her drink on the table as she wagged a finger in Molon's face.

"Don't play coy, Lobo. Undercover or no, you know full well Tede's regulations against non-humans are going to grate on her. She'll be scouring the horizon for any excuse to out herself and flaunt it in the face of authorities. She's likely to get us kicked off this rock before we even have a chance to get paid."

"Come on," Molon said shaking his head, but half fearing Twitch was right. "Voide will do her job. Sure she gets to chafing when people try to bind her up, but she knows the drill. Besides, the call's already been made. What would you have me do?"

"Think of something, anything, to give her a reason to be on this ship, or with you at the port. Pick any one of a dozen human marines to escort the doctor home and back. But if you send her on this mission, you are just asking for trouble."

Molon set his glass down on the desk, grabbed the arms of his chair, and exhaled a long breath.

"In all our years together I can count on one hand the number of times you've misread a situation."

"Darn, straight," Twitch said, nodding.

"But this is my call. Who knows how many locals might be involved with Dawnstar. Sure we've got some good marines, but you can't honestly sit there and tell me there is another person on this ship, the two of us included, that the doc would be safer with if things go all pear-shaped."

Twitch shook her head and drained her glass. Her silence was affirmation enough.

"Yeah," Molon continued. "I thought as much. Look, Twitch, I appreciate you coming to me. I rely on your input, but you're wrong about Voide. She's been with us almost since the beginning and she hasn't let us down yet."

Twitch laughed.

"That depends on your definition of letdown."

"Aw, knock it off. Yeah, she's volatile, and I won't pretend she hasn't made a few situations a lot more interesting than they had to be—

"Interesting? That what you call it?"

"Okay, chaotic," Molon scowled, flailing his hands in frustration. "You happy?"

"Better...still euphemistic."

"Whatever. Truth is I'd rather have her on my side making things *chaotic* than not have her around at all. She'll behave."

Twitch stood and walked toward the door.

"Okay, Lobo. It's your call. But I've got that 'I told you so' all queued up and ready."

"Well pack it away for safekeeping. It'll be a while before you need it."

"We'll see," she said as she opened the door to leave. "Good brandy, by the way."

"Glad you approve. I would get you some, but I figure why bother when you'll just keep drinking mine."

"Good point. Good night, partner."

"G'night, Twitch."

If she turned out to be right on this, he'd never hear the end of it.

Five – Unexpected Guests

John entered the lower deck of *Star Wolf*'s shuttle bay, which housed the larger cargo STS. The smaller STS, which Molon had used to extract them from Ratuen, was docked on the upper level above them.

As he approached the larger STS he observed a number of *Star Wolf* crew members milling about and prepping the shuttle for departure. A striking raven-haired human woman, her arms crossed, looking impatient, bearing a Lieutenant Commander's insignia, stood near the entry hatch. She was dressed in a black jumpsuit of the type used by commandos on night runs, at least in the military holovids John had seen. He approached the woman and gasped as he realized why she looked so familiar.

"Voide?" he asked, shocked that her gray skin and bright yellow eyes had been replaced by an even, light-tan skin tone with piercing green irises in the center of human-looking white eyes.

"I told you it wouldn't be a problem," she answered, "as long as I don't smile. These," she said flashing her vampiric canines, "are a little harder to hide."

"Amazing," John replied, his head reeling at the astounding disguise. "But how?"

Voide looked at him like something she had just scraped off the bottom of her shoe. John stood up straighter, threw back his shoulders, and returned her gaze. He refused to wither beneath her condescending stare.

"Keep up, pale," Voide replied. "Molon told you I used to work for GalSec. Infiltration is a core survival skill for spies. Don't worry, I'll be out of this horrid, pale coloring and back to my beautiful gray complexion as soon as we finish up this house call on your xenophobic little ball of dirt."

Just then, Molon entered the cargo bay dressed in the hi-tech advanced boarding vac-suit he was wearing when they escaped Ratuen. The sergeant rank insignia had been removed, but otherwise it looked just as John remembered it.

60

"Souvenir?" John asked, nodding at Molon's attire.

"You kidding me?" Molon replied, sweeping his hand in front of his suit as if it was on display and he was the salesman. "This is TL14 stuff. Can't find gear like this very easily since the Shattering. I consider it a bonus, courtesy of Dawnstar."

John laughed. He supposed looting was just part of the mercenary trade. Molon was right, TL14 equipment didn't come easy or cheap anymore on any non-core world. TL14+ medical equipment was something John had rarely even seen at conferences or trade shows. Since the Shattering, Tede had reverted to a self-sustaining tech level of six.

John sometimes regretted how badly the Shattering had impacted the technological and economic structure of the galaxy. Post Shattering, star systems had been divided into those which served as home bases for the megacorps, called core systems, and everybody else, now called frontier worlds even though many were deep in the heart of Humaniti space. Frontier systems were only useful for strategic location or raw resources, but otherwise were left to fend for themselves. Having studied and done his residency in the core Sarren system, the high-tech lifestyle and abundant wealth didn't seem like they were in the same galaxy as struggling frontier worlds like Tede.

Interstellar trade, so much a hallmark of the hundred and thirty-eight years of the Halberan Dynasty, had almost collapsed completely post-Shattering. This was doubly true on worlds like Tede, located so close to a contested border. Pre-Shattering, cooperative economics were the order of the day. In the eight years since, self-sustaining had become the mantra in frontier regions throughout the sprawl of Humaniti space. The prosperity of the Humaniti Empire had been killed by blocked trade routes, scorched earth warfare, and the selfish greed of the megacorps.

John's musing was cut short as the newly-humanized security chief brushed some dust flecks off Molon's shoulder.

"It looks great on you, captain," Voide said, snapping John back to the moment. "You don't even have to cut a hole in the back for your tail."

Molon scowled, and then let it slip into a grin.

"Do you have any idea how hard it is to find Lubanian fitted armor outside of Lubanian space? You tailless sophonts don't exactly go out of your way to stock tailed vac suits."

John chuckled at the exchange, but was anxious to get back to his home. Most of the crew appeared to be the the final stages of loading the STS. John did a quick mental recheck of

61

his own but could not think of anything he forgot to handle.

"Are we departing soon, captain?" he asked.

"Now good with you, Doc?" Molon asked, motioning toward the STS's entry hatch. "We will have you dirtside by midafternoon."

John liked that "Doc" had become almost a de facto call sign for him. It made him feel more like a part of the crew. He certainly preferred it to the pejorative "pale" which most non-human sophonts used as slang for humans, and which seemed to be Voide's preferred manner of address for him.

Soon the STS, with its resupply crew, Captain Hawkins, and John's disguised escort, was wending its way toward Tede's surface. The shuttle ride went smoothly, and they had received the landing clearance codes from the governor's office just as Ben had promised. Soon they touched down at the starport, located about four hours by surface transport outside Elucia City proper. An express mag-rail train could reach the city in twenty minutes, but John wasn't going to the city.

"Okay," Molon said as the hatch opened." You kids run along and stay out of trouble. The crew will take care of resupply while I haunt whatever passes for a bar in this starport and wait for our payday."

"You got it boss," Voide answered. "Grab your ruck, pale, and let's hit the road."

John started to ask what a "ruck" was when Molon grabbed his shoulder and turned him to look into the captain's eyes.

"Straight home and straight back, Doc. No sightseeing. I don't want you in the wind any longer than necessary."

"No problem, captain," John said, nodding. "As scintillating as I find Voide's company, I'll try and rein in my wanderlust. I just want to make sure the house is secure and grab a few personal things. We should make it there and back by dusk."

John angled toward the starport exit with Voide tight on his heels. *Star Wolf's* security chief, in addition to her commando-like jump suit, had added a bandolier, slung from right shoulder to left hip, with some sort of mechanical device attached to the front of it. From her right hip swung a quiver with a dozen arrows. In her left hand she carried a long, sheathed, single edged sword with a black cloth-wrapped handle and matching duraplast scabbard. John's curiosity got the better of him concerning her gear as they walked toward the starport exit.

"You look like you are dressed for combat."

"And you look like a victim." Voide snapped. "I prefer to be prepared. Is that a problem?"

"You do know this is a peaceful hermit-world, right?" John replied with a shake of his head.

"So?"

"So, we are simple folk, farmers and craftsmen mostly. I'm afraid you won't find much to fight hereabouts."

"Maybe so," Voide responded, with cold steel in her voice. "But don't forget, whoever snatched you off this rock was counting on simple folk. Should they return, they will find me considerably less peaceful."

John refused to let the matter drop. After all, this was his city and he was going to have to return here. What would people think of him going around with a hostile-looking female bodyguard armed to the teeth? John stopped walking toward the gate and turned to face Voide.

"Look at you."

"Beautiful, ain't I?" Voide teased.

The comment made John flush slightly. He sighed and tightened his face. He had never wanted to hit a female this badly before in his life, but knowing who Voide was and valuing his life, John found restraint.

"You're practically a one-woman war party," John said, motioning toward her sword and quiver of arrows. "I'm not even sure they are going to let you walk around in public like that."

Voide glanced at her accoutrements as though noticing them for the first time. She gave John a derisive smirk.

"Look, pale, I'm touched by your concern, but if you are worried about me getting arrested, don't be. I did my homework."

"Your homework?" John asked, raising an eyebrow.

"Yes," Voide replied, pulling out her datapad and handing it to John. It displayed the section of Tede's legal statutes dealing with legal and illegal weapons. "Your world prohibits energy weapons and automatic slug-throwers. Everything I am carrying is perfectly legal here."

John rubbed the back of his neck as he scanned the datapad. The legal codes did seem to allow for everything Voide was visibly carrying.

"I suppose you did," John said, his irritation growing but starting to realize he was not going to win this argument. "But what about that?" he said pointing to the odd device attached to the center of the bandolier. "That looks pretty dangerous and high tech. What is it, some kind of explosive or

63

something?"

Voide shifted her sword to her right hand and reached up with her left to detach the device from its cradle. With a snap of her wrist, the complex gadget unfolded and stretched from top and bottom into a black, metallic, high-tech bow.

"It's still legal, but more convenient than carrying around a wooden longbow. This is less conspicuous."

"Wow," John marveled. "I'm a sporting bow-hunter myself. What kind of pull weight does that thing have?"

"Adjustable up to thirty kilos," Voide replied, flipping a switch on the grip. The bow once again collapsed and folded into a form she reattached to the bandolier.

"You know something, Voide," John quipped with a shake of his head as he resumed his march toward the starport exit. "You're an odd person...and more than a little scary."

"You have no idea," Voide replied, flashing him a close-lipped smirk, keeping her elongated Prophane canines concealed.

They approached the exit port. John recognized the young officer manning the security checkpoint. That was one of the advantages to being a big fish in a low-population, hermit-world pond.

"Hello Max," John called out to the young man.

Max was a spindly young man with slicked back black hair and a serious case of acne. He was dressed in a starport security guard's uniform that looked at least one size too large for him.

"Hey, Dr. Salzmann," the young man answered, smiling and waving a hand in welcome as he recognized John. "I didn't realize you had been off world. Welcome home."

"Thanks, Max," John replied curtly.

He had no desire to go into any more detail with the port security officer than was necessary. The fewer people asking questions right now the better. Unfortunately, Max was not so quick to rush unquestioningly through the entry logistics.

"And your friend..." Max said, nodding at Voide.

"She's just that, a friend" John answered as he offered a mental prayer that Max would let the matter go at that. "You should have the authorization from High Governor Perry's office in your system."

Max punched up something on his computer screen.

"Sure enough, Dr. Salzmann, I've got it right here. Um, ma'am," Max said, eyeing the sword in Voide's hand. "Would you like to check that weapon into one of our convenient port lockers? They are normally two theocreds a day, but I would be happy to issue you a complimentary guest voucher. It will be perfectly secure until you return."

"No thanks," Voide mumbled, keeping her mouth mostly closed to avoid flashing her fangs. "It is more secure with me holding it."

The young officer looked back and forth between Voide and John, not quite sure how to respond.

"It'll be fine, Max. Everything is within Tede's legal regulations," John bluffed, hoping that Voide had been as thorough with her research as she claimed. "We are just making a quick run to my house to pick up some things and will be back shortly. Is there a ground vehicle available?"

John's ploy worked. With the transportation question the security officer was back in his comfort zone.

"Certainly, Dr. Salzmann. PT or CUV?"

"There was some construction out our way before I left. Road clearance might be a bid dodgy with a personal transport. Let us have a full-size cargo and utility vehicle, Max."

"You got it!" The youth entered some information into his terminal and passed a set of keys to John. "Take the dark blue CUV in spot six. It was recently serviced and I washed it just this morning. Should I bill Salzmann Pharmaceuticals?"

"No, Max, this trip is not a business trip. Bill it to my personal Tede Central Bank account, if you would."

Max punched a few more keys on his keyboard.

"Done and done. You're all set. Have a nice trip, Dr. Salzmann."

John breathed a sigh of relief as he and Voide exited the starport proper and headed into the parking lot.

They traveled for nearly two hours, bouncing lightly down the road in the large CUV. Tede's lower gravity made for a floaty ride, but John was accustomed to handling a vehicle in this environment. Tede's automobiles came standard with extremely dense undercarriage plating, giving them greater maneuvering stability.

As they traversed the largely pastoral countryside between Elucia City's starport and the city proper, John broke the silence that had engulfed them since leaving the starport.

"Can I ask you a question, Voide?"

"You can ask," Voide replied, glancing sideways at John and crossing her arms. "Whether or not I answer depends on the question."

That sharp, snarky edge she projected both annoyed and intrigued John. He had made a few faux pas with her, but her disdain for him seemed out of proportion to any minor slips

65

that might have set her off. No way around this but through it, he supposed.

"You don't like me very much, do you?"

She laughed. John caught a hint of derision hidden in there somewhere.

"To be honest, pale," Voide replied with a tone that projected the resentment bundled into that sneer on her face. "I don't have much of an opinion about you at all. I'll like you more when whoever arranged for us to snatch you away from Dawnstar pays up. I can't wait to get off this backward rock."

John chose to ignore the dig at his homeworld's lack of sophistication. There was something hiding under that cool exterior, and his natural curiosity goaded him to dig it out.

"So tell me something, why do you do it?"

"Do what?" Voide snapped, looking perturbed at John's insistence on making conversation.

"Be a mercenary. I mean you are a beautiful, determined, and intelligent woman. I have no doubt you could succeed at anything you put your mind to. Why would you choose to fly around the galaxy endangering your life for pay?"

"Do you always answer your own questions?"

John wasn't sure if Voide was being serious or sarcastic.

"What do you mean?" he pressed, starting to wonder who was mentally dissecting whom.

"For pay!" she answered. "You just asked why I would endanger my life for pay. That's exactly why any merc does what they do: to get paid."

"There are many ways to make money that don't involve killing or the risk of being killed."

John caught Voide's feral smile out of the corner of his eye. It made his skin crawl as her voice dropped into a smooth, haunting rhythm.

"Yeah, but I'm very good at killing."

Silence fell for a few brief moments as John pondered her statement. He did not doubt her sincerity, but chose to adjust the focus of his inquiries onto a less morbid target.

"Life is about more than getting paid."

"Really?" Voide replied. "That might be a more credible philosophy if it wasn't coming from a multi-billionaire."

Apparently Voide had done her homework on more than just Tede's weapon laws. Salzmann Pharmaceuticals was a publicly traded company so its records were open, as were much of John's holdings. She was clearly trying to rattle him, but being an experienced gambler gives one a passable poker-face, even when the cards start going against you.

66

"Money can't buy everything," John said, returning to his point. Suddenly a sad nostalgia fell over him as he thought about how true that statement had proven in his own life. "Trust me, I know."

"What it can't buy, it can rent; for a few hours at least," Voide quipped.

John kept his focus on the road and off her sly grin. That buy-vs-rent joke was one John had heard too many times before, usually from people living payday to payday. It never got any funnier. Voide was clearly ducking any serious questions, but he wasn't about to fold his cards just yet.

"Can you be serious for one minute? You are far too complex a woman for there to be nothing more to your career choice than just money. What about the Prophane? They are your people. Don't you ever wonder what it would be like to go back to them? You could be instrumental in bringing peace between the Prophane and Humaniti."

Voide gave John a not-too-gentle smack on the back of his head, startling him and causing him to swerve. The maneuver nearly sent the CUV off the road and into a ditch.

"Hey!" he interjected.

"Do you have brain damage, or just memory issues?"

"What are you talking about?" John felt his face flushing as he gripped the steering wheel tighter.

"I already told you, pale, there is no going back. I am a Pariah. That's not just a fun nickname I use at parties. Any Prophane would try to kill me on sight. Molon and the crew of the *Star Wolf* are my people now."

She flashed a deep scowl. John started to respond but Voide raised her voice and interrupted before he could form his next sentence.

"Okay, you really want to know about me?"

John nodded.

"Fine. Here's a history lesson you won't find in any books. I was on one of the first Prophane ships that crossed the Stygian Rift into Humaniti space. Ours was a colony ship and I was an infant at the time. My real family, and every other adult Prophane on board, fought to the death when Empire Marines on patrol boarded our ship."

John's heart wavered at her story. Were there really such things as Prophane colonists? He only knew of stories about maniacal, war-mongering Prophane. He'd never heard tell of a civilian Prophane ship.

"That was what, like thirty years ago?" John asked. "How did you survive?"

"The young marine officer in charge of the boarding action, Lieutenant Ikei Matsumura, found me. Our colony ship was well armed and had ignored communication attempts, destroying three Humaniti Navy ships before we were boarded."

"Tough colonists," John remarked.

"Yeah, I'm not the only Prophane good at killing. So you can understand why the commanding officer of the patrol group wasn't in a forgiving mood."

"Yet you survived?"

"Barely. Lieutenant Matsumura disobeyed the order to take no prisoners, instead ordering his marines to stand down when they found me in my parents' quarters."

"An Old Empire Navy captain ordered the slaughter of civilians? What kind of insane order is that?" John gasped, wondering if Voide was relaying some type of hoax to make him look naive.

"It is the kind given by a captain who has had a lot of his buddies ripped to bits by the few other Prophane ships they had encountered without so much as a hello in response to hails. For the Prophane, there are no civilians. Every adult is a combatant."

At least this latest revelation helped to reconcile Voide's story with what he knew about Humaniti's history of encounters with the Prophane Ascendency.

"But you weren't an adult. Surely murdering infants couldn't have been a legal order."

Voide scoffed. "You think some vengeance-minded officer cared about legal? Legal or not, disobeying orders gets young officers court martialed, which is exactly what happened to Lieutenant Matsumura."

"Was he found guilty?" John asked, reeling at the revelation that such injustice might exist within the Empire of Humaniti.

"No, but it didn't matter. Even after a court martial found that he rightfully disobeyed an unlawful order, his reenlistment was denied. Despite an otherwise stellar service record, he was issued a general discharge rather than an honorable one. No further pay, no military benefits."

John mentally connected the dots with Molon's introduction in their first meeting. The truth clicked as he put the pieces together.

"In our first meeting, Molon introduced you as Yasu Matsumura, I assume that surname is no coincidence?"

"You are a quick one, you are," Voide replied, snapping

68

back into her sarcastic tone.

John choked back his response to her sarcasm. He was on a trail here, and didn't want to do anything that might break the momentum. As he mulled over what she had said, John spotted a potential hole in her story that once again raised suspicions that he was being led on.

"But Lieutenant Matsumura was a marine serving aboard an Empire Navy ship. Even if he chose to resist the order, how could he smuggle you aboard and protect you from a bloodthirsty captain?"

For the first time since their conversation started, the sharp edge dropped out of Voide's tone. She sounded pensive.

"He never did tell me how he hid me or kept me alive until he could smuggle me off that ship. I suspect cooperation from loyal men under his command had a lot to do with it, but he would never betray their trust, even to me. It cost him his career. Father wasn't the type of person to take anyone down with him."

Father. That was the first time she had used that term. John couldn't resist attempting to reach a tender emotion buried beneath her gruff exterior.

"So you consider this human who killed your biological family your father?"

Surprisingly, John didn't receive the violent response he half expected. Instead, Voide's voice remained distant and nostalgic.

"He raised me. He was the only father I remember."

"So you were reared on a human colony?"

"Yes. Just like Molon, I grew up among humans. Father lived in Adirs sector, subsector O, on the subsector capital world of Asbis. He had me smuggled to his wife, and they reared me as their own daughter after his discharge."

John saw an opening to revisit his earlier point.

"You see, your adoptive father quit being a soldier and still provided for a family. Why is this so strange a possibility for you?"

With that, John managed to sever whatever rapport he had built with Voide. The sad, thoughtful tone disappeared and she growled her response.

"You have no idea what you are talking about. Father opened a training studio to teach martial arts and personal combat."

"So he was a teacher," John pressed, refusing to surrender the point.

"A teacher of war," she snapped. "His family's roots went

69

back centuries, to Old Earth. I grew up learning the code of *bushido*, the way of the warrior."

"So that's where all the super-spy stuff comes from? Some ancient warrior code?"

John noticed Voide eyeing him as if she was contemplating smacking him in the head again. Fortunately, she chose instead to just ball up her fists and sneer.

"I said soldier, not spy, you idiot. Father tried to teach me the warrior code of his *samurai* ancestors, but as I researched this history, I became much more fascinated with another aspect of that ancient culture, the *ninja*."

"Weren't the *ninja* spies rather than warriors?" John asked.

"They were assassins who prized stealth and improvisation as much as the *samurai* prized honor."

"So you rebelled against your father's teaching, then?"

John was glad the contact lenses disguising Voide's Prophane eyes were not weaponized. He could feel her burning gaze as he blundered through the minefield that made up every attempt at conversation with the security chief.

"I learned and honored everything my father taught me. I just went above and beyond. I studied *bushido*, but in my free time I focused my efforts on learning many more things that father never intended to teach."

Bringing the conversation out of personal and back to practical territory seemed to John the best way to salvage the situation without dragging her into resenting him more deeply.

"Soldier or spy, you are in a truly unique position, Voide. Why are you so certain there is no way to become a bridge? You understand humans, and even if you could not personally meet with the Prophane due to their hatred of Pariah, you can help human diplomats to the Prophane understand them better. You are living proof our races can co-exist. Maybe God has put you in this place for just such a moment."

Voide laughed.

"From what I know of your God, I doubt he has any plans for humans to reconcile with the Prophane."

"What makes you so sure?" John replied, fighting hard to bite back his frustration with Voide's incessant sarcasm and skepticism. "I have found that with God anything is possible. Might you not be at the center of that plan?"

Again, John wound up increasing Voide's ire without quite understanding how he had managed it. Her face took on a look that was half grimace and half the face you make when you find a cupboard full of spoiled food.

"You're not pretending, are you?" she snarled.

"What's that supposed to mean," John asked, desperate to understand what he had said that had set her off so badly.

"You really are this ignorant!" Voide said, shaking her head.

"Hey!" he responded, having had enough of her insults. "I'm just asking the question. Unless you know everything, you can't possibly know what God has planned. Do you know everything?"

"I know this much. I know I am the reason humans understand how much the Prophane hate Pariahs."

John took a deep breath. Was this some exaggeration or braggadocio on the part of the security chief? Despite the churning feeling in his gut that Voide wasn't embellishing, he had to challenge her assertion.

"Oh come on. Of all the Pariahs Humaniti has captured, somehow you are that special? How do you figure that?"

Voide took a deep breath before responding. Her calmer tone had returned. All trace of sarcasm was gone from her voice as her eyes focused not on John but somewhere beyond him.

"I was the first Prophane taken alive that didn't die within a week. Only Prophane kids younger than around ten years old don't die in captivity. That's how the scientists theorized the existence of a Prophane suicide gland, or maybe some type of surgical implant, that is present in adults but not children."

"So what in the galaxy does any of that have to do with you discovering this deep-seeded hatred by the Prophane towards Pariahs?"

"When I grew up, I joined the Empire Navy."

"You joined the military that rode your adoptive father out on a rail?"

"Yeah," Voide said, scowling. "I did it to try and redeem my father's family name. I graduated first in my class. I was a recruit fresh out of the academy six years before the Shattering. At that time, the Prophane Ascendency's advance across the Stygian Rift was pushing the tailward borders of Empire space. I was the weapons officer on the flagship of an assault fleet. We'd been sent to the Lowery Sector to engage a Prophane invasion force that had been capturing planets there."

"You don't mean the Lowery Rout, do you? That's Empire-wide history, and you are telling me you were there?"

Voide folded her arms across her chest and rolled her eyes. Her tone was not angry, but John could tell her emotions were simmering just below the surface. If he wanted to keep this rapport up, he'd need to be a little more careful how he phrased things.

"Doubtless you have heard the romanticized, fairy-tale version of the battle Humaniti has dubbed the Lowery Rout. Do you want to know what really happened?"

"Absolutely," John said.

He was focused on Voide's every word and suddenly found it hard to concentrate on keeping their CUV on the road. Being a history buff, John loved when situations arose that gave him the opportunity to talk with people who were part of the events. Somehow the personal accounts never seemed to reconcile completely with the official versions of events.

"We had reports that the Prophane were tearing their way through a large cluster of worlds in Lowery subsector J, the Dotrend subsector. We dropped out of voidspace in the Teklu system, a slightly more remote system with a major Empire Navy base. We thought to levy additional ships from there and gather intel on where the Prophane were last spotted."

"Teklu? That was the system where the Lowery Rout happened."

"Yes. We arrived to find the Naval Base at Teklu destroyed and ourselves badly outnumbered. The Prophane ships were in perfect formation to wipe us out, like they somehow knew where we would be jumping into the system. Previous encounters showed the Prophane to be disciplined and cunning enemies, and given their superior command of voidspace tactics, retreat wasn't really an option."

"Well, you survived," John replied. "So, they couldn't have hated you too badly."

He was feeling a bit snarky that this tale was dragging out without any hint of the evidence that Voide was the catalyst for Prophane hatred of Pariahs. If she was leading him on, he was determined to call her bluff.

"Listen, pale," Voide answered, her invective proving that this was no joking matter to her. "Do you want to hear the story or not?"

"Okay," John blushed. "I'm sorry. You were saying?"

"Our CO tried hailing the Prophane, hoping to negotiate a surrender and avoid a complete slaughter. The Prophane had never, in two decades, answered a hail or shown any interest in communicating whatsoever, but the captain was desperate enough to try anything."

"Did it work? Did they answer?"

"We got an answer, all right," Voide said with that sly tone of sarcasm creeping back into her voice. "My weapons position was located just forward of the captain's seat. I was in clear view during the broadcast hail. The Prophane didn't give any communication acknowledgement to the hail, but as soon as it went out, their fleet completely broke formation and launched a suicide run straight at our flagship; you know, the ship with me on it."

"Suicide run?" John asked.

"Yeah. They went berserk, abandoning their crossfire formation and every ship made a run straight for our fleet."

"Why would they do that? I'm no military strategist, but surrendering a superior tactical position makes no sense."

"And enlightenment dawns," Voide said with a smirk.

"Knock it off," John said, chafing at her implied insult to his intelligence but finding he was so caught up in her story he no longer cared if she was just making it up. "What happened next?"

"Fortunately, our captain was a seasoned naval officer. He quickly recognized that the pattern and focus of their all-out attack run was our flagship. Beginning a steady withdrawal to draw the Prophane forward, he ordered the rest of the fleet to arrange themselves into an extended gauntlet of crossfire between the Prophane fleet's starting position and our flagship."

"The tactic worked?"

"It was surreal," Voide recounted, her voice transforming into a far-off tone of recalled memories. "The Prophane took a few pot shots at ships that strayed too close, but otherwise they didn't even engage in evasive maneuvers to avoid the crossfire. They just charged full speed after the flagship firing missiles, blasters, slug-throwers, and everything else they had, at or beyond maximum effective range, in single-minded pursuit of destroying one ship—the one with me aboard."

"From what I remember of the account," John said, raising an eyebrow. "The Lowery Rout was a decisive tactical victory for Humaniti. The commanding officer was awarded the Galactic Naval Cross for combat victory, and the Empire Navy was later able to cut through the Lowery sector and push back the Prophane advance after wiping out that fleet, at least for a year or so."

Voide smiled and shook her head. John got the feeling that her demeanor this time was more pity than anger.

"That's what the history logs show, isn't it?" Voide said, her voice far calmer than John had expected.

"It is," John affirmed.

"Let me clue you to how the world works outside your hermit world. History and truth are rarely synonymous. The gauntlet shredded the Prophane fleet and turned a slaughter into victory. The humans lost two ships, and those only because they strayed a little too close to the intercept route and were accidentally locked onto by Prophane missiles that had gone ballistic after losing lock on the flagship. That's the truth of the lauded Lowery Rout. It wasn't Empire Navy brilliance and strategic tactics that won the day but Prophane psychotically pursuing a Pariah."

"You."

"Me."

"That is incredible!" John said, taking a deep breath and trying to process what he had just heard. "But how can you be certain it was seeing you that triggered that response?"

"And the mental sluggishness returns."

"Enough with the insults! It's a serious question."

"Because, genius, this has only ever happened when there was a Pariah officer on the bridge during a broadcast hail. The Navy repeated the experiment several times with myself and with other Pariahs. It happened every time there was a Pariah on board the broadcasting ship, and never under any other circumstance."

John's skeptical mind was going off the charts. Either he was being duped for the enjoyment of a sociopath, or he was sitting in the vehicle with a key person in the shaping of galactic history. For all the awe and wonder he battled to contain, he just couldn't believe the former wasn't the best explanation here. Furthermore, of all the things to shine him on about, something so deeply personal just seemed out of character for Voide.

"Then why is this the first I have heard of this?" John probed, letting his skepticism have a little leash.

"I'm sorry, pale," Voide replied, her ascerbic sarcasm returning in full force. "Is the Empire Navy in the habit of informing every citizen of its top secret mission briefings and its experimental combat tactics?"

She had a point. Even the Old Empire was not above secrets and coverups. If a commander had lucked into turning a massacre into a victory, it was doubtful that would be what showed up in the reports.

"Okay, point made. But Molon said you were with GalSec before, not the Imperial Navy. How'd that happen?"

"Once the Navy confirmed this thing they called the *Pariah effect*, they started using us as bait to set traps and turn the tide of battle. That's the only reason they have managed to slow the Prophane Advance as much as they have. Once this became common practice, I resigned my Naval commission and joined GalSec."

"I can understand why 'bait' isn't exactly an endearing career choice. Were you thinking the Empire's covert operations division would treat you more fairly?"

"No," Voide answered, flashing her signature feral grin. "I figured if I was going to be bait, I might as well be somewhere I could shoot back. GalSec was thrilled to have a dual-purpose Pariah agent and lab rat all rolled into one."

Suddenly a deep blush came over Voide's face. John wasn't sure how that was possible with her disguise, but figured it must be built into the technology to register her biometric responses and relay them into the human illusion.

"Are you feeling all right?" he asked.

Voide spun her gaze toward him. Apparently he had done it again. Her burning anger washed over him as John wracked his mind to figure out what he had said to warrant such a response.

"Look, you inquisitive *pale*," Voide said with more invective than John had managed to elicit previously in this roller-coaster conversation. "I have no idea why I just dumped all that out to you. Maybe you're some kind of brain-twiddler like that blue-skinned scarecrow of a comms officer. Whatever the reason, if you breathe so much as one word of this to anyone, I promise you will wear your lungs as a hat."

"Hey, I won't say a word," John assured her.

He meant it too, not merely fearing her threats of bronchial haberdashery, but because he was moved that Voide would trust him with such an intimate part of her history.

"You won't if you like being alive," she reiterated.

"I do," John affirmed, "and I swear."

"You won't have to keep that promise long, pale," Voide said, suddenly relaxing in both tone and posture.

Not sure exactly how to take that statement, her change in demeanor gave John the willies as much or more than her angry outburst had. Was she planning to kill him?

"What do you mean?" John asked, not entirely sure he wanted the answer.

Voide must have sensed his apprehension. She laughed aloud and gave his shoulder a playful shove.

"Relax, pale. I'm not going to eat you. I only meant that by tomorrow we will get paid and you will be gone. So, I suppose it doesn't make any difference if some hick doctor on a backwater dirtball world knows the truth. I mean, who are you going to tell, your pigs and chickens?"

John had never seen this side of the icy security chief. It intrigued him. He was no psychologist, but she was clearly trying to cover up letting her guard down. Deep down he felt an instinct to provoke her, given her unwarranted hostility toward him, but instead his compassion won out.

"Voide, whatever you think of me, I am glad to listen if you need to talk. It's just you and me out here. I'll treat whatever you say to me as I would anything under doctor-patient privilege. Keeping confidence is part of being a doctor. Besides, bottling up your emotions can affect your health in very real ways."

"Listen you glorified veterinarian," she almost spat the snarl in his face. "If you want to psychoanalyze someone, analyze Mel. That mawkish waif loves that kind of crap. Me, I got a job to do: get you home and get you back."

"There's no need to get angry, Voide."

"You wouldn't survive seeing me angry. Face it, pale, you're cargo. You might as well be a crate of cabbage or a sack of seeds. We get paid, you get delivered, and that is that."

Was that truly how she viewed him, as nothing more than cargo? What about Molon and the others? They seemed genuine enough, but they were mercenaries after all. In John's estimation, these mercenaries didn't overly value their own lives. Why should they value his?

"Look, I get it," John said, unwilling to surrender the possibility that he might be on the verge of real progress with the Prophane security officer. "You are all hard and terrifying. Be that way if you want to. It was a long drive, I was just trying to make conversation, and I genuinely wanted to know more about you."

"Get this, pale," Voide's hardness remained unwavering. "I'm not interested in forming any bonds of camaraderie or swapping spit in the shower with you. You're a job, period. By tomorrow, you won't even be a lingering memory."

"Not even a lingering memory?"

"That's right."

"Harsh," John risked a joke, hoping to lighten the mood. "Are you sure we haven't dated before?"

The scowl he received in return was much less violent a response than he had expected. Voide shifted in her seat, turning to look at the road ahead and once again folding her arms across her chest.

"Look, Doc," she said, her voice once again calm and

collected. "Just focus on the mission. How much farther to your house?"

For someone who didn't care, Voide had a lot to say. Furthermore, this was the first time he could recall that she'd addressed him as "Doc" instead of the pejorative "pale". He doubted that Voide would be his best buddy anytime soon, but maybe there was some hope of rising above the status of cargo in her estimation.

Still, pointing out her change in how she addressed him, or mocking her sudden just-business stoicism would likely prove unwise. Whatever else she was, Voide was genuinely dangerous. Her orders might keep her from doing him harm, but John wasn't ready to be the test subject for that particular experiment.

"Not far," he succinctly reassured. "Another couple of kilometers. My house is about midway between the starport and the city proper."

The glowing ball of Tede Alpha settled lower on the horizon. John slowed the vehicle upon approaching a mid-sized farmhouse set back about fifty meters from the road. The sun had set the sky ablaze with an orange glow, igniting in stunning brilliance the wispy fingers of clouds floating in the dusky sky. Unfortunately, there was no time to lay out on the mesa awaiting the beautiful Tede sunset, and no suitable company for it even if there had been enough time.

John suddenly tensed and pulled the CUV off the road just before the driveway leading to the farm house.

"This it?" Voide asked, eyeing the modest abode. "I thought you were rich?"

"We choose to live simply. And yeah, this is it, but something is off."

"What's wrong?" Voide asked, visibly tensing.

"You see those personal ATVs?" John asked, nodding toward a quartet of single-rider, four-wheeled all-terrain vehicles parked in front of the farm house.

"Yeah."

"They aren't mine."

Voide reached into a satchel attached to the waist of her jumpsuit, pulled out a small revolver, and tossed it to John.

"Stay here!" Voide said, the tone of command unmistakable in her voice.

Without another word, she slipped quietly from the CUV, touching a button on the belt of her suit. John watched through the vehicle windows as Voide instantly faded to a shimmering, transparent silhouette. Where a moment before had stood *Star*

Wolf's chief of security, now was nothing more than a roughly Voide-sized light-distortion slipping silently toward the house.

"Stealth suit!" John whispered to himself, fascinated by yet another high-tech toy in the hands of a *Star Wolf* crewmember.

As Voide drew close to the point halfway between the vehicle and the house, John saw the outline of someone inside the house move past one of the windows. Suddenly all the rage and frustration he had suppressed and tried to forget since his escape from the Dawnstar facility boiled to the surface. The inquisitor on Ratuen had stolen almost everything from John when that devil's spawn had killed Elena. There was no way John was going to sit idly by while some roving band of punks invaded his home to take whatever was left.

John opened the driver's side door of the CUV and started toward the house. Following in Voide's footsteps, he awkwardly fumbled with the small slug-thrower Voide had tossed to him before giving up and shoving it in his jacket pocket.

Voide's translucent silhouette slipped silently up to the side door, bounding across the terrain easily in Tede's low gravity. John did his best to stay low and approach the house as quietly as she, wanting to help her any way he could.

The small handgun weighed oddly in his pocket. He was a healer, not a killer, and while he regularly enjoyed sport bow hunting, he had never discharged a firearm in his life. Still, judging from the vehicles, there clearly were at least four intruders inside, and he felt that he could not simply leave Voide facing those odds alone.

Voide's stealth-suited shadow disappeared against the side of the house when one of the intruders again crossed in front of the large front windows. John dove flat onto the grass to attempt to preserve surprise. The lower gravity made the fall seem to last forever. There was no indication he had been spotted, but he had lost sight of Voide. Only the side door, now slightly ajar, gave him indication she had already slipped inside.

John regained his feet and bounded lightly across the last few yards to the house. Suddenly, sounds of battle rang out from inside; gunfire and clanging steel. John reached in his pocket and extracted the pistol Voide had given him. It still felt foreign in his hand, and he hoped there was nothing more complicated to its operation than pointing and pulling the trigger.

As John reached for the doorknob, a masked man in black,

bleeding from a long slash across his chest, barreled out the door. The masked man bowled into John, forcing him to grab hold of the man in an attempt to keep himself from falling. In the process, John dropped the revolver and it skittered several yards away from the jumble of falling bodies.

The two men tumbled into a tangled pile, their momentum carrying them several yards from the door before rolling to a halt. Fortunately for John, the man was more intent on making his escape than fighting. Half scrambling, half crawling, the masked intruder crossed the ten yards to one of the ATV's and hit the starter switch.

The man was halfway across the field to the west, heading for the woods, when the sound of breaking glass rang out. John saw a small, thin, black blur fly straight from his front window and strike the man in the shoulder as he drove away. Despite being clearly wounded and in pain, the fleeing intruder did not let off the throttle of the ATV. Slumping over the handlebars to provide a smaller target for any further shots, he continued to weave his way toward the woods.

Moments later, two more bloody and battered masked men crashed through the already damaged front window, stumbling and tumbling toward two more ATVs. One of the men held a machine pistol set to full auto, and he spun mid-bound to empty his entire magazine in a deadly spray back into the house.

John crawled for the revolver, intending to try to get at least a shot or two off at the fleeing bandits. By the time he had picked up the pistol and turned, the men were well off across the field behind their fleeing cohort. John squeezed off a few rounds anyhow, to no effect, with the recoil from the pistol stinging his untrained hands.

Voide, having disabled her stealth field, rushed out the side door, her bloody katana in one hand and her bow in the other. She made no attempt to nock another arrow.

"Stop wasting bullets," she half-growled at John. "You couldn't hit them from this distance even if you knew how to shoot, which you clearly don't. One won't get away though."

"You caught one?"

"Not exactly," Voide answered. "He's dead inside."

"We need one alive to question. Can't you shoot one of them with your bow before they get away?"

"I can't judge the drop right in this half-gravity," Voide replied with a shake of her head as she pressed the button to fold her high tech bow and replace it in the bandolier. "My first shot was meant to take out a tire but I nearly overshot him

79

entirely. Those three are gone, but we need to move quickly. They might be back with reinforcements soon."

John eyed the lone one-man ATV still parked in front of the house, handed the pistol back to Voide, and rushed inside. He stood in stunned silence as he surveyed the wreck his home had become. Obviously, they had been searching for something, and had left nothing undisturbed in the course of their search. Holes were bashed into walls, furniture had been shredded, every box or container in the house was opened and emptied. He had seen tornados that did less damage.

There in the middle of his living room lay a masked man, blood pouring from a hole in his chest where his heart should have been. John moved swiftly to him, physician's instincts taking over, but there was nothing John could do.

He sensed Voide's presence slipping up quietly behind him as he knelt beside the fallen intruder. A bit of red and black ink on the man's collarbone was visible in an area where his mask had separated from his shirt.

"What's that?" Voide asked.

John pulled down the man's collar and gasped. The man's upper chest bore a tattoo of a lion's head in red and black. The words *Fratres Leonis* were etched in a banner below the emblem.

"You've seen this tattoo before?" Voide asked.

"Yes. It is the mark of the Brothers of the Lion."

"Religious monks?"

"A radical sect," John answered with a sigh.

"I take it they do more than just pray for change?"

"You could say that. They are fierce resistance fighters. The Brothers have been waging guerilla actions against the Provisional Imperium and the New Halberan Empire since shortly after the Shattering."

"Aren't you a Faithful, too? What's their quarrel with you?"

John shook his head as he looked into Voide's eyes. He was used to defending his faith against unbelievers and scoffers, but her inquiry seemed genuine. None of the usual condescension he had seen from unbelievers resonated in her voice. She seemed genuinely puzzled why fellow Faithful might be behind this raid on his home. John shared her confusion. He had expected Dawnstar goons, but for Faithful to be ransacking his home...

"I honestly have no idea," John admitted. "The Brothers are allied with the Theocracy of the Faithful. Tede is a Theocracy-held world. This makes no sense...unless."

"Unless what?"

John didn't answer. Instead he sprinted toward the back of the house. Bursting into the master bedroom, as equally trashed as the rest of the house, John made his way toward the large double closet. He knelt down and tore back the carpet, revealing below it a subtle, rectangular outline in the flooring boards. Clawing at the edge, he freed the section of floor and tossed it aside revealing the face of a safe sunk into the concrete foundation. John punched in an eight-digit code and the safe door beeped and popped open.

Reaching inside, he tossed aside several folders filled with documents and a couple bundles of Tede paper currency. He turned toward Voide, holding in his hands a small decorative cube pendant dangling at the end of a necklace chain.

"This had to be what they were after."

"And this bit of costume jewelry is what, exactly?" Voide asked.

"All of Elena's research on malmorphsy. It's a modified datacube made to resemble a simple pendant. It was Elena's idea."

Suddenly Voide dropped into a crouch and began to look around. She pulled a small electronic device from a zippered pocket, activated it, and began scanning the room.

"No electronic surveillance," she announced after a few moments. "They might not know yet that you have the datacube. Grab whatever you need. We leave in five minutes."

Voide exited the room before John had a chance to argue. He hung the datacube pendant around his neck, grabbed his spare medical bag from his closet, and tossed a few shirts and socks into another satchel along with the bundles of cash he had pulled from the safe. The smell of smoke wafted into his nostrils as he made his way toward the front room.

"Oh, what now?" He mumbled before he rounded the corner to see Voide busy setting curtains, carpet, and furniture stuffing on fire.

"What are you doing?" he screamed at the security chief. "Are you insane? This is my house!"

"Not anymore, Doc. It's a target. If we leave the place standing, those monks will figure out they missed something, and that you have it."

"So what?"

"So then you become the target."

"And burning my house down changes that?"

"Yes. If we leave this place a smoking pile of ash, they won't know if what they were looking for was even here."

John could follow her logic, but his house burning to the

81

ground before his eyes clouded the argument. Before he could reconcile it all, Voide grabbed his arm, forcing him out of the door and back toward their vehicle.

"I'll drive," she announced, pushing John toward the passenger side of the vehicle.

He climbed in, too stunned to object or ask any questions. Voide started the vehicle, spun it back in the direction of the starport, and gunned the engine.

"Not too fast," John mumbled, his mind still processing the reality of his home being destroyed as he fumbled with the seatbelt. "We will get a citation."

"Zealot monks just tried to kill us and you are worried about a traffic ticket?" she replied, not letting up on her speed in the slightest.

Voide's wristband sounded an alert. She glanced down at the small display screen, shifting her eyes briefly off the road ahead.

"Well, that's good news, I suppose," she said.

"What news?" John said, snapping out of his daze.

"Our patron made contact. He wants to meet with Molon for the payoff later today in the Greenway Lounge at the starport. Molon wants us to report there as soon as we get back."

"Did he say who it was?"

"No," she said as she tapped an acknowledgement into the comm band. "We will know soon enough."

*****

John released his white-knuckled grip from the dashboard of the CUV as they pulled into the rental lot at the starport. They had reached it without receiving a citation for Voide's speedy and reckless driving. She guided John, still reeling somewhat from the loss of his home and the inexplicable involvement of the monks, back toward the entry portal.

"Where am I supposed to go now?" he asked, still halfway in a daze. "I have no life, I have no home."

"You're rich, aren't you? Buy a new one, or hide out on *Star Wolf* until you sort this all out. Molon has a heart for strays."

"Me on a mercenary ship?"

"Just a thought."

"Why would I do that?" John asked, both relieved and confused by the security chief's change in attitude toward him.

"To stay alive."

John stopped in his tracks. In all this, the thought that the events at the house might have been more than just a robbery

82

attempt had never occurred to him. What would have happened if he had stumbled upon the intruders alone? Would Faithful monks truly have killed him?

"Do you really think I am still in danger?"

"If I was after you, you would be."

"That's comforting."

John didn't doubt her assessment. Still, this was Tede, a peaceful hermit-world. Things like this didn't happen here. How had his world gotten turned so upside down?

"You've got to figure," Voide explained. "Even after this mystery patron pays up, Tede is the last place in the galaxy you want to be."

"But if the monks are after Elena's research, I can address that with their High Abbot. I'm sure this is all just a big misunderstanding."

"It is not just the monks," Voide replied.

"How do you figure that?" John asked.

Voide sighed and shook her head.

"It seems like there are way too many people interested in you not living out a peaceful life on Tede. You said yourself these Brothers of the Lion have been waging war against the Imperium. Do you really think they are the ones who handed you over to Dawnstar?"

"No," John replied after briefly thinking it through. "That wouldn't make sense. So I suppose there are two groups after me now."

"At least," Voide replied. "You are a popular guy."

John sighed. Maybe a gunship full of mercenaries was exactly where he needed to be, at least until all this craziness got sorted out.

Six – Brothers of the Lion

Molon Hawkins sat facing the door of the private room in the rear of the Greenway Lounge. Twitch had finished her oversight of the supply run and had joined him. As the chime announced a request for entry, she flashed Molon her signature look that resonated through him like a call to battle stations.

"Ready for trouble?" Twitch asked.

"Cynic," Molon grumbled. "You know sometimes things go smoothly."

Twitch flashed Molon a patronizing grin and gave him a gentle pat on his jowls.

"Not with an anonymous patron and us holding half the cargo they don't, but your optimism is just so cute."

He could have done without her smug jibe, but he trusted her instincts. To that effect, he slipped his automag out of its holster and laid it in his lap below the table. Twitch similarly cradled a palm-sized blaster with a four-shot energy cell sufficiently low profile to slip past most weapon detectors. She had nicknamed that tiny blaster 'Plan B', and it had been the deciding argument in quite a few rocky negotiations the last few years. Hopefully they wouldn't need Plan B today.

"Come in," Molon announced.

A salt-and-pepper-haired man with a closely trimmed beard entered the room. He was slightly below average in stature but in fit shape, wearing a suit reminiscent of the brown cassocks of old-Earth monks. The garb was more tunic length than a full cassock, with functional, matching brown pants below. There was a kindly glint to the man's green eyes, but Molon sensed something deeper.

"Captain Hawkins?" the new arrival inquired.

"That's me," the Lubanian captain replied without rising. "And this lovely lady is my executive officer, Commander Jane Richardson."

"Twitch," she added, with a cordial nod.

"I suppose you are our mysterious benefactor?" Molon

84

inquired.

"Yes, I suppose I am. Call me Brother Martin. I am a representative of the Brothers of the Lion," the man said as he glanced around the room.

"Looking for something?" Twitch asked.

"I'm sorry," the monk said, clearly somewhat distracted. "Is Dr. Salzmann en route?"

"The doctor should be here momentarily," Molon said, shifting a bit in his chair. "I trust you have brought the transfer pad and files to release the funds on the contract?"

"Yes, of course," Brother Martin affirmed with a grin and a nod. "I will release those the moment Dr. Salzmann arrives and I confirm she is safe and sound."

Molon's stomach hitched.

"She?" Twitch asked, giving voice to the thought in Molon's head.

"Why yes. Captain Hawkins did say Dr. Elena Salzmann would be joining us momentarily, did he not?"

The fur on the back of Molon's neck stood up. He hated it when Twitch was right. Time to face the music.

"Um, actually," Molon replied, "Dr. John Salzmann is on the way. Unfortunately there were complications on Ratuen. Dr. Elena Salzmann didn't make it."

Brother Martin's smile disappeared. He had been in the process of taking his seat, but Molon's revelation froze him halfway between sitting and standing. He grabbed the edge of the table with both hands.

"What do you mean Elena Salzmann didn't make it?" There was no longer any trace of congeniality in the monk's tone.

Just then, Voide and John slipped quietly in the door behind Brother Martin. He gave no indication he was aware they had entered. Molon flashed a brief but subtle furrowing of his brow to Voide. She motioned for John to be quiet and not to announce their arrival just yet.

"I'm sorry, Brother Martin," Molon explained. "There was nothing I could do. Dawnstar's interrogator killed her moments after I arrived. In truth I was lucky to get John out alive."

"This is...unfortunate," Brother Martin replied, gazing at the center of the table as though his mind had already left the meeting.

Molon knew now only solid bargaining might salvage a partial payment out of this deal. He hoped the Faithful monk would be reasonable and they would at least get some

85

compensation for rescuing John. While he was still mulling over where to go next, his faithful partner took the lead.

"We recognize this is only a partial fulfillment of the contract," Twitch interjected, in her best rules-and-regs tone. "And we understand if you feel the need to adjust the contract payout accordingly."

Brother Martin locked eyes with Twitch. He returned to a fully standing position but did not release his death-grip on the table edge.

"You think this is a partial success?" Brother Martin fumed. "John Salzmann is a foppish dandy who flits through life playing at being a good Samaritan when he's not camped out at a card table. He is useless to us, as he is to most anyone who knows him as more than a casual acquaintance. We issued that contract to retrieve Dr. Elena Salzmann. This is not a partial success, it is a complete failure."

John started to move in, but Voide quickly and quietly grabbed his arm and held him back. Molon was glad because he didn't want the Doc in between himself and this rude, arrogant monk at this particular moment. Molon raised an eyebrow and drew his lip back into a lupine semi-snarl, which elicited a nervous glance from the frustrated clergyman.

"I bet to differ," Molon argued. "The contract, as written, was for both Salzmanns."

The flustered clergyman, apparently realizing Molon was still fighting only with words and unlikely to jump across the table and take a bite out of him, pounded a fist on the table.

"Of course we had to issue it for the both of them," Brother Martin replied. "I doubt Elena Salzmann would have taken it very well if some literalist mercenary had rescued her and left her useless husband behind."

"You know," Twitch replied, her brow furrowing in suspicion. "That raises an interesting question."

In Molon's mind there were far more questions than answers about this whole situation. Wherever his XO was going with this, he mentally prepared himself to back her play.

"What question is that, Commander Richardson?" Brother Martin said, clearly struggling to remain civil.

"How did the Brothers of the Lion even know the Salzmanns were missing and who had kidnapped them?"

Twich could always be counted on to find the 'gotcha' in any situation. Molon knew legally the monk had them dead to rights. The contract had stipulated both Salzmanns. John without Elena was a busted contract and by rights Brother Martin could refuse to pay. Still, from the paleness in Brother

Martin's face following Twitch's probing question, they might be able to wring a partial payday out of this after all.

"W-well, you see...b-but," the monk sputtered.

Twitch had flushed their prey. The hunting instinct in Molon surged to the surface and he pounced.

"Twitch is right. This contract is evidence you know more than you are saying about the Salzmann's abduction."

"That's absurd," Brother Martin objected as his face went from pale to flushed.

"Not really," Molon pressed. "You see, Salzmann Pharmaceuticals, with all their money and connections, didn't know. Even High Governor Perry had no idea who had taken them. Yet your contract states that they were in the custody of Dawnstar headed for the detention facility on Ratuen. How did you know that when no one else had the first clue what had happened to them?"

Brother Martin settled visibly, cleared his throat, smoothed his cassock, and took his seat. He took several slow, deep breaths, folded his hands in front of him and turned toward Molon.

Molon slipped his right hand into his lap, placing the automag firmly into his grasp. He saw Twitch had Plan B leveled under the table, aimed at Brother Martin's midsection. They both smiled patiently at the monk, waiting for a response, but Molon knew enough to be cautious. Even the tamest animal could be dangerous when cornered. Brother Martin let out an exasperated sigh and finally spoke with a cool collectedness in his voice.

"Your executive officer has a keen mind, Captain."

"No arguments there," Molon replied.

"It is perfectly simple, really," Brother Martin continued. "The Brothers of the Lion have had Dr. Elena Salzmann under observation for some time. When our observers saw Dawnstar ships land and take them, one of the brothers managed to plant a magnetic tracker on one of the raider ships before it took off."

Brother Martin paused as if that snippet resolved the query. Molon and Twitch looked at each other. Molon could read Twitch's skepticism in her eyes. It matched his own.

"You see there, Twitch," Molon quipped as he flashed a sarcastic grin at his XO. "Perfectly simple."

"Downright elementary," Twitch agreed, following his lead. "Why didn't we think of that?"

They turned and shot a pair of patronizing smiles back at the monk. Despite their mocking, Brother Martin resumed his explanation as though he had intended to continue all along.

"Upon leaving Tede, the Dawnstar ships proceeded to the registered jump point to Hatacks. Hatacks is too high profile a location to hide prisoners, so it wasn't hard to guess they would push on to Ratuen where they would have privacy for whatever they planned for the Salzmanns."

"So wait a minute," Twitch replied, crossing her arms. "You mean to tell me that you posted a high-paying rescue contract based solely on an educated guess?"

"Yes, we did," Brother Martin affirmed, with only the slightest waver in his voice. "We dispatched the contract on every System Express jumper leaving Tede in hope that someone would pick it up in time to make a rescue attempt before any ill befell Elena." Both Brother Martin's head and voice dropped slightly. "She was very important to us."

"Based on that contract payoff," Molon said, "I suppose she was."

"However," Twitch added, "that still doesn't explain why you were monitoring Dr. Elena Salzmann in the first place."

John broke free from Voide's restraining hand on his elbow as he stormed over to where Brother Martin was sitting. He spun the monk around in his chair and locked eyes with him intensely as John drew his face close to Brother Martin's.

"Yes, Brother," John growled, "why were you monitoring Elena?"

Brother Martin, clearly startled at John's sudden appearance, flashed an appeasing smile. A slight flush returned to the monk's face.

"Oh, Dr. Salzmann," Brother Martin said, fidgeting slightly under John's proximity and intensity. "I'm so glad you are alive."

"Hah!" John exclaimed. "I just overheard how glad you are to see this useless, foppish dandy alive. Now answer the question. Why were you watching Elena?"

Brother Martin stared unblinkingly at John. Molon guessed the monk was scrambling to figure out how to defuse this situation as diplomatically as possible. Molon's ears flipped back as he released his pistol back into his lap. Outnumbered four to one, it was doubtful the monk would turn violent here. Twitch didn't follow suit, keeping Plan B aimed at squarely at Brother Martin just below the surface of the table.

Folding his hands, Molon formed a toothy grin as the drama unfolded before him. John was more on fire than Molon had ever seen him, and the smug monk was clearly reeling. Molon couldn't wait to see how this played out, even if it cost him a payday. At least the show should be entertaining.

"We had been in discussions with her over her research," Brother Martin continued. "The Brothers of the Lion felt it could be key to the war efforts against the Daemi and possibly one day even the Prophane."

John's face went semi-slack, as though processing a distant memory. He stood up, letting go of the arms of Brother Martin's chair.

"I remember a couple of the Brothers of the Lion leaving our house as I arrived home about a month ago."

"That was about the time of our last discussion with your wife," Brother Martin affirmed.

"Elena was extremely upset after that visit, but wouldn't tell me what was going on. She wasn't herself for a week after that meeting."

"I'm terribly sorry to hear that," Brother Martin replied, sounding genuine. "We had no intention to cause her anxiety."

"Well you did," John replied. "If she was that upset by whatever you were proposing, I can't imagine what it was. Elena was no shrinking violet, so if you rattled her that badly, whatever you wanted must have been horrific. There is no way she would have agreed to whatever it was."

"Which may be why," Voide interjected, stepping toward the table, "four Brothers of the Lion dressed like commandos just trashed and burned Dr. Salzmann's house to the ground."

"What?" Brother Martin asked, jumping to his feet. "What are you talking about?"

"Don't deny it," John snapped. "One was killed and the rest tried to kill us before running away. The dead intruder had a *Fratres Leonis* tattoo. That is the mark of your order, is it not?"

Brother Martin extended both hands, palms down and motioned for calm as he sat back down at the table. He indicated empty seats, to his right and left, somatically urging John and Voide to follow suit.

"All right," Brother Martin said, his amiable façade regaining control. "Honestly, if we all will settle down, I can explain."

John took a seat beside Brother Martin, but Voide reached for controls on her belt.

"As long as we are being honest," Voide said, "let me go first."

Prophane-gray skin emerged as her stealth suit's chameleon field dissipated, and her human complexion faded. She reached up and removed the colored contacts, revealing her bright yellow eyes. Brother Martin gasped and scooted as

89

far away from her as he could within the confines of his chair.

"Now then," Voide said finally taking a seat on the other side of Brother Martin from where John was as she smiled broadly revealing her vampiric canines, "you were saying something about the Prophane?"

Twitch leaned over in her chair and whispered to Molon.

"See, I told you she would look for any excuse to break cover."

"Doesn't count," Molon whispered back. "Brother Martin isn't the Tede authorities. Besides, we're inside the 'aliens-allowed' starport, so not actually illegal."

"Technicalities," Twitch replied.

Molon fought back a grin. He knew Voide's move was calculated to put the monk into an uncomfortable state. If he was in fear for his life, he was more likely to let something slip that might give them some edge in the discussion.

It achieved the desired effect.

Brother Martin shifted nervously in his chair and stared at Voide for a long moment. His voice and hands both bore a slight tremble at the very idea that he was sitting next to a living Prophane.

"Brother Martin," Molon said, straining to hide his amusement. "Allow me to introduce Lieutenant Commander Yasu Matsumura, my security chief. She's a Prophane Pariah, as I am sure you noticed. Anyway, I believe you were about to enlighten us on the details of what happened at John's home and what business you had with Elena Salzmann?"

"Um, yes," the monk said, gaining a tentative grip on his composure.

Brother Martin grabbed the arms of his chair tightly, possibly attempting to steady his hands. Although he was addressing Molon, and the room in general, his eyes remained steadfastly focused on Voide.

"We approached Dr. Elena Salzmann with a proposal to pay for access to all her research data to date."

"To what end?" John prompted.

"We discussed possible applications that might aid in our fight against the Daemi."

"Possible applications?" John snapped. "Meaning biological warfare, right?"

"Something like that," Brother Martin said, nodding. "We felt sure one of the Faithful would rally behind the idea."

"Yet she didn't," Twitch responded.

"No," Brother Martin admitted. "She did not."

Molon saw John's face turn red as he balled his hands into

fists. John was clearly struggling to maintain his composure and his seat. Molon tensed slightly and prepared to intervene if the doctor lost control of his emotions. Pounding on a patron was no way to negotiate a partial payday.

"Elena took an oath to do no harm," John interjected through gritted teeth. "She was a healer, not a mass-murderer."

"Destroying demons is hardly murder," Brother Martin said as he tore his gaze from Voide and faced John. "As one of the Faithful and a follower of the Lion, you should know that, Dr. Salzmann."

Molon growled under his breath. Not this religious hokum again. His adoptive parents had been Faithful and were good people, but sometimes the Faithful party line could be used to justify all kinds of atrocities. Human history was full of wars started because one group thought another group worshipped the wrong god.

"'*Demons*' is a superstitions term," Molon interjected. "Both the Angelicum and the Daemi are sophont races who visited Earth early on in its history. Some believed they were messengers sent by the Creator. Others say the visits were interstellar reconnaissance missions. Either way, they're sophonts, not spirits, good or evil."

Both Brother Martin and John turned and stared with surprise at the Lubanian captain. He liked surprising people who weren't aware of his upbringing. Growing up away from other Lubanians had come at a cost, but there were a lot of advantages growing up among humans as well.

"What?" Molon laughed. "I was raised by humans. I've studied your history and your Scriptures. Now can we get back to the question at hand. Elena turned you down, so I'm thinking maybe you arranged for her and John to be removed so your agents could grab her data while they were away."

"Nonsense," Brother Martin answered, waving his hand in a dismissive gesture as if to fan away the very idea. "If we wanted them removed, why would we have put up a contract to pay for their rescue?"

"Makes a great alibi," Voide offered. "Plus, it sounds like you never intended to pay off the contract."

"Ridiculous!" Brother Martin objected, turning a pleading gaze toward Molon. "We are freedom fighters, captain, but we are not kidnappers. I was thrilled to get your message about completing the mission."

"Yeah," Twitch reasoned, "so thrilled you dispatched those monks to Dr. Salzmann's house after you received the prearranged mission complete signal. That's why you didn't acknowledge it as soon as we hit orbit yesterday."

Brother Martin flushed. He was struggling under the multi-front barrage of questions. He hung his head slightly before turning to address Twitch.

"Admittedly," the monk explained, "I thought it might be worthwhile to send a few of the brothers to Dr. Salzmann's home to make a thorough search before we concluded our business. I am sorry the encounter went poorly. Perhaps they mistook you for Dawnstar forces trying to get their hands on the data. However, I assure you I gave no orders for the house to be destroyed and I most certainly had nothing to do with the abduction."

Brother Martin turned his gaze to John. "Were you able to retrieve the data from the house, Dr. Salzmann?"

"No," Voide said, cutting off whatever response John started to make. "By the time we got there, the house was ablaze, and the arsonists were fleeing. If your men didn't retrieve the data, then it is gone."

With a brief scowl at Voide's statement, Brother Martin stood up and turned to leave. Molon had been through these types of situations enough times to know the monk wasn't buying what Voide was selling. Once they were in a secure location, Voide would fill Molon in on the details she obviously was keeping from Brother Martin. In the meantime, it looked like their payday was about to walk out the door.

"The contract as written was not successfully completed," Brother Martin said, a business-like efficiency returning to his voice. "It was for both Salzmanns, which you were unable to secure. I expect you will issue the release of funds back to us, Captain Hawkins, along with acknowledgement of failure to complete the mission."

And there it was. His XO didn't look eager to let the matter drop quite so easily. Twitch leaned forward in her chair, her left hand on the table and her right still firmly gripping Plan B below.

"So you intend to stiff us completely?" Twitch said. "For a monk, you sure are a crook."

"When you send the release, captain," Brother Martin said to Molon, ignoring Twitch's insult, "if you will also send along an itemized list of costs you incurred on the mission, I will issue a reimbursement voucher for that amount, payable in Theocreds. I am a reasonable man."

With that, Brother Martin turned and briskly exited the room without so much as a backward glance.

"But I still have questions," John called after the monk, his petition going completely unacknowledged.

"Well, mystery solved," Molon said, holstering his automag and walking over to pat John on the shoulder. "At least we know who grabbed you and who sent us to fetch you."

"We still didn't get paid," Voide griped. "I told you we weren't going to get paid."

"Don't worry about funds, captain," John replied. "I will issue a credit voucher against any supplies you need that are available on Tede. It is the least I can do."

"Thank you, John."

"It is not a problem, captain."

Molon liked the doctor. He was a decent man, a true Faithful like Molon's own adoptive parents. Who knew when knowing a multi-millionaire might come in handy in the future.

"You are a good man, Doc," Molon said, patting the doctor on the shoulder. "Let me know if there is ever anything we can do for you."

"Actually, captain, there may be."

"Really," Molon raised an eyebrow, wondering if his polite offer of assistance was about to come back and bite him already. "What can I do for you, John?"

"Well, on our trip back from my house, Voide made a suggestion that suddenly makes a lot of sense to me."

"Oh really?" Voide added, her voice filled with warning.

"Tede clearly is not the safest place for me anymore. I would like to take Voide's suggestion and join *Star Wolf*'s crew."

"What?" Voide snapped. "When did I—"

"If you still need a ship's doctor, that is," John continued, cutting off her objection. "I would be happy to fill in for a while, at least until you find a proper replacement."

Star Wolf really could use a proper doctor aboard. The corpsmen were top notch, but still they were field medics, not real surgeons. They had lost a couple of good crewmen for want of the difference between a corpsman and a surgeon. Besides, if it flustered Voide this much, the amusement value alone would be worth the price of admission.

"Great idea, Doc," Molon answered, trying to suppress a devilish grin as Voide's complexion seemed to go even grayer than usual.

"But," Voide spluttered, "that's not what I—"

"You are welcome on *Star Wolf* as long as you earn your keep like the rest of the crew," Molon continued.

"I will, captain," John said shaking Molon's hand vigoursly and flashing a brief grin in Voide's direction. "Thank you."

"Captain," Voide said, looking like she'd eaten a bag of lemons. "I said hide on *Star Wolf*, not join the blasted crew."

"Either way, it's a good idea," Molon answered.

"But— " Voide started to argue but Molon cut her off.

"With that settled, I believe you have a good bit of debriefing to do about your little foray."

"Oh, yeah," Voide replied, dropping any further arguments against John coming on board. "I might have been a little loose with the truth on some of the details."

"Really?" Twitch jibed. "You are usually so forthcoming and open."

"Yeah, that's me," Voide answered.

"Let's leave that discussion until we are back aboard *Star Wolf*," Molon said, glancing around the private room they had been using. "Too many ears here."

The captain moved toward the lounge exit. John followed close behind, leaning in toward Voide and whispering to her as he passed. Molon's superior Lubanian hearing caught the comment.

"Guess tomorrow I'll be a little more than just a lingering memory after all."

Molon smiled. He didn't understand the full context of John's taunt, but guessed it was a continuation of some private exchange the two had shared. Whatever it was, Voide's fuming silence, rather than a violent outburst, hinted that John might be making progress building bridges with the volatile security chief.

Seven – Back to the Stars

Molon and Twitch entered *Star Wolf*'s conference room just aft of the bridge. Voide and John were close on their heels. The Lubanian captain proceeded to the control panel beside the hatchway leading to the bridge and activated the controls.

"Command protocol blackout CR1, authorization Molon Hawkins, captain."

A digitized voice answered.

"Voice recognition accepted. Input verification code to initiate blackout protocol for Star Wolf room CR1."

Molon punched an alpha-numeric code into the control panel, using his body to block line of sight to the panel."

"Verification code accepted. Star Wolf room CR1 is in blackout protocol."

Inside the room, the sound of heavy magnetic locks sounded from both the fore and aft doors. A shimmering energy field coated the walls. The droning hum of white noise emanated from the room's audio system speakers. Above each door, a tiny LED light flashed alternately red and bluish-black.

"So what—," John started.

Twitch held a finger up to the front of her lips and shook her head, silencing the doctor. At a nod from Molon, Voide pulled out the small device from a zippered pocket on her stealth suit which John had seen her use to scan his bedroom before she burned his house down. It flashed and hummed quietly as she walked around the room moving the device close to every square meter of the walls, the conference table, and each chair in the room.

"All clear," Voide announced, putting the scanner away.

"Isn't this your ship?" John asked, skewing his face into a puzzled gaze. "You think your own people would bug the room?"

"Standard procedure in a situation like this," Twitch replied.

Molon took at seat at the head of the oblong conference table. He motioned for his crewmates to do likewise. Voide and

Twitch sat down on either side of Molon, but John remained standing, pacing back and forth. Whatever had happened down on Tede, it had rattled John badly. Molon only hoped the doctor's agitation came from the Brothers and not from Voide.

"Look, John," Molon said. "I can see you are upset, and with good reason. Dangerous people made a bold raid across the Theocracy border to kidnap you. Then allies of the Theocracy burned your house down and tried to kill you."

John bellowed an exaggerated interjection souding like something midway between a mocking laugh and an indignant harrumph. He stopped pacing, slapped both hands on the table, and faced Molon.

"The Brothers of the Lion?" John replied, shooting a scathing glare in Voide's direction before returning his attention to Molon. "It was your pyromaniac security chief who burned my house down."

Oh, well. Voide not being at least partially responsible for John state of mind was wishful thinking. Molon shook his head before glancing in Voide's direction.

"Hows that again?" Molon queried as Voide flashed a sheepish grin. "Maybe you two'd better bring me up to speed from the beginning."

Voide and John vollied comments like a game of netball as they recounted their trip to John's home, including John having recovered Elena's disguised datacube, which he now wore around his neck. As they completed their story, Molon pulled absent-mindedly at the fur on his chin, considering the implications of the chain of events. There was a far deeper motive to this matter than Dawnstar and a group of militant monks haggling over some research notes.

"I suppose you are lucky Elena made that backup," Molon said, hoping to soothe John's growing agitation. "At least that gives you a starting point to unwind this thing."

"Yeah, but since the custom reader for it mysteriously burned up in a freak house fire," John said, shooting Voide another sour look, "I don't really have any way to access the data."

"That's no problem," Twitch replied. "Dub should be able to rig something up to dump the data onto a more standard medium."

"I'll ask him about that," John answered, appearing to relax a little.

The room grew silent as Molon stared off into nothing for a few moments, mentally assembling pieces of this puzzle. Twitch, and Voide sat in patient silence awaiting his next words. Even John finally sensed the awkwardness of him standing, dropped quietly into a seat next to Twitch, and waited.

"I think I see what may be going on here," Molon finally piped up just as the others were beginning to look a little uncomfortable in the extended pause.

"So you gonna share with the class, or are we playing twenty questions?" Twitch snarked.

"The Brothers of the Lion want Elena's research to make a bio-weapon against the Daemi. Brother Martin said as much. Dawnstar probably had a similar motive."

"Dawnstar space doesn't border the Daemi, or the Prophane advance for that matter," Twitch replied.

"No, but they are allied with the Provisional Imperium, which borders both," Molon reasoned. "That would be a lucrative toy in Dawnstar's war chest."

John slapped the table, startling his companions.

"That was their plan all along!"

"Whose plan?" Voide asked.

"Dawnstar's. That's why they were funding Elena's research."

"You said that was before the Shattering," Molon replied. "You think Dawnstar was seeking a bioweapon pre-Shattering?"

"Yeah, maybe," John answered. "The Daemi malmorphsy bio-weapon was destroyed centuries ago, but the genetically inherited components of malmorphsy remain an ongoing problem. Pre-Shattering there was no reason to think their interest in Elena's work was anything other than altruistic. The Prophane advance had only started to seriously impinge on the far tailward edge of human space, and the Daemi had not been an active threat for over a century and a half."

"So, you don't believe Dawnstar was looking to develop a marketable cure for malmorphsy?" Molon asked.

"I did at the time, I suppose, but I see clearly now," John replied. "The Dawnstar representatives were never interested in Elena's breakthroughs with human malmorphs, even though curing humans was her passion. They only brought her genetic samples and data from non-human malmorphs."

"They only brought data," Twitch asked, "not live subjects?"

"Tede's laws prevented them from bringing live non-human subjects on planet."

"Why not just move her research to a more open system?" Twitch asked.

"They tried," said John. "Despite many attempts to get her to move, Elena loved our life on Tede. She wouldn't even consider uprooting. With such a focus on the transmission of the malmorphsy mutation in non-humans, it is likely Dawnstar had ideas of developing a targeted bio-weapon even before the Shattering."

"Well," Voide replied, "our little misdirection about the fire might have thrown the Brothers off for a bit, but once they debrief about the encounter, they will know we burned the house, and will suspect John has the data."

"Yep," Molon affirmed, his gut tightening in a knot. "That's not the worst of it."

"It gets worse?" John asked. "How?"

"Dawnstar has well-paid soldiers outfitted with the best tech money can buy. They won't give up easily if Elena's research was what they were really after."

John dropped into a chair, grasping the sides of his head with his hands. Molon knew after everything the human had been through, this was likely only the beginning of the road. He had run up against Dawnstar's forces before, and not all were like the rejects and wannabes on Ratuen. There were some top notch mercs, ex-spooks, and former shadowrunners on Dawnstar's payroll. If they came for John while he was aboard *Star Wolf*, this would not just be the doctor's problem.

"Something still doesn't make sense," John said, lifting his gaze once again to face Molon.

"What's that, John?" Molon asked.

"If Dawnstar wanted Elena's research, why didn't the inquisitor on Ratuen ask about it? He didn't mention it once. All he cared about was the location of the Brothers of the Lion."

That was a good question. Molon wished he had a good answer. Still, "I don't know" just didn't feel like the response John needed right now. Unfortunately, that's the only one Molon had.

"Maybe they got wind the brothers had contacted Elena and figured, with her being Faithful, that she had already turned it over to them," Voide said, not sounding overly convincing or convinced.

"There is more to it than that," Twitch replied. "Tubal may be a spineless puppet of High Archon Zarsus, but he is not stupid, and no stranger to corporate espionage."

"The Daemi are allied with Zarsus and the Provisional Imperium, which also includes Dawnstar," Voide said. "Maybe Dawnstar found out the Brothers were looking to develop a Daemi-targeted bio-weapon and tried to stop it."

"Maybe," Molon answered. "But whatever the reason for their involvement, they aren't done with this yet."

"Neither are the Brothers," John added. "They are relentless guerrilla fighters and fanatical about destroying the Daemi and restoring Humaniti to a unified force in this region of the galaxy. If they even suspect I might have what they are looking for, they will be back."

Molon stood and walked back to the control panel.

"Sounds like a good reason to jump this system as soon as possible."

"What about Elena's research?" John asked.

"I would keep the knowledge of that pendant datacube's existence on a need-to-know basis. Just keep it to the four of us and Dub, since you will need him to rig a reader. Get settled in, Doc. You may be with us a while."

"I've been in worse places," John replied with a confident smile that belied the fear and confusion Molon could see lurking just below the surface.

"Disengage blackout protocol room CR1," Molon said, accessing the panel. "Authorization Molon Hawkins, captain."

"Voice recognized, verbal commands accepted. Blackout protocol disengaged for Star Wolf room CR1."

"Twitch," Molon said, "oversee the wrap-up of the supply run. The rest of us will get to the bridge and get us out of here before we find any more trouble."

Twitch nodded and padded out the aft door while Molon, Voide, and John headed through the forward portal connecting the conference room to the bridge. As they stepped through the forward hatch, Z-Man, manning the helm, jumped to his feet, saluted, and opened his mouth to—.

"Ensign!" Molon snapped at the young officer. "If you announce '*captain on the bridge*' you will be scouring the refuse hold with a microscrubber for the next month!"

The young man flushed and returned to his post. Molon turned to address the ensign staffing the astrogation station.

"How soon can we hit voidspace, ensign?"

"That depends on the destination, captain. What is our heading?"

Before the captain could answer, an alert sounded from the communications station.

"Captain, a System Express boat just arrived with a standard news and communications packet," Mel announced.

"Any merc contracts close enough for us to pick up?"

"There are no contracts listed, but there is a secure communication within the packet relevant to us."

99

"What is it?"

"An encoded message addressed to Tede system, Elucia City, attention Dr. John Salzmann," Mel replied. "Since you filed John's travel documents with the Tede starport, their comms center forwarded the communication to *Star Wolf.*"

Eight – A Voice From Beyond

"Mel," John said approaching the communications officer station. "Does it say who sent it?"

"It does," Mel replied, "but there must be an error."

"What do you mean?"

"The message says the sender is Dr. Elena Salzmann."

John grabbed the back of Mel's chair to steady himself.

"When was it sent," John asked, "and from where?"

Mel paused. She turned toward John, her face pained and compassionate. He felt waves of sorrow and comfort swirled together emanating from her.

"The origin shows Ratuen," she said softly.

"The Dawnstar detention facility?" John said.

His stomach tightened and his head swam. His brow furrowed as he rubbed the back of his neck, puzzling through the implications.

"Apparently," Mel answered. "The time and date stamp on the file shows it was sent the day we rescued you, about seven hours after we left orbit."

This was impossible. Elena was dead before Molon and he had made their escape from Ratuen. How could she send a message seven hours later?

"John," Mel said, placing a hand on his, calling him back to reality. Her touch filled him with a warming calm that fought against the chaos of his confusion. "Time and origin tags can be easily counterfeited."

"This has to be Dawnstar's idea of a sick joke," Voide snapped from the security station. "I wouldn't put it past those twisted techies."

"John," Molon said. "We can patch this through to your cabin if you want some privacy."

"That won't be necessary, Captain," John replied.

John sighed and braced himself before straightening himself up with help from the bolstering of Mel's touch. He took a deep breath, smoothed the front of his shirt, and spoke.

"Voide is probably right. Dawnstar may have sent this as a

101

parting shot. Open it please, Mel, so we can see who is behind such a twisted act."

"I'm sorry," Mel responded with a shake of her head. "I cannot open the file."

"Why not?" John answered, his voice rising slightly in frustration. Whatever this message was, John didn't believe it had the remotest possibility of actually being from Elena. Still, it was best to get to the bottom of it as soon as possible.

"The file requires a security code to access," Mel answered. "Do you know the code?"

"How would I know that?" John replied.

"Get your head in the game, pale," Voide commanded, pounding a fist on the edge of her console.

"What do you mean?" John growled back at the security chief, not understanding what he was missing that Voide saw.

"For a doctor, you aren't very bright," Voide replied. "This was set to be delivered to you personally. There's no payoff unless you can access it. Whoever is behind this expected you would know how to open it."

"John," Mel said, the waves of her voice lapping at his mind like gentle swells on a calm shore, ebbing away his annoyance at Voide's chafing demeanor. "What if it really was from Elena?"

John jerked his hand off Mel's shoulder, taking a step back from the communications officer. As soon as he broke contact, the ebb of calm that had held back his frustration and confusion flowed away, leaving only his raw emotion.

"That's impossible," he said, fighting back the tears threatening to fill his eyes. "Elena is dead. I saw her die."

"John," Mel interjected with a glisten in her eye. "I only meant that if you had received a message from Elena, something she wanted to send for only you to see, how would you have accessed the message?"

John could feel Mel's voice trying to break through, but the walls of pain that had sprung up from the memory of seeing the interrogator slit Elena's throat right before his eyes were like the bastions of a fortress holding back an invading army, refusing to let the calm breach the gates. Still, the analytical part of John's mind fought to be heard.

"How would anyone know Elena's security key?" John mused aloud. "That makes no sense."

"Unless you have any better ideas," Voide interrupted, "then quit rationalizing and try it."

John felt the frustration inside him focus into a white-hot point of light aimed at the center of the gray-skinned security chief's forehead. He had just reached the same conclusion, but her outburst robbed him of the opportunity to act on his decision. Now, in everyone's eyes, he would be acting on her command.

There was nothing to be done about it for the moment, but if he planned to stay on *Star Wolf* for any length of time, a stern talk with the security chief would be part of that. Without another word, he returned to Mel's workstation, careful not to touch her again lest whatever effect she had on him return against his will. He punched in the sixteen digit alphanumeric code he and Elena always used to send secure messages.

"Security code accepted. Accessing message," Mel's panel announced.

John wavered on his feet, dizziness threatening to engulf him. His and Elena's private code had worked. How was this possible? Could she really be...?

"Put it on the main screen," Molon said.

"I cannot," Mel replied. "The message is audio only."

"Play it," John demanded.

He had lost patience with this whole ruse. Why would someone try and trick him into believing, even for a second, his Elena was still alive? Would this recording be demands for her research, or threats against his life?

Whatever John expected might be on that recording, he wasn't prepared for what he heard as Mel routed the message through *Star Wolf*'s comm system.

"John, I...," came an almost whispering voice.

By the Lion of Judah, it was Elena's voice! John's chest tightened. He couldn't breathe. The edges of his vision began to blur and dizziness threatened to engulf him. He pushed back the overwhelming flood of sensations through sheer will, but he wasn't sure how long he could hold it back as the sound of her voice continued.

"I don't know if you will hear this, but I found a way to uplink to the...to the System Express boat in orbit. I looked for you when the explosions freed me. You weren't in our cell. I...I don't know how long I can stay hidden. I'm afraid, John...If you get this messa--"

As suddenly as it started, the message ended.

"Why did you stop?" John said, spinning Mel in her chair, tears streaming down his face. "Play the rest of it!"

Nausea churned his gut. Elena had always been so eloquent. To hear her stammering and confused, she must be at the limits of her endurance. Why had he left her there?

"I am sorry, John," said Mel's sweet voice, a single tear of her own sliding down her powder-blue left cheek. "That is all."

"It's a hoax," Voide said. "Dawnstar must suspect John has Elena's research. They are trying to lure him back to get their hands on it."

"She's alive," John whispered.

The numbness in his soul transferred itself to his tone. He stared blankly at the forward bulkhead, his mind reeling with the implications.

"John, that's impossible," Molon added. "We both saw her die. I don't know what their game is, but this recording is definitely a fake."

"No. *No.* That voice was Elena's. She's alive!" John insisted. "I have to go back for her."

"It can't be her," Molon argued. "We saw the inquisitor slit her throat."

"I know that!" John screamed, clenching his fists in rage as he spun toward Molon. "But no one else would have her encryption key. How do you explain that?"

"Maybe they tortured it out of her," Molon reasoned. "They had been tuning you two up for quite a while before I found you."

"But never alone," John said, shaking his head. "Always together. They never split us up, and they never asked about encryption codes or anything else. The only thing the inquisitor cared about, when he bothered to question us at all, was the location of the Brothers of the Lion base on Tede. I'm telling you, captain, Elena is alive."

"You're insane," Molon snarled.

John's face brightened as he spun and beamed a hopeful look at Molon.

"I may well be, but you are mercenaries, aren't you? I have money. Name your price. I will hire *Star Wolf* to take me back to Ratuen to look for her."

A hush fell over the bridge. For a moment John wasn't sure if anyone had heard him, until Voide replied in an angry tone.

"We're mercs, not a suicide squad. You want us to fly back into Dawnstar territory after you and Molon dropped a grenade down their shorts less than a week ago?"

Something in John snapped. Weren't these types of people supposed to be fearless? Hadn't Voide said during their time together on Tede that it was axiomatic for mercenaries to risk their lives for a payday? Well John had no shortage of funds, so this sudden reluctance to help him get back to Elena was enfuriating. John reached deep for his best poker-bluff attitude and turned to face the gray-skinned security chief.

"Well then," John said, a menacing calmness overtaking his voice. "If you don't have the guts, then set me down on Tede. I will catch the next freighter to Furi and find a more courageous crew of mercenaries there. Either way, I'm going back for her."

Voide, with murder in her eyes, took a step toward John before Molon turned to face the security chief. The hackles on the back of Molon's lupine neck stood straight up. His upper lip on both sides pulled back into a snarl, flashing his deadly canines. As Voide moved toward John, Molon took a half step toward her.

"Stand down, Lieutenant Commander!" he growled.

"Is there something wrong with your ears, captain?" Voide spat, halting her advance. "This sniveling pale just called us cowards."

"I heard him," Molon replied. "I was also with him when he saw his wife killed in front of his eyes less than a week ago. Now he gets sent a recording of her voice calling for him to come back for her. That's enough to shake anyone into saying something..." Molon turned his head to face John before adding, "suicidal."

"However," Molon said returning his gaze to Voide, "he's right. We're mercs who just got stiffed on a job. As captain, I need to make payroll so, Lieutenant Commander, unless you have a boatload of cash and want to pay me to take *Star Wolf* someplace else, then we've been offered a paying gig to return to Ratuen, and I'm taking it."

"You've got to be kidding," Voide replied, her body tense as a spring as she stepped back to her station.

"Last time I checked I'm still captain, so that's my call."

"It's a bad call," Voide snapped as she lowered her head to her controls, deliberately not looking at Molon.

"You got a problem with it, Voide," Molon replied, "I'll be happy to put you dirtside before we leave."

Voide looked up from her station and hurled a killing gaze at John before returning her attention to Molon. She suddenly affected a terse smile and cocked her head.

"As security chief, it is my duty to respectfully inform my captain that he is being an idiot ordering our ship into a trap and is about to get us all killed."

"Of course it's a trap," Molon said, the snarl slipping more into a wolfish grin, ignoring Voide's blatant insubordination. "Have we ever taken a job that wasn't rigged to get us killed?"

"Fine," Voide said, busying herself with the controls at the security station. "You are the captain and I will follow your orders, as long as you don't order me to take a bullet for this irrational pale. I already saved his pathetic life once today. That meets my altruism quota for the month."

Molon looked like he was trying his best not to laugh.

"One good deed a month, Voide?" Molon quipped. "Did you up your quota without telling me?"

Voide widened her yellowish eyes, tossing him an exaggerated smile. He responded with a wink before turning his attention to the forward bridge stations.

"Ensign," Molon addressed the young officer manning astrogation. "Change of course. Take us to Hatacks, then queue up a heading for the rabbit trail entry point to Ratuen."

"Aye, captain. ETA two hours to the jump point to Hatacks."

"John," Molon said.

"Yes, captain?" John replied warily, expecting Molon to lay into him for his provocative outburst.

"Meet me in my quarters in ten minutes," Molon instructed. "We have some things to talk about."

"Yes, captain," John answered, feeling like a prisoner who had just been called to the gallows.

"Lieutenant Commander Matsumura has the conn," Molon announced, nodding to Voide.

The captain proceeded toward the port-side forward hatch leading from the bridge and made his exit without another word. Voide moved from her security station to the captain's chair and put out a call for a security officer to report to the bridge to take her place.

"John?" Mel said.

Her soft voice cut through the fog in his mind. Suddenly he realized he wasn't angry anymore.

"Yes, Mel?"

"I think it is brave that you would go back for Elena, even if there is only a slim chance that this is true."

John didn't know much about the Fei, but if they all were as compassionate as Mel, he felt they were a race worthy of their Creator. Just her soft, sweet voice filled him with warmth. Unfortunately that warmth blended with John's consuming sadness over Elena. His insides knotted over the possibility that she was still alive and he had left her there in the hands of that brutal torturer.

He was shocked to realize that some small part of him, down in the depths of his heart, hoped that this was a hoax. If it were not, how could he ever face her again? How could she ever forgive him for leaving her behind?

"I have to know," John answered, hanging his head and releasing a deep sigh.

"I understand," Mel said and a wave of comfort washed over John along with her words. "In the meantime, I will run full diagnostics on the message file. If I find any evidence the recording was fabricated or altered, I will let you know."

"Thanks," he said, starting to put a hand on her shoulder.

He suddenly remembered how irresistible the emotions were every time he touched her. How could she make him feel this way? Elena was killed less than a week ago, and now there was a possibility she was even still alive. Why did he feel like a swooning schoolboy around the blue-skinned Fei communications officer? He withdrew his hand, instead simply nodding to her before turning to follow after the captain.

Whatever Molon had to say to him, it was unlikely to be pleasant. At least the captain had the decorum to chew him out in private. John appreciated that.

Every step of the short trip from the port bridge door, down the short corridor, and around the corner to Molon's quarters was dreadful. However this discussion went, he had to watch his temper. The last thing he needed was to mouth off and cause Molon to reconsider taking him back to Ratuen.

John stood outside the door to the captain's cabin, took a deep breath, then pressed the panel button announcing his arrival.

"Enter," came Molon's voice from inside.

As far as John could tell through the door, Molon didn't sound furious. That was a good sign, right? He stepped toward the hatch, and it slid open before him. Molon was already seated in a mag-locked swivel chair at the desk beside his bed. The captain's quarters were large enough to also accommodate a three-seat sofa, which Molon nodded toward.

"Have a seat, John."

"Look, captain, I—"

"Have a seat," Molon insisted, sternly but still with no hint of anger in his voice.

John took a seat on the end of the couch nearest Molon. He found himself fiddling with his hands, unsure of exactly what to do with them. John cleared his throat, fixed his gaze on the floor at Molon's feet, and strained not to sound too sheepish.

"Not the best start to my first day as acting ship's doctor, I suppose?"

Molon laughed. This put John at ease enough to raise his

eyes and meet Molon's gaze.

"Don't worry about Voide," Molon said, grinning. "She hates everyone."

"Even you?"

"Hah, at times especially me."

"So how does a ship function like that?"

"Surprisingly well, actually."

"She just seems so angry all the time," John remarked.

"She's Prophane, John. She may have been raised by humans, but anger is in her DNA. What amazes me is how well she manages to rein it in most of the time."

"Most of the time?" John asked, raising an eyebrow.

"Yeah, she has her moments, but she has yet to murder a crew member, as far as I know. I doubt you will be the first."

"As far as you know?" John inquired, hoping Molon was being facetious.

"Eh, there are rumors..." Molon said with a chuckle.

Molon had to be kidding. At least the humorous banter served to lighten John's mood. Maybe he wasn't in as much trouble as he had feared.

"That's comforting," John replied, playing along.

"Ain't it though?" Molon grinned. "Still, it would be in the best interest of your continued good health to avoid ever again even so much as remotely implying Voide is a coward."

The sudden serious shift in Molon's tone and the stern look in his eyes conveyed to John in no uncertain terms that this part was not just witty banter. There was a genuine warning embedded.

"Everyone has fears, captain," John said, not sure he was ready to kowtow to the security chief's temperamentalism just yet.

Molon shook his head before locking eyes with John.

"I'd buy that, Doc, if you were talking about a human, or a Lubanian, or heck even a Daemi. But, I'm not sure the Creator even put a fear gene in the Prophane. If He did, I've never seen it."

As a doctor, John knew the fear response, fight or flight, was a part of every living creature. As a gambler with a knack for reading truths and bluffs in the faces of his opponents, he believed Molon wholeheartedly.

"Anyway," Molon said, the casual tone returning to his voice. "I didn't call you here to talk about Voide; I called you here to talk about you and me."

"What about us?" John asked.

"If you are going to serve aboard *Star Wolf*, there are some

108

things I need to know, and some things you need to know.

"Okay," John said, intrigued by the change in direction. "What things?"

"I understand you have been through a lot...are going through a lot, so your judgment isn't very dependable right now."

Apparently John wasn't getting out of the consequences of his actions on the bridge that easily. Still, Molon seemed fair and reasonable so hopefully whatever dressing down was coming may not be as bad as John had feared.

"You think going after Elena is a mistake?" John dropped his gaze and sighed.

"I think Voide is right, it is a trap. Taking you back to Ratuen puts every member of this crew at risk."

John's heart sank. Had the captain decided to abandon the mission already? John hadn't done anything to provoke Molon, at least as far as he knew, and they were already en route. Molon had already agreed to take the job, but was a verbal agreement enough? They hadn't signed a contract. No compensation or security had changed hands. No terms had been reached or price even set. There was nothing binding Molon to continue.

"So you changed your mind, then?" John asked, hoping he had misread Molon's intentions.

"No, I haven't," Molon replied, to John's great relief. "I just want you to know I am not going into this blindly or out of some sense of misguided sympathy."

"Then why go, captain?" John said, fighting against his temper threatening to resurface. "Why take such a risk for someone you just met?"

Molon folded his hands, resting his muzzle on his fingertips. He sighed and slowly blinked his eyes. John got the impression he was trying Molon's patience.

"I'm not doing this for you," Molon finally replied. "I agreed to take you back to Ratuen, but I am not recklessly tossing my crew into danger over your emotional hysterics or just for a payday."

"Then why are you heading into what you already said you believe is a trap?"

Molon shook his head before giving John a sidewise stare.

"Do you think being mercenaries is a safe and secure job choice?"

"Not particularly," John admitted.

"We get paid to go where people are trying to kill us. Risk is part of our life, but this isn't just a paying gig, John, it's a

109

mystery."

"A mystery?" John said, raising an eyebrow. "You mean Elena's message?"

"I mean all of it," Molon said, leaning forward in his chair. "Nothing about this rings true, and I hate being lied to."

John's head was spinning trying to follow Molon's reasoning. He agreed this was a mystery, but did Molon really believe solving it was worth dying for?

"Being lied to?" John again attempted to catch up to Molon's train of thought. "You mean Brother Martin?"

"Yes and no," Molon replied, shaking his head. "He's up to something, but Brother Martin is just a tiny piece of the puzzle."

John was an accomplished people-reader, but he found the captain baffling. He gave off all the airs of a simple, straightforward person, but there were deeper layers to this Lubanian.

"So you agreed to take on this potentially deadly mission just to assuage your curiosity?" John probed.

Molon's look soured as he sat back in his chair and glared at John. The captain's extended pause and withering stare were intensely disquieting.

"Did I say something wrong, captain?" John asked finally, breaking the awkward silence.

"I'm trying to decide if you are being sarcastic or antagonistic," Molon said. "I'm going to give you the benefit of the doubt and assume you are just slow-witted."

"Thanks," John said, choosing not to rise to the insult.

He might be a hermit-worlder who wasn't familiar with how life worked on a merc ship, but he was getting a little tired of people insinuating he was mentally sluggish. He graduated in the top five percent of his class in medical school. He was an accomplished surgeon and president of an interstellar pharmeceuticals company. He may have many flaws, but lack of intelligence was not among them.

"Do you really want to know why I do what I do?" Molon asked.

"I admit, I'm curious," John replied, glad to get to the end of guessing what Molon was thinking.

"Well, to understand me, you need to understand a bit about my history and why I'm captaining *Star Wolf*."

John perked up. He had wondered about that quite a bit, actually. This little talk might prove enlightening. Besides, if Molon was reminiscing, he wouldn't be focused about John's antagonistic outburst on the bridge.

"I actually am a bit of a history buff. I'd love to hear your story, Molon."

"Well, it starts before the Shattering. My birth father was a Lubanian soldier who served in the Humaniti Imperial Navy. He was killed during a peacekeeping mission near the Daemi border, but his best friend and comrade-in-arms, a human soldier, kept a promise they had made to each other.

Soon after my father's death, this human came for my mother and me. He gave up his military career, brought us to a human colony world, and he and his wife raised me like their own child. My birth mother had been sick for a long time and died a few years later, but my adoptive father taught me the same ideals under which he served Emperor Halberan."

"He sounds like a good man," John remarked.

"He was a good man, and a faithful soldier who taught me to believe in the Empire. I joined the Imperial Scouts, and like my birth father and my adoptive father before me, I devoted my life to serving the Empire of Humaniti.

"When Emperor Zariah and Empress Rhia were assassinated on the day Zariah was to name which of his four children would succeed him as heir apparent, it changed the course of human history. The Shattering changed my life too."

"How so?" John asked.

"I tried to be a good soldier, to maintain my position with the scouts under the Provisional Imperium, but High Archon Zarsus wasn't a shadow of the man Zariah Halberan had been. I lost hope. Zarsus wasn't leading a provisional anything. Stringing that technocrat Tubal Halberan along as if he might one day name him heir was a farce. Mathua Zarsus had seized power and had no intention of giving it up."

"At least we agree on that," John interjected. "Tubal is a businessman, but nothing about him would inspire or command the loyalty of an interstellar empire. I believe Zarsus staged the assassination and used the confusion over the culprit to keep power from all of the rightful heirs."

"I eventually came to that same conclusion," Molon agreed. With the more capable Halberan heirs opposing him, and Zarsus refusing to name a rightful successor, Humaniti will remain divided for the foreseeable future. The final nail in the coffin of the Provisional Imperium was when Zarsus made a pact with the Daemi, Humaniti's oldest and greatest enemies."

"So you left the Scouts and picked up your own ship?" John asked.

"Not exactly," Molon sighed. "It took a while for me to

111

overcome all the loyalty ideology my adoptive father instilled in me. I had to do what I could to salvage the Empire if possible."

"An ambitious goal for a lone Scout. How did you expect to manage that?"

"I started voicing dissension from within. I thought respected citizens and soldiers like Twitch and I could inspire those loyal to the former emperor to band together. United, we might amass enough political pressure to force High Archon Zarsus' hand, compelling him to name an official heir to the Empire and so end the fighting."

"I guess that didn't exactly go according to plan."

"No, it didn't. Once word got out that some Lubanian Scout officer was stirring up trouble, they set me up for a fall."

"Who did?" John asked.

"I have my suspicions, but no proof."

"I see," John replied. "So, what happened?"

"I was working deep-cover against a pirate network," Molon explained, "when a false report came out claiming I was in league with the pirates. I was accused of skimming off them and lining my own pockets with their pillage while feeding them information to stay ahead of authorities."

"Ouch," John remarked. "So that got you kicked out of the Scouts?"

"Worse. My identity as an undercover Imperial Scout was also leaked to the pirate leader, Razdi Chadra, scourge of the Hinterlands. I guess it was Zarsus's way of making me disappear."

John's respect and appreciation for his Lubanian rescuer was growing by the minute. He could understand why Molon's crew held him in such high regard.

"How'd you get out of that mess?" John asked.

"I owe my life to Twitch and to a group of GalSec agents who had infiltrated Chadra's pirate network. They had been operating outside the chain of command and without High Archon Zarsus's knowledge."

"GalSec?" John said, raising an eyebrow. "You said Voide used to work for GalSec. Is that where you met her?"

"Yeah, but a bit later. Once I was burned, Twitch and the other undercover agents pulled me out. Later, I was sent back in with a GalSec task force to take out Chadra and break the pirate ring once and for all."

John scowled. This tale had just taken a turn for the remarkable. He wondered if he was being played, or if Molon was really just that good at what he did.

"You were accused of treason," John said, "and GalSec still

trusted you enough to send you back in undercover? That strains credulity, not to mention the question of why Chadra would let you back in after you betrayed him."

"To your first question," Molon replied, "GalSec has its own factions. Voide's former commanding officer had been watching me since I started voicing dissidence against Zarsus. So when GalSec got evidence I had been set up, Voide's CO was determined to try and set things right."

"Okay," John said, still scouring Molon for any hint that he was spinning a tall tale. "Let's say I buy that part, but what about Chadra? Why would he let you back in?"

"GalSec fixed that too. They ran with the bait Zarsus had laid about me being a traitor. Publicly I was dishonorably discharged from the Scouts and arrested for treason. GalSec staged a highly publicized incident where I, with Voide's rather violent help, broke out of custody and went on the run."

"And Chadra fell for it?"

"GalSec also set up a very convincing paper trail for Chadra to find, tying me to many of the anonymous tips he had received about raids. Turns out someone in GalSec had been helping the pirates all along, for what purpose they never told me. They just made it look like that someone was me."

"And that cinched it?"

"With a little help from a certain rogue Pariah," Molon replied with a grin. "Voide was assigned as GalSec team lead on that mission. She had previously met with Chadra's people to feed them the some of that intel I mentioned. They trusted her, and she put me forth as the brains behind the whole deal."

"But you are not still a fugitive. If you had been, Tede's system alerts would have triggered the moment you logged our landing. So how did you unwind all this mess?"

"During our second undercover op, the one Voide led, we got intel on Chadra's whole organization. GalSec set up a huge, inter-sector sting that shredded Chadra's pirate network. I saved Voide's life in a firefight as we seized Chadra's flagship, *Star Wolf*."

John's jaw dropped. This merc vessel formerly belonged to a pirate leader. John fancied himself an adventurer because he had played with live kalo-cats at a game preserve and hunted zuma pigs with only a bow and arrow. All these things now seemed frivolous to John compared to Molon's story. To think someone who had been through the stuff of legends was sitting here chatting with him was mind boggling.

"You stole his ship?" John asked, unable to suppress his widened eyes and even wider smile.

113

"Confiscated...and conveniently forgot to report on our mission logs, as per my agreement with GalSec senior leadership. It was part of my retirement package from GalSec along with a generous mustering-out payment."

"That's quite a reversal of fortune," John remarked, shaking his head as he tried to process it all.

"Yeah. Anyway, after all the hullabaloo, I recruited a crew and tucked *Star Wolf* safely away in a remote system while the dust settled."

"So you got to arrest Chadra?"

"Yes and no," Molon answered.

"That doesn't sound good," John said. "What happened?"

"Chadra was slippery. We burned his organization to the ground, but he had enough loyalists left to break him out of custody during his transport to Corialis for trial."

"So he's still on the loose, and you likely aren't one of his favorite sophonts. Aren't you worried he will come for you?"

"It's a big galaxy, and I've got his ship. Ships aren't cheap, and it may be years before he can scrape together the scratch for another one."

"But what about you? You never told me how you cleared your record."

"Once the mission was over, the GalSec director fixed that, putting out a statement affirming that I had been working undercover with GalSec the entire time and the arrest was part of a ruse to establish my cover. Heck, they even gave me a medal."

"How'd that fly with High Archon Zarsus?"

"Zarsus had no choice but to go along and amend my record to an honorable discharge with full retirement benefits."

"And that's when you took up the mantle of mercenary?"

"Yep. Twitch also resigned her commission in the Scouts to join me. A few months later, Voide showed up. She left GalSec and started tracking us when her deputy director, the guy who put together the whole undercover operation and my vindication, wound up dead, poisoned in his own home."

"Fascinating!" John said, tentatively testing the waters with the captain once again. "I have to say, though, I'm still fishing for how this relates to your agreeing to return to Ratuen with me, and I'm coming up with empty nets."

"It relates because running this merc crew was never about the money for me, John. When I mustered out I was set for life. If I sold *Star Wolf*, I'd be set for a life of luxury. But I have no intention of retiring."

"Why not? Why continue to risk your life? I'd think you've

just about used up all your luck and then some, Molon. You sure you want to keep rolling the dice?"

"Because, I left the service to do whatever I could to restore Humaniti space to rightful rule. There was honor and purpose in the Old Empire. Zarsus and his lust for power have ruined the remnants of the Empire of Humaniti. So, I pointed *Star Wolf* spinward searching for a way to help set things right."

"So then you headed where, exactly?"

"Seth Halberan had joined forces with his sister Phoebe. They were claiming to be the Halberan Empire reborn. Two of the rightful Halberan heirs allied against Zarsus; that sounded hopeful."

"Let me guess what shattered that hope. Alpha Pack?"

A fire lit behind Molon's eyes. His answer came as a deep growl in the back of his throat as he gazed somewhere far beyond John.

"Yeah, Alpha Pack."

Molon took several deep breaths, returning his gaze to John before continuing. "Sorry. Sore subject."

"I understand," John replied.

"When Ghost Fang pulled together a Lubanian uberpack and allied with Seth and Phoebe's New Halberan Empire, I was elated. Lubanians and humans fighting side by side; it seemed like an ideal setup for me. Or so I thought."

"I'm guessing you weren't on board with Ghost Fang's whole rape, loot, and pillage plan, huh?"

"You could say that. When Ghost Fang began seizing Fei colonies, I realized he was a thug using the humans to advance his own ends. When the New Halberan Empire started launching scorched earth attacks against Enoch Halberan and the Theocracy of the Faithful, they proved themselves no better than Zarsus."

"In all fairness," John objected. "Seth and Phoebe have denounced Alpha Pack's invasion of the Fei and have called for a cessation of hostilities against civilian targets. The Halberans claim Ghost Fang and the officers who carried out the scorched earth attacks acted of their own accord. Many of those human officers had historical, anti-Faithful family ties going back a hundred and forty years to the Parvisian Dynasty."

Molon gave John a skewed look.

"Were those officers ever prosecuted?" Molon asked.

"Not as far as I am aware," John admitted.

He knew what Molon was implying. In fact, he had often wrestled with that fact as he spoke with Faithful who saw the

115

New Halberan Empire as no better than the anti-Faithful Dawnstar sympathizers.

"So what happened to those officers, John? Do you know?"

"According to the news reports," John replied, "they were dishonorably discharged."

"That's comforting," Molon said, his tone dripping with sarcasm. "I'm sure they feel duly chastised."

"Okay, so they got off light. I see your point."

"Oh, that's not even close to the point, John. The real point is does the New Halberan Empire alliance with Alpha Pack still stand?" Molon asked, rhetorically.

"It does."

"Well there you go."

"Yet you are still heading spinward," John remarked. "If you are disillusioned with the New Halberan Empire, where are you going?"

"I'm convinced that the best hope for restoring any vestige of the Empire of Humaniti lies with Enoch and the Theocracy."

John was surprised to hear that. Given Molon's coolness in the Faithful discussions with Brother Martin, John had assumed Molon was an anti-faither. To learn Molon intended to join the Theocracy's war effort just yanked whatever tentative grasp John thought he had on Molon right out of reach again.

"You are in the minority with that opinion, Molon."

It was Molon's turn to look shocked. He furrowed his lupine brow and cocked his head slightly sideways.

"That's a surprising sentiment," Molon replied, "coming from one of the Faithful at least."

"I'm a realist," John replied. "I am not sure Enoch is any more capable of uniting the factions of Humaniti than Tubal is."

"Enoch is a good man," Molon replied. "Despite the scorched earth attacks against him, he refuses to respond in kind. That says a great deal about his character."

"So," John asked, thinking he finally was tracking with Molon's motivation, "you see helping me as somehow helping Enoch?"

"In a way."

"In what way?" John asked. "I'm a Faithful, but I have no ties to the Theocracy or Enoch beyond our shared faith."

"Helping you is a way to stick my finger in the eye of Tubal and his Dawnstar Technocracy. By extension, messing up Dawnstar's plans indirectly works against Zarsus. If there is even a remote possibility that Faithful guerilla fighters like the

Brothers of the Lion are also turning against Enoch, then helping you will put a twist in their tails as well."

John smiled and shook his head.

"And that's why you agreed to risk your life helping me? To twist a few tails?"

Molon laughed.

"Sounds petty when you put it like that," Molon replied. "Whether Elena is still alive or not I don't know. Lifting a leg on the collective plans of Tubal, Zarsus, and that deceitful Brother Martin is a nice bonus, and I help the Theocracy in the process."

"So you are helping the Theocracy. Are you a member of the Faithful, Molon? Because I got the impression you weren't on the same page theologically when we met with Brother Martin."

Molon laughed as he stood up, walked to a cabinet in the corner, and pulled out a decanter and two glasses.

"Brandy, John?"

"No thanks," John declined with a raised palm.

"That's right. A hermit-worlder and genuine Faithful. Teetotalers through and through."

Molon replaced one of the glasses in the case and filled the other with the amber liquid. He swirled it in the glass, giving it a loving sniff as he returned to his seat.

"Abstinence from the joys of drunkenness for the rest of my life might be enough to keep me from ever being one of you."

John frowned at Molon's flippancy. He was used to dealing with anti-faithers when traveling away from Tede, but it was never pleasant no matter how accustomed one grew to the attitude. Molon's jibes, at least, were much milder that what John was used to dealing with.

"Joke if you want to," John said. "It was a serious question. Few outside the Faithful have any desire to see Enoch take power, even those who disagree with the rabid anti-faith movement."

"True enough," Molon said, taking a deep draught from his glass.

"Enoch is a clergyman at heart," John continued, "not an emperor. He has no desire to ascend his father's throne."

"That fact," Molon replied, "might be precisely why he is the only one of the Halberan heirs worthy to sit upon it."

John nodded. Molon was right, of course. The problem with Zarsus was his lust for power and refusal to relinquish it. The main issue with Seth and Phoebe was Seth's dogged insistence that he was to be named the rightful heir. Tubal was simply a sycophant who would do anything for the chance to rule, even as a puppet. Enoch was the only Halberan heir who had chosen to fight to establish a safe zone for the Faithful fleeing the anti-faithers. He had no desire to rule beyond it being a path for establishing security for the Faithful dispersed throughout the reaches of the Old Empire.

"Now," Molon continued, "to answer your faith question. I don't know for certain what I believe."

"How does a man not know his own mind?"

"Easy, when one's mind is filled with more questions than answers. My adoptive parents were human Faithful. Growing up I studied the Bible right along with history, math, and science. One question I never found an answer to is why, other than the Angelicum and Daemi who are mentioned in quite metaphorical and allegorical terms, are none of the other races, worlds, or galactic empires even mentioned in the Bible?"

John's heart sped up. This was what every true Faithful hoped for; an encounter with someone genuinely seeking truth. John was no evangelist, but he felt he knew how to answer this question. Might this be a turning point for Molon? John knew that the Lion used all things for good for those who love Him and are called to His purpose. Could the chance to lead Molon to faith have been the reason behind this whole experience?

"That is your barrier to faith, Molon?" John asked, his mind already working up his answer.

"That's not enough?" Molon asked. "That seems like a pretty big question to me."

John quickly crossed and uncrossed his hands, as if waving off the misunderstanding that had just taken place.

"That's not what I meant."

"When the Bible was written," Molon explained, "humans hadn't even left earth, but Angelicum, Daemi, and who knows how many others already had interstellar empires. Lubanians and Fei even beat Humaniti to the stars. Other major races, Dractauri, Doppelgangers, Prophane, none of them are even hinted at, not to mention the races we haven't encountered yet, or the thousands of minor races scattered across thousands of worlds. If the Lion of Judah came to redeem all of creation as the Faithful claim, then why aren't they even hinted at in the Scriptures?"

"That is a great question, Molon," John replied, grateful that his verbal hiccup hadn't shut down the conversation. "You know the Creator is revealed in the history and writings of every race known, except for the Prophane. Who knows, if we

118

ever found a way to get them to stop killing long enough to talk to anyone, we might find Him there too in some form."

"I know," Molon said, draining half his glass. "But then why do we only see three races mentioned in the Bible?"

John took a deep breath. All his life, part of his training and study with the Faithful was to prepare him for this type of conversation. He lifted a quick prayer heavenward and began.

"You said you studied the history of Humaniti, right?"

"Yeah," Molon answered, "so?"

"Did you study what the homeworld of Humaniti was like before we reached the stars?"

"It was a tiny world hell-bent on ripping itself apart. Until the discovery of voidspace opened the door to the stars, humans squabbled over one ball of dirt, willing to kill anyone who wanted to take their piece of it away from them."

"A bit of an oversimplification," John laughed. "The point is there were ancient cultures, entire nations, and important people who profoundly shaped the course of human history. The Mayans, Incas, Aztecs, Zulu, Mauri, Chinese Emperors and Japanese Samurai. The Russian Czars, American Presidents, European Monarchs, and Viking Conquerors. Without all of these, Humaniti would never have learned how to work together to forge itself into a vast interstellar empire. Yet where in the Bible do you see any of these mentioned?"

"Nowhere," Molon answered after a thoughtful pause.

"Exactly," John replied. "These were people, nations, and cultures on the same ball of dirt that the Lion of Judah visited. The place where He lived, taught, and died for all of us. Yet there, in the book of His story, they aren't mentioned."

"You didn't answer the question," Molon replied. "You just added another one to the list."

"Not really, Molon. It doesn't mention these, or the interstellar races, because the book is His story, not all of history. God gave us the Bible to help us know the Lion of Judah, the Messiah. He told us what we needed to understand about Him. He left it up to us to discover what we needed to about the rest of His creation."

Molon sat quietly scratching the fur on his chin for a long moment. John could almost see the wheels of his mind wrapping around John's answer.

"I don't know," Molon said at last. "That's a lot like a politician's answer, it sounds nice to the ear but at the end of it all you aren't sure if you heard anything at all."

"Please understand," John replied. "The Lion of Judah loved and came for all the people and nations. All of creation suffered in the fall, and all of creation groans for His return. The promise is that *whosoever* believes can become one of the Faithful. Redemption is not based on genetics."

Molon drained the rest of his glass and set it on his desk.

"I think you missed your calling, John," he said with a wry grin. "You should have been a proclaimer."

"Every Faithful is a proclaimer," John replied.

"Well, now you understand me better, and I understand you better. Get settled into your quarters and get some rest. Whatever is waiting back on Ratuen, we're all going to need to be at our best when we get there."

"But did I answer your question?"

John sensed that he had gotten as far with Molon as he was going to at this point. The captain had suddenly erected a defensive wall barring further discussion and John wasn't sure how to move past it.

"You gave me an answer, John," Molon affirmed, "but a lifetime of skepticism won't disappear in a flash. You gave me something to chew on for now. We'll talk again later."

"As you wish, captain," John answered, wishing his words might have had a greater impact on the affable captain. Perhaps the seeds he had sown just needed time to grow. "Thank you for taking me back to Ratuen."

"Thank you for offering us a job," Molon replied. "I like you, John, but don't think for a second you are getting a discount on our rates. I've got a crew to keep from starvation and mutiny."

John laughed. There was something likeable about Molon Hawkins. Molon was searching for answers. John did not know if he was the man to provide them, but would do his best. He turned toward the door when Molon called out to him.

"Oh, and John."

"Yes, captain?"

"Give Voide a wide berth for a few days. She probably won't kill you, but best not to find out the hard way I was wrong."

"Good advice."

"You might want to give Mel some room too, while you are at it."

John understood Molon's warning about Voide, but Mel?

"Really?" he asked, hoping Molon would elaborate.

"You don't know much about Fei, do you?"

"Nothing beyond what I read in the medical journals on our trip back from Ratuen the first time."

"Fei are empaths. Nobody really knows much about the

120

extent of their abilities, and the Fei don't like to talk about it. Still, Mel has an effect on people."

"That's an understatement," John replied, thinking of the strange feelings he had every time he came near her.

"Folks are a lot more agreeable when she is around," Molon continued. "I don't question Mel's motives, but given you are pretty much an ion storm of emotions just at the moment..."

"I'll keep that in mind, captain," John said as he exited and headed for his quarters.

So Mel was an empath. That explained a lot. This might be a fascinating medical topic to explore at some point, but for now, heeding Molon's advice seemed like a good idea.

Nine – Friend in the Fold

Before John went to settle in to his quarters, he took the elevator down to *Star Wolf*'s middle deck, heading toward engineering. He wandered into the room filled with control stations, monitors, and more gauges, dials, and digital readouts than he had ever seen in his life. His head was abuzz with recent events, but if he intended to remain on *Star Wolf* for any length of time, he would need friends. Molon was friendly enough, but he was also the captain. John understood that Molon would have to maintain a certain distance to reinforce the chain of command.

With the mess he had made thus far of his interactions with the security chief, and Molon's warnings about Mel, he was running out of options for allies among the command crew. Twitch was all business and by the book, plus—with what Molon had told him about their history together – talking to *Star Wolf*'s XO was no different than talking to Molon himself. That left Dub, *Star Wolf*'s malmorph chief engineer.

Despite an awkward start, he had connected with Dub in their initial meeting. Cultivating that seed and growing it might be the key to at least one ally in *Star Wolf*'s command crew.

The chief engineer was hovering over monitoring panels near the main engine controls. He looked up as John approached.

"Hiya, Doc. Come to see how the freakishly mutated have adapted to work among real humans?"

Ouch. Apparently, Dub had not forgotten John's indelicate first impression. But the impish grin on the chief engineer's face put John's mind at ease that this was merely a manifestation of Dub's overactive sense of humor.

"How'd you guess?" John replied, gambling with a verbal riposte. "I was thinking of writing a paper on how the critically mutated can emulate human behavior, within limits of course."

This drew a full on laugh from the jovial malmorph chief engineer. His mechanical glove hands continued working, but his gaze stayed focused on John. How, without the assistance of tactile senses, could Dub work without watching what he was doing? Could those glove hands actually transmit sensory data? It was a distraction from his purpose, but his analytical mind couldn't help but toy with this enigma.

"Tell you what, Doc," Dub said, snapping John back to the moment. "I'll grant permission to use me in your paper in exchange for a cut of the royalties when you publish it. It should be worth a laugh or two in a science rag somewhere."

John sighed as subtly as he dared, relieved that he had read Dub correctly. Given his own sardonic bent, maybe Dub was indeed his best shot at a friend around here.

"I'll give that some thought," John replied. "Five percent tops though, since I'll be doing all the work."

Dub laughed and glanced back down at the guts of the panel he was currently working on. The chief engineer frowned at something he saw there.

"Speaking of work, Doc, how about you reach in that toolkit over there and hand me the portable voidspace thread calibrator. I knew I felt a shimmy that didn't belong during that last jump. Danged kids have been tampering with my mix again. Every time we get a new engineering recruit, they fiddle with things, convinced their textbooks are to be followed like the word of God. Operations manual specs be spaced, I know how my bird flies best."

John scrunched his brow as he found the aforementioned box filled with an array of unfamiliar technical devices.

"The portable whatsawhosit?"

Dub shook his head and pointed with his chin.

"That gray box that looks like an oversized communicator with an oscillator screen."

"Oh, why didn't you just say so in the first place?" John quipped as he retrieved the device and placed it in Dub's extended robotic glove hands.

"Thanks."

"No problem."

John found himself staring at Dub's mechanical gloves. They perfectly mimicked the dexterous and delicate movements of human digits. It was like watching a living hand whose skin had been peeled away to leave only its bones, muscles and sinews.

"Enjoying the show, Doc?" Dub quipped, snapping John out of his distracted trance.

"I'm sorry, Dub. I've just never seen any tech like those glove hands before. Do they have tactile sensors?"

"Eh, sort of," Dub replied, raising one of the gloves away

from the compartment he was working in and wiggling the robotic fingers. "I did put some biofeedback proximity sensors into the fingers, but couldn't really do a full work-up. Had to keep things small and protected from external damage."

"Wow, that's some seriously advanced stuff, at least tech level ten or eleven. Where did you get them?"

Dub snorted and shook his head.

"Hermit-worlders don't have much tech-sense, huh?"

"What do you mean?" John asked.

"These are more like TL fourteen at least, and you haven't seen anything like them before because they are one of a kind, or two of a kind I suppose since they're a pair. I invented them."

John raised an eyebrow and bit back his instinct to call Dub out, wondering if the jocular chief engineer was razzing him again.

"Really? That's extraordinary," was the response he finally settled on.

"Don't look so shocked, Doc. I've got a knack for toy making. Designing them wasn't the problem. Building the things was the challenge. Malmorphsy made my actual hands way too large and cumbersome for most engineering work and definitely too awkward for building intricate mechanicals. I admit I had some help with the final assembly."

John's face flushed red. He wanted to build trust with the chief engineer, but so far his no-holds-barred honesty hadn't exactly endeared him to the rest of the crew. He had a feeling Dub was different, so just said what was on his mind.

"I guess I never expected someone suffering from malmorphsy could accomplish something like this."

Dub sighed and looked up from his work long enough to frown in John's direction.

"Doc, you gotta stop using that phrase."

"What phrase?"

"*Suffering from malmorphsy.* Look, I get it. A whole lot of malmorphs have it real bad, but if your wife spent her life researching malmorphsy, you ought to know that for most of us the condition gives and takes."

John scratched his head as he tried to recall the handful of live patients Elena had seen in their home after hours. Mostly she was a researcher and dealt with data only, but she did see a number of human malmorphs at her office on Tede. John had generally been too busy carousing and gambling to take much interest in her office work, but occasionally the situation required examinations in the evenings at their home.

124

Unfortunately, in those early days when Elena was working with live patients, John was generally deep into his cups when he was home at all, so any details about individual patients were foggy at best.

"To be honest, Dub, I never really dug deeply into Elena's work. That was her thing. What do you mean when you say it gives and takes?"

Dub finished calibrating whatever technical gizmo he had been working on. He closed the cover panel on the console and returned his tool to its box. He then released the mag-locks on an oversized, heavily reinforced chair in front of the control panel he had just repaired and glided it over next to John, taking a seat there and motioning for John to do likewise with another oversized chair at a neighboring engineering station. John obliged, noting how heavy these seats were even with the mag-locks disengaged. Given Dub's size and weight, all the stations in engineering had been modified to accommodate him.

"It's like this," Dub explained once John had sat down. "Malmorphs all have various degrees of physical deformities, some pretty severe. Truth be told, I'm pretty far down the normal end of the scale as far as that goes. I need these biomech gloves to do some parts of my job, but some malmorphs can't function at all without major technological assistance. But the side effects the Daemi never anticipated when they made the original Hellfire bioweapon were the enhancements."

"Enhancements?" John said, raising an eyebrow.

"Yeah. Nobody has figured out all the determining factors yet. They seem to vary a lot by race and sometimes by individual. Fei tend to manifest greatly amplified psionic abilities at a cost of seriously debilitating physical impairments. Lubanians tend to gain enhanced physical abilities, mostly strength and stamina but often have impaired cognitive function. I've heard of Dractauri malmorphs that have lost almost all sense of pain, their bodies able to endure tremendous amounts of physical damage, but their lifespans are drastically shortened and their physical senses damaged."

"Dractauri?" John said shaking his head. "Sorry, Dub, you had me going for a minute, but I'm a history buff. Humaniti didn't encounter the Dractauri refugees until almost seventy years after the end of the Demon War and the destruction of the Hellfire weapons."

"Well," Dub said, his normally irrepressable grin fading for a moment, "here's a little fact they don't put in the history

125

books. The psychotic Emperor Parvis, during his five-year reign of terror, came into possession of a cache of Hellfire weapons."

"That's impossible," John argued. "They were all destroyed during Operation Purge."

"Apparently crazy ran in his family. Parvis's great-grandfather was in charge of one of the strike groups raiding Daemi production facilities and decided to seize a cache of the weapons rather than destroying them. During the Dractauri Confinement, Parvis had a number of them sent to the Tecfianed system in the Igses sector. That's only a few parsecs from my homeworld. He used the Hellfire weapons as part of the torture of the Dractauri, to get them to reveal their advanced VS drive secrets and admit to being scouts for an invasion force preparing to go to war with Humaniti."

"That's abominable!" John replied.

"That's typical emperor Parvis, and these types of abuses were what ended the Parvis dynasty in five years and opened the door for the Halberans to rule from then until the Shattering."

John was aghast. How had such a thing happened without it becoming common knowledge?

"I didn't know."

"Most don't. No-one ever seems to raise the question how we got Dractauri malmorphs. Most just assume the Daemi went beyond the borders of Humaniti and attacked them as well. I'm surprised though, if your wife had a malmorphsy research library, she surely would have come across Dractauri case studies."

"Elena's work focused on humans for the most part."

"Ah, human malmorphs," Dub said, his smile returning, "a subject near and dear to my heart. Humans often get enhanced cognitive abilities, becoming skill-based savants, but enduring a wide range of physical impairments in exchange."

"So you think that is the reason for your talent with building things?"

"Pretty much. I actually hit the mutation jackpot. I'm physically functional and I got more than my fair share of enhanced strength too. I've got the muscle power of a trained and fit Lubanian. My size impairs my manual dexterity, which the gloves make up for, and I am not going to win any beauty contests anytime soon, but all in all I came out with a win, all things considered."

John stared in wonder at the huge mutated chief engineer. He would have to put in a lot of listening time to fully understand his new friend, but the past few minutes had given him more of an education on malmorphsy than his medical studies and life with Elena combined.

"I guess I need to spend some time digging through Elena's research," John said. "I might have a considerable amount of misunderstanding that needs correction."

The change in Dub's demeanor was palpable. His smile disappeared as his eyes widened.

"So you have your wife's data?"

"Yes."

John was suddenly reminded of the reason for his visit to engineering. He pulled out the small pendant from around his neck, where he had hidden it beneath his shirt.

"I have it right here," John said, dangling the stylized datacube pendant like a pendulum before Dub's eager gaze.

"That necklace is your wife's research?"

"It's a modified datacube. Elena had it designed it to look inconspicuous in a form she could keep with her as she went about her daily business. She would lock it up in our safe before we went to sleep. If Dawnstar hadn't snatched us out of bed in the middle of the night, they'd have gotten this too."

"Lucky break, that," Dub replied.

John's stomach tightened. He knew the engineering chief meant no offense, but to think anything about Elena's abduction and death could be considered 'lucky' was absurd. Still, he seemed to be bonding with Dub, so he let the comment slide. No sense burning this newly built bridge over a slip of the tongue.

"Yeah, I suppose," John replied, trying hard to repress a frown. "Not sure they would have deduced what it was, but almost definitely it would have been destroyed or at least still been in their possession. So, do you think you could rig up something to read it?"

"Sure, Doc," Dub replied, pointing at a machine to John's right. "Drop it in the scanner right there and push that blue button."

John saw a small attachment on the station from which he had liberated his chair. It looked similar to a medical sample analyzer. John placed the datacube into the fist-sized compartment and pushed the activation button. The machine whirred to life, emitting a web of yellow holographic lights that swept over the necklace. The lights blinked out after a few seconds, the device having completed its scan.

"Okay, Doc, now I've got the specs on the cube. I should be able to put together a cradle that can dump the data in a few days. Will have to work on it in my spare time, though, unless the captain okays work time for it."

"No rush, Dub. I appreciated the help," John answered, returning the pendant to its place around his neck and tucking it inside his shirt once again. "Captain says to keep knowledge that I have it on a need-to-know basis. Apparently there are a number of people with an unhealthy interest in this data."

"Gotcha, Doc," Dub said with a wink. "My lips are sealed. Say, that modified cube pendant is a pretty nifty idea for keeping data close while disguising it."

"Yeah," John laughed, "Voide and I recovered it from my home on Tede. Elena had a custom reader on our home data terminal, but I didn't get a chance to download the data onto more conventional media before Voide burned my house down."

Dub laughed aloud and slapped his knee with his mechanical hand.

"She burned down your house?"

"Yeah, she did," John said with a scowl.

"Voide usually settles for a simple beat down or an occasional arrow to the knee to make her point. If she burned your house down, you must have really ticked her off."

John fought the urge to smile as he cocked his head to the side and cast a sideways glance at Dub.

"Be honest with me, is it possible not to tick her off?"

Dub chuckled and rubbed his chin with a mechanical hand before shaking his head.

"Not that I've seen," he concluded. "On edge is pretty much her default setting. She is good at what she does, though. Saved Cap's bacon more than once."

Dub gently wiped a tear of laughter from the corner of his right eye with his mechanical appendage. John was once again drawn into fascination at how Dub had acclimated to this augmentation. As a doctor, John was familiar with mechanical prosthetics, but this was different. Dub's actual hands were still attached and functional, albeit within the limits of their mutation. This was like adding an additional pair of limbs to a fully functioning body.

"As fun as it is to reminisce about our psychotic security chief," John remarked, "I am more interested in discussing your glove hands. The way they mimic human movement is astonishing."

Dub raised his appendages as if modeling them at a booth at a tech convention. His exaggerated poses, feining delicacy and grace, were comical given his uncomely physical appearance.

"During the design phase," Dub explained, ceasing his antics, "I used medical scans of human hands in operation to form the basis for my schematics. They tap into the nerves in my arm that normally would control my real hands. Electronically copying the signals to and from my brain allows me the same precise control you have over your hands. They are also braced and anchored to my arm bones so hold up under a great deal of stress without getting pulled off."

John noted how perfectly and dexterously the mechanical glove-hands mirrored genuine flesh-and-blood movements. Were they covered in a layer of artificial skin, they would be nearly indistinguishable from human hands.

"So you just naturally adapted to their use?"

John was startled as Dub let out a loud, sharp, "Hah!"

"Not on your life, Doc," Dub continued. "Took years to get used to these things. I had all the subtlety of a sledgehammer at first. After months of practice I finally mastered basic functionality. After that, I tweaked the interface for years before I got to the control I have over them today."

"What are they made of?"

"Tempered indelium."

"Indelium?" John raised an eyebrow. "Indelium is hyper rare. How did you afford that much of it?"

Dub paused for a second, nodding and glancing off at nothing in particular. It seemed as if he had slipped briefly into a daydream or distant memory. A slight glassiness came over his eyes.

"That credit goes to Cap," Dub said, emerging from his reverie.

"Captain Hawkins?"

"Yeah," Dub replied with a slow nod. "I was part of the first crew he hired after he nabbed *Star Wolf* from that scoundrel Chadra. Soon after Voide joined the crew, she worked with some GalSec contacts to get us assigned to an off-book mission taking down a smuggling operation in Igses sector. Word was there were smugglers sneaking tech and information across the coreward border to the Daemi."

"Mission accomplished, I suppose?" John asked.

"Eh, sort of. Made a right mess of things for the smugglers anyway. All their identity data and location information we sent to GalSec. Anyhow, along the way we popped a corvette bound for Daemi space. In the hold were six bars of refined indelium, among other things."

John struggled to catch his breath. John was no stranger

to wealth, but even at a rough calculation the value of six bars of refined indelium was staggering.

"Six bars?"

"Yep," Dub confirmed. "We had permission from GalSec to seize any contraband we encountered, save for any TL12+ weaponry which had to turn in to GalSec. Molon gave me three bars of the indelium to temper into the parts I needed to craft these hands."

John shook his head in disbelief. This went beyond generosity, beyond altruism. Who was this Molon Hawkins? What possible motivation would a marauder captain have for such a disregard for profit? What kind of crew were on this ship that wouldn't mutiny over such an act favoring a single crewman to the financial detriment of the rest of the crew. Something seriously did not add up here.

"Dub, I'm sorry but out of all you have told me today, that story is the hardest to swallow. Six bars of refined indelium is worth more than *Star Wolf.*"

"Yep," Dub nodded, unwavering in his sincere demeanor.

"And Molon just handed you half that haul, for no reason at all?"

"Not for no reason," Dub objected, a hint of annoyance creeping into his tone. "I had titanium and steel prototypes for the hands, but they were heavy and with my enhanced strength, I kept wrecking the things every time we got into a tussle and would have to build new ones. Molon reasoned that if I used tempered indelium, even I wouldn't be able to break them. Hopefully these are the last pair I will ever need."

John always tried to see the best in people, but Molon was not even a Faithful. Had he heard a story like this about a renown Faithful leader or activist, it might have strained credulity but John granted it was possible. For an unbeliever to act so selflessly was beyond John's comprehension.

"I just can't get my head around this," John confessed. "A mercenary captain drops half a ship's worth of loot on a single crew member just because he is feeling magnanimous? I don't know many Faithful that would do something like that, even though by the Lion we are supposed to."

"That's what you are not seeing, Doc. This isn't just a crew, it's a family."

"A family?" John asked.

"Yeah, that's right, a family. In four years you know how many crew members have left *Star Wolf*? I'm not talking about casualties or the occasional treacherous slagger that had to be spaced out an airlock, I'm talking about ship-jumpers voluntarily moving on. Guess how many."

"I have no idea," John replied. "From your tone, I suppose it's a low number. Maybe twenty or thirty?"

"Zero."

"Zero?" John asked, puzzling through the implications. "I'm sorry I have been a grounder most of my life and know little about ship crews. I take it this is unusual?"

"Unusual? Try impossible. Look, mercs jump billets all the time, it's part of life. This one pays better, that one is going somewhere I want to go, my girl wants me home, family duties call, whatever. There are thousands of reasons mercs leave ships, and not all of them negative. On average, an independent captain can expect fifteen to twenty percent turnover per year. Well-paying and successful captains might get it down to ten percent."

"And you are saying nobody has voluntarily left *Star Wolf* in four years?"

"Yep," Dub nodded. "So what does that tell you, Doc?"

"It tells me something," John said, rubbing his chin. "I'm just not sure what."

Dub stood from his seat and wandered over to a large wall of readouts and engineering controls that had just started beeping and flashing with yellow lights. Dub appeared unperturbed as he went to address whatever had just happened.

"When you figure it out, then you will understand a bit more about Cap Hawkins. When you embrace it, you will know you are home."

John watched a serpentine umbilical extend from Dub's right glove hand and jack into one of the engineering panels as he input commands into the console with his left.

"Hey," John interjected. "I didn't notice that feature before. Is that some kind of data jack?"

Dub glanced back over his shoulder and grinned at John.

"This?" he said, pointing at the umbilical with his left hand. "Yeah, sort of. It is called a NID, Neural Interface Device. Mechers use them to interface with rigs to remotely control machines."

"Mechers?" John asked, racking his brain to dig out anything from his time in the high-tech Sarren system to give him a frame of reference for the term but coming up empty.

"Gosh, Doc, you *are* a hermit-worlder. Mechers are also known as riggers because of the control rigs they use. Maybe you've heard that word."

John nodded even though he hadn't really. A vague

memory tickled at the back of his mind of one of the tour guide drivers back on the Sarren main world who had driven without using his hands. John remembered being somewhat unsettled but the driver had assured him the vehicle was 'rigged' for it. John had assumed the vehicle was computer controlled, as were many on Sarren, but maybe this was what the driver meant by 'rigged'.

"We, meaning mechers or riggers as you like," Dub continued, "have cybernetic implants that allow us to remotely control vehicles and machines via a control rig. The rig converts our own biomechanical signals into a frequency and form which the remote vehicles or drones are set up to receive."

"So the rig acts like a biological to mechanical translator of sorts?"

Dub rubbed his chin, thinking for a moment before responding.

"Yeah," Dub concluded. "That's one way to look at it."

"But you are plugging right into the ship. Where is your rig?"

"For a hermit-worlder, you catch on quick, Doc. There might be hope for you yet. This panel has a rig built in. This is one of several control interfaces I installed throughout the ship to allow me to remotely control my engineering drones. I use them to get into all the hard-to-reach places for cleaning and maintenance. That little alarm was a reminder that the ventilation systems are due for routine cleaning and anti-bacterial sanitization."

John thought back to what he had noticed at the base of Twitch's skull. This seemed as good a way to assuage his curiosity without giving offense.

"So, Dub, I saw a data jack on Twitch's neck. Is she a mecher too?"

Dub grinned widely.

"Nope, Twitch has a decker augment, but she's not really a proper decker. She's just 'decked out' like one," Dub said, before laughing at his own pun.

"Decker, mecher, enough with the slang. Can you put things in plain speech?" John laughed, feeling more than a little out of his league with technology so far beyond what was found on Tede. "She interefaces with machines, doesn't she? What is the difference?"

"Well, sort of. Her implant is called a CID, Cerebral Interface Device. She doesn't interface with a rig controlling drones or vehicles. Instead, she is actually able to enter directly

132

into a computer system and interact at the speed of thought. Whoever built *Star Wolf* had a love for tech and no qualms about an augmented crew. There are CID interface remotes on every system on the bridge, and quite a few others throughout the ship. Most go unused right now since Twitch is one of the few current crewmen with a CID implant."

"So how is her implant different than yours? Aren't you issuing commands directly from your brain to the drones?"

"Sorry, Doc," Dub said, his mouth twisting even more out of shape than usual as the engineer tried to think of a way to explain. "This is a little like you trying to discuss an appendectomy with a mechanic."

"Ah, different vocational vocabularies. I see."

"Let me explain it this way," Dub continued. "Have you ever played with a remote control car? Surely they have those even on a TL6 world like Tede."

"Yes," John said, biting back his irritation. "We are hermit-worlders, not Neanderthals."

"Okay, well my interface, when attached to a control rig, kind of works like an RC car controller. I'm giving commands but I'm just sending them right from my nerve interfaces, freeing up my hands for other things. It is not really any faster than using a remote control. Deckers are a whole other matter."

"How so?"

"Deckers are the evolution of historical computer hackers. As computer systems got more advanced, and AIs started to really develop, anti-intrusion software advanced, so that some guy trying to hack into a computer system with a keyboard and a few worm programs didn't stand a chance. As cyber-security evolved, so did the hackers.

"A group of whiz kids developed something called a cyberdeck. It's basically a portable box containing a virtual reality environment that deckers use to hack computer systems. Via a CID wired directly into their brain, they plug into the cyberdeck, and then jack the cyberdeck into a computer system. The cyberdeck takes the actions of the computer system's anti-intrusion programs, the data files it contains, and the thoughts of the decker, using them to create a virtual, 3D environment that a human mind can relate to. The commands from the decker's brain operate at the speed of thought in this cyberdeck space, and deckers are able to exist in cyberspace as if they were walking around inside the computer systems."

"So what does that have to do with Twitch and *Star Wolf*'s

system interfaces? Is there a cyberdeck built into the ship's systems?"

"Not exactly. With the right interfaces, CIDs can be used like a rig on steroids. *Star Wolf's* CID stations can accept either manual inputs or take the commands directly from the mind of the operator via a CID. Twitch is the only pilot aboard who controls this bird at the speed of thought."

John thought back to the technology regulations he was aware of. Technological prosthetics were considered quite different than augmentation. Prosthetics that simply replaced normal human functions were widely accepted. Cybernetics that allowed humans to function far beyond normal human abilities were more restricted even on high-tech worlds, and were banned outright on planets like Tede.

There was still a lot of debate about data jacks given the potential for abuse as a drug replacement on high TL worlds. "Enhanced Reality" parlors offering programs which submerged the customers into a virtual reality world of pleasure stimulation for as long as their credits held out had become the modern equivalent of opium dens. Reports of ER junkies dying from malnutrition or dehydration while jacked into an Enhanced Reality station were widely publicized and were the focus of the argument against data jack augmentation.

"So how many augmented crewmen are there aboard *Star Wolf*?"

"Got a problem with augments, Doc?" Dub said, adopting a much less congenial demeanor than they had been enjoying.

"I mean no offense, Dub. I understand your hands to be within the realm of cybernetic prosthetics, although the built-in NID clouds the issue. During my medical training however, I came to understand that with cybernetic augmentation there is a danger of cyberpsychosis manifesting in the augmented individual."

Dub shook his head and raised his voice slightly. John didn't sense Dub was angry, but he was clearly perturbed.

"Cyberpsychosis only happens when somebody gets implants out the wazoo, enhancing function way beyond human norms. Also it is far more common with people using sub-cute augments that can't be clearly observed externally."

"I do recall the cyberpsychosis rate being much higher with extensive sub-cutaneous augments," John admitted, "now that you mention it."

"That's because sub-cute auggers jack around with their own perceptions of themselves. Their mind no longer knows if they are man or machine. A few augments here and there,

134

especially ones as common and externally conspicuous as NIDs and CIDs, don't create cyberpsychos."

"I'm sorry, Dub. You are right," John said, once again mentally kicking himself for letting his hermit-world preconceptions get in the way of fitting in with *Star Wolf*'s crew. "It is just I have had to process quite a few changes since I came aboard."

Dub visibly calmed and the jovial grin once again graced his large, mutated smile.

"Apology accepted, Doc. To answer your question, we have a couple of other augments with CIDs, one of the sensor operators and a heavy infantry marine who jacks into his mechanized armor. Beyond any gizmos that might be in the crew's medical records, I think we four are the only cyborg threats to the existence of humankind aboard right now."

John laughed.

"Okay, okay, I guess I deserved that. I clearly have a lot of adjusting to do. I appreciate your patience with my learning curve."

"Null sweat, Doc. You'll get used to it. Honestly, high-tech worlds are few and far between. We see a lot more backwater rocks like Tede than we do places where mechers and deckers abound. We ever make it to a techno-paradise, I'll have to get you drunk and see what kind of implants we can fix you with before you sober up."

John hoped Dub was joking, but a devilish glint in the malmorph's eye was enough to make John wonder. Still, best to play it off for now and not risk what had been a good session of friend-making thus far.

"That's a good reminder not to go drinking with you, Dub," John chided as he stood to leave. "Take care of yourself and let me know when you have that datacube reader put together."

"You got it, Doc."

John patted Dub on the shoulder, thanked him for the talk, and made his way toward his quarters. He had quite a bit to chew on. Digging deeper into Elena's research was a priority, not only to possibly help Dub, but possibly uncovering answers as to why so many were willing to go to such lengths to get it. There was also the generosity of *Star Wolf*'s captain to ponder. Molon's ability to inspire such incredible loyalty was like nothing John had ever seen. What had he signed up for?

Ten – Firefight

Molon strode onto *Star Wolf*'s bridge. Twitch was at the helm, her CID interface jacked in and blinking furiously. With the exception of Dub, who Molon wanted in the engine room in case anything went wrong, the most experienced senior officers for each station would be manning the bridge for this transition out of voidspace.

Voidspace was in effect another dimension. It could not be entered and exited at will, but rather the voidspace drives were tuned to utilize points of connection between voidspace and real space called jump points. They were basically places where the two dimensions drew together, figuratively at least, and the barrier that separated the two was porous enough to cross. These places, called VEPs or voidspace entry points, were fixed places in real space. Since the discovery of the first VS drive, Humaniti had been mapping these VEPs.

The voidspace drive also utilized the unique, malleable nature of voidspace, which could be manipulated to fold together upon itself, effectively negating the concept of distance. Those anchor points within voidspace, pulled together in a certain order, allowed ships with VS drives to enter voidspace at one VEP, and exit at another, which might be a vast distance from the entry point, without having to cross the real space distance in between. Only a small fraction of these VEPs had been mapped, along with the calculations tying them to other fixed and recorded VEPs.

These mapped and recorded routes had been assembled into a huge shared database that Humaniti used to connect its vast empire. Ships willing to experiment might enter an unmapped VEP and grab available anchor points, exiting from another unmapped VEP elsewhere. Sometimes this dumped a ship into the middle of nowhere, but other times this led to the discovery of rabbit trails, shortcuts through voidspace to nearby star systems.

Their path from Hatacks to Ratuen was just such a rabbit trail. Their arrival point in Hatacks from Tede, however, was

136

fixed and mapped as a standard VS route. If someone was planning to ambush a ship jumping from the Theocracy border system of Tede into the Dawnstar-controlled Hatacks system, this is where they would be waiting.

"Captain," announced Lieutenant Marie "Warbird" Warberg, currently manning the astrogation station. "Voidspace transition in three minutes."

Molon's command officers were the top five in *Star Wolf*'s chain of command. Warbird was sixth right after Mel, so not technically a command officer, but without doubt capable of assuming the captain's seat if needed. She had served with the Empire Navy and had been one of Molon's earliest recruits.

The starboard forward door opened, and in walked Dr. John Salzmann.

"Captain," John said, nodding a greeting.

"Couldn't take the suspense?" Molon asked.

"Mel let me know we were about to enter Hatacks. Word is if we are going to hit trouble anywhere this side of Ratuen, it'll be here."

"That's about the size of it, Doc," Molon replied. "Warbird, how long from transition until we can get to the rabbit trail VEP to Ratuen?"

"Just a hair shy of forty minutes, captain. It is very close."

Molon growled under his breath.

"Forty minutes is a long time in enemy space with our tail flapping in the breeze, lieutenant. Have that course queued up and drop it in as soon as we complete transition."

"Aye, sir. I'll shave the time as close as I can."

"Twitch, punch it the microsecond we clear the VEP and beeline for that rabbit hole."

"Aw, and I was thinking I might do a few barrel rolls, loop-de-loops, and laps around the nearest star first." Twitch snarked.

Molon ignored her quip and tapped at the communication panel on the arm of the captain's chair.

"Bridge to engineering. Dub, you there?"

"*Aye, Cap,*" came the reply across the comms. "*Whatcha need?*"

"As soon as we read all green post- transition, push those engines to the red. My hackles are up on this one, and I want the trip to the rabbit trail VEP to be the shortest forty minutes in history."

"*Already on it, Cap. I might get you to thirty-two if I can keep from blowing the ship up or having anything critical fall off in the process.*"

Molon couldn't help but smile. Dub knew this ship like no one else. There wasn't a person in the galaxy he'd rather have in the engine room.

"You know where we keep the glue if you need it, Dub. Bridge out," Molon said, as he closed the comm channel.

Molon turned to face Peter "Boom-Boom" Trang, currently manning the bridge engineering station. After Dub, Peter was the senior engineer aboard.

"Boom-Boom," Molon said, addressing him.

"Yes, captain?"

"Watch those engine load readings. Once Dub takes us hyper-hot, you let me know if anything even hints of trouble. The last thing we need on this run is to blow an engine."

"Aye, captain," Boom-Boom responded, turning his attention fully to the array of panels in front of him displaying every aspect of the ship's engine and energy functionality.

"Dub was joking about the blowing up part," John asked, having turned a slight green. "Wasn't he?"

"Probably," Molon answered, fighting to hold back a grin.

He liked John. Whatever happened after this mission, he hoped the doctor would decide to stay aboard. It was a refreshing change to have a civilian around.

"Starrrting transition," Twitch announced.

The slight slur in her speech and her hands resting motionless on the console in front of her told Molon that she was more than halfway on the cyber-side of her interface with *Star Wolf's* helm controls. As of now, every movement of the ship was being controlled directly from her CID.

"Put it onscreen."

Mel accessed the vid screen controls on her comm panel and the forward wall of the bridge came to life with light. The swirling colors of voidspace appeared, having already begun to align, signaling that transition was imminent.

Molon watched the window to normal space appear ahead. Nothing but stars showed through the narrow portal, but any experienced spacer knew enough to keep clear of the dead-on front of a voidspace jump point. There was a lot of space they wouldn't be able to see until they had completed the transition back into real space. An entire fleet could be waiting outside the VEP, and they wouldn't know it.

"Warbird."

"Yes, captain?"

"Have a secondary course plotted back into this VEP to Tede. How long will it take to reverse course at best speed?"

"We will hit normal space with considerable momentum.

138

Maybe two minutes tops to reverse course and get lined up to hit the VEP again."

"Queue that up. If sensors pick up anything bigger than a System Express boat near that jump point, don't wait for an order, drop in that secondary course."

"Aye captain."

"Twitch, if it comes to it I need you to shave that two minutes as close as you can while readying evasive maneuvers."

"Mmm," Twitch responded.

Molon knew Twitch was mostly gone from the bridge now. Her mind was immersed in the helm control system. She was tied into the external sensors, astrogation, and more, feeding her all the info she needed to pilot *Star Wolf*, but she wouldn't be an active contributor to any conversation until she knew they were safely on course and not in need of speed-of-thought piloting anymore. There wasn't a better pilot in the galaxy to have in that chair.

Molon had taken ships into known danger hundreds of times. That was never as bad as the waiting when he had no idea what to expect. Even with Twitch at the helm and jacked in, and even with every one of his top officers at their stations, Molon couldn't stop himself from revisiting his mental checklist to make sure he had taken every precaution to ready them for whatever might lie ahead.

The nausea that always accompanied transition peaked and suddenly subsided. This time, the quiet *fwwp* sound the VS drive normally sent shuddering through the ship, marking the completion of transition out of voidspace, was drowned beneath a blaring crescendo of alarms.

"Holy crapoli!" announced Lieutenant JG Jerry "Hoot" Barundi from the bridge sensor station. "We got a *Nova*-class cruiser, ten kilotons, and a squadron of long-range assault fighters in close proximity."

Hoot was the last senior bridge officer and right behind Warbird in the chain of command. He was good, if sometimes a bit over-excitable. A whiz kid with ship's sensors, he was also the most broadly skilled bridge officer on board. Hoot's background with System Defense Command gave him a wide spectrum of skills, and the ability to fill in at any bridge station aside from security and engineering. The more relaxed discipline of the SDC also freed him from the communication formalities observed by most former military officers.

"ID on that cruiser?" Molon asked.

"Transponder shows *ICR Revenge*."

"Dreck!" Molon snarled. "A Provisional Imperium ship. Twitch, back into voidspace now!" Molon barked at the helmsman.

"Mmm," Twitch mumbled, the helm interface plugged into her CID flashing wildly in response.

"No joy on reentering this VEP, captain," Hoot interjected.

"Why not?" Molon growled, his face showing irritation at being countermanded by his sensor officer.

"Those fighters have voidspace disruption emitters. They fired them up as soon as helm punched in that reverse course. This door is closed."

"What the...?" Molon started. "VDE's are tech fifteen toys. Since when does the Imperium have half a dozen of them to mount on fighters?"

"Fighter transponders show Dawnstar IDs" Hoot replied.

"Of course they do," Molon snapped. "Who else would it be? Warbird, lay in the course for the rabbit hole. Twitch, evasive maneuvers but get us hauling hull toward that jump point. We can outrun the cruiser, but those fighters are another matter. If they pursue, those VDEs are going to lock us out of voidspace anywhere we go."

"Fire orders, captain?" Voide asked.

Star Wolf's security station was also the station that commanded ship's weapons.

Clearly the Pariah was itching for a fight.

"Load two blinder missiles, and drop them between us and that cruiser. That'll buy us a minute or so before they can target their big guns. We aren't sticking around to slug it out here, not in range of that cruiser anyway."

"Aye sir," Voide answered, clearly disappointed at the distract-and-run orders.

If it were up to Voide, she'd fly Star Wolf right up that cruiser's exhaust ports, guns-a-blazing. Retreat wasn't in her vocabulary. Fortunately for them all, Molon was in charge, and he was a firm believer in discretion being the better part of valor.

"Hoot, is that big son-of-a-gun sporting a spinal mount weapon?"

"Not as far as I can tell."

"Double-dreck!" Molon swore. "This just keeps getting better. Voide, get your security teams geared up and ready to repel boarders. If that cruiser ain't carrying a spinal, she'll be chock full of assault craft. We won't be able to outrun this fight."

Voide nodded, punching up the remote status transmitter

from her bridge panel to her wrist module. She called for Lieutenant JG Angelica "Halo" Dickenson, to report to the bridge and take over as weapons officer, before sprinting out the port forward portal.

"Captain," Mel said. "The cruiser is hailing us."

"I doubt they want to talk about the weather. Broadcast the PI signal code for comms down. Let them suck on static for a while. We can always exchange pleasantries if we run out of other options."

"Aye, sir. Transmitting comm damage code now."

"Good. Now switch comms control to my station, and get John to engineering. Tell Dub I want the two of you dressed like deck hands and into vac-suits. If we're lucky these guys won't know John by sight, so a little masquerade ball can buy us some time if we get boarded."

"No, captain," John objected. "This is my fault. If we can't get away and the ship gets boarded, trade me for your freedom. I never meant for anyone else to get hurt because of me."

"A noble gesture," Molon replied, "but useless. PI troops don't negotiate, and you already know what Dawnstar's hospitality feels like. Do what I tell you. You've had vac-suit training, I hope?"

"Yeah, the basics anyways."

"Then get to engineering now and suit up."

"But captain, I—"

Molon turned to Mel. He couldn't believe what he was about to do.

"Mel," he said, cutting John off mid-sentence and giving his Fei communications officer a knowing look, "get him out of here now, whatever it takes."

Before John had a chance to complete his objection, Mel grabbed his hand.

"John, come with me to engineering."

"Yes," John said, with a hazy tone in his voice. "Let's go to engineering."

The two of them exited through the same door Voide had, passing Halo on her way in.

"Lieutenant JG Dickenson reporting as ordered, captain," Halo announced, not waiting for acknowledgement before assuming her post at the security and weapons station.

"Halo, if you can get a missile solution on any of those fighters, fire at your discretion."

"Aye, captain."

Molon punched up general comms on his chair panel.

"Attention all personnel: report to your assigned anti-boarding battle stations. All shifts report, this is not a drill. Vac-suit protocol initiated. Hull depressurization in ten minutes."

He reached into the compartment under his chair and retrieved his fitted vacuum helmet, attaching it to the collar seal on his boarding vac-suit. All other bridge officers did the same, even Twitch who was careful to maneuver her vac-suit helmet gingerly around the interface module currently jacked into her CID.

"*Hoot,*" Molon asked via the suit comms. "*Those fighters aren't firing on us yet?*"

"*Nope. Half are hanging around the VEP to Tede, the other half are following us toward the rabbit hole. Those VDE's are one heck of a power drain. I doubt they can keep them powered and fire energy weapons at the same time. Scans show they're not equipped with slug-throwers, lucky for us.*"

"*And the cruiser?*"

"*Big boy ain't firing either. They should have a firing solution on us by now. They seem more interested in keeping us here than blowing us to pieces.*"

"*That's what worries me,*" Molon replied. "*Keep an eye on the bow of that cruiser. She's going to puke assault craft any minute now. Let me know when that happens.*"

"*You bet!*"

"*Twitch,*" Molon said, knowing that even when fully jacked in, his XO could still hear his commands. "*We aren't going to outrun the fighters to the rabbit hole, but if we can draw the fighters out from under the protection of the cruiser's guns, we can turn and engage them. Make best vector to get and keep us as far as possible from that beast.*"

"*Already...on...it,*" Twitch replied, a little sluggishly as she pulled out of VR enough to respond. "*Been dropping klicks between us and that cruiser since we arrived. Now if you will excuse me, I have an exciting VR program to return to. I think a starship battle is about to happen and I don't want to miss a second of the show.*"

"*Smart aleck,*" Molon replied but was grateful Twitch was at the helm. If they needed evasive maneuvers, he would rather *Star Wolf* be executing them as fast as Twitch could think.

"*Hoo-whee, you called it, captain,*" Hoot announced.

"*What now?*" Molon asked, growing a little impatient at Hoot's casual communication style.

"*Six assault transports and four heavy gunboats just left the cruiser headed our way. Assuming current speed and the class of those ships, we'll be in range of the gunboats in twelve minutes. The assault transports will close to boarding distance in twenty-three."*

"Boom-Boom," Molon called to the engineering station. *"Prepare to depressurize all decks."*

"Aye, captain. I already cued depressurization to match your earlier command. Depressurization in eight minutes."

"Gotta love a crew on their toes," Molon remarked. *"We might get through this yet."*

"You do realize," Hoot responded, *"we're still in range of that cruiser. Those blinders are long expired. If the big boy hasn't vaporized us yet, chances are those gunboats aren't going to open fire either."*

"Half a dozen long-range fighters locking down any VEPs and a half dozen assault transports en route, why waste the energy?" Molon answered; not even sure he was convincing himself but liking the alternative even less. *"Maybe they want to pick through the scraps. That cruiser's guns wouldn't leave enough of Star Wolf to recycle."*

"Yeah," Hoot replied, *"but they only need one of those fighters on each end to keep a VDE field up and lock us out of voidspace. They could have switched the rest to guns hot if they wanted to engage. They mean to take the ship intact."*

"I noticed that," Molon said, resigning himself to the fact that the all-too-familiar pattern in their tactics told a tale he had hoped never to hear again. *"Rest assured, I fully intend to test their resolve on that point."*

Molon knew there was one sure way to confirm if his instinct was correct.

"Halo."

"Yes, captain?"

"Calculate a full firing solution on the two leading assault transports, all weapons. Thirty seconds before we hit the weapons range of those gunboats, Twitch is going to do an about-face and blow past the gunboats full speed. I want you to say a weapons-hot hello to our inbound guests. We have a range advantage, so let's see how determined they are to keep their fingers off the trigger."

"Aye, captain," Halo replied. *"If Twitch can give me a forward firing vector, I'll light 'em up."*

"Twitch," Molon said, turning once again to his helmsman and executive officer. *"Assuming they don't go guns hot after our little greeting, they definitely intend to board us. Make them work for it, would you?"*

"Mmm," Twitch mumbled and gave the slightest hint of a

143

nod as the control module plugged into her CID continued to pulsate wildly as it processed her mental piloting commands.

"Halo, after that initial howdy, you have free-fire orders. Be ready, though. With Twitch flying evasive, it's going to be a bit like shooting darts, during an earthquake...while drunk."

"No worries, captain," Halo replied with a smirk. *"I've had practice at that."*

"I bet you have," Molon laughed.

*****

John watched hazily as the corridors scrolled by them. It was like a calm-filled dream. The faces of the crewmen they passed looked grim and determined, but all John felt was the warmth and peace of Mel's hand in his. He could not escape the nagging thought struggling to break into his consciousness that there was something important he was forgetting, but somehow, strolling hand in hand with Mel, none of that mattered. Without knowing why, he was reassured that things were exactly as they were supposed to be.

They walked into engineering. The large, malmorph chief engineer snapped a glance in their direction as he was struggling to don an oversized vac-suit.

"What are you two doing here?" Dub asked, flashing a familiar sarcastic smile. "Did Cap lose the bridge already?"

"Molon asked that I bring John here," Mel replied, "He wants him disguised as a deck hand. Boarding is imminent, and the captain suspects John is their target."

"Ah, hide and seek; fair enough. In that room there," Dub said, gesturing toward a door marked EMERGENCY GEAR, "you'll find lockers with spare deck crew jump suits and engineering vac-suits. Hurry up and get changed. Cap's gonna depressurize this place in about five minutes."

Mel gently tugged John's hand. He found himself compelled to follow her toward the door. Once inside the room filled with storage lockers, she released her grasp.

John's emotions pounded him like a tsunami. He remembered leaving the bridge and the journey here, but giving up without a fight was not in his nature. He recoiled from the blue-skinned comms officer.

"What'd you do to me?"

"John, please, there will be time to explain later."

"Explain now!"

"If you do not get into this vac-suit immediately, you will be dead, and the explanation will no longer matter."

John was far from done, but reality was what it was. He retreated around a row of lockers, using them as a visual

144

barrier between himself and Mel while they changed. He wasn't sure what the Fei rules on modesty were, but at the moment they also served as a barrier between himself and whatever witchery Mel possessed that robbed him of free will.

Once changed and vac-suited, John returned to main engineering, not sparing Mel so much as a sideways glance on the way out of the locker room. The vac-suit felt cumbersome. He had been through deep-space training before. He remembered it was standard procedure to shunt the ship's internal atmosphere into a special, pressurized room when under attack. This kept the vacuum of space from ripping any personnel out through hull breaches caused by battle damage.

Book knowledge never replaced actual experience, however, and John found the reality of his current predicament almost overwhelming. He lumbered over to Dub, who had also finished suiting up, and addressed the engineering chief through the suit comms.

"Where do you want me?"

"Out of my way," Dub answered. *"You and Mel head for the upper deck of the hangar. There will be plenty of cover there, as well as several of the flight crew battle stations, so you won't look out of place."*

John's heart sank at the thought of going anywhere with Mel.

"Um, what if I just hang out in a corner here, I'll stay out of the way."

"No, you won't," Dub snapped. Any hint of his normal jovial nature was nowhere to be seen. *"Engineering wasn't designed with extra space, and the half second it takes to dodge around you could be the difference between saving and losing the ship. Go to the hangar, the barracks, the mess hall, or anywhere else. You ain't gotta go home, but you gotta get the heck out of here."*

John nodded and headed for the exit. While he had been speaking, Mel had slipped up beside him. He heard the suit chime a request for a private comms channel. Against his better judgment, John acknowledged it as they made their way out of engineering and toward the upper hangar.

"John, please listen."

"Listen to what, Mel?"

"Listen to me."

"I've heard enough. The captain warns me to be careful around you, and then he puts you on me like an attack dog or something. When you grabbed my hand, I lost myself. I don't want to be anywhere near you right now."

145

"*I understand. It can be quite a discomfiting experience at first.*"

"*Discomfiting? You forced me to do something against my will. Discomfiting doesn't even scratch the surface.*"

"*John, I can influence you, and I can strengthen some of your emotions while suppressing others, but I cannot make you do anything you don't want, on some level, to do.*"

"*I didn't want to leave the bridge.*"

"*Yes, you did,*" Mel replied.

All emotion had left her voice. John recoiled at her stark reply. What was she implying?

"*This crew is about to fight, and maybe die for me. I never wanted that. Going back for Elena was my burden. I never thought it would drag you all into such danger.*"

"*Yes, you did, John,*" Mel repeated.

A flash of anger jumped into John's throat. This Fei had just called him a liar. Yet somewhere in his gut he knew there was truth in her words. On some level he had known that returning to Ratuen would lead to this.

The ship lurched wildly, with the gravitic stabilizers straining to compensate. The shudder of the ship's weapons firing vibrated through the now-depressurized, soundless corridor. Whatever he had left behind on the bridge, it was clear that *Star Wolf* was now fighting for her life against whatever was coming.

John and Mel steadied themselves before moving onward as the ship continued to buck and roll in the inevitable battle dance. The stabilizers kept them from being tossed around like rag dolls, but the pitching and yawing in John's stomach remained. He wasn't sure how much was due to the movement of the ship and how much was due to Mel's stunning accusation.

"*I'm not a liar,*" was all the reply he could manage as they resumed their trek toward the upper hangar.

"*No, John, I don't believe you are. But you are out of your element. You trust Molon, so you wanted to obey his order. Whether or not you admit it, you are also drawn to me above and beyond whatever my abilities have caused. You trust me too. Your memories of Ratuen are fresh wounds. The idea of a disguise possibly keeping you safe was a powerful draw. I only eased your reservations, John. You wanted to come with me.*"

Mel had just laid his mind bare. Part of him wanted to run as far as possible from this alien from whom he had no secrets.

"*So you're a telepath?*" John asked, fear and wonder filling his voice.

"*I am an empath,*" Mel corrected. "*I sense feelings. I have a limited ability to push and pull what is there, but I cannot create feelings, nor can I force you to do anything against your will. I would never harm you.*"

They reached the doors to the upper hangar half-deck. It led to a large platform above the main hangar floor where the smaller STS Molon had used to extract him from Ratuen was docked. The light in his vac-suit's display panel showed the atmosphere in the hangar had also already been vented.

John paused as realization hit him that for now, the necessities of life were contained in this single, cumbersome second-skin. Death loomed inches away. The thought almost overwhelmed him, feeling none of the calm from Mel that had bolstered him earlier.

As they entered the upper hangar, a vac-suited crewman approached. A merc assigned to security, his sleeve bore the rank insignia of a sergeant.

"*Who in blue blazes are—*" the non-com started, before spotting Mel's unmistakable powder-blue skin through the clear faceplate of her vac-suit helmet. "*Oh, I'm sorry Lieutenant, your suit wasn't marked with your rank. What can I do for you?*"

"*Sergeant, the captain instructed that we dress as enlisted deck crew and come here for the duration of the battle. He wants to protect Dr. Salzmann's identity from our attackers.*"

"*You can hang out with us, ma'am, but you might as well make yourself useful. Can you handle weapons?*"

"*Not really,*" John answered.

"*I am trained with handguns, though I prefer my needler pistol. I can retrieve it from my quarters if need be.*"

"*No time,*" the sergeant said, pulling his sidearm and handing it to Mel. "*This will have to do. Same principle, point and pull the trigger. You two won't need to hold the line. Set up back by the STS. Open the hatch, take cover inside, and shoot anything that gets past us.*"

"*Thank you, sergeant,*" Mel replied.

"*Doc,*" the sergeant continued, turning toward John. "*My corpsman is down below with the team on the hangar floor. If you are willing, grab the med kit from the STS, and be on standby in case we have casualties up here. I would feel better having another medic close by.*"

"*That I can do, sergeant,*" John replied.

At least with a med kit in hand, he would be earning his

keep. John might be able, in some way, to repay the *Star Wolf* crew for risking everything to fight his battle.

"*All right then,*" the sergeant said. "*Take your positions and keep alert. Captain called all hands on this one, which means we're in for one heck of a fight.*"

*****

"*They are getting close,*" Molon announced through his vac-suit comms. He watched the array of small ships on the tactical display currently filling the bridge's main screen. "*Ladies, they are all yours.*"

"*Halo,*" Twitch said, pulling herself momentarily out of her deep interface with the ship's systems.

"*Aye, sir?*" Halo answered, using the genderless masculine address common to the military.

"*I'm about to give you a fixed target forward arc on the bogey painted Alpha 1 on tactical. Be ready with pulse lasers on that one. I'll set a thirty-five degree pitch on the maneuver so you can sweep plasma cannons for the other bogey tagged Alpha 2.*"

"*But we're out of range for the pulse lasers, Commander,*" Halo answered.

"*Trust me kiddo, I've danced this tune before. We're about to get real close, real fast. You get one shot with the pulse lasers. After that, I won't be standing still long enough for another.*"

"*Aye, commander,*" Halo replied, her hands hovering over the ship's weapon control panel. "*Ready when you are.*"

Twitch slipped back into her deep interface trance. Suddenly, *Star Wolf* yielded under her mental commands as the ship pulled a turn that strained the gravitic compensators and intertial dampeners to their limits. Fortunately, the bridge crew was well strapped in, but elsewhere aboard, Molon suspected there might be more than a few loose lunches among the crew after this maneuver.

As soon as *Star Wolf*'s bearing aligned on the leading assault shuttle, the thrusters fired to maximum acceleration for a half second before backing off to maneuvering speed once again. The effect was an almost instantaneous closing on the assault shuttle directly in front of them. Proximity alarms sounded, and a collision warning flashed on the main screen as it switched from the tactical display to a visual representation of what was going on outside the ship.

Halo was an experienced and disciplined weapons officer. Molon watched with satisfaction as she followed Twitch's anticipated maneuver by releasing a full array of weapons fire from her console right on cue. The four fixed position pulse lasers blasted a streaming barrage into the craft directly ahead, while the plasma turrets turned and acquired a targeting solution on the second assault shuttle.

Hoot let rip a shout commensurate with his call sign as moments later both enemy ships were reduced to scrap metal and molten debris. The proximity alarms silenced, and *Star Wolf* flew through the shredded cloud of what a moment before had been a fully manned assault shuttle.

Molon noted the weapons launch notification flashing on his HUD. *Star Wolf* had just fired another barrage of missiles.

"*Where are those birds headed, Halo?*"

"*Launched twin tethered nukes at the gunboats. Not that I don't trust your instincts about them not blowing us to shreds, captain, but figured I'd give them something else to shoot at while they think it over.*"

Hoot switched the display to an aft view as Twitch once again accelerated to gain some distance, and then began a rolling evasion pattern. The gunboats unloaded with point-defense batteries against *Star Wolf*'s missiles. One brief, large flash flared on the screen, while three smaller ones marked the destruction of three of the missiles.

"*Hoot,*" Molon called out to the sensor officer. "*One missile connected. How solid was that hit?*"

"*Glancing blow. Ablative armor took the brunt of it. It was a nuke though, so probably some crew casualties and minor system damage from radiation. That assault craft is dropping back from pursuit though.*"

"*Great job, Halo. That was as good an opening volley as we could hope for.*"

"*Uh-oh*" Hoot interrupted, "*two of the three fighters shadowing us just dropped their VDEs and are closing.*"

Molon's heart jumped in the hope that his worst fears might not be manifesting after all.

"*They on an intercept course?*"

"*Nope,*" Hoot replied. "*They are moving between us and the remaining assault shuttles. The gunboats are also not firing. The remaining assault shuttles are closing fast with the gunboats flying cover. That little trick put us a lot closer to them. They'll be in range to lock on for boarding in less than three minutes.*"

"*Yeah,*" Molon said, with no hope now of stopping the dread growing in his stomach. "*I've seen this before.*"

"*Where, captain?*" Warbird interjected. "*These aren't standard Imperial Navy tactics.*"

149

"*GalSec. It's called a dead-stick order. They use it against pirates when they mean to capture critical cargo. Those gunboats and fighters are going to run point-defense for the assault shuttles. We blow up that last assault shuttle, it kicks in a free fire order for every ship out there, including the cruiser.*"

"*Why would a Provisional Imperium cruiser be using GalSec tactics?*" Warbird pressed.

"*That's a good question,*" Molon replied. "*My guess is a GalSec spook is giving orders on that ship, not a navy captain.*"

"*That's.... a... capital.. class ship!*" Twich objected, wrenching her consciousness out of her interface long enough to speak. Her normally calm, professional demeanor showed a hint of a stress crack. "*No way in creation Zarsus handed the reins of a capital class ship to some GalSec spook.*"

"*If Zarsus didn't, someone did.*"

"*So,*" Twitch replied, "*our choices are to let them board or force them to destroy us. You got an option C floating around in that fur-covered skull?*"

"*I'm working on it,*" Molon replied. "*In the meantime, we are done here. Kill the maneuvering drive, and put Star Wolf into a three-axis roll with a randomized thruster fire every sixty to ninety seconds just to make it interesting.*"

"*That will buy us some time,*" Twitch replied. "*But it won't stop them for long.*"

"*I know,*" Molon replied. "*Just lock the helm controls once you've established the roll. I will set a distress code to transmit that we lost helm control as well. That should at least stall any 'comply or die' ultimatums.*"

"*Then what, captain?*" Halo asked.

"*All bridge crew prepare to repel boarders. Halo and Hoot, head for the port side airlock, and join up with Voide and her security teams there. Boom-Boom, I want you in engineering helping Dub with anti-boarding protocols and security locking systems. Warbird, you and Twitch follow me to the starboard airlock. We will meet up with Master Gunny Tibbs and his troops.*"

The crew all acknowledged Molon's orders and secured their bridge stations before moving for the exits. He knew his crew were among the best, but if GalSec was running this op, there was no telling what they were in for.

"*We will be outnumbered but we have home field advantage. In the end it may not make a difference, but they aren't taking Star Wolf without a fight.*"

Eleven – Close Quarters

Voide looked through the clear vac-suit helmets of her security team and the infantry troopers around her. Some of these mercs she knew, but most she only recognized. The life of a mercenary was dangerous, and Voide's policy had always been to forego bothering to learn names until you had been through a few scrapes together. Untested mercs came full of enthusiasm and left in body bags more often than not. She doubted today would be an exception.

The ship lurched wildly with whatever breakneck maneuver Twitch was pulling on the bridge. The vibrations of *Star Wolf*'s weapons firing resonated through the hull, but no impacts from incoming fire shook the troops positioned and waiting with her near the lower deck port side airlock.

One of the newest recruits, a young Private First Class full of more bravado than brains, failed to cut to a private comm channel before whispering a question into his helmet.

"Hey, sarge. How come Lieutenant Commander Matsumura isn't wearing combat armor or even a vac-suit?"

Gunnery Sergeant Raul "Rockjaw" Manolo flashed a smile through his helmet at Voide, recognising the comms protocol error made by the PFC, who had only joined *Star Wolf* just over a month ago. Rockjaw just nodded to Voide, leaving her to administer the education lesson.

"Listen up, boot," Voide snapped through the comms unit in the rebreather mask she wore, using the Empire Marine term for someone new to a billet. *"You got a question about me, you ask me, and next time you want to gossip, open a private channel."*

"Yes, Lieutenant Commander," the PFC replied, flushing a bright red.

"But since I want to keep your mind off wetting your armor before combat even starts, I'll answer you. See this gray skin?"

"Affirmative."

"Well then you know I'm Prophane, a Pariah. Prophane

151

physiology is built to withstand vacuum pressure and a lot of other weirdness affecting bodies that transition voidspace."

She focused her mind on a voidjump, disappearing from in front of the rookie trooper and stepping through voidspace to reappear immediately behind him. She grabbed the shocked mercenary by the shoulders and spun him around, careful to control the barrel of his weapon so it didn't point at anything vital in case the startled recruit accidentally hit the trigger. Fortunately, his self-control held, even though the wide-eyed look on his face said he had never seen a Prophane teleport before.

"*Boo,*" Voide taunted playfully through his helmet's clear faceplate. "*I don't need a pressurized suit, but I still need to breathe, which is why I wear the rebreather mask. The combat armor is very dense. It takes a lot more effort for me to shift it into voidspace, so I prefer lighter, stealthier attire. Oh, and before you ask why I am not carrying a weapon, I assure you I am well armed.*"

She pulled two stilettos from waistband sheaths behind her, waving them in front of the young merc's faceplate. Choked-back laughter echoed across the squad comms channel as the veterans enjoyed watching their security chief toying with the new recruit.

"*But,*" the young man inquired, "*these guys are going to be boarding in combat armor at least, probably even full battle dress. We will have a hard enough time ripping through that with ACRs, no way you get through with knives.*"

A chorus of "ooh"s rippled across the comms. A chiding lesson was one thing, but challenging Voide so boldly was a sin the rest of the team knew better than to commit. Still, they were keyed for battle, and this pup wasn't likely to live out the day. If he survived, she would be sure to instruct him a little more forcefully, but for now she kept her humor.

Voide poised one of her stilettos near his faceplate.

"*You see how fine a blade this is, private?*"

The young private nodded.

"*Well imagine that very vulnerable area at the base of your neck, where your helmet joins your pressurized combat armor. Now imagine such a fine, tempered blade being inserted forcefully at just that point*" she said, adding a little flourish as she pantomimed an attack thrust. "*Then, a little twist, and suddenly an invader, whose sole thought was killing everyone in front of him, is now focused on surviving. Every alarm in his suit is suddenly screaming at him that he is going to suffocate and decompress unless he hauls it back to the shuttle's life support systems."*

"Oh, I see," the young soldier answered.

"Oh, do you now? *Or maybe you don't,"* Voide taunted as she touched the controls on her stealth suit belt and faded to nothing more than a shimmering shadow before the merc's eyes. *"Do you know how disruptive it is to an assault plan when your point man runs screaming back to their shuttle swearing he was attacked by ghosts? It screws up firing lines, clearing patterns, and wreaks all kinds of dreck with general morale, giving you boys a chance to light them up while they get themselves sorted. We on the same page now, private?"* she asked as she turned off her suit's stealth mode.

"Yes, Lieutenant Commander," the wide-eyed trooper replied, hanging his head.

"Don't go getting all hangdog on me, boot," Voide scolded. *"If you live through today, you will have a tale to tell your grandchildren about how you fought side by side with one of those hell-spawned Prophane."*

She gave the young mercenary a good-natured clap on the shoulder.

"All right, jarheads," Rockjaw said through the comms. *"If we are done with supplementary boot camp training on Prophane tactics, then I want everyone locked and loaded. You feel that odd little queasiness in your gut?"*

A chorus of "Yes, gunny" echoed through the comms prompting Rockjaw to continue.

"That means the helm just put the ship into a three-axis spin. Those boarding shuttles are going to be locking onto the hull and breaching these airlocks any minute, so look alive. We are going to be outnumbered and probably outgunned, but that don't make no difference. You hold this position until you're dead or I tell you otherwise. Any of you boots breaks rank, I'll shoot you myself. Welcome to the merc life, boys."

They didn't have to wait long before the subtle vibration of magnetic locks attaching to the hull reverberated through the airlock door. Voide reached down, reactivating her stealth suit displacement field.

"Rockjaw, I'm going radio silent," she announced over the local comms assigned to their position. *"I'll look to mess up their advance. Try and keep these boots from shooting me."*

"No promises, LTC. Might want to keep a boarder between yourself and these new guns, just in case."

"You're all sunshine, Rockjaw."

"Sunshine and roses."

Voide liked Rockjaw. He was a solid combat veteran who had been with *Star Wolf* almost as long as she had. Master Gunnery Sergeant "Handsome" Hank Tibbs was the senior staff non-com in charge of all deployable infantry aboard, but Rockjaw had been put in charge of the security teams. He was a good leader and as tough a fighter as she had ever served with. She hoped he made it through today alive.

As Voide teleported through the sealed door and into the airlock proper, she slipped into the shadows opposite the airlock portal, where the boarding shuttle was now attached to *Star Wolf*'s hull. Voide knew the security forces were as ready as possible for whatever was coming.

Star Wolf was designed for defense. The two lower deck external airlocks were adjacent to the main personnel barracks on both the port and starboard sides. On a merc ship, that meant first contact for anyone entering would be the security forces. It also minimized readiness time in the event that unfriendlies were the ones using the airlock. The smaller, secondary airlocks on the middle deck port and starboard were near the NCO quarters. While slightly less secure than the ones on the lower deck, they were also much smaller and less conducive to allowing a stream of battle-armor-clad marines to come pouring aboard.

Voide settled into her position in a darkened corner of the airlock. She had disabled the lights, her stealth suit camouflaging her visual appearance as well as her heat signature. This would give her the best chance for a surprise flanking attack once the outer airlock door was breached.

The bright interior lights from the assault shuttle's adjoining airlock bay spilled into *Star Wolf*'s airlock, as the outer door opened to allow the boarding party access to the airlock. The light was too restricted by the narrow, circular doorway to put Voide's hiding place in jeopardy.

Tentatively, weapons at the ready, the first boarders slid cautiously into *Star Wolf*'s lower port airlock. Most were wearing combat armor suits, though one was armed with a heavy weapon and outfitted in full powered battle dress. She could see more queued up in the assault shuttle waiting for enough room to board.

These were not pirates or renegades. Molon had radioed ahead to be alert for a possible GalSec shadow squad leading the boarding party. That wasn't the case either. This was by the book Imperial Navy boarding tactics, and these invaders were wearing the markings of Empire Marines serving the

154

Provisional Imperium.

Voide would have to wait for an opportunity. Even though they gave no indication that their sensors had detected her stealth suit, two of the boarders continued to monitor and sweep the airlock with their weapons at ready. Another raider worked at the panel to open the interior airlock door, to the room full of security officers and mercs waiting on the other side.

Having cleared the airlock and not detected her, they should have relaxed and turned their focus on the next room. Their continued readiness could only mean one thing. They had fought Prophane before. Only one question remained. Given the rarity of Pariahs, especially this far spinward, were these marines merely maintaining cautionary protocol or did they know she was on board?

Voide moved her fingers across the armband controlling her intra-aural communications system and linking her to the ship's security systems. By memory, since she couldn't see her hand any better than the boarding troops could, she input the command to set her receiver to scan for local communication band signals, excluding the frequency her own troops were using. She then sent a text-only signal to Rockjaw to let him know an airlock breach was imminent and to be prepared.

Her communicator soon locked into the signal band the invaders were using. As she had suspected, it was scrambled and encoded. She blindly punched in the commands to run the signal through the ship's security decryption program before routing it to her earpiece.

The point invader continued to work on the airlock access panel for another minute or two before *Star Wolf*'s security system finally cracked the encrypted channel and began routing clear audio to her from the invaders. The perimeter troops, in the meantime, maintained a ready-alert status, outward facing and tightly packed to give no opportunity for a sneak attack.

"*Hurry it up, would you?*" came a gravelly voice through her earpiece. *Star Wolf*'s security decryption program had found the correct digital cypher to unscramble their comms.

"*I'm doing the best I can, sergeant. This is no simple freighter lockout. Someone who knew what they were doing upgraded these security locks. We might have to breach the door.*"

Voide smiled at the unintentional compliment. She had indeed brought the latest and greatest GalSec security and encryption protocols to *Star Wolf* when she came aboard. That was a few years ago, but given that GalSec made it a point to stay a decade ahead of the regular military forces, it was not surprising that even these outdated protocols were confounding the PI marines.

"*We are not going to breach the door,*" the gravelly voice replied. "*Our orders are to take this bird intact, so you go blowing holes in the airlock we're all going to answer for it.*"

"*Then you better get the spook out here, because I can't get through this door, sergeant.*"

"*Simmons,*" the gravelly voice called out, "*you monitoring comms?*"

"*What do you require, sergeant?*" answered a voice as smooth as glass. "*Have you secured a position? I haven't heard any weapons fire.*"

"*Negative. Someone upgraded the security locks on the airlock doors. This looks like GalSec level stuff. If you wouldn't mind, could you suit up and give us a hand?*"

Voide was shocked to hear a gruff Provisional Imperium Marine sergeant speak so politely. GalSec was generally treated with grudging indifference by the military. If this Simmons commanded that kind of respect from marines, he was one to keep an eye on.

A dark-skinned man, hair impeccably groomed, stepped out of the shuttle. He was wearing what appeared to be a business suit. Only the tiniest glimmer of refracted light near his head told Voide this man was not super-human with no need to breathe in the empty atmosphere of the airlock, nor someone with a Prophane-like body built to withstand the vacuum of space. He was wearing a type of tailored vac-suit that Voide had never seen before. She had seen the latest TL15 tailored vac-suits, but even the lightest and most sophisticated were nothing like this.

Voide watched in fascination as the seemingly unprotected man approached the panel. The hardened marines parted for him as though he was the High Archon himself.

"*What seems to be the problem, sergeant?*" the creamy smooth voice inquired.

"*I told you, they must have their own in-house spook. This door encryption is beyond what our top tech has seen before.*"

"*I'm sure,*" came the smug reply. "*Step aside, and let me solve your problem so you can get on with your task.*"

The new arrival approached the security panel. He detached the marine code-breaker and discarded it like it was a

156

dead rat the cat had left on the doorstep. He attached a tiny, black square to the panel and punched in a quick command. To Voide's amazement, she heard the magnetic security locks disengage immediately, but the door remained closed.

"*Once I am back in the shuttle, please complete your job.*" The man reached into a pocket of his suit and produced a black and yellow oval, handing it to the sergeant. "*Oh, and since your incompetent delays have given them all the time in the galaxy to prepare a welcome, you might want to use this.*"

The man detached his tiny code-breaker and turned back toward the shuttle, while the sergeant handed the oval to the marine on point. Voide's stomach sank as she recognized the device: a neural grenade. In the tight confines of the barracks beyond the airlock, one neural grenade would take out the entire security team. Neural weapons were at least TL14. Whoever these guys were, they were well trained and better outfitted than most military.

Star Wolf's security forces had no psionic shielding in their combat armor. Mercs could rarely afford the latest tech, and psionic shielded combat armor was strictly controlled by the military. Even mercs rich enough to afford it would have trouble finding black market units in sufficient quantities to outfit an entire shipboard force.

Once the suited agent was clear, the point man reached for the airlock door controls. The door irised open, and the lead marine pushed the activator on the neural grenade and tossed it through the doorway.

They were answered by a barrage of weapons fire from Rockjaw's men. The energy weapons bounced harmlessly off the reflective surface of the boarders' combat armor, but Rockjaw had anticipated as much. A handful of his mercs were cutting loose with flechette rifles. The tiny, needle-like projectiles were ripping into even the solid combat armor, with only the invading marines in hardened battle dress escaping the effects.

Flechette rifles were extremely effective provided there was no sensitive equipment in the area. They wouldn't penetrate the hull of the ship, but they could really mess up any type of sensitive pressure tanks or piping. Needlers, the common name for flechette weapons, lacked the ballistic damage potential of conventional slug-throwers, but they had a massive penetration and fire rate. Getting ripped through by fifty tiny flechettes could easily cause as much or more damage to internal organs as a tumbling lead round.

Three of the leading boarders went down in the initial

volley, twitching and screaming into their comms channel, after which the remaining boarders pulled out of line of sight of the door while they waited for the neural grenade to clear the room beyond.

There was no time to waste. Voide had only seconds to react before her entire team would be disabled. She quickly tapped her wrist controls, returning her communicator to their own frequency.

"Rockjaw, hold your fire, I'm coming through."

Voide had no doubts the veterans would honor the order. She had much less confidence in the restraint of those twitchy-fingered boots. At this point, however, there was no choice. If she didn't get that grenade out of there, this fight was over.

Voide focused and phased into voidspace. She transitioned, still cloaked, into the barracks beyond the inner airlock door. The bunks closest to the door had been unbolted from the floor and upturned to form a makeshift barricade against the boarders. It would provide no protection whatsoever against the neural pulse that was about to rip through this room.

Quickly spotting the grenade lying just beyond the first bunk, Voide bent and grabbed the black and yellow oval, focused her attention once again, and dragged the device with her into voidspace.

For a split second, the thought crossed her mind to release the grenade into voidspace and transition to clear herself, but she had no idea what the consequences might be. The everywhere and nowhere structure of voidspace might amplify the effects and leak them through into real space. She could end up inadvertently turning a localized weapon into something that took out the whole ship. She knew exactly what the capabilities of the weapon were in real space, however, so opting for the solution with the fewest variables was the best choice.

Transitioning back to real space in the airlock behind the boarders, Voide mentally prepared to step back into voidspace as soon as she released the neural grenade. She had no idea how much time was left before it detonated, but all she needed was another second or two.

It was time she never got.

Out of the corner of her eye, she caught a glimpse of a silhouette in the shuttle doorway. She found she could not turn her head to look, but was able to roll her eyes to the side enough to see the suited GalSec agent standing in the shuttle doorway. He was pointing a small device in her direction. A

158

tiny, white light pulsed from the end of it. To her amazement, a voice came across her own private comms channel. It was the silky-smooth voice of the agent, Simmons.

"*Well, hello my dear. Aren't you a surprise.*"

Her stealth suit was still activated, but the agent stared directly at her as though she were not cloaked at all. Voide found that not only could she not turn her head, she also could not release the neural grenade still in her hand. Neither could she summon the mental focus to transition back into voidspace. She was trapped.

"*Not quite the surprise you were expecting?*" the dark-skinned agent said as the shuttle's door closed in front of him, putting a shielded portal between himself and what was about to happen in the airlock.

The neural grenade in her hand emitted a whining crescendo before flashing a pulse. Voide saw the airlock full of boarders still standing, obviously protected by psionic shielding in their combat armor. As pain slammed into her head and unconsciousness overtook her, Voide had one final comforting thought. At least she had given Rockjaw a fighting chance.

*****

As they waited for the boarders to breach the shuttle bay, John gripped the medical bag in his hand and leaned back against the interior of the small STS that had delivered him from Ratuen. He took several deep breaths.

"*Are you all right, John?*" Mel asked reaching out a gloved hand to rest it on the arm of his vac-suit.

His instinct was to draw away, knowing the effect the Fei communications officer's touch had on him, but apparently, the suit provided a barrier her touch couldn't breach. Or perhaps she was just holding back her abilities. Either way, John felt completely in control of himself when he responded.

"*I'm fine. It's just that growing up on a hermit-world didn't exactly prepare me for everything that has happened recently. I'm not a soldier.*"

"*No one expects you to be. We all have an essence, an essential identity, that defines us. You are a healer, John. Just heal. That is your purpose. You must learn to heal yourself as well.*"

"*So, 'physician, heal yourself', is it?*" John said with a laugh.

He wondered if the Fei had ever read the Scriptures or if she even realized the allusion to the gospel of Luke.

"*Why do you find this amusing?*" Mel asked, cocking her

159

head slightly to the side.

"*No reason. This is just advice I have heard before and should have remembered. It is easier said than done, though.*"

There was no time to continue their dialogue. The shudder of the cargo bay doors opening resonated throughout the deck. The lack of atmosphere left it a tactile sensation without any accompanying sound. John and Mel switched off the private comms channel they had been using in order to monitor the general comms which the mercenaries defending the cargo bay were using.

"*They overrode the cargo door controls!*" barked a commanding voice. "*All lower level troops fan out and establish a firing line. I want forward fire arcs, and don't get crossed up. Get two and two spread to flanks for a crossfire. Topside troops rain dreck down on their heads.*"

"*Yes, sergeant,*" came a chorus of replies.

John peered out the open hatch of the STS. The troops on the upper landing platform fanned out along the railing, all their rifles trained on the cargo opening at the front of the ship.

John tore his eyes away from the gaping maw of the cargo door and aimed his vision back toward the deck. The stars outside were tumbling and whirling by as the ship continued its three-axis spin. Overwhelmed by the nothingness between himself and the dark void of space, John fought to control his fear. If anything happened to *Star Wolf*'s artificial gravity, the momentum might send them all tumbling out of the cargo doors and into open space like grains of salt from a shaker. What in the name of the Lion of Judah was he thinking joining the crew of a star ship?

John stood for a moment, taking deep breaths to calm himself and listening to the sound of his own battle with hyperventilation resounding inside his vac-suit. His heart pounded a gentle, insistent rhythm that was simultaneously soothing and terrifying. That serenity lasted only a few seconds before the cargo bay erupted into chaos.

"*Here they come!*" was the only warning that came across the comms channel.

With the atmosphere vented, there was no medium through which sound could travel. John thought it odd that a major battle raged all around him, weapons pouring out death from the mercenaries along the railing and being returned from the invading forces below, yet only the sound of his own breathing accompanied the conflict. It gave the deadly exchange playing out before him a surreal feel, as though he were watching a holovid with the sound turned off.

Then it became all too real. One of the mercs along the railing, thrown back from his position, landed sprawled out upon the upper half-deck of the cargo bay. The trooper dropped his combat rifle and lay there on his back, writhing against whatever wounds had just been inflicted.

John did not hesitate, his fear now forgotten in a sudden rush of adrenaline. He sprinted toward the downed man, dropping beside him and quickly assessing the situation. Air poured from a grape sized hole in the left shoulder of the merc's pressurized combat suit. Escaping air combined with the spray of blood from the wound below it to form a crimson mist of ruddy crystals in the freezing vacuum of the cargo bay. Thousands of tiny ice balls of water and blood formed and, coming under the pull of *Star Wolf*'s artificial gravity, rained down through the grating to shatter like sanguine hail upon the deck of the main cargo floor below.

John felt the back of the man's shoulder to see if there was a second puncture marking an exit wound. The rear of the suit was intact. He ripped into the med kit and grabbed a surgical patch, slapping it across the opening to stop the vac-suit's air loss and the influx of cold to the fallen trooper.

Mel ran up and crouched beside him.

"*Is there anything I can do to help, John?*"

"*Just keep me from getting shot. I need to focus.*"

She nodded and took up a kneeling, defensive crouch, pointing her weapon in the direction of the starboard side access lift to the lower cargo bay.

John had studied this type of situation in medical school, and reviewed the procedures again from the medical manuals aboard *Star Wolf*, but many bouts of drunken debauchery lay between medical school and the man he was today. He hadn't always been a devout Faithful.

Procedures in some manual were very different from reality. He was a trained surgeon, but had been more of a consultant philanthropist for years. John had not seen the inside of an operating room for a long time. On top of all that, he was far outside his element in the airless hull of a star ship under siege.

"*Am I gonna die, Doc?*" the man said, tapping over to a private channel.

John was anything but confident. He didn't even know what had caused the wound or how serious it was. Still, he knew the only answer appropriate to the situation.

"*No, son, not on my watch.*"

The trooper visibly relaxed as John activated the heads up

display in his suit and linked it to the camera on the laparoscopic surgical attachment built into the medical patch. Injecting a strong, local anesthetic, John probed the wound. A large, metal slug was lodged in the man's shoulder. Fortunately, it hadn't damaged any of the bone but was deeply embedded in the soft tissue. As wounds go, this one was fairly minor.

Then John saw it. A dark reddening around the wound was deepening. Despite the mercenary's combat armor having administered a coagulant gel to the wound area, the gel was dissolving, and the bleeding continued. John grabbed a strong coagulant medication from the med kit and injected it through the surgical patch. There was no effect. Only one thing could cause something like this.

Turning on the diagnostic probe's radiation monitor, his helmet's HUD filled with flashing warnings. What kind of savages still used irradiated rounds? They had been banned for decades on most civilized worlds. With the levels bathing this man's body from that round, John had to get him to a fully functional hospital or he would be dead in a matter of hours. It was doubtful *Star Wolf*'s medical bay even had the equipment to treat this, but if John didn't get this projectile out immediately, it wouldn't matter.

"*What's your name, son?*" John said, fighting to maintain some semblance of calm in his voice.

"*PFC McGhehey.*"

"*No, your name. What do your parents call you?*"

"*Name's Robert Liam, but everyone calls me Bobby Lee. My call sign is Cowboy—*" at the end of his introduction, the boy coughed, and John saw the light spray of blood across the inside of the man's faceplate. The radiation was already starting to damage blood vessels and capillaries.

"*Well you listen to me, Bobby Lee. I've got to get that slug out of your shoulder. You might start to feel pretty bad, nausea and cramps, but you have to do your best to hold still for me. I've got to get it all out of there, you understand?*"

"*Yeah, Doc,*" the man nodded weakly. "*Won't move...a muscle.*"

John quickly extended the surgical probes through the patch and focused on taking out the projectile and all the tissue around it. He couldn't risk missing even a small splinter. The strong local he had given the man would keep him from feeling it now, but it would be months before he would use this arm normally again, even if he somehow survived the radiation.

Surgical suit patches were designed with enough mobility

to pull out shrapnel and projectiles and leave them rattling around inside a suit until they could be extracted later. But John couldn't leave this irradiated round anywhere near exposed flesh.

"*Bobby Lee, you still with me?*"

"*Yeah...I reckon so. Don't feel so good though, Doc.*"

The man's groggy slur was not encouraging. He had lost a lot of blood, and the radiation would continue to bombard his system as long as the slug was inside the suit.

"*I'm going to need to change patches, so don't get nervous. Hang in there another minute with me.*"

Only the slightest nod came in reply. John ripped off the surgical patch, the clamps tearing out the chunk of flesh he had cut away with the irradiated round buried at the center. He tossed the patch, flesh and all, toward the railing, then grabbed a second surgical patch, slapping it over the hole in the combat armor currently spewing a volcano of air and blood from the man's shoulder.

"*Bobby Lee, you there?*"

No answer. The young man's eyes were closed, but his suit system still showed respiration and a steady, if slightly erratic, heartbeat. With the source of radiation gone, John administered another injection of coagulant. To his relief, he saw on the video feed from the surgical patch camera that it was working. The blood flow was slowing, and the wound was sealing up. Bobby Lee was far from out of danger yet, but this was all John could do for now.

John pulled his attention from the downed trooper to assess where things stood in the battle. The rest of the troops at the railing still held their positions, with the only hole being the spot where Bobby Lee had stood. Yet there, splayed out on the upper decking, was another fallen body.

"*Mel!*" John cried out as he rushed to her. There was a tear in the abdomen of her unarmored vac-suit, and she was trying to maintain pressure on the wound. Bluish tinted blood dripped through the grated decking from where she lay, freezing into icy blue droplets on the way to the main deck below.

"*I am sorry, John... I should have been...more careful.*"

"*Stop that. Let me see.*"

He rolled her slightly toward him and saw an exit wound on the back side of her suit. She was venting air fast, but at least there were no irradiated rounds still lodged in her system. Even though it was an unarmored vac-suit, the suit itself had already begun self-sealing against the atmospheric breach.

163

John quickly grabbed another coagulant injector and delivered a shot of the gel to the front and back wounds through Mel's side. He wracked his brain trying to remember everything he had read about Fei physiology since coming aboard. To the best of his recollection, there were no vital organs where the round had passed through.

"I will be fine, John. I have had worse injuries. You have stopped the bleeding. My suit will seal in a few moments."

Her words were comforting, but the soft yet strong quality of Mel's voice was somehow diminished. There was pain and weakness that she was clearly working to mask.

"Doc, get over here," came the voice of the sergeant who had greeted them when they arrived in the cargo bay.

John looked up and saw two more troopers had fallen from the fire line at the railing. John pulled himself away from Mel and ran to the two men. He heard a *tink* sound from the side of his helmet and saw with dismay a tiny hole at the very edge of his faceplate. His suit alarms began sounding indicating a suit breach, but the pressure levels were dropping very slowly. The suit should self-seal shortly. He had larger things to worry about.

Approaching the man closest to him, John knew it was already too late. Four grape sized holes pierced this merc's suit, with one of them being in the faceplate. The man's right cheek was shattered and from the angle of impact John knew the round that hit him had continued on into his brain. His suit showed flatlines on all vitals. John moved toward the second downed soldier.

At first John was confused as there were no apparent entry points for the large caliber slugs that had taken out Mel and the others.

"Flechettes, Doc. Suit already sealed the holes, but he's gotta be torn up inside," the sergeant said on a private channel.

John had little experience with flechette weapons. They were a higher technology than was commonly available on Tede, though he understood the principle. The problem with these wounds were finding the damage and repairing it before the patient bled out internally. He couldn't do this on the field.

"Sergeant, I've got to get him to sick bay. I can't treat this here."

John saw through the sergeant's faceplate the non-com's eyebrows furrow deeply. He knew the man was weighing the decision of saving one man at the cost of one of their medics leaving the field.

"All right. Corporal!" he barked out. One of the troopers at the railing approached. *"Help Doc get him to sick bay, then get back here double-time."*

"Yes, sergeant," the corporal answered.

Then John saw a small oval object land near their feet and rattle down the decking.

"Grenade!" the corporal shouted and started to move toward the object.

There was a bright flash. John's world went black.

*****

Molon entered the lower deck starboard barracks with Twitch and Warbird right behind. Master Gunnery Sergeant "Handsome" Hank Tibbs strode stoically up to greet them.

"Captain," the man said through the local comms channel.

"Master Guns," Molon nodded to the merc leader. *"Sitrep?"*

"They latched on just before you got here. I figure they've made the airlock by now but are trying to figure a way around Voide's security upgrades on the door."

"No breach?" Molon asked. It was unusual for boarders to take such care. Standard procedures was to breach the doors with an acetylene torch or flexiplast explosives.

"Not yet," Tibbs said with a disturbing grin rolling across his horribly scarred visage clearly visible through his helmet's clear faceplate. *"Looks like they are trying their best not to break her. No doubt they are coming in one way or another, just a question of when."*

"Well then, we stay sharp and wait," Molon answered, nodding for the leader of the shipboard mercs to return to his ready position behind the makeshift barricade of bunks facing the door leading to the airlock.

Molon wasn't sure if Hank's call sign, "Handsome", was from his days as a fresh-faced youth when the handle might have suited, or if it was a nickname clearly mocking what he had become. Oddly enough, it fit either way.

Hank might have been handsome once. He certainly had the dark eyes capable of snaring prey of the opposite sex. The face that now held those eyes, however, bore the deep furrows and jagged remnants of a man who'd had a front row seat to the enemy's version of tender mercies. Half his face looked like a tent flap stitched together in the middle of the night by a drunken soldier whose fingers had been frozen too numb for delicate work.

Hank's biography of battle was written in the scars that wriggled and danced up his face from chin to hairline. This

165

man had more than enough reasons to go home. The fact he was still here spoke as much about his character as his face told about his war record. Molon didn't feel sorry for him though. He was saving that sentiment for the first poor fool to dare express pity for Master Gunny Tibbs.

Molon waited for what seemed like hours, but his chronometer argued it had not even been five minutes. Then, across *Star Wolf's* own encrypted, secured general coms came a voice he did not recognize.

"Attention, captain of the independent mercenary frigate identified by your transponder as the UFR Star Wolf. This is Rear Admiral Richard Starling of the Provisional Imperium cruiser Revenge. If you check the situation with your crew, you will see things are going badly for you. I expect, Captain, that your thoughts were to take out the boarding parties from the shuttles, and turn those ships against us."

Molon wasn't sure which disturbed him more, the fact that this man had managed to take control of *Star Wolf's* secure internal comms system, or that he had read Molon's plan like it was a cheap datapad novel.

"While an admirable strategy," Starling continued, *"your plan has two major flaws. First, the shuttles are rigged to remote detonators, so if any of them detach from your hull without confirmation from the assault teams that they have control of your ship, the shuttle won't make it five klicks before it is floating debris."*

"Your second issue is believing that you only have to repel four shuttles' worth of boarders. Those shuttles hold fifty marines each. I believe the entire crew complement for a frigate of Star Wolf's class, before any casualties, is fifty-eight. I just dispatched four more shuttles. You can see, captain, the odds are clearly against you."

Molon growled to himself. He had been bested before, and didn't mind losing to a better commander. It just stuck in his jowls when some smug dreckhead punctuated the defeat with taunts. Whoever this Starling was, Molon figured he owed the man a punch in the mouth before this was all over.

"So, Captain," Starling continued. *"Let me be clear. I intend to capture your ship intact. Whether your crew lives or dies is irrelevant to my purpose. Therefore, I leave their fate up to you. You can opt to order them to stand down, and open all remaining airlocks to my boarding parties, surrendering yourselves immediately. If you do this, I will order that no further harm come to your crew. Alternatively, you can continue to fight, in which case I will order my men to kill*

166

every single person on board, no exceptions. The choice is yours. What say you, Captain?"

Molon's chest burned with helpless rage. Were he alone, he would choose to fight to the death, but as captain, he was responsible for his crew. There was no victory here. What the Provisional Imperium wanted with a ten-year old frigate was beyond him. Whatever it was, it wasn't worth more than the lives of his crew. If this admiral was lying and they surrendered, they were all dead. If they fought on, they were all dead anyway, just with a handful of PI Marines brought along for the ride.

The only chance for anyone rested on the word of a Provisional Imperium officer. Molon knew there were a few honorable officers that still served in the Imperium. He could only hope that this Admiral Starling was one of them.

Molon accessed the comms channel in his suit and set it for shipwide broadcast.

"Attention all Star Wolf personnel, this is Captain Molon Hawkins. Stand down all stations. Surrender your weapons, and turn yourselves over to the Imperial Marines at port and starboard airlocks and the cargo bay. All personnel not at forward combat stations, secure your stations and report to one of those three locations to surrender yourselves. Any further hostilities against the boarding parties will result in the execution of every Star Wolf crew member. I am surrendering the ship."

A private channel opened up directly into his combat armor comms. It was Admiral Starling's voice.

"A wise choice, captain. You may not know me, but I know you. I was an officer under Emperor Halberan, and you have my word no-one else of your crew will be killed, as long as they follow your orders to surrender peacefully."

"My crew follows my orders," Molon replied, hoping Voide was already unconscious or captured. He was certain of most of his crew, but he had never had to order the Pariah to surrender before.

"I have no doubt, Captain Hawkins, as does mine. Understand, though, I am not the only one giving orders."

Molon's stomach sank, and his hackles stood on end.

"What's that supposed to mean?"

"We will discuss it once you are aboard, captain. I will do all I can to see you are treated well while aboard the Revenge."

Molon noted there was a sincerity in Starling's voice, but he couldn't help but wonder what else was going on. No one

167

lower than a Rear Admiral was given command of a cruiser-class capital ship. If this guy was that high up the food chain and still taking orders from someone else aboard, that could only mean someone way up the GalSec food chain was in command.

Twelve – Friend or Foe?

Pain ripped Voide from her peaceful unconsciousness. She seethed as her guard, dressed as naval enlisted with his right shoulder emblazoned with the golden lion patch of the Provisional Imperium, continued to strike her with the side of his baton while his comrade watched. Her wrists were tethered to the ceiling by corded bonds. Thick, high-tech wristlets encircled her forearms, separate from the manacles that suspended her. These wristlets had a few embedded readouts in a cryptic, alphanumeric code, but she had no idea of their purpose.

Additional restraints secured her ankles to the floor, leaving her little ability to defend herself or resist. She flashed her tormentor a malicious grin, already picturing her revenge as she focused her concentration on phasing into voidspace. She would materialize behind this ignorant fool and snap his neck while whispering some witty quip to his companion about why one should never mistreat a lady.

Unfortunately, she never got that chance. Her mind was buzzing, bombarded with sensory and memory data, preventing her from achieving the focus she needed to phase. Whether this blockage of her abilities was due to the after-effects of the neural grenade, some drug they had given her while she was out, or something else entirely, for the moment she was at the mercy of her captors.

The watcher, Jasper, addressed her tormentor as Alex. Alex would occasionally switch from striking with the side of the baton to instead using the electrified end to deliver a wracking shock to her abdomen. Voide was still wearing her stealth suit, but Alex had opened the seal which attached her torso armor to her leggings, exposing just enough of her stomach to apply the electric shock from the baton directly to her gray skin. The smell of her own electricity-seared flesh wafted into her nostrils, fueling her determination to survive long enough to exact her revenge.

As Voide endured Alex's sadistic exercise, she changed her

169

mind about his fate. He would not be granted anything as quick and easy as a snapped neck. She would take her time. GalSec had taught her many creative ways to prolong a painful death, and she had added a few of her own in the years since. It had been a long time since such a worthy volunteer as Alex had come along on whom she could test them.

Star Wolf's crew was mostly still unconscious, dispersed in groups between two large cells adjoining the open area where Voide and Alex were getting acquainted. Starling had taken no chances and had gassed them all as they cycled through the airlocks before coming aboard Revenge. Only Captain Hawkins had regained consciousness. He had a clear view of Voide's beating in the central area of Revenge's brig.

"Release my crewman immediately!" Molon demanded.

"Quit your barking, dog-breath, or I'll turn the hose on you," Alex answered.

"Admiral Starling assured me none of my crew would be harmed. You will answer to the admiral for this."

"Hah, that was before the old man knew you had a gray-skin on board. Everybody knows all bets are off when one of these yellow-eyed devils is concerned."

"Maybe we should rethink this, Alex," Jasper whispered.

"Shut up, you dimwit," Alex replied.

Alex then enthusiastically returned to administering his personal brand of hospitality to Voide. Voide remained silent, not acknowledging the torture at all. She was determined to deny her abuser any satisfaction on that front. She smiled at him, her mind filled with joy at her thoughts of revenge.

Her silence and sweet smile only fueled Alex's desire to break her. Too bad for him, he was out of his league. While his cruel ministrations were not pleasant by any stretch of the imagination, Voide was a former GalSec agent, trained in resisting torture and interrogation. She had experienced worse at the hands of her training instructors than anything Alex's feeble imagination could concoct. If he expected to break her with a shock baton and a few love taps, he was in for a disappointment.

"Wahoo Jasper," Alex said as he delivered another punishing jolt of electricity. "You ever seen anything like this? Heck, most humans would've passed out already. This gray-skinned devil is built tough. Kind of pretty too, for an alien freak I mean."

"I dunno," said Jasper, looking and sounding much less enthusiastic about the situation. "Admiral Starlin' said hold them, he didn't say nothin' about workin' 'em over. We might wanna put her back and wait for orders."

"Are you kidding?" Alex snapped. "You see that gray skin and them yellow eyes? This is a bona-fide Prophane Pariah. How many friends have we lost to these soulless fracks in the border wars against the Ascendency? Don't you think it's time for a little payback?"

"Pariahs ain't with the Ascendency no more, Alex. Heck, their people hate them worse than they hate us, which is sayin' somethin'. She ain't the enemy, Alex. Let her go."

"She sure as heck ain't our friend. Besides, how do you know the Ascendency didn't plant these Pariahs right in the middle of us so they can wipe us out with our own weapons once our guard is down, huh? Ever think of that?"

"I don't think the PI would be usin' 'em on our ships if they was enemy agents."

"Shut up, you inbred huckleberry. You wouldn't know an enemy from a relative. Besides, don't worry yourself about what I am doing. Do you have any idea what them GalSec spooks are going to do to her? Heck, man, I'm just getting her warmed up for the main event."

Alex took the end of the baton and ran it tenderly down Voide's cheek. She clenched her teeth expecting him to activate the electrified tip. Fortunately, the shock never came.

"Besides," Alex said eyeing Voide closely, "she looks like she kind of likes this, don't you honey?"

Voide's mind raced as she saw a chance to turn the tables. Forcing through her pain, she summoned her most alluring closed-lipped smile, not wanting her oversized canines to look threatening. She licked her lips while sending a provocative ripple down the length of her body. If she could draw Alex closer, she might be able to strike back and buy herself a much-needed reprieve from his attacks.

"I don't know what your friend is talking about, Alex. I thought we were having fun," Voide said, then dropped her voice to a whisper as she continued. "Fun always makes me hungry."

Voide edged her head forward, parted her lips slightly, and partially closed her eyes. Alex fell for the ruse.

"See, Jasper, I told you. Come here, sugar, and give old Alex a kiss."

As Alex's face drew close and tilted slightly to meet Voide's lips, she lashed her head forward, baring her extended canines as she bit fiercely into the soft flesh of Alex's nose. She tightened her bite with all her strength as her captor recoiled, struggling to retreat from the unexpected attack. A large chunk

171

of flesh tore away from his face and blood gushed from where Alex's nose used to be.

Voide spat the chunk of flesh on the deck in front of her as Alex collapsed into a screaming pile on the floor desperately trying to stem the tide of blood pouring from his face. Jasper stood frozen, gasping in horror with clearly no idea what to do next.

"Aw, come on Alex," Voide taunted, blood trickling down her chin as her tone changed from sensual to sneering. "Don't you want to play anymore?"

"Why you crazy—" Alex's invective was cut short when the door to the brig opened.

A thin, dark-skinned man in a black business suit entered, flanked by four security officers dressed in black with shoulders bearing the black shield and inverted gray triangle emblem of GalSec. Voide recognized the swarthy man as the GalSec officer, Simmons, who had disabled her during the attack on *Star Wolf*. Simmons motioned toward the downed Alex and the stupefied Jasper.

"Remove these imbeciles and confine them to quarters. I'll decide later if they should take a walk out of an airlock."

Simmons spoke just as calmly as he had during the assault. He clearly did not need to raise his voice to inspire obedience and fear.

"Oh, and take this with you." he said, toeing Alex's detached nose toward one of the security personnel, who stooped to retrieve it. "The surgeons might want to reattach that if I decide to let him live."

Two of the security officers took hold of Alex, dragging him from the room still bleeding and screaming. The other two escorted Jasper, leaving Simmons alone in the brig.

"I'm terribly sorry about that," Simmons said.

He pulled a handkerchief from his suit pocket and wiped Alex's blood from Voide's chin. She thought for a brief moment about taking a finger or two off this cocky agent, but something deep in the back of her mind sent a ripple of caution through her, keeping her from acting on any violent impulses.

"I can see you are struggling with the desire to continue to fight," Simmons said. "You being Prophane, it is to some degree genetic, so I cannot blame you. I would, however, strongly advise against it."

"Who are you?" Voide asked.

"I am Senior Special Interrogator Simmons of Galactic Security."

"This is a PI ship," Molon shouted from behind the

security grating of one of the large holding cells currently housing the majority of *Star Wolf*'s surviving crew. "*Star Wolf* is an unaligned vessel and we are PI licensed free traders. Our vessel has been unlawfully seized. What does the Provisional Imperium want with us?"

"What the Provisional Imperium wants and what I want are not necessarily the same," Simmons said, the first hint of a subtle smile gracing his stoic features as he answered Molon's question without ever taking his eyes off Voide. "I cannot speak for Rear Admiral Starling's wants and desires, but on this journey, he is merely our chauffer. This cruiser is under the command of Galactic Security, not the Provisional Imperium."

"Fantastic," Voide replied, flashing what she hoped was her most professional and least insane-looking smile. "I am a former GalSec agent, so we are on the same team. Release me and let's talk about how we can help you and be on our way."

"If only things were that simple," Simmons replied with a shake of his head.

"Hey, Simmons," Molon yelled from his cell. "Admiral Starling promised that no-one else from my crew would be hurt if we surrendered. Is this how the Provisional Imperium honors its commitments?"

"Captain Hawkins," Simmons replied, finally acknowledging Molon with a subtle nod in the direction of the holding cell. "Unfortunately, Admiral Starling was not in a position to make such a guarantee."

"Then why did he," Molon growled.

"I suspect to reduce casualties for his marines boarding *Star Wolf*. For such a small ship and crew, the resistance you managed proved quite troublesome."

"Yeah," Molon replied. "Being attacked without cause tends to bring out that inconvenient survival instinct. Sorry our will to live caused you such grief."

"Nevertheless," Simmons continued, ignoring Molon's jibe, "we have no reason to harm you. What was done to your crewman," he said, motioning a hand toward Voide, "was neither Galactic Security's orders nor Admiral Starling's."

"So those two dreck-eaters thought that up all on their own, did they?" Voide snapped, battling to control the rage rising within her.

"I am afraid that your race inspires unseemly behavior. The *Revenge* has spent considerable time on the tailward front engaging the Prophane Ascendency. They have an understandable basis for ill feelings toward your people."

"They aren't my people," Voide replied. "Like I said, I

served for many years with GalSec, and right now *my people* are the ones locked up in those cells."

"Yes," Simmons said, glancing off for a moment with a wistful look in his eye. "Nonetheless, rest assured the two guards responsible for your mistreatment will be disciplined accordingly."

"You said letting us go was not that simple. Can you tell us why are we being held?" Voide asked, her voice calm and her face painted with a soft smile.

She was working hard to suppress her rage. She needed to build a rapport with the GalSec Interrogator. If she could get him to trust her, perhaps Simmons would free her. Then she could repay his kindness by snapping his neck.

"That is a complicated question. Before I address it, I have a question of my own. You claim you are a former agent?"

"Yes, that's right."

"I know of several Pariahs who have served with Galactic Security. What is your name?"

"Senior Agent Yasu Matsumura. I was a field agent under Special Agent Mark Russel. I'm sure you know of him. I hear he is deputy director of the Intelligence Division now."

Voide had no idea if name dropping would work out to her benefit or not. She had left GalSec under less than optimal conditions, but to her knowledge, her GalSec record was clean and they had no reason to be openly hostile. Mark's rank might carry some weight in her favor.

"Really?" For the first time Voide detected an excited fluctuation in Simmons's normally dead-level voice. "This is quite a coincidence."

"What is?"

"Listen carefully, Agent Matsumura," Simmons continued, ignoring her question. "I am going to release you from this uncomfortable position and escort you to a cell for the moment. I am afraid I must leave the wristlets on, however. They dampen your voidspace transition ability. Admiral Starling made that point quite non-negotiable I am afraid. I am sure you realize why a teleporting Pariah running around on board might make the admiral somewhat ill at ease?"

"Understood," Voide said already running through in her mind half a dozen scenarios to take out Simmons and free the crew as soon as her hands were loosed.

Simmons first freed her feet from their restraints. He paused, however, as he reached up toward the clasps on the manacles attached to Voide's wrists.

"Of course, I know you are a trained agent," Simmons said,

his voice dropping again into that eerie calm tone as he gave her a subtle, knowing smile. "You no doubt are working through what you plan to do as soon as I release your hands. I admire your adherence to your training, Senior Agent Matsumura, but I would strongly advise, for the moment at least, that you curb those thoughts. I am not your enemy...yet."

The icy calm in Simmons's voice as he delivered the veiled threat caused Voide's chest to tighten. He was an interrogator. They went through an entirely different preparation process from the regular GalSec agents. She had no idea what he might be capable of, but it was not in her nature to miss an opportunity, no matter how much she believed his veiled threat.

As soon as he pressed the release button on the manacles holding her wrists, Voide snapped into action. Slashing downward with both hands, she hoped to catch Simmons off guard and drive him to the ground with a double-fisted hammer blow. Once he was down, she could move to gain control of him.

The blow never landed.

Quick as thought Simmons sensed the unseen blow, stepping in toward Voide and spinning behind her. Even as she fought to check her downward swing and adjust, Simmons grabbed her waist, thrust a leg out behind hers, and hip-tossed her to the ground.

Voide was shocked at Simmons's quickness and strength. Speed was usually her advantage in hand-to-hand combat. Prophane were naturally stronger than most humans. Simmons, though, was insanely forceful and reacted faster than she had ever seen anyone move. Voide could sense a bridled power in Simmons belied by his wiry frame. There was something extraordinary, inhuman, about him.

Before she could even twist to position herself and regain her feet, he was on top of her, grabbing her left arm and forcing it behind her back. He was not only strong and quick, but also precise, applying pressure just shy of dislocating her shoulder. She knew if she continued to struggle, he could apply the minimal additional pressure needed to pop her shoulder out of its socket and send her into agony.

"I told you, Miss Matsumura," Simmons said without the slightest hint of agitation or windedness in his voice. "Resistance is unwise. I have no desire to injure you, but if you insist on attacking me, I will incapacitate you, and it will not be pleasant. Do you understand me?"

Voide nodded, trying to analyze what she could have done

differently that might have changed the outcome of their brief altercation. She drew a blank.

"I am about to release you," Simmons continued. "You are going to rise to your feet and advance to the cell in front of you. I will open the door, you will step inside, and I will close it again. Any deviation from this plan will result in regrettable and completely avoidable pain for you. Are we clear?"

"Yes," Voide said through gritted teeth.

She found herself fighting her instinct to continue resistance as soon as she was back on her feet. A well-trained agent not only knew how to fight, but also when restraint was the better choice. She was not sure she could trust Simmons, but she was positive she could not best him one on one.

"Very well," Simmons replied. "I will work to expedite the release of you and your crewmates as quickly as possible, provided you continue to cooperate."

Simmons released his grip on Voide and was on his feet before she could even brace her arms against the floor to get up. He stood above her, poised and ready to react to anything Voide might try. She rose slowly and cautiously, measuring the situation to see if any possible opening to overcome Simmons presented itself. Nothing had changed. As soon as she was secured in the cell, Simmons turned and left the brig without another word.

"Voide, I'm shocked," Molon murmured. She could hear the subtle sarcasm oozing in his voice. "I've never seen you give up a fight while conscious. You sure those GalSec spooks didn't fix you up with some subliminal brainwashing in case they ever had to face you again?"

"Spare me your feeble wit. As fast as he moved and as strong as he was, Simmons had to be a sub-C auggie."

"Sub-cutaneous augmentation?" Molon replied. Voide heard no lingering hint of humor in his voice. "SCs are illegal within the military and Empire government. That would include Galactic Security."

"You of all people ought to know, laws don't always apply to GalSec. I could tell you things about GalSec that'd make your fur fall out. Besides, do you honestly think High Archon Zarsus is concerned about the Provisional Imperium following Old Empire laws?"

"You got that right, *Senior Agent Matsumura*," Molon replied, obviously mocking Simmons's chosen form of address for her. "So, you know GalSec. What's their game here?"

Voide spun and faced the bars separating her cell from Molon's. She bit back the bilious response she almost launched at him and tried to remember that the captain rarely asked stupid questions. Sometimes he just looked to Voide or Twitch to confirm what he was already thinking.

"You are kidding, right? An impossible, cryptic message arrives luring us back toward Ratuen. Upon arrival at Hatacks, an unavoidable bottleneck en route to Ratuen, a GalSec commanded PI cruiser and a Dawnstar assault force equipped with VDEs just happens to be waiting for us. This whole thing stinks of a GalSec setup. You know good and well what they are after, or at least who they believe can lead them to it."

"So," John said groggily, struggling to consciousness within Voide's cell. "Turn me over to them. Maybe they will let the rest of the crew go."

Several other crewmembers, including the five Lubanians who were more hearty and resistant to chemical agents than humans were, also showed signs of regaining at least partial consciousness. John, somehow, was ahead of the recovery curve for the humans.

"That is unlikely, John," Molon called out from the other cell.

"Yeah, pale," Voide snapped in John's direction. "Even if we turned you over, no way GalSec lets a ship full of witnesses just fly away."

"You know," John answered, scratching his cheek and blinking like he was trying to shake the sleep from his eyes. "There is a band playing a marching tune with nuclear instruments inside my head at the moment. You could stand to be a little nicer...and quieter."

"Suck it up, pale," Voide responded. "It's your fault we are here in the first place."

"Also, for the record," John continued, taking no note of her accusation, "when someone offers to exchange their life to save yours, I believe *thank you* is the appropriate response."

"Thank you?" Voide answered, not bothering to wring any of the sarcasm out of her tone. "I didn't realize useless gestures fell under the thankworthy category."

"Knock it off, you two," Molon barked from the other cell. "John, if you have enough of your wits about you, see if anyone in your cell has anything worse than a narcozine gas hangover. Voide get a headcount. I need a casualty report from the boarding action."

"Eighteen, captain, counting me and doctor damsel in distress here."

"Hey!" John snapped.

"Dreck," Molon replied. "Twenty-six here. We were three

177

short of a full complement before the boarding. That means we lost eleven people."

"Might lose two more," John answered, glaring sideways at Voide while he examined the other crewmen in their cell. "Kid I patched up in the cargo bay, Bobby Lee, has severe radiation sickness. I need to get him to a med bay soon or he is done. Mel was also hit and isn't looking too good either, but at least her wound was a through and through. Can you believe those devils were using irradiated ammo?"

"Rad rounds were outlawed in the Empire decades ago," Molon growled.

"You are such an idealist, Molon," Voide answered. "I told you this is GalSec. They make their own rules. Oh, and in case you missed the news update, there hasn't been an Empire for eight years. There was this thing called the Shattering..."

"Don't patronize me, Voide," Molon growled. "The Provisional Imperium has maintained that it is the legal successor to the Old Empire until a rightful heir can be identified. I knew Zarsus was a rat, but marines using rad rounds? Has his insanity really gone that far?"

"If they ever let you talk to Starling, you can ask. Like I said, though, I'm not sure the Provisional Imperium has much say with GalSec in command of this cruiser."

*****

Molon worked in his cell, Voide and John in theirs, to get as many of the crew conscious as possible. There were other wounded besides Mel and Bobby Lee, but none so critical.

"Captain," John called out. "I have to see if they will give me a med kit to treat them, or maybe even access to the cruiser's sick bay. Bobby Lee will die without treatment, and Mel might."

Molon was grateful those two were in the same cell with John, but without medical tools there was not much he could do. Molon couldn't risk exposing John by asking for medical supplies to be given to him either. If Voide was right, they were looking for John, and they had to know he was a doctor. Maybe this was all part of their plan to identify him.

"No, John," Molon answered. "You are dressed as deck crew, so keep playing at being one."

"But I am a doctor, I can't just—"

"You can, and you will," Voide snapped, grabbing John by the neck and slamming him against the wall. "Otherwise those eleven crewmen died for nothing. You paid us to get you to Ratuen so you could chase your dead wife's ghost, so obey the captain's orders, pale. You blow this mission after talking the

178

captain into it, I'll gut you myself."

"Enough, Voide," Molon replied, summoning that commanding, captain tone that supposedly conveyed he was in charge. "Stand down, now. He's a doctor, not a soldier. He took an oath to heal; he can't just turn that off. Give him a break."

Molon didn't quite catch what Voide's mumbled response was, but the words "...break his..." wafted through to Molon's cell. He saw through the bars that Voide had released her grasp on John's neck.

"Besides, John," Molon added, "Bob is in the cell with you and coming to. His uniform is clearly marked as a corpsman, so if we can get supplies, he can treat them without raising suspicion. Patch can help once he wakes up. You can assist if no one is watching."

Bob was a Lubanian corpsman whose real name was Rzorf Ffranzawu. His call sign came from his tail having been cut off. This was a Lubanian custom when prisoners were taken in battle and turned into slaves. A bobbed tail was a permanent sign of servitude.

Molon had liberated Bob during the same *Star Wolf* raid on Tetoyl that had freed Mel. Molon had granted Rzorf his freedom, and the grateful Lubanian medic had joined *Star Wolf* as a corpsman, taking the call sign Bob as an inside joke.

"Voide is right though," Molon continued. "You hired us to do a job, and we knew the risks. The casualties aren't on your head, they are on mine. I figured this for a trap but still took the most obvious route from Tede to Hatacks. It was too predictable a move."

"You couldn't have known, Captain," John replied.

"I should have. A captain is supposed to know, but we are where we are. For now, just let us complete the job you hired us for. Voide knows GalSec, and if anyone can figure the angle to get us out of this, she can."

The brig doors opened. In walked Simmons and another GalSec officer all too familiar to both Molon and Voide. His tall, fit build, gel-slicked black hair, bright blue eyes, and too-perfect smile was enough to turn Molon's stomach. Mark Russel.

"Yasu!" Russel said, using Voide's given name rather than her call sign as he rushed toward the bars of her cell. "When Simmons told me you were here I thought he had grown a sense of humor."

"And Molon Hawkins," Mark said, turning toward the other cell, "I heard Voide joined up with you after she left GalSec, but I had no idea you'd secured your own ship. A

179

Scimitar class frigate? That is a hefty hull for a private merc vessel. You have done quite well for yourself, Molon, or I guess I should say Captain Hawkins."

Molon could almost feel the seething rage emanating from Voide as she stared intently at Russel. He mentally commended her for her self-control. Mark Russel had been a large part of Voide's decision to leave GalSec. He had fallen hard for her, and his fixation with pursuing a relationship had made sticking around problematic. She wouldn't have stayed in GalSec with Mark as her superior even if Molon hadn't made her a better offer as *Star Wolf*'s security chief.

"Mark, good to see you again," Molon lied. "I wish it was under better circumstances. However, since we are all old friends I trust you will release my crew and allow my injured crewmen the benefits of *Revenge*'s sick bay?"

"Oh, I wish it were that simple, Molon," Mark said, shaking his head.

Molon realized he was about to be in a yarn-spinning contest. He would have to pretend that *Star Wolf* wasn't doing anything against the Provisional Imperium, which included their Dawnstar allies. Mark would have to pretend he actually wanted to release Molon and his crew but that somehow the Deputy Director of GalSec's Intelligence Division didn't have that authority. As accomplished a liar as Russel was, Molon might not be on par with an opponent of such skill.

"I tell you what," Russel continued. "If Yasu would be so kind as to join me, we will discuss what can be done to resolve this situation quickly and equitably. In the meantime, Simmons, do be so kind as to arrange to have the ship's doctors see to Captain Hawkins's injured crewmen."

To Molon's surprise, Simmons nodded and exited. How a clearly brilliant, possibly augmented interrogator like Simmons wound up taking orders from a hyper-ambitious sycophant like Russel had to be quite a story.

"Now, Yasu," Russel continued. "If your crewmates would please step back from the door, I can let you out. We have so much to talk about."

Molon clenched his jaw. Voide's once-held feelings for Russel were long past. His stalking obsession had driven them away long before Molon met them. Now the mission was on the line and this was the break they needed. Could Voide play along until an opportunity to secure the release of *Star Wolf* and the crew presented itself?

"Of course, Mark," Voide answered in a tone Molon had only once heard her use before.

180

It bore a striking resemblance to the one she had used on the sadistic guard Alex to lure him to his surprise rhinoplasty. What shocked Molon even more was that once Mark opened the cell door, Voide did not immediately dismember him. She walked calmly out of the cell, brushing a hand gently across Russel's chest as he locked the door again from the security panel.

"After you, Yasu," he said, placing a hand lightly on her waist and motioning toward the door to the brig. As they exited, Voide flashed Molon a half-smirk and a quick wink.

"What the heck is she doing?" John choked. "Just like that she is off with the enemy?"

"Relax, Doc," Molon replied. "She is playing along looking for a way to spring us."

"It didn't look like she was pretending."

"Voide is a trained GalSec agent. She's very good at pretending."

Besides Bob, two Lubanian marines, Tracker and Frosty, shared John's cell. In Molon's cell, a Lubanian communications officer, Snips, and two Lubanian engineers, Midnight and Scraps, had mostly recovered from the narcozine. Lubanians had a greater resistance than humans did to the effects of chemical agents, but even Molon and the Lubanians were in less than optimal condition.

It was up to Voide to find a way to get them out of this. Molon knew she was struggling against her conflicted feelings for Mark Russel. Controlling her emotions wasn't exactly Voide's forte. Despite his assurances to John, Molon was not completely convinced that even Voide's GalSec undercover training would enable her to get *Star Wolf*'s crew released without handing John over to the Provisional Imperium or GalSec.

Thirteen – Spies and Lies

Voide followed Mark Russel in silence down a long corridor outside the brig. As they approached an elevator, he finally broke his reticence, turned to face her, and reached out as if he meant to take her hand.

"It's been a long time, Yasu. I've missed you."

Her jaw clenched as she struggled to settle the unfamiliar twitch in her stomach. She left his partly extended hand hanging awkwardly, ungrasped, until he realized her reluctance and withdrew it. He led her into the elevator and punched in a destination code.

Once, she had held hope that they might be more than friends. Long ago she had cherished a vague, fleeting belief that somehow in a galaxy filled with sophonts who wished to see her dead, there might be one person with whom to share hopes, dreams, and, dare she imagine it, even love.

"Mark, I..." she started, then paused in thought as the elevator doors closed.

She remembered the day, years before, when it had all changed. They had been dancing the night before. She'd floated home, her heart lighter than she ever remembered it being. Had she ever been as happy as she was holding his hand while they strolled back to the GalSec barracks?

But the next morning, she had walked out of the communal shower room wrapped in a towel. On her way back to her room to get ready for the day she discovered Mark just sitting on the floor in the hallway outside her room with the stupidest looking grin on his face.

"Good morning, beautiful," he had said to her without even getting up off the floor, as though this was the most natural thing in the world.

She had greeted him awkwardly, told him she was late, and excused herself as she went into her room to get ready for work. When she had dressed and come back out, he was gone. From that point on, however, she was never again fully at ease with Mark. What had been so joyful became creepy. Her romantic man had become an obsessive stalker.

"Look, Yasu," Mark said, snapping her out of her reverie. "I know this is an awkward reunion."

"Awkward? That's one word for it," Voide responded, thinking that capturing her ship and imprisoning the whole crew went a few steps beyond awkward.

"I want you to trust me," Mark continued. "We just need some information. If you help us, I will make sure Molon and the rest of your crew are released unharmed."

Voide knew Mark was a professional liar. Everyone in the GalSec Information Division was, including herself. Despite her instinct to loathe him and doubt anything he might say, on some level she believed he was being sincere, at least as much as Mark understood sincerity.

The elevator opened onto *Revenge*'s expansive bridge. Two armed security officers reached for blasters until Mark raised a hand to signal them to stand down.

"At ease, everyone," Mark commanded. "Miss Matsumura is former GalSec, and my guest. I assure you she poses no threat."

From the captain's chair an older man, slightly heavy set with white hair and a closely trimmed full beard, stood to his feet. On his uniform was the golden lion emblem of the Provisional Imperium. His shoulder epaulettes bore the rank insignia of a Rear Admiral in the Imperial Navy.

"I will be the judge of that on this ship, Deputy Director Russel," the older man said. "It is highly irregular to bring any prisoners out of the brig, much less to the bridge. You can rest assured I will be filing a grievance with High Archon Zarsus as well as with the Overdirector of Galactic Security. You may be in charge of our destination and mission, but I am responsible for the security and safety of this ship."

Admiral Starling motioned to the two security officers nearest the elevator door.

"You two, I want weapons charged and unholstered at low-ready position as long as this Pariah is on my bridge. Set your weapons on maximum power. If she comes within two feet of any operational panel, makes any attempt to remove those wristlets, or otherwise moves to threaten any member of the bridge crew, deadly force is authorized. Acknowledged?"

"Yes sir," echoed the two security personnel.

The men immediately drew their weapons, changed settings on the laser pistols, and kept them in hand. Their intense gaze never left Voide.

"Yasu, I am sorry about this," Mark said with a smile

somewhere between sympathetic and patronizing. "I do have considerable leeway, but security measures rest with Admiral Starling."

"I understand," Voide answered, quite sure Mark was manipulating Starling as much as he was trying to manipulate her with this charade.

"Admiral," Mark said, dropping the affected smirk and projecting so everyone on the bridge would hear him clearly. "By your leave, I would like to utilize the ready room adjoining the bridge for a private conversation. Please instruct the stewards to bring us something to drink and some light food. I am sure Miss Matsumura is quite hungry by now."

Voide doubted if, in the worst fit of anger she had ever managed to summon, she had conjured up a more murderous gaze than the one in Starling's eyes. He stared at Mark for several seconds before giving a silent motion with his hand that sent an ensign scurrying off via the elevator that had brought her and Mark to the bridge. Mark motioned toward a door to starboard and nudged Voide gently in that direction.

"Security, stay with her," the admiral ordered.

"I am sorry, admiral, I cannot allow that," Mark answered, warning the security officers off with a glance. "What I need to discuss with Miss Matsumura is an eyes-only GalSec matter. I am afraid your men are not cleared to attend. Come to think of it, neither are you."

Mark flashed a condescending grin at the admiral, who flushed a more sanguine shade than most humans were able to achieve.

"Why you arrogant—"

"Now, now, Admiral," Russel interrupted. "I assure you GalSec takes full responsibility. You are welcome to have your security officers monitor the room, video only mind you, and have them stand ready outside the door if it makes you feel any better. I assure you *Revenge* is in no danger from this particular Pariah."

Voide and Mark exited the bridge and entered a small conference room. While actual windows on a starship were a structural vulnerability few were willing to risk, monitors on the wall currently displayed a projected image of what a window would have revealed. Natural space, rather than the swirling colors of voidspace, showed they were still in the Hatacks system.

Ahead were the larger glowing globes of the red main-sequence dwarf star, and the red subdwarf, which were the two

184

primary stars in the Hatacks system. The third star in this trinary system, a brown sub-stellar dwarf object, was too far and dim to be seen from this position. Though Voide could sense they were moving at high sub-light speed toward the Hatacks mainworld, the view from the monitors appeared nearly as still as a painting.

They were millions of miles from the red twin stars. Without any of the ten inhabited worlds in the Hatacks system anywhere nearby, there was nothing in close enough proximity to gauge relative movement. Normal space was funny that way.

Voidspace was so full of color, lines, and movement, like a swirling mass of painted clouds. Distance was meaningless in voidspace as it was constantly in flux, folding, bending, and changing. There was always a sense of movement that Voide found comforting. Normal space was also in constant motion, but the vast distances stole any perspective of that movement and left the viewer feeling alone and stagnant.

"Yasu, are you all right?" Mark asked, placing a gentle hand on her shoulder.

Voide snapped back to the reality around her and fought the instinct to grab Mark's arm and snap his wrist. Part of her wanted his touch, but that part was buried deep beneath the raging essence of her Prophane genetics.

"All right, Mark?" Voide replied, furrowing her brow as the slightest hint of agitation slipped into her tone. "You capture our ship, leave me to be tortured, then ride in to the rescue and take me away while my crew sits stewing in the brig. Exactly how all right do you expect me to be?"

Normally Voide was disciplined and could control her feelings when she focused on doing it, at least for the most part. Now, it was almost like she was a passenger inside herself, watching the journey but with little control over the destination. Her wandering mind and lack of focus was probably a side effect of the voidspace inhibiting wristlets. Then again, maybe it was the wrestling with some lingering feelings for Mark, other than loathing and revulsion, that was keeping her off-balance.

Mark flashed a brief look of anger at her mention of being tortured by the crewmen, but then moved to take a seat at the end of the small conference table. He gave Voide a sympathetic smile.

"Those men will be severely disciplined, I assure you."

"And that is supposed to make it okay?" she snapped.

He didn't respond verbally, but simply nodded toward the chair closest to her. After a few moments locked in a futile stare

185

of resistance, she relented and took a seat.

"First off let me say I had no idea you were on that ship. Neither Admiral Starling nor I gave orders for anyone to be mistreated. The crew was to be held until Simmons and I could question them. I am truly sorry about what happened."

"You didn't know I was on that ship?" Voide reigned in her shock. "GalSec must be slipping. It is standard procedure to know targets inside out before making any move. I would have expected you to know everything down to what we all had for breakfast this morning."

"You are right," Russel replied with a smile, "but not this time. I only learned about you when Simmons told me we had an old acquaintance of mine in custody. I came straight to the brig once I heard you were there."

Maybe they weren't as burned as Voide had feared. If Mark hadn't known she was on the ship, maybe he didn't know about John either. She didn't believe in coincidence. It was time for some counterintelligence questions to establish how deep they had stepped in it this time.

"So what is an Imperial cruiser doing under command of GalSec, and why are you capturing ships coming out of voidspace without so much as a courtesy hail?"

Mark's brow furrowed. His formerly pleasant tone took on a more serious inflection.

"A courtesy hail? Are you kidding me? The moment *Star Wolf* came out of voidspace and spotted us your helmsman put in a reverse course. If we hadn't had the Dawnstar fighters there with VDEs, you would have been back in voidspace before there was time to say hello. Then you dropped two missiles with blinder loads in between *Revenge* and *Star Wolf*. We tried to hail but got your EM transmission code for comms down, a suspicious condition on an otherwise undamaged ship. Those are typical pirate cut and run tactics, Yasu, you know that. What did you expect us to do?"

Voide ignored the question. How much did Mark actually know about their recent activities? Time to push the issue.

"We drop out of voidspace into what is clearly an ambush setup? Do you blame Molon for going defensive? You were obviously waiting for someone, so if it wasn't us, who *were* you expecting?"

Mark's face grew cold and Voide began to feel her familiar loathing returning. It gave her a confidence boost, finally being back on familiar, antagonistic turf with Mark. She was determined to continue her counter questions while doing her best to avoid answering his. At least the nagging flutter in her stomach had receded.

"Who we were expecting," Mark said, annoyance rising in his tone, "was irrelevant once *Star Wolf* blasted two escort shuttles into scrap metal. You were hostiles at that point, and enemies of the Provisional Imperium."

"Dractauri scat! Those were as much escort shuttles as Lubanians are house pets. I think you meant to say boarding assault shuttles. Or did you forget they were stuffed full of armed and armored marines?"

"*Star Wolf* shot first, Yasu."

"What did you expect us to do? You blocked us from entering voidspace with VDEs and launched assault shuttles and gunships at us. You can't honestly maintain we weren't under attack. You forced Molon's hand."

"It makes no difference," Mark said, his exasperation clearly rising. "You were behaving like pirates and you attacked Provisional Imperium ships. Starling initiated anti-terrorist protocol at that point."

"Anti-terrorist protocol?" Voide jumped to her feet and leaned over the table, pointing an accusing finger as she stared Russel down. "Since when does any lawful protocol include irradiated ammunition? Your troops were the ones using illegal weapons. Who are the real terrorists?"

"You might want to calm down," Mark said, furrowing his brow and nodding for Voide to sit back down. "I'm positive Starling is watching us. If he thinks I have lost control of this debriefing, he will send security in here weapons blazing."

Voide stood fuming, waiting for an answer, but it was clear Mark wasn't saying another word until she calmed down. She retook her seat but did not relent with her piercing stare.

"That's better," Mark said, with a smug grin that showed how much he relished being in control of the situation. "And yes, overkill boarding shuttles, irradiated ammunition, neural grenades, narcozine gas during decontamination in the airlocks, etc. That is all part of the new anti-terrorism protocol. A lot has changed since you left GalSec, Yasu."

"Apparently so," Voide was disturbed at the new measures Zarsus had instituted, but wasn't surprised.

"Honestly, Simmons and I had a hard time convincing Starling to take you all alive. If he'd had his way, as soon as you destroyed those two shuttles, this cruiser's guns would have made sure there wasn't a big enough piece of *Star Wolf* left to identify with a molecular scanner."

Voide knew there was some truth behind this. Military types tended to throw restraint out the window when they lose

187

soldiers. In this, at least, they were lucky Mark was in oversight command of this cruiser.

"Listen, Mark," she said, calming her tone and hoping to edge them back toward less antagonistic turf. "We are an independently registered mercenary vessel. Did you even bother to check out our registered transponder ID? We are a neutral ship with clearance to cross Provisional Imperium borders. We have a legal PI trade license. We are not terrorists."

"Really?" Mark scoffed. "Just over a week ago the Dawnstar prison colony at Ratuen was attacked and a prisoner extracted from that facility. Ratuen's long-range monitors reported a *Scimitar* class frigate leaving the system via a rabbit hole shortly after the attack. A day later Hatacks long-range sensors detected a *Scimitar* class frigate entering the Hatacks system via a rabbit hole and leaving via the Tede jump point. We received credible intelligence that these raiders might return so we set up to intercept them at the jump point from Tede."

Voide's stomach tightened. This wasn't coincidence or a blind fishing expedition. The question was, how did they know whoever had taken John would be coming back?

"You mentioned a report about the perpetrators returning. What was the source of that credible intelligence, Mark?"

Mark's smile revealed he was onto her. Mark had received the same GalSec counterintelligence training she had. Her last question was too bold, too direct. She had tipped her hand and the game was up.

"Nice try. You know I can't reveal that, so you can stop fishing. But I can tell you what you already know. A few days after we set up to act on this lead, *Star Wolf*, which happens to be a *Scimitar* class frigate, pops out of that jump point and starts cut and run maneuvers as soon as it spots *Revenge*. I want to help you, Yasu, I do, but this doesn't look good."

Voide scrambled to come up with some angle to talk her way out of this. Mark hadn't said anything about John or Elena Salzmann, so maybe he wasn't sure who or what he was looking for yet. Perhaps they were just responding to a possible security threat. It would be hard to explain what *Star Wolf* was doing here without revealing more about John than she intended to.

"So what now, Mark? You know Molon and I are not terrorists. Read us in on the situation. Whoever you are looking for, maybe we can help you."

Mark laughed. It wasn't a good-natured laugh. He knew

188

more than he was saying. Mark gave the appearance that he was in complete control of the situation.

"Tede is a Theocracy of the Faithful colony," Mark expounded. "Enoch and the Theocracy are known to supplement their regular forces with mercenaries. I have techs combing through *Star Wolf*'s travel logs right now. If you haven't been to Ratuen recently, you and your crew will be on your way in a few hours with our sincere apologies for the misunderstanding. If you have been, then you are in real trouble, Yasu, and I am not sure even I can help you."

"What do you mean?" Voide asked, reflexively. She already knew the answer.

"I mean that if you are associated with terrorist actions against Dawnstar, a protectorate and ally of the Provisional Imperium, then jurisdiction over *Star Wolf* and its crew revert to Senior Special Interrogator Simmons."

Voide swallowed hard.

"You outrank Simmons. He is a Senior Special Interrogator, but you are a Deputy Director."

"I am Deputy Director of the Information Division. Simmons reports to my peer, the Deputy Director of Interrogation. If you are officially labeled terrorists, I have no authority whatsoever. Terrorism falls under the jurisdiction of the Interrogation Division."

Voide knew that spelled trouble. Interrogation was known for being able to break even the most stalwart of enemy agents. That was the core of their existence. Whatever happened, she had to try and keep things in Mark's hands.

"Simmons seems like an intelligent and reasonable man. Surely, Mark, you can make him understand we pose no threat to the Provisional Imperium."

A genuine look of nervousness filled Mark's eyes. He could hide behind words, but his eyes could not lie to her. Rank notwithstanding, Mark feared Simmons.

"Don't let Simmons's polite demeanor fool you, Yasu. He is a space-cold killer. He's the most ruthless interrogator I have ever met."

"He's also an SC augment," Voide snapped, hoping to throw Mark off his game as she fished for leverage. "Did you know that? What happened to the prohibition against SCs serving in GalSec?"

"As I said before, a lot has changed. Sub-cutes were banned from service in the Old Empire out of fear of cyberpsychosis. Apparently, being psychotic isn't a detriment to service in the Interrogation Division."

189

Voide noted Mark's glib remark belied the anxiety resting just below surface of his voice. She was running out of ideas how to gain Mark's trust while diverting him from discovering anything further about John's presence on *Star Wolf* or Elena's research.

"But Mark, we aren't some unknown gunslingers looking to make a fast buck or dissidents promoting a cause. Molon, and most of the crew, served either with the Scouts or the Imperial Navy, and I was with GalSec."

"Molon was drummed out of the Scouts under suspicion of collaborating with pirates."

Voide slammed her fist on the table and started to stand again before remembering that might draw armed security into the conversation.

"Molon was exonerated. We worked with your predecessor, Deputy Director Mertz, to bring down Razdi Chadra's entire pirate network. The charges against him were proven false. Zarsus himself issued Molon's pardon."

"A pardon is a piece of paper," Russel said, shaking his head. "You and I both know a blot like that never goes away, especially not from the minds and records of the Interrogation Division."

Mark lowered his voice and leaned closer to Voide.

"Yasu, if you have anything to tell me about where *Star Wolf* has been or what you have been up to the past week, now is the time. If you come clean I may be able to spin it as a misunderstanding and plead for leniency."

Voide stared at the unmoving projection of the Hatacks system on the wall panels. She had not wiped the logs. It had not even occurred to her, but it was not really her job. Had Molon ordered any of the other authorized officers to do it?

Voide mentally kicked herself. She had suspected a trap before they left Tede. To not take care to clean up logs showing their visit to Ratuen was a rookie mistake. She should have taken the initiative. After all, she was in charge of security, which sometimes meant erasing footprints. Voide could only wonder if this would prove a fatal oversight for them all.

*****

John watched as the medical team from *Revenge*, with Simmons in tow, entered the brig. The doctors had anti-radiation medical kits at the ready and headed straight for the cell where most of the wounded, including Bobby Lee and Mel, were. John fought his instinct to demand one of the medical kits.

"Simmons," Molon called out.

"Yes Captain?" the interrogator answered with his usual calm, monotonic voice.

"With all due respect, PI troops caused this damage. I would feel much better if your medics would leave the med kits and anti-radiation supplies with us and let *Star Wolf*'s corpsmen care for our people."

Molon was trying to get the medical kits into John's hands while concealing his identity. John appreciated the captain's concern and steeled himself for whatever answer came. He owed it to Molon and the crew of *Star Wolf* to do his part not to blow his cover.

"*Revenge* has a team of top-notch doctors, Captain," Simmons answered. "I am sure they will give your crew the best medical care possible."

"Maybe, or maybe they finish what those marines with the illegal rad rounds started."

A thin smile crossed Simmons's face.

"If we wanted you dead, you would be."

"Still, I have Lubanians here," Molon replied. "They don't take well to being kicked while they are down, and having the enemy patch you up after shooting you up, that's a hard ball of fur to swallow."

Simmons raised an eyebrow. John was sure he suspected something, but Molon's gamble was worth a shot. If John couldn't keep his mouth shut and rein in his instinct to help his crewmates, this all might wind up for nothing.

"Very well, captain," Simmons replied, his half-smirk showing he suspected more was at play than simply appeasing Lubanian pride. "There is nothing in the medical kits that will assist you in effecting an escape, if that is what you are thinking. But if you insist, we will do as you ask."

Simmons gave the order. *Revenge*'s medical team handed the med kits to Bob and Patch, the two corpsmen in the cell with John. Simmons gave a curt nod in the direction of Molon's cell, then departed with the cruiser's medical team in tow.

As soon as they were out of sight, John grabbed one of the kits and went straight to Mel's side.

"You two," he called to Bob and Patch. "Start level five anti-radiation protocols on Bobby Lee. Check for radiation exposure in any other crewmen who suffered projectile wounds during the boarding action. The boarders in the shuttle bay were using irradiated rounds, but I have no idea what went on at the airlocks."

John raised Mel's head slowly and fed her a dose of

191

potassium iodide. She opened her eyes and flashed him a weak smile. Her powder blue skin had taken on a dark and bruised look. John couldn't be sure if this was due to the radiation or just some effect of her overall mood.

"What is this for, John?"

"It is potassium iodide. It'll help fill vacancies in your system so whatever radiation is floating around in there will have fewer places to hide. If you can sit up for me, I need to give you a DTPA injection as well. It will bind to the radioactivity in your system and help your body to get rid of it faster. How are you feeling?"

"Cold," Mel answered as her lip quivered slightly. "Very cold."

"You are going to be fine. I promise."

John pulled the Fei comms officer close, using his own body heat to try to warm her although the ambient temperature in *Revenge*'s brig was quite comfortable.

He held her hand and felt none of the out-of-control feelings that had previously given him such an aversion to her touch. He wondered if the effect was hampered due to the radiation coursing through her, or if Mel was consciously suppressing it.

"Thank you, John," Mel said, giving his hand a gentle squeeze as she slipped into fitful unconsciousness.

John had no idea what the effects of these radiation rounds might be on non-human sophonts. He wished he had studied the NHS medical library more closely during their travel time. He cared deeply for Mel even though he had only known her a few days. He couldn't bear the thought of losing her so soon after losing Elena.

But that was the whole point of all this, wasn't it? Had he really lost Elena? Was she still alive? Was GalSec's command of a cruiser waiting for them along the route part of a plot to recapture him? Doubtless they would know soon enough.

Fourteen – Who Watches the Watchmen?

Voide stared at Mark, torn between ripping his throat out with her teeth, or continuing to try and manipulate him into releasing *Star Wolf* before their recent travel to Ratuen was confirmed. Conversation was ahead of violence by a hair, but the gap was quickly closing.

"Suddenly nothing to say?" Mark Russel chided at Voide's extended pause. "No biting quips, no witty banter? Come on, Yasu, just tell me the truth, I spin it to Simmons, and you and Molon will be spared the worst of it."

"The truth about what, Mark? What do you think I am hiding?"

Russel frowned and shook his head. Reaching into his inside jacket pocket, he pulled out a datapad, scanned it, then locked eyes with Voide once again.

"*Star Wolf* was responsible for the breakout at Ratuen. Do you deny it?"

Voide stared back unblinking and unflustered. Mark was fishing. If he knew as much as he pretended to know, this would not be an interrogation. She would already be in the custody of Senior Special Interrogator Simmons. Time for classic counterintelligence; answer a question with a question.

"Are you asking a question or making an accusation?"

"Cut the games, Yasu," Mark snapped, clearly losing patience with their GalSec-trained verbal sparring. "I know you were at Ratuen. In another hour or so we will have decrypted *Star Wolf*'s logs, which will confirm it. Witnesses say a Lubanian engineered the prisoner breakout."

"So, Molon is Lubanian, thus he's fit to play your patsy for this? Is this some kind of vendetta against Molon for luring me away from GalSec? Lubanians aren't exactly a rarity along the spinward border, Mark. They have a vast interstellar confederacy right next door, galactically speaking."

"Molon is not just any Lubanian. He is a Lubanian with the skills and experience to pull off this kind of prison break. He also happens to be the only Lubanian in this subsector

193

commanding a *Scimitar* class frigate."

"Circumstantial garbage, Mark. You try and hang a case on that, the Adjudicator General will make sure your next assignment is on some waterless pit on the edge of the Hinterlands."

"Enough with the indignant denials, Yasu. As soon as we process the logs, you and Molon are nuked, so own up now and save yourself. What were you doing there? Who put you up to it? Was it Enoch? What does the Theocracy want with John Salzmann?"

There it was! In his enthusiasm to press the question, Mark admitted to what Voide suspected all along. They were after John. On the other hand, maybe Mark dropped this revelation on purpose. While he was no hero, Mark was never careless. To assume this slip was unintentional would be a mistake. Voide knew better.

Mark was still fishing. He had just swapped bait. He was trying to put Voide off her guard and get her to admit she knew John. Right now Mark was studying every muscle in her face, every blink of her eyes looking for some hint that he had hit a nerve. It was GalSec training at its finest. The game was on, and it was her move.

"What in the bowels of the universe are you on about, Mark? Molon is the captain of *Star Wolf*, so if you want to know her destination, ask *him*. As for what we are we doing here, I imagine he had a line on some work."

"You are *Star Wolf*'s security chief. Do you expect me to believe you don't know where she was headed?"

"The captain plays things pretty close to the vest now. That probably has something to do with getting sold out to the pirates he was infiltrating."

There had been no proof Mark was the one who had sold them out to Chadra. Still, that was Molon's working theory, and it was not without merit.

As Voide sent that stinger in, she looked for any reaction. She spotted a slight twitch in Mark's face at her insinuation, but he quickly dodged the barb.

"Seriously?" Mark replied, furrowing his brow as he dropped his datapad unceremoniously onto the table and returned to his earlier line of questioning. "Looking for work here in Dawnstar space? That's the best you can do?"

"Yeah, why not?" Voide pressed. By maintaining the offensive, she deferred having to answer his pointed questions. "We are a registered, unaligned merc ship. Hatacks has direct, mapped, voidspace jumps to Tede, Hececcrir, and Corespoun.

Corespoun is a PI system with a Class A starport and military supplies. If you are asking me to guess, he was planning a Corespoun resupply run and maybe looking to find us a gig out of Hatacks or Hececcrir. Dawnstar pays pretty well from what I hear."

"Sorry, Yasu, you overreached with that one," Mark answered, a smug, cat-ate-the-canary grin crossing his face as he folded his hands and sat back in his chair. "Class A starport notwithstanding, all three of these systems are border systems, technological dump holes where you aren't going to find work unless you are a janitorial crew."

"Dawnstar is rich," Voide answered, but knew she was breathing thin atmo with this line. "They have high-tech core worlds just rimward of here. Jobs would filter to the border systems via System Express quickly enough."

"Dawnstar hasn't used mercs since it allied with the Provisional Imperium. They hire direct. Scooped up every shade merc and ronin as would trade in the freelance lifestyle for a steady paycheck."

"Is that so? I guess I had better let Molon know."

"He knows full well, and so do you. Besides, Hatacks also happens to have a mapped jump point to Furi. I noticed you are also licensed for Theocracy contracts."

"Yeah, so?"

"So, playing both sides is dangerous."

"Now who is playing dumb? Eighty percent of free mercs have opposing faction licenses. That's the only way inter-faction trade happens. There is nothing illegal about that."

"I don't think you are running purely corporate contracts, though." Mark said, shaking his head. "I think it is much more likely you are working directly for Enoch and the Theocracy. Using a PI contract to gain access to PI systems for the purpose of conducting military operations for an opposing faction, that would not only be terrorism, but treason."

This was no passing threat. Voide knew independents were allowed to run civilian, corporate contracts across faction lines. But they were expressly forbidden to take military contracts directly from any factional government if they entered another faction's territory under a commercial trade license. They had really taken a gamble with an anonymous contract to rescue the Salzmanns from Ratuen in the first place. Fortunately, it had been the Brothers of the Lion who had issued the contract. Who knew how the PI or GalSec would view that?

"If you already have all the answers, Mark, then why are

you even bothering with questions?"

Voide was still fighting to contain her rage. Indignation was at least a plausible reason for her to keep stalling any straightforward answers, but her rising fury was threatening her control. Losing it now would not only jeopardize the entire *Star Wolf* crew, but might just land her a quick execution by trigger-happy security teams aboard *Revenge*.

"Enough, Yasu," Russel said, pounding the table in frustration. "Just tell me the truth! I promise to protect you. We will consider you a cooperating witness and can arrange immunity from prosecution if you testify."

Voide seethed, the balance within her tipping suddenly toward violence. Mark's suggestion that she dishonor herself and sell out Molon and the rest of *Star Wolf*'s crew pushed her to the brink.

Mark knew her better than that. She would never sell out her captain. Was he trying to rile her in order to put her off her game and force a mistake? That had to be it. Ripping his throat out would not be the most productive response, but she wasn't ready to rule out that possibility just yet.

As Voide pondered her next move, warning claxons sounded throughout the conference room. *Revenge*'s computer announced the situation on a ship-wide broadcast.

Warning. Proximity jump detected. Initiating red alert.

"A proximity jump?" Mark announced as he jumped to his feet, dislodging the lightly magnetized base of the conference room chair and sending it toppling behind him. "That's a Prophane tactic."

Voide's mind had leapt to the same conclusion. Her heart pounded and she felt her skin go cold. It couldn't be. Not here.

"It is," Voide answered, scrambling to think of any more feasible explanation than Prophane all the way on the spinward border of Humaniti space. "But with enough time and preparation, non-Prophane have pulled it off as a system defense tactic."

"Impossible," Mark said, shaking his head. "We're on a Provisional Imperium ship in allied Dawnstar space. This is no defense maneuver."

With that, Mark Russel turned, sprinting toward the bridge. Mark was right. Dawnstar had no reason to execute a proximity jump near a PI cruiser, but the alternative was unimaginable.

With the alert drawing Mark's attention away from the interrogation, Voide followed him instinctively toward the bridge, disregarding the possibility of armed security waiting to kill her at the first sign of trouble. She could only hope they were more concerned with reacting to a proximity jump alert than executing a visiting Pariah. As they entered the bridge, the security officers were nowhere in sight.

"Admiral Starling," Mark shouted above the sound of the warning alerts. "What is going on?"

"You heard the alert, Russel," Starling replied from the captain's chair on the bridge. "Some blasted fool ship just dropped out of voidspace not a thousand klicks off our port bow. Lieutenant, do you have an ID from their transponder yet?"

"Yes, admiral," the sensor officer replied. "It's a *Hive*-class pocket carrier flying an unaligned transponder code, *UCA Hornet's Nest*."

Voide did not recognize the ship name, but she knew an unescorted pocket carrier attacking a cruiser one-on-one was madness. It would be giving up six thousand tons at least, and even with a full complement of fighters, the pocket carrier would be severely outgunned.

"What's her status?" Starling replied.

"She just pulled a rapid dump deploy of fifty short-range assault fighters flying unaligned transponder codes. The carrier just raised screens."

"XO sound battle stations," Starling commanded, yelling above the clamor of alarms. "Raise screens and deploy intercept fighters from aft bays. Reinforce and harden forward and broadside screens port and starboard."

"Aye, sir," a tall, thin man near the admiral, with the uniform markings of a captain, responded and began barking orders to various stations.

Mark grabbed Voide's arm at the elbow with a vice-like grip. She bit back a yelp of pain and surprise.

"Are they with you?" he whispered through gritted teeth.

"No, Mark," Voide hissed, wrenching her arm free and meeting his gaze while reining in her instinct to throat-punch him. "I have no idea who they are. We have nothing to do with this."

His eyes belied his suspicion. Trust came hard to GalSec agents. That was part of the training: distrust everyone. Fortunately, the ambient noise and chaos of prepping for battle had kept their conversation, as well as Voide's presence on the bridge, off the admiral's mind. Suddenly, that became a decided disadvantage.

"All hands suit up. Emergency decompression in five minutes," Starling ordered across general comms. "And shut off that claxon, I can't think straight with all that racket."

The young sensor officer touched the panel in front of him and silenced the audible alert, while red lights above the doors and main screen continued to flash a silent warning of the alert status. The carryover ringing in Voide's ears was the least of her concerns at the moment.

"But admiral," Voide interjected with far more passion than she generally exhibited. "What about *Star Wolf*'s crew in the brig? They still have vac suits on, but our helmets were confiscated when we were taken aboard. You need to send a security team to return those helmets or the crew will die when you vent atmo."

"Not my problem, Prophane," Admiral Starling replied with a steely satisfaction in his tone. "You should have thought of that before you violated Dawnstar space and engaged in acts of terrorism."

Voide spun toward Mark Russell, grabbing his arm nearly as hard as he had grabbed hers.

"Mark!" she pleaded. "By Imperial law *Star Wolf*'s crew are innocent until proven guilty. You can't let this happen."

"She's right, admiral," Mark said, turning his attention to Starling and adopting a commanding tone. "Those prisoners have not yet been interrogated, and it is believed they have information vital to Imperial security. By order of GalSec, every effort must be made to ensure their safety. Deploy a security team at once to return their vac suit helmets and delay depressurization until you have confirmation the prisoners are prepped and ready."

Admiral Starling stood up and faced him. His left arm hung at his side but ended in a balled fist. He snapped at Mark, pointing with his right index finger while his face reddened.

"You sentimental idiot, are you trying to kill us all? Do you know what happens if a hull breaches while pressurized?"

"Yes, admiral, I do," Mark replied with a matter-of-fact tone. "Therefore I suggest you stop wasting time arguing and issue the order, so we can avoid that eventuality."

Starling loosed a frustrated snarl and spun to address his executive officer.

"XO, make it so, double-time."

"Aye, sir."

The gangly executive officer stepped to the security station and issued the order via the bridge security officer. Suddenly, another alert blared through the bridge, this time changing the flashing warning lights to a rapidly blinking pattern accompanied by a repeating, whooping siren.

"We are out of time, admiral," announced the lieutenant manning the sensor station. "Those fighters just launched a full barrage of missiles."

"Are screens up?" Starling asked, taking his seat in the captain's chair once again.

"Yes sir, up and hardened, but at two missiles per fighter, we are going to take a serious pounding. I'm not sure the screens will hold if even a third gets through point-defense."

"Any idea of their payload?"

"Negative, admiral. The missiles are shielded. We won't know what type of warheads they are carrying until they hit. If they are nukes, this is bad news."

Voide's brow furrowed. A rapid-dump deployment was always a risky maneuver, even for only deploying a few fighters. Too many things could go wrong that could have catastrophic impacts to the carrier, especially if the fighters were armed with tactical nukes. However, a pocket carrier pulling a rapid dump, fifty-fighter deployment was sheer madness. Still, there was something very familiar about this maneuver. Where had she seen this before? Every part of her tingled a warning, but she could not pinpoint why this scenario filled her with déjà vu.

"Where are we on weapons? Have intercept fighters deployed yet?" Starling asked, addressing the weapons officer. "Bring all forward main batteries to bear on that carrier."

"Fighters are deploying now but out of position to intercept the missiles. They won't get there in time. Main batteries are still powering up, sir. Four minutes to firing charge and a confirmed targeting solution. Point defense guns and secondary batteries are online and ready."

"Set all forward and port side point-defense turrets and even the secondary batteries to target those incoming missiles."

"Sir, secondary batteries are too slow to track missiles. We won't hit ten percent."

"Don't lecture me, boy. Secondary batteries won't pierce their screens, but every missile we hit is one less that hits us."

"Aye sir, secondary batteries and point defense targeting incoming missiles."

As *Revenge*'s bridge officers scrambled to execute the admiral's orders, Starling turned his attention toward Mark once again.

"Russel, we can't wait anymore, I am sorry about your prisoners, but this ship comes first."

Mark nodded and flashed a sympathetic look toward

199

Voide. She was a bridge officer and understood the admiral had to depressurize before those missiles hit. She could only hope the security teams got to the crew in the brig in time.

"XO begin depressurization," Starling commanded. "Prioritize the brig section last. Tell those security teams to move like their feet were on fire."

"Aye, sir. Security teams report they have already reached the brig. They've started distributing the helmets."

Voide breathed a sigh of relief. At least the crew would not suffocate in the stockade. She just hoped *Revenge* survived long enough for it to matter.

The bridge crew began attaching helmets to their vac suits. Mark stepped to a closet at the side of the bridge. Pulling a breathing mask and tank from the shelf, he tossed them to Voide before himself stepping into a vac suit.

"You remembered?" she said, noting Mark had not offered her a vac suit.

"Yeah. Prophane biology is hard to forget, especially yours."

Voide cracked a smile as she affixed her ventilator. Mark had once seemed so kind. Where had that young man gone? It was hard to look at him now and see that eager young GalSec officer in the man he was today. Ambition and living as though life were one big chess match had forever warped the good man she once knew.

Other than the buzz of bridge officers carrying out their duties, all hands silently awaited the impact of the incoming missile barrage. The high-pitched, stuttered whine of the point defense batteries quickly faded in Voide's ears as the atmosphere vented into the pressurized and heavily armored compartment of the ship designed for that purpose. She placed the intra-aural comm link attached to the breathing mask in her ear. She was the only one on the ship now openly exposed to the depressurized atmosphere on board. She was also the only one whose body was built to survive it.

Voide had heard that Prophane military vessels ran continuously in a depressurized state, outfitting the crew with respirators and intra-aural communicators. That way, even an ambush would find the Prophane ready for battle. She often wondered what it would be like flying through space in a ship full of her own people. Unfortunately, unless enough children were captured and raised to crew a ship full of Pariahs, that would only ever be a dream.

In their current situation, depressurization might not make a difference. Depending on the quality of the hardened screens *Revenge* was sporting, the skill of the point defense gunners, and the type of payload those warheads were carrying, surviving this first volley was by no means assured. Even if the point defense and secondary batteries took out half, a good showing at that, fifty missiles would overload the screens with enough payload left over to shred the hull and irradiate most of the crew on the port side if they were carrying tac-nukes.

On the other hand, if they were merely standard laser loads, hardened screens on a cruiser the size of *Revenge*, not to mention her reflective armor, should be enough to repel the attack almost completely. The captain of the pocket carrier had to know that a cruiser would be running hardened screens over a reflec hull, so the hope that these missiles were carrying laser loads was slim. That is, unless the carrier captain was some novice idiot. Voide seriously doubted that an idiot would be capable of pulling off a proximity jump and a fifty-fighter, rapid-dump deploy.

Still, there was something unshakably familiar about this whole situation. It was maddening that she could not place exactly why.

The missiles shook the ship violently as explosions peppered the cruiser down its port side. No radiation warning sounded across the comms, but excited chatter and damage reports rolled across the bridge's local channel.

"*Admiral,*" the security station announced. "*The port broadside and bow screens are down, but ship reports minimal damage. It looks like they were carrying standard high-explosive warheads sir, not nukes.*"

"*What about the fighters? Are they advancing? Are our interceptors in position yet?*"

"*Intercept fighters closing, admiral, but...*"

"*But what, lieutenant?*" the frustration in the admiral's voice was clear, even across the comm line."

"*The enemy fighters, sir. They've disengaged. They have hit a straight Z axis vector away from us.*"

Suddenly Voide's memory clicked. She knew where she had seen this before. This was not a standard military maneuver; this was a GalSec, Psi Ops tactic!

"*Spin the ship, admiral!*" Voide shouted across the comm line, her voice carrying the weight of command as though she were one of *Revenge*'s bridge officers rather than a prisoner.

"*Who said that?*" the admiral snapped. "*What twinkle-toed dreck-eater is mucking up my comm lines?*"

"*This is your Pariah dinner guest, and I just figured out*

what is happening. Spin this ship and get the hardened starboard screens between you and that carrier, now!"

Starling spun to glare at Voide through the visor of his vac suit. His face was red and the admiral looked like he was ready to rush Voide that very moment.

"It's bad enough I have to take orders from some GalSec spook," Admiral Starling screamed over the bridge comms, spittle spattering the inside of his helmet visor. *"But I'll be spaced if I am taking orders from a Prophane prisoner!"*

"Gunner," Starling said, turning to face his weapons officer. *"Do we have a firing solution on that carrier for port side and forward batteries yet?"*

"Targeting confirmation coming through now sir. Firing all port side and forward main batteries in sixty seconds."

"You don't have sixty seconds," Voide pleaded to no avail. *"Spin the ship now, admiral,"*

She saw through the visor on Mark's vac suit a look of comprehension cross his face. He had come to the same conclusion.

"She's right, admiral," Mark said emphatically. *"You need to do an emergency one-eighty roll along the spinal axis, now!"*

"I'm about to have weapons lock, Russel," the admiral responded. *"The guns on that carrier won't put a dent in our armor even with screens down, and the fighters have disengaged. In less than a minute our main batteries will fire and that carrier is going to be floating scrap. I'm not about to wreck a perfectly good firing solution and chance to end this battle on the word of a Prophane Pariah and some GalSec desk pilot."*

"You're a fool, admiral," Mark protested.

"You may have operational command, Russel, but this is a combat situation. I'm in charge. Now, get off my bridge!"

"Admiral," the sensor officer announced. *"The carrier has dropped forward screens and opened a bow porthole. It looks like some type of spinal mount assembly, but the weapon is like nothing I have seen before, sir."*

"What?" Starling shrieked. *"A spinal mount on a carrier?"*

"It's a neural cannon," Voide announced, matter-of-factly. *"Congratulations, admiral, you've just killed us all."*

"Helm," Starling snapped. *"Spin the—"*

Suddenly the bridge was filled with officers grasping their helmets in both hands and writhing out of their seats before collapsing onto the floor. A piercing pain ripped through Voide's skull.

Subjecting prospective agents to neural weapons at the GalSec academy was part of the training. The feeling was not unlike the neural grenade that had taken her out in the boarding action on *Star Wolf*. Well, that is, it would have been similar if someone taped that grenade to five of its friends, shoved them inside her skull, and then set them off in a chain reaction one at a time. Fortunately, she did not endure the agony for long as the merciful darkness of unconsciousness engulfed her.

Fifteen – Out of the Frying Pan

Molon's head throbbed worse than the morning after a three-day bender. Groping blindly to gain a purchase on the world around him, it took him a few moments to realize he was no longer wearing a vac-suit. A strong smell of antiseptic filled the air, and soft linens engulfed him. Unsure of the last time he had eaten, he smacked his lips and tried to swallow away the coppery tang coating the inside of his mouth. Whatever contents might still be in his stomach were lobbying aggressively to make an encore appearance.

Straining to open his eyes, seeking confirmation that he was still alive, he squinted at the bright, recessed ceiling lights. Blinking several times helped to clear the glaze blurring the world around him. He found himself in what appeared to be a sick bay bed. Beside him, monitors were emitting a gentle, rhythmic pulse, displaying vital signs that seemed to be compelling evidence that he was not, in fact, dead. However, given how he felt, death might be an improvement.

Molon sat up slowly, trying not to jog what was left of his brain out of his ears. On an identical bunk to his right lay Voide, just now starting to twitch as though she were fighting off her own hangover. Her forearms had been freed of the devices placed on her by the crew of *Revenge*.

John lay on a bunk to his left. The doctor had half kicked off his sheets to reveal he was still wearing deck crew coveralls. The chain partially visible around his neck gave Molon hope that the disguised datacube with Elena's research had not been discovered. John moaned groggily, showing early signs of returning to consciousness. Molon was impressed that the human was fighting off whatever had robbed them of consciousness almost as quickly as Voide was. No one else from the crew was anywhere in sight.

A middle-aged human woman dressed in a white nun's habit entered the room.

"Oh, you are awake, dear" the nun said, beaming. "That's good. So, how are we feeling today?"

204

Her voice was excessively cheerful given Molon's current state. Now he really felt like throwing up.

"I don't know how you feel, sister. I feel like I've been kicked in the head by a Dractauri and set on a three-axis tumble through space, but thanks for asking. By the way, where exactly am I?"

"You are in safe hands, dear," she replied, with Molon's sarcasm not deterring her grin in the slightest. "I'll fetch the doctor. I'm sure he can answer all of your questions."

Without another word, she scurried out. Molon glanced around. It looked like the recovery room of a sick bay, but far roomier and better equipped than *Star Wolf*'s claustrophobic infirmary. From the subtle hum and the almost unnoticeable vibrations running through the flooring and into the bedposts, they were on a ship. Was this still *Revenge*? Given that the nurse wore a habit like the nuns of the Faithful, he doubted it.

In walked a man dressed in a white monk's cassock, followed closely by the grinning, overly chipper nurse. On the monk's left breast was the mark of a lion, but not the golden lion of the Provisional Imperium. It was the fully maned, red and black lion's head with an underlying banner bearing the motto *Fratres Leonis:* Brothers of the Lion.

Voide grumbled and mumbled as she sat up in bed, sniffing loudly. John rubbed his head and moaned, smacking his lips and scrunching up his face as he struggled to sit up as well. The monk flashed a placating smile as if he were mimicking the nurse's. Molon wondered if they practiced that in front of a mirror.

"How are you three feeling?" asked the monk, presumably the doctor whom the grinning nurse had promised.

"Lousy," Molon answered, while nothing more than unintelligible moans and grunts came out of Voide and John. "But if you're a doctor, you probably guessed that."

The monk laughed, and the nun-nurse covered her mouth to suppress a giggle.

"I imagine you have quite the headache. The captain assures me the neural cannon was set at a level to incapacitate the crew of the *Revenge* without causing permanent damage. Unfortunately, that means you all received the same treatment. Regrettable, but unavoidable. I'm afraid neural weapons aren't particularly selective. Don't worry. Preliminary cerebral scans of you and your crew show no permanent damage. Still, you should take it easy for a few days nonetheless."

"So, I'm still waiting for someone to tell me where we are. And speaking of my crew, where are the rest of them?"

"You are aboard the *UCA Hornet's Nest*," the monk-doctor answered.

"And my crew?"

"They are safe, I assure you, captain."

"You will forgive me if I want more than your assurances, doctor. Who's in command of this ship?"

Just then, into the room walked Brother Martin wearing a brown monk's cassock with the same emblem above the left breast as the doctor wore. He nodded a greeting to Molon.

"Captain Hawkins, it is so good to see you again. I wish it were under more pleasant circumstances."

Molon could not quite choke back a laugh that set his head ringing once again. He knew Brother Martin, and the Brothers of the Lion, were in this deeper than they let on. Their showing up and ambushing *Revenge* was no coincidence.

"Just happened to be in the neighborhood, huh? What a lucky break for us I suppose." Molon made no effort to hide his sarcasm.

"On the contrary, Captain Hawkins," Brother Martin said shaking his head and flashing a smug grin. "It was no coincidence at all. We have been following you since you left Tede. I suppose it is a good thing we were."

Well, at least he was honest about following them. The question of the day was why. Molon expected he would find out what they really wanted soon enough. Had they figured out John had Elena's research, or did this oubliette run even deeper?

Voide, having finally regained what passed for consciousness after a neural weapon brain scramble, cleared her throat.

"So," she began in a raspy voice, clearly fighting through considerable pain. "How'd you pew-warmers manage to pull off a proximity jump?"

"Ah, yes, Captain Smythe is quite something, isn't he? While technically a mercenary captain, he is also a member of the Faithful, a high-ranking officer in our defense forces, and a wonderful servant of the Lion of Judah. When our brotherhood was based in the Tede system, Smythe had a number of small, jump-capable ships working secretly in the Hatacks system to thoroughly map out rabbit holes in local voidspace. While he was there, he put up shielded micro-transmitters throughout the Hatacks system. We thought it a waste of time, given our plans to relocate our base of operations further within the borders of the Theocracy, but fortunately for you his insistence proved quite providential in the end."

"That map would be pretty handy to have," Molon said, nearly salivating as he considered what he might be able to trade for such a useful combat tool. "Knowing all the rabbit holes near Hatacks would surely give Enoch enough of an edge to retake that system for the Theocracy."

"Why of course," Brother Martin replied. "Naturally, we sent the information on to Haven as soon as it was completed, Captain. We are on the same side after all. Unfortunately, Enoch isn't particularly interested in a marginally useful system like Hatacks."

"Why not?" John asked, finally composing himself enough to speak, albeit groggily. "Hatacks would make a far more suitable border base than a hermit-world like Tede."

"I agree, Dr. Salzmann," Brother Martin replied, "But Hatacks, with mapped jump points to Hececcrir and Courspoun, would be far too strategic a system for Dawnstar and the Provisional Imperium not to spend considerable resources to retake it. Tede still stands on the Theocracy side of the border only because your hermit-world has nothing worth taking. If it did, I doubt Enoch would commit the resources to defend it. He has his hands full with his Fei allies trying to recapture the worlds occupied by Alpha Pack. He's entrenched, fighting purely defensively everywhere else."

"So, Brother Martin," Molon interjected, changing the subject away from distant politics and more to immediate concerns. "I'm still waiting for someone to tell me the location of the rest of my crew."

"Safe and sound," answered Brother Martin. "They are receiving the best medical care our order can provide. We didn't have the bunks aboard *Hornet 's Nest,* so I have had your uninjured crew housed back aboard *Star Wolf.* Our engineers are making repairs to your ship as we speak, assisting your malmorph engineer, Dubronski I believe his name is. Remarkably resilient character that one. He was conscious and alert before we even finished getting the rest of your crew off *Revenge.*"

Molon knew malmorphs often received boosts to some of their physical or mental attributes as side effects of the malmorphsy. Dub was highly resistant to intoxicants, a fact Molon had discovered the hard way. Maybe he had some innate resistance to neural weapons as well.

"Where are our wounded?" John asked. "We had two with severe radiation sickness due to those Imp Marines using radiation rounds."

"They are in good hands, doctor, I assure you. Why don't

207

you all just rest a bit? Brother Zebedee, our senior Brother on board, wants to speak with you as soon as you are up to it."

"I want to see our wounded now," John snapped. Taking a deep breath, he added, "Forgive my rudeness, Brother. I just feel it is my duty to oversee their care personally. They are my responsibility."

"So you have joined *Star Wolf* as the ship's doctor then, have you, John?" Brother Martin asked, his smile slipping a little.

"Yes, I have," John answered.

"Well, good for you. Everyone needs a place to serve."

"I'm glad you approve," John replied. "So I would appreciate being taken to see my patients now, if you would be so kind."

"Fine. Brother Landrus will see to it," Martin said, losing his smile completely while nodding to the white-cassocked doctor. "And Brother Zebedee will send for you all shortly, captain. Please let Sister Agnes know if you are hungry or require anything at all."

Brother Martin turned and left. Brother Landrus, his grin unwavering, spoke softly, extending a hand toward an internal door leading to an adjoining room.

"Your wounded crewmates are next door in the Critical Care Bay. Our CCB is state of the art, I assure you. We have initiated a Zotroxin system flush and anti-radiation medication. They should be fine in a few hours. I have them scheduled shortly for a regeneration bed session to work on the tissues already damaged by the radiation."

"Wow," John exclaimed as he followed the doctor out of the main sickbay. "Regen beds are TL14. What are monks doing with that kind of tech?"

"We are ascetics, doctor, not primitives. Quality medical equipment is no more a luxury than starships. Besides, they came with the ship, so it would be wasteful not to use what the Lion has provided."

Molon turned to Voide as Brother Landrus escorted John out of the room, with Sister Agnes close behind.

"So, Security Chief Matsumura," Molon asked with a lupine grin on his snout. "In your expert opinion, have we been rescued or just upgraded to a more comfortable hoosegow with more congenial jailers?"

Voide laughed, followed by a grimace that showed it still hurt to do so.

"I'm a pessimist, captain. The bright side is usually just the side closer to the flames."

208

****

The CCB on board *Hornet's Nest* was positively dazzling. John had rarely seen planetside hospitals, even on worlds far more advanced than Tede, that were this well outfitted. Much of the equipment here was unfamiliar to him. Was that complex-looking console with spiral leads attached to shining silver discs some type of resuscitator?

The beeping machine in the corner holding various liquids in an array of tubes, with leads running to beds housing two of his crewmates, must be the apparatus administering the Zotroxin flush. That, at least, was John's best guess by the color and consistency of the fluids being dispensed. This was a far more complex system than the simple IVs he was used to, but he conjectured this gave precise monitoring and control of the rate of flush, which could be dynamically tailored to each patient's physiology. This was seriously impressive gear.

Against the far wall sat two TL14 regen beds, powered up and ready for use. Suddenly, amidst this collection of technological finery, John felt like a dirt-covered farm boy at a high-society cotillion.

Bobby Lee and Mel were in two of the four CCB beds. Both had forearm-mounted IV cuffs connected to the complex flush machine. John had seen these types of cuff at a medical convention once on Furi. The elongated cuff wrapped around the forearm, keeping the needle safe from accidental removal from the vein while the self-contained medication compartment allowed the patient mobility. In this case, the cuffs were not using the self-contained medication dispensers, but were bypassed by the feeds from the Zotroxin machine.

"Brother Martin tells me you are from Tede, Dr. Salzmann. You wouldn't happen to be affiliated with Salzmann Pharmaceuticals, would you?"

"Yes," John said, shifting uncomfortably but seeing no reason to lie to a fellow Faithful. "That's my company."

"Really? Well then, doctor, you are treating our patients already. The Zotroxin we are using comes from Salzmann. It's the most effective radiation flush available. Hard to believe this came from a TL6 world."

"Yeah," John snapped. "Sometimes our backwater moss and dung remedies really work."

John was used to condescending attitudes toward hermit-worlders, but coming from a fellow Faithful, it just seemed out of place.

"Forgive me," Brother Landrus replied, sounding sincere. "I meant no offense. I was only marveling that it is not always

209

necessary for man's latest and greatest technology to provide the answers. Sometimes the Lion provides through humble means."

"I'm sorry, Brother Landrus," John said, sensing his overreaction to such an innocuous comment. "I suppose that neural cannon or whatever your ship hit us with has me a bit out of sorts. If you don't mind, I'd like to check on my crewmates."

"Certainly," Brother Landrus nodded, guiding John to the beds containing Bobby Lee and Mel. "I'm afraid the lad is out cold. Between weakness from radiation and the neural overload, he may not wake up for several hours. The Fei, however, does seem to be coming around. I will leave you alone. You can find your way next door once you are satisfied. Be sure to call Sister Agnes if you need help with anything."

Landrus turned and left. John approached Mel's bed with a wrenching in his stomach that matched the one in his head. As he approached, Mel cracked open her eyelids and smiled weakly.

"Hey, you," John said, sitting beside her on the bed but reluctant to take her hand. "Captain Hawkins says no sleeping on the job."

"Hello, John," she said, her voice barely above a whisper. "Where are we?"

"Safe for now. You are in good hands," John repeated the platitudes from the Faithful caretakers. "You should be feeling as normal as you can with a bullet hole in you within a couple of hours. They are flushing all the radiation out of your system and repairing the damage."

"John, there was a psionic attack. Are you okay?"

John puzzled at Mel's statement. She had not been privy to the details about the neural cannon attack. True, it was a weapon that simulated some psionic effects, but how did Mel know what happened? Molon mentioned the Fei being empaths. Was that it, or was it something more?

"We were hit by a neural cannon. I imagine it is a lot like a psionic attack. How did you know?"

Mel dropped her eyes. John could see her tense visibly.

"Just a guess. I'm very tired, John. Can we talk later?" She was clearly dodging the question.

Mel reached for his hand, and John fought his every instinct to pull away. As he gently took her hand, none of the confusion or powerful sensations he had felt before flowed from her. Maybe that had all been his imagination, or maybe Mel was too weak to duplicate her previous effect on him.

Either way he was glad for a normal touch. Her powder-blue skin was soft and cool, and oh so pleasant.

"Sure, Mel. You rest. I will check on you again in a little while."

He stood and turned to go, but his grasp on Mel's hand lingered as long as possible. He wanted more than anything to stop himself from letting go. John's head was spinning, not from anything emanating from Mel this time, but from a wave of emotion rushing from his gut to his head. This was crazy.

He loved Elena with all his heart, and if there were even a chance of getting her back, he would move the galaxy to make it happen. Yet even without any strange, possibly empathic emanations from Mel, her touch stirred feelings in him he could not suppress.

John walked out of the CCB, glancing back over his shoulder at the waifish Fei communications officer. So gentle, so delicate, but there was far more to this azure enchantress than he had yet seen.

Sixteen – Brother Zebedee

Molon, Voide, and John followed Brother Martin through the corridors of *Hornet's Nest*. The ship was much roomier than *Star Wolf*, though only around twice the tonnage. Even full-sized carriers were normally cramped, but this degree of spaciousness was particularly out of place on *Hornet's Nest*; a tiny, *Hive*-class pocket carrier.

Yet *Hornet's Nest*, according to what Voide had told Molon, had executed a proximity jump in order to ambush *Revenge*. She had been on the bridge during the attack and the sensor officer hadn't mentioned a battle carrier or any other support class ships. Apparently, *Hornet's Nest* had undergone a refit even more extensive than the tweaks he had done to *Star Wolf*. This piqued his curiosity.

"So, Brother Martin," Molon asked as they wound their way through the ship. "*Hornet's Nest* has an internal voidspace drive? That's an extremely unusual configuration for a *Hive*-class carrier."

"Ah, yes," Brother Martin replied. "Well, I am afraid I don't know much about all that. I know we came through voidspace to get here, but I am only a simple cleric, trained as a bookkeeper and administrator, so starship particulars are beyond my purview. You would have to ask Captain Smythe about *Hornet's Nest's technical details.*"

Molon wasn't sure if Brother Martin was just engaging in pleasantries or if he genuinely foresaw an opportunity for Molon to speak with the carrier captain. If it were the latter, they might not be in quite as serious a pickle as Molon feared. On Tede, Brother Martin had been a stiff-necked negotiator and the whole involvement with the Brother's of the Lion with the raid on John's house was shady, but overall Molon had no reason to suspect that the Brothers were not on the same side as the Theocracy. If they were genuine Faithful, the likelihood of *Star Wolf* and her crew just disappearing was much lower than when they were in the hands of the Provisional Imperium or GalSec.

"So we will be meeting Captain Smythe, then?" Molon pressed.

"Once we are done with Brother Zebedee, I shall see if I can arrange a private dinner with the captain, if you like. I'm sure that once he knows we are all on the same side, he would be happy to share details with a fellow shipmaster."

There was the rub. This was not going to be just a friendly meet and greet. Apparently, Brother Zebedee was going to lay conditions on the table for continuing to be "on the same side". If those conditions proved untenable, the rest of their stay aboard *Hornet's Nest* would doubtless turn considerably less cordial.

Brother Martin tapped a door panel. The portal opened to reveal a respectable-sized conference room. An older man, slender of build and dressed similarly to Brother Martin, sat at the table. The fellow had a long flowing white beard and soft brown eyes, with a slight, but sincere, smile. His bronzed, leathery skin and plethora of wrinkles bore witness to someone accustomed to planetary life under a proximate, blazing sun.

A slightly rotund man, in an Old Empire Navy formal dress uniform, sat next to him. His high-and-tight salt-and-pepper hair and clean-shaven face marked him as a career military man. Only his slight paunch bore evidence of at least a few years in the private sector. The epaulettes on his uniform bore the rank of captain, but also carried the emblazoned leonine emblem of the Brothers of the Lion.

"Captain Molon Hawkins," Brother Martin said, motioning to direct Molon's gaze toward the elderly monk, "allow me to introduce the High Abbot of our order, Brother Zebedee. And this is our beloved friend and host, Captain Malachi Smythe, shipmaster of *Hornet's Nest*."

Smythe stood and offered a smile and deep nod in Molon's direction. Brother Zebedee took a moment or two longer to rise, leaning heavily on the table, aided finally by a steadying hand from Captain Smythe.

"Captain Hawkins," said Brother Zebedee in a soft but strong voice. "Or may I call you Molon?"

"Sure, call me Molon. After all, we're on the same side, right?"

Molon flashed an insincere wolfish smile at Brother Martin before returning his attention to Brother Zebedee. The opportunity to make a dig at Brother Martin's earlier comment, while simultaneously setting a tone of cooperation with Brother Zebedee, had been irresistible. Molon's response brought a tender smile from the aged monk.

"Yes, I certainly hope so," Brother Zebedee replied, wavering a bit on his feet. "I must apologize for my instability, I'm a born and bred lightworlder, and Malachi's dogged insistence on maintaining one-G is giving me quite the workout. No mercy at all for an old man from this one, I tell you," Zebedee noted with a fond smile toward the captain.

"Oh, quit your bellyaching, Zeb," Smythe replied, matching Brother Zebedee grin for grin. "A week or two aboard *Hornet's Nest* will do you good. A farmer should have some muscle about him, even one as old as you."

"Brother Zebedee, Captain Smythe," Brother Martin interjected, interrupting the exchange and looking dismayed by Smythe's casual attitude toward High Abbot Zebedee. "Allow me to introduce our other guests. This young woman," he said, motioning toward Voide with the slightest tremble in his voice, "is Yasu Matsumura, *Star Wolf*'s chief of security. And this gentleman," he said nodding toward John, "is Dr. John Salzmann, about whom you have heard so much recently."

Molon's hackles raised, and he fought the instinct to curl his lip back over his canines. If John had been the subject of some recent discussions among the Brothers, then Molon suspected that a battle over control of the doctor, or at least his wife's research, was behind this rescue. Molon prepared himself mentally for a continuation of his aborted conversation with Brother Martin back on Tede.

"Please, everyone," Brother Zebedee said, motioning to the empty seats to his right. "Take a seat, and make yourselves comfortable. I am afraid I cannot stand for very long in this gravity myself. Malachi is a great friend to the Brothers, but he is obstinately unaccommodating toward his guests. Possibly the least gracious host the Creator ever made."

Zebedee sunk heavily back into his chair, his aged muscles succumbing to the one-G. Zebedee slipped a slight but definite sideways glance at Captain Smythe, who responded with a wide grin, obviously taking the good-natured jibe as a compliment.

"That's right, Zeb. Ship's gotta fly straight, and crew's gotta be on their game at all times," Smythe said. He turned to Molon, apparently looking for understanding or affirmation. "I don't tone down the lights for darkworlders, or turn 'em up for brightworlders. A captain can't rightly go pitching his crew all stagger-jacked just because some weak-legged, lightworld landlubber climbs aboard. Ain't that right, Hawkins?"

"Captain's call," Molon replied, deciding not to join in whatever game of mutual chiding was being bandied between

214

Zebedee and Smythe.

Zebedee's smile showed this verbal roughhousing did not faze the elderly abbot. From the ease with which these two interacted, they had known each other a long time.

After Voide found a seat, Smythe, courteously deferring to the only female present, settled into his own. Molon remembered that human custom of politeness taught him by his adoptive father. He shook his head in wonder at Smythe's queer blending of manners and maladroitness.

"A Pariah for security chief, huh?" Smythe said to Molon, shaking his head. "That's a dangerous proposition, ain't it?"

"Yeah," Voide interjected, "kind of like proximity jumping a PI cruiser with a lone pocket carrier."

"Touché," Smythe said beaming a huge grin in Voide's direction before turning to Molon once again. "I like her, Hawkins. A captain needs officers not afraid to speak their minds, and to blazes with propriety."

"Honey," Smythe said, returning his gaze to Voide. "If you ever decide to jump billets, I'll find you a bunk aboard *Hornet's Nest* even if I have to toss a raggedy old monk or two out an airlock to do it."

Brother Zebedee showed no sign of offense at Smythe's rough manner, but Molon noted Brother Martin's face darkening a shade or two.

"It's good to know a girl has options," Voide parried playfully.

Molon realized the jibe was more for his benefit than Smythe's. Voide often joked about leaving, but in truth he knew that, aside from himself and Twitch, Voide was the most loyal officer aboard *Star Wolf*. That was saying a lot.

"Molon," Zebedee began once everyone had taken their seats. "Please excuse Malachi. He is notoriously uncouth; quite unsuitable for mixed company, actually."

This drew another smug smile from the boisterous captain.

"Nonetheless," Zebedee continued, "I hope his medical team has amply seen to your recovery?"

"As well as can be expected, I suppose," Molon answered, his ears darting forward and his tail raising slightly, signaling his readiness for a fight. "Especially considering it was his neural cannon that put us in need of medical assistance in the first place."

This drew a wry smile from Zebedee and a loud laugh from Smythe.

"Hah, I suppose that is on me," Smythe said, slapping the

table with his palm. "But then again, given my crew pulled everyone but Miss Pariah here out of the brig, danged if we didn't improve your situation, give or take a good brain scramble in the bargain."

Molon had to admit, even if they did just exchange jailors, they were certainly in no greater danger from the Brothers than they had been from Mark Russel and some GalSec interrogator.

"Why, heck fire," Smythe continued, "if Martin here hadn't told us to look for your gray-skinned girly there, we'd have probably left her behind thinking she was part of the Imp crew."

Adopting a sly smile, Smythe tilted his head slightly and locked his eyes on Voide. His jovial demeanor took a dark turn.

"Now I wonder what exactly you did, little missy, to get yourself sprung from the clink all by your lonesome, hmm?"

Voide curled her lip, baring one of her fangs. Her voice dropped into a cool calm that set Molon's ears back on his head just hearing it. He could sense violence swimming just below the surface of that tranquil tone.

"I snapped the neck of some officer who made a sleazy insinuation. Apparently, that gets respect aboard an Imp ship."

Smythe smacked the table with both hands and let rip a hearty belly laugh, leaning so far back in his chair that only the magnetic locks anchoring it to the deck kept it from toppling over.

"Flaming supernovas, Hawkins you've got a real fire-spitter right there. I haven't had this much fun since I dropped a class of newly ordained Brothers off on a nudist colony world! By the Lion that was a riot."

Brother Martin reddened deeply as he cleared his throat, trying to regain some sense of decorum. Brother Zebedee seemed utterly unperturbed. Molon mused that Brother Martin's blush might be an indication he had been a member of the ordination class Smythe just referenced.

"Ahem, Captain Smythe," Brother Martin interrupted. "Your past questionable antics aside, I am certain our guests are anxious to know why we have asked to meet, and Brother Zebedee has many other duties to attend to, so if we may..."

"Yeah, sure, junior. Don't go getting your cassock all twisted. Go ahead, Zeb, and get on with your business. I'll watch my P's and Q's, don't mind me none."

"I never do, Malachi," Zebedee quipped through just a hint of a smirk. "But as Brother Martin has said, Molon, we do have serious matters to discuss."

Molon's whiskers twitched. Here it was.

"Brother Zebedee," Molon began before the monk could pose any uncomfortable questions about John or his late wife's research. "Please don't think for a moment I'm ungrateful for your intervention on our behalf, but let me be direct. Brother Martin informed us we've been followed since we left Tede. Your order relocated off Tede months ago, yet here I sit with the High Abbot of the Brothers of the Lion. That makes me more than a little curious what it is about *Star Wolf* that warrants such attention."

Brother Martin tensed, but Brother Zebedee remained undaunted by Molon's bluntness. Giving Molon a kindly look, he folded his hands and leaned slightly forward over the table.

"Yes, friend Molon, as you rightly guessed, you have become embroiled in a matter of great importance to the brotherhood and to Faithful everywhere. I actually arrived on Tede some time ago, just before agents of Dawnstar abducted John and Elena Salzmann. I had wanted to meet with her in hopes of succeeding where others had failed in persuading her to lend her efforts to our cause. I believe Brother Martin spoke to you on Tede about our interest in Elena's research?"

"Yes," John sat forward in his chair, interjecting before Molon could respond. "And Elena told the Brothers who visited us before; she had no interest in her research being used as a platform for committing genocide."

Molon saw the slightest flash of annoyance snap into Brother Zebedee's soft, brown eyes, but he maintained remarkable composure. His calm tone continued as he turned toward John.

"If you say so, John. I hope you don't think it too forward if I call you John. Titles can be so divisive."

"You can call me whatever you want, but it's not going to change the answer. The point is moot. Elena is dead, and her research died with her."

Molon knew that had to sting John to say, especially since the entire reason they were in this system to begin with was chasing the source of a ghost recording on the chance Elena might somehow still be alive. Unfortunately, lying was not John's strong suit, and his lack of conviction in that statement permeated the room.

A slight huff from Brother Martin belied his suspicion that John was not being truthful. Smythe was more subtle, with just a twitch of his mouth indicating he was weighing John's words heavily. Zebedee's visage, however, unwaveringly pleasant, was unperturbed by John's statement that their efforts to gain possession of Elena's research were in vain.

"Please understand, John," Zebedee continued, "objection to genocide was not the reason for her refusal."

"What are you talking about?" John replied, puzzled at what Brother Zebedee might be insinuating.

"Only that your wife was a woman of complex convictions. Elena did not fully understand the gravity of the situation. You two were Faithful, yes?"

"We were, and I still am," John answered.

"Then you know the demons have been a plague on humanity since the fall of Adam."

"Every Faithful knows that."

"Well, as is so often the case, the demons have once again become the agents of their own downfall."

"How's that, exactly?" John asked, raising an eyebrow.

"It's really quite simple, you see," Zebedee explained. "Lucifer sealed his fate and the fate of his entire rebellious faction when he enticed humanity to kill the Lion of Judah. His own hand delivered the eventual stroke that marked his destruction. And now, again, when the demons developed the malmorphsy bioweapon, they gave us the means to destroy them."

"I think you got your facts flipped, Brother Zebedee," Molon interrupted. "The mutavirus was genetically designed to affect everyone *but* Daemi, with the Angelicum apparently still being close enough genetically to also remain unaffected."

"Exactly!" Zebedee's eyes lit with excitement. "Which means it was capable of recognizing Daemi genetics, don't you see? Elena Salzmann's research can help us redesign and repurpose a mutavirus specifically targeting the demons rather than ignoring them. This would end them once and for all, freeing humankind to reunite and expand our border coreward among the stars until the Lion returns. Surely you see this, don't you?"

"What I see is this," Molon replied, fighting to keep his lip from curling in disgust at how casually Zebedee was proposing genocide on a galactic scale. "The Daemi are sentient beings, just like the rest of us."

"Yes, but—" Brother Martin interjected before Molon cut him off.

"Hold your tongue," Molon growled, baring his teeth at the younger monk. "I ain't done talking yet."

Brother Martin paled and remained silent.

"As I was saying," Molon continued. "I believe the Daemi are the demons of your Scriptures. I also believe the Angelicum are the angels the ancient humans wrote about, but we know now neither are supernatural spiritual beings. They are sophonts as much as any of the major races, Lubanians, Fei, Dractauri, Doppelgangers, Prophane, as well as the thousands of other minor, non-voidspace-capable sophont races we have encountered on other worlds. If you create a weapon that biologically targets a specific race, you have become no better than those you seek to destroy."

"And why stop there?" Voide added, aggression rising in her tone. "When you are done destroying every man, woman, and child of the Daemi, what's to stop you from tweaking your bloody new toy again for use on, say, Prophane, or Lubanians, or anyone else you view as a threat?"

"Please calm down," Brother Martin said, breaking his silence and trying to defuse the rising discord in the room. "Brother Zebedee has done nothing to earn your ire, so I would ask that you treat the High Abbot with the respect his station deserves."

"So much for setting aside titles," Voide quipped.

Brother Zebedee shot Brother Martin a warning glance. The older cleric clearly felt he had matters well in hand without help from his junior. Captain Smythe was rocking back in his chair wearing a face-splitting grin and obviously using every ounce of willpower within himself to keep from laughing aloud.

"I meant what I said about titles," Zebedee continued, "and Brother Martin has spoken out of turn. This is a deep and troubling topic. It is perfectly understandable that emotions would run high. Yet let me assure you, we are only here to discuss possibilities. I had hoped simply to persuade, not coerce."

"Well you persuade in vain," John answered. "I have already told you, Elena is gone, and her research was destroyed. You missed your chance at justifying your genocide."

"Not to mention," Molon added, "doesn't the book of Jude say that not even the Arch Angelicum Michael dared to bring so much as an abusive condemnation against the leader of the Daemi? If Michael wasn't even willing to use harsh language, what makes you think the Creator would endorse you making a genocidal mutavirus? If God wanted them gone, it seems to me the Lion could remove them without your help."

This drew shocked stares from John and both the monks. A genuine, surprised laugh came from Brother Zebedee as he emulated Captain Smythe's earlier table slap, albeit with much less vigor.

"Well, Lion be praised," Zebedee said, still grinning. "You know your Scriptures, Molon. Are you one of the Faithful as well?"

"I'm not sure what I am," Molon answered, with a shake of his head. "But I was raised by humans. Both my adoptive parents were devout Faithful, so yes, I know the stories."

"Ah," Zebedee replied with a sagely nod. "Knowledge is one thing, but faith is another matter altogether, eh?"

"Yeah," Molon half-muttered. "Something like that."

"Fair enough," Zebedee answered. "No-one comes to faith who isn't led. Perhaps it is just not your time yet, friend. Nevertheless, to answer your question, the Creator's restrictions on angels have no bearing on the Lion's instructions for us."

"Is that so?" Molon answered, trying to hold back his skepticism.

"Why, yes," Zebedee shifted in his seat.

Molon couldn't tell if the elderly monk was ill at ease with the line of reasoning or just trying to find a comfortable position in gravity heavier than he was accustomed to.

"Molon," Zebedee continued. "If you know the stories, then you are aware that God often uses men as instruments for His will. He could have given Noah a boat, but He instead gave him instructions to build one. He could have created the tabernacle for Moses, but in lieu of that, He permitted a situation where they had the materials, and gave them the instructions on how to make it. He could have sent angels to spread the gospel to all of Earth, but He instead chose human apostles to do it. Is it beyond reason for Him to give men the means to destroy our ancient enemy?"

"So, just a minute" Voide interjected, raising an eyebrow in that way Molon knew she used when interrogating a prisoner and fishing for a confession. "You're saying the Creator told you to eradicate the Daemi?"

Zebedee shook his head, spreading his hands open before him.

"Sadly, child, no. Man has not heard the clear, audible voice of the Creator for ages, at least as far as I am aware. The book of Hebrews tells us He spoke in many times and various ways in the past, but in the last days, He has spoken through His Son, the Lion. We have the words of the Lion in the Scriptures and the leading of the Holy Spirit in our hearts. They, and our faith, must guide us while we await His return."

"God would *not* have us completely destroy another race!" John snapped, fervent conviction flooding his voice. "That is *not* His way. Whatever spirit is leading you to that conclusion, you can be sure it is not the Holy Spirit!"

Molon sat back in wonder. John was energized in a way that reminded him of the fiery preachers his adoptive father had taken him to hear as a youth. He had no idea what he himself might need to overcome his own hurdles to unwavering belief, but when he witnessed genuine Faithful speaking, filled with the passion of their convictions, Molon could not help but envy their faith.

"That is the way of the radicals who nearly destroyed Earth before we even reached the stars," John continued, his voice rising in impassioned crescendo. "That is the sentiment that fueled the split of the Empire of Humaniti after the Shattering. It is why Dawnstar, the Provisional Imperium, GalSec, the Brothers of the Lion, and who knows who else, would destroy each other, and us, just to be the first to twist Elena's attempts at finding a cure for malmorphsy into an instrument of destruction."

"Is that what Dawnstar wanted with you?" Brother Martin asked, sliding to the edge of his seat.

"I have no idea what Dawnstar wanted with us," John replied, sounding less sure of himself than he had just moments before. "All they asked us about was the location of the Brothers' base on Tede. Yet, given they were funding Elena's research before the Shattering, and then we get kidnapped and wind up in a Dawnstar detention facility, it stands to reason."

"So you see," Zebedee added, "Tubal and Dawnstar were persecutors of the Faithful long before the Shattering, and now even our enemies see the potential for this research."

"Wrong there, Brother Zebedee," Molon said, shaking his head. "Both the Daemi and Dawnstar are allies of the Provisional Imperium. If they are looking for Elena's research, either they want it for use against someone other than the Daemi, or maybe Zarsus and the Imperium want a little insurance policy in case their Daemi allies decide to show their true colors."

"All the more reason," Zebedee replied, "to keep John out of the hands of the Imperium and quickly move toward destroying the demons forever."

"That is *not* His way!" John insisted.

"Is it not?" Brother Zebedee replied. His soft expression sharpened a bit. "Surely you remember God repeatedly commanded his people to wipe out the inhabitants of Canaan. Certainly, if the situation calls for it, it can be within the realm of His way."

John exploded to his feet. The move was so sudden and unexpected that both Molon and Voide half jumped up as well, expecting violence soon to follow. Even Smythe stopped smiling and reached for where his sidearm would be were he not in dress uniform.

"You call yourself a High Abbot?" John accused, wagging a finger at the high abbot. "How dare you pervert God's word that way? As a teacher, you know those were specific commands at a specific time, situationally given as a preemptive strike against those who would threaten the Creator's plan to bring the Lion into the world. Once the Lion arrived, His commands were to love our enemies, and to return good for evil. Unless you have personally heard God command it, which you have already admitted is not the case, then it is the ultimate in hubris to presume that destroying every man, woman, and child of our enemies is somehow His will."

Zebedee shook his head and gestured for John to take a seat. His face offered no sign of matching John's tension. However, Brother Martin and Captain Smythe did not look nearly as eager to resume civil discussion.

"Calm yourself, friend John," Zebedee urged. "I was not advocating this line of reasoning as the definitive factor in our decision to pursue this course. I was merely reminding you that, under certain circumstances, it is not outside the breadth of God's will. Knocking over tables and striking with a whip of cords was within the realm of possibilities, even for the Lion of Judah."

John did not look mollified in the least. Molon laid a calming hand on John's arm and silently urged him back into his seat.

"Scriptural interpretations aside," Molon said, "there is a greater question."

"That question being...?" Zebedee prompted.

"If we believe the history," Molon explained, "the Daemi and Angelicum were one race before Lucifer led his rebellion, right?"

"That is correct," Zebedee affirmed.

"In fact they were genetically similar enough so that the original malmorphsy bioweapon ignored Angelicum as well as Daemi."

"Correct again, captain."

"So then, what's to say a weapon designed to destroy the Daemi could not also be turned against the Faithful and used to wipe out your Angelicum allies? If their version of the mutavirus couldn't tell the difference, the one you are proposing might not be able to either. I daresay explaining that to the Creator on Judgment Day might prove problematic."

Zebedee's face saddened.

"That, friend Molon, is the greatest area of concern in pursuing this course. While we know from our angel ambassadors that the demons have changed much throughout the millennia, it would be difficult to say if such a weapon could be designed with the ability to discern between demon and angel."

"Then the responsible thing to do," Molon replied, "would be to ask the Angelicum ambassadors. Are they, or Enoch, or the leadership of the Theocracy, even aware you are contemplating this?"

Smythe cleared his throat and broke his silence.

"Enoch is a good man, but he is weak."

"The leader of the Theocracy is weak?" John asked, clearly still perturbed over this whole discussion.

"Yes, weak. Now before you clench up and get your skivvies in a bunch, understand that I've known Enoch since he was little enough to bounce on his daddy's knee. I served as an Imperial Navy officer under his father in the Old Empire pushing the edges of our border into the Hinterlands, and I served for a while under Enoch and the Theocracy after the Shattering. Nonetheless, that jelly-legged lad just won't do what it takes to win."

"Like genocide," snapped Voide.

Molon saw she was no more calm about this line of reasoning than John was. Likely she was stewing over how a genetically targeted mutavirus could be just as easily turned on the Prophane next. Bioweapons don't give special treatment to friendlies.

"Yes, by Hades," Smythe furrowed his brow and locked his gaze onto Voide. "If that is what's necessary. Enoch's unwillingness to make the hard calls is what drove me to set *Hornet's Nest* to aiding the Brothers of the Lion. Zeb may appear a kindly old fart, but deep down he knows what needs to be done and has the steel to do it."

"So in other words," Molon said, his voice dropping dangerously close to a growl, "the Angelicum and the Theocracy have no idea that the Brothers of the Lion are contemplating walking in the footsteps of the Daemi by creating a bioweapon that could inadvertently wipe out the Angelicum Host as well. Is that right?"

"No!" John pounded his fist on the table before either

223

Zebedee or Smythe could confirm Molon's assessment. "Humaniti, the Lubanians, and the Angelicum worked together two centuries ago to destroy every bit of the Daemi bioweapon that created the malmorphsy mutations as well as the plans and facilities to reproduce it. Operation Purge cost hundreds of thousands of lives and incalculable funds to plan and execute. I'll not hand over Elena's research, meant for curing people, to misguided terrorists intent on undoing everything those brave sophonts died to accomplish."

Like a used-starship dealer who just sold a junker to a group of tourists, a slimy smile crept onto Brother Martin's face. Even Brother Zebedee folded his hands and sat back in his chair.

"So," Brother Martin's words oozed out of his sly grin, "you admit her research is still available to be handed over, or not, as you see fit?"

John's jaw dropped, and Molon tensed his grip on the arms of his chair. Had that wily old abbot taken the conversation down this road in order to coax John into a slip? Molon suspected this was the case. That doddering grandfather routine was a smoke screen for the shrewd dealer resting within.

"Hot dog, he got you there, boy," Smythe said, slapping the table again. Molon was starting to find that habit a bit grating. "I tell you, don't ever play chess with old Zeb. Slicker than whale crap, that one is!"

Had it wind behind it, the look of genuine annoyance Zebedee shot at Smythe would have knocked him out of his chair. This was the first evident divide Molon had seen in the pair's jocular partnership.

"Enough, Malachi!" Zebedee chastened the captain.

Then, as if flipping a switch, Zebedee turned on a gentle face once again as he addressed John.

"I assure you, despite Malachi's exuberance, there was no intentional manipulation here. However, let us not look at this revelation as a reason for dismay. The Lion would have us be honest with each other, so perhaps the Spirit within you would not tolerate living in a temple of dishonesty. He helped you bring out the truth of the matter, so we might all decide together on the best course."

"I think the best course," Molon said, taking command and relieving John from having to trip over himself backpedaling, "is that we agree to disagree. We appreciate you rescuing us from the PI cruiser. We are grateful for your medical care for our wounded and for your help repairing *Star Wolf*. However,

I think it is best that we be on our way. We wish you well, but John's mind is clear; he won't assist you in pursuing this course."

"That is most unfortunate," Zebedee answered, all semblance of cordiality dropping out of his voice. "We are already in mid-VS jump, so you couldn't rightly leave anyway at the moment. Aside from that, I am afraid you must remain our guests until you change your mind, or until the teams currently scouring *Star Wolf* locate where you have hidden Elena Salzmann's research."

Molon's tactical mind began to buzz. The Brothers had erred in removing Voide's restraints that kept her from phasing into voidspace. Apparently, either they did not guess at the true function of the restraints or they weren't familiar with what fighting a Prophane entailed. This gave Molon's side at least one advantage.

"So, we've gone from guests to prisoners then, have we?" Molon said, crouching slightly, ears forward, ready to spring into action if they had to fight their way out.

"Not at all, friend Molon," Zebedee continued, maintaining his calm demeanor. The abbot nodded toward Smythe who began tapping commands into his wrist module. "But you know of our plans now, and we simply cannot be swayed from our course. We mean you no harm, unless you intend to forcibly resist."

Voide leapt out of her seat, dropped into a fighting stance, and bared her fangs.

"Forcibly resisting is my favorite sport!"

"I'd stand down if I were you, missy," Smythe snapped in a commanding tone only a man accustomed to unquestioned authority could manage. "Those nice marines who just joined us aren't armed with party favors. Besides, my engineering teams have already rigged your ship to blow if you disengage without my authorization codes. Oh, and don't worry none about *Hornet's Nest*. They're directional charges set to blow away from us. But you might like to remember that, besides the other two in CCB, the rest of your crew are still aboard *Star Wolf*. So you might want to think hard about your next move so this turns out best for all concerned."

Smythe was a shrewd commander. Molon mentally bit himself for getting lulled into thinking this encounter was a friendly one. They were arguably better off than on *Revenge*, but a prison was still a prison no matter the gilding on the bars.

A small, armed squad of Smythe's marines, accompanied by Brother Martin, escorted them back to sickbay. Marines stood post outside the sickbay and the outer doors of the adjoining CCB. Fortunately, the doors to the room holding Mel and Bobby Lee were left unlocked and unguarded. This gave John access to tend to their wounded crewmates.

"Make yourselves comfortable," Brother Martin said with just a hint of condescension. "Marines will be stationed outside these doors and the outer doors to the CCB. You can use the call signals on your beds to alert Sister Agnes or one of the nurses if you need anything, but any aggressive action will carry severe repercussions."

"You're a real peach, Martin," Molon snapped.

"Brother Martin," the monk corrected as he turned and walked out the door, having the marines secure it behind him.

"You ain't my brother," Molon said to Martin's back. The monk gave no indication he had heard the comment.

"Well I'll give them one thing," Voide said, her smile dripping distaste as she jostled Molon with her shoulder. "These are about the politest people who have ever locked us up."

"There is that," Molon answered, not overly in the mood for joking.

John flopped down on his bunk, face down, burying his head in his pillow. Molon reflected that the doctor had not looked this discouraged even when he pulled him out of that Dawnstar detention facility. He knew John's faith was important to him, so for fellow Faithful to be their captors must be a devastating blow for him.

Part of him wanted to comfort and encourage John, to stoke the passionate fire he had seen this man exhibit during their discussion with Zebedee. However, if Molon understood anything about the Faithful, he knew that their true strength and capacity for resilience had to come from the Spirit within them.

Besides, he could not worry about John's emotional well-being right now. Molon was *Star Wolf*'s captain. His responsibility was to bend his mind toward figuring a way to get them all safely off this suddenly-not-so-friendly vessel.

Seventeen – Breakout

Molon pondered all the possible angles of getting himself, John, and Voide, as well as their two injured crewmen in the CCB, out past the guards and back on board *Star Wolf*. It was a multi-faceted challenge.

First there was the fact that he had no idea how to find where the docking bay was that led to *Star Wolf*. Then there was the matter of finding and disarming the charges Smythe's men had set, and all before their absence was noted. That accomplished, they would have to somehow disengage mid-VS jump, cold-start *Star Wolf*'s VS drive, hope to get their bearings, and find an exit from voidspace that didn't land them somewhere the other side of the Stygian Rift. Child's play, right?

Voide had been scanning the room, peeking through the glass in the door, and generally taking account of their current security situation. She could move through voidspace, but doing so blindly could be ugly, and dangerous. Normally she only moved within line of sight, and who knew if *Star Wolf* was close enough to reach, even if she knew the direction to jump.

Her curiosity apparently satisfied for the moment, she moved to the bed where John was still laying with his head engulfed in his pillow. Voide gave the bottom of the bunk a hard kick. While the bed's legs were mag-locked to the deck, the force of the blow underneath his bunk, plus John's own jolt at the unexpected disturbance, sent him flailing off the opposite side of the bed onto the floor.

"What is wrong with you?" he screamed at Voide.

"Get up, Nancy-boy. Crying time is over. We need to break out of this place, so you need to assess the operational mobility of Mel and Cowboy next door. While you're at it, see if those medicos left anything useful in the CCB that we can use to knock out a marine or two. I mean, snapping necks works just fine for me, but Molon tends to get antsy about rising body counts, especially when our jailors have been so polite."

Molon had never fought so hard in his life to keep from

laughing. A mother hen Voide was not. She was, however, correct. They couldn't leave without Mel and Cowboy, so John needed to get in the game.

"You have real issues, lady!" John muttered, picking himself up off the floor and stomping toward the CCB in a huff.

"Too rough?" Voide asked, flashing Molon a smile.

"Aren't you always? Give him a break. He's a civilian, and between Elena and this group of renegade Faithful, he's had a pretty rough time."

"What don't kill us makes us stronger," Voide said.

"Or makes us wish we were dead," Molon replied. "I've turned this every which way, Voide, and I just don't see a way to navigate all the variables and get away clean."

"Eh," Voide shrugged. "Assuming Smythe pulled everyone from the brig, we've got forty-two reasonably healthy crew somewhere on this tub, and two next door that hopefully John can get fit enough to move and maybe hold a weapon. What's the crew compliment on a *Hive*-class carrier?"

"Standard configuration?" Molon said, shaking his head. "Sixty-two crew plus pilots. But we already know *Hornet's Nest* ain't standard."

"They popped fifty fighters in a rapid deploy," Voide replied. "As far as I know we were hit by the neural cannon before *Revenge*'s fighters could engage, so figure at least fifty flyers not counting any reserves, and flyboys always have reserves."

"Well," Molon pulled thoughtfully at the fur on his chin. "You said they didn't use a battle carrier. That means an internal voidspace drive. That VS drive will take up some crew space, and with the wide corridors and that spacious conference room, he has to have given up twenty-percent standard crew complement at least in this refit. So even with ten percent reserve flyers, at fifty crew and say fifty-five flyboys, we're over two to one against."

"Null sweat, boss," Voide laughed. "I'll cover my two, Doc's two, and one of yours, easy."

"I admire your optimism, but unarmed, John basically a non-combatant, two wounded to carry, and the rest of our crew inside *Star Wolf*, which from here is Lion only knows which direction, I hope you have a better plan than the two of us chewing our way out one throat at a time."

John stomped back in, arms crossed. His cloud of despondency had been replaced by a firmly set scowl of annoyance focused on Voide.

"See," Voide whispered to Molon. "I helped. He's gone

from whiny and useless to ticked-off and motivated."

Molon bit back a laugh.

"So what's the medical sit-rep, Doc?"

"Mel and Bobby Lee are mobile. Their wounds are closed and the radiation treatment has flushed their systems. They can move, slowly, but they aren't in any condition to run an obstacle course anytime soon."

"Blast it!" Voide exclaimed. "Cowboy is a good merc. We could have used his help."

Molon mentally echoed her concern. Recalling his conversation about Mel's potential mental frailty and John's general unfamiliarity with anything combat related, they would need every able body they could muster.

"Sorry to ruin your plans for a violent rampage, Lieutenant Commander Psycho," John snapped, apparently still ruffled from Voide's earlier rough handling, "but you will have to figure out another way for the five of us to take over *Hornet's Nest.*"

Molon shook his head. These two were going to take a long time to learn to play well together.

"Did you find anything in the CCB we might use to quietly put the guards out?" Molon asked.

John's face grew more despondent as he shook his head.

"There are anti-radiation meds, some painkillers, and a few vials of antibiotics. It looks like they already pulled out anything potentially dangerous. I might be able to mix an injectable cocktail of pain meds, but they would take a minute or so to kick in, and that might not do much more than give a full-grown marine a buzz. Regardless, there are four guards, and I maybe have enough to make up two doses, even if we had the syringes to deliver them."

"You have a long-winded way to say, 'no'," Voide quipped.

John frowned at her and started to respond, but she cut him off.

"No matter. I can bust through the door, snap the first guard's neck, then use him as a body-shield while I take out the others with his rifle. Then we find a terminal, hack in, find the closest route to *Star Wolf*, and get out of here. We will have four rifles off the guards, plus sidearms. Cowboy may be injured, but he can still point and shoot. Surely powder-puff can handle a pistol at least, and Doc Useless here can play body shield."

"Or here's a thought," John snapped. "According to the medical journals, Prophane can voidspace jump without a ship. Why don't you just jump back to *Star Wolf* and bring help?"

Voide scowled.

"Weren't you paying attention, pale? Unless the monks were lying, we are already in voidspace. I could phase back to normal space, but that would be suicide."

"Sounds like a plan. Why don't you give that a shot," John growled.

"Okay, you two, knock it off," Molon said as he pulled his chin whiskers and scrambled desperately to formulate a plan. "I admit, I had a similar thought to John's."

"About me killing myself?" Voide teased.

"You know what I meant. I hadn't thought about us already being in voidspace. That's probably why they removed those bracers inhibiting your jump ability. They knew you wouldn't be able to use it anyway."

Something tugged at Molon's mind. Maybe their captors weren't so careless when they removed Voide's restraints. Perhaps they were counting on Voide trying a teleport as a way to take her out of the picture and keep their hands clean. Molon hoped he was reading too much into it, but Smythe and Zebedee were crafty and clearly not to be underestimated.

"Sorry, Molon," Voide replied. "I can't sidestep physics."

"It's not your fault," Molon said. "Zebedee might appear a doddering fool, but he hasn't done anything since we got here that wasn't sunk in three layers of calculation. So, either he lied or he figures that if you call him on it, it'll give him one less enemy to worry about."

"I doubt it is as sinister as all that," John replied, clearly bothered by Molon ascribing such devious motives to the High Abbot. "Faithful have gathered in the Theocracy, on the spinward edge of Humaniti space and have little experience with Prophane. He might have just been honest, not trying to trick Voide into killing herself. In fact, Voide, I'm sorry for even joking about that."

"Oh, that was supposed to be a joke?" Voide quipped. "Give me a warning next time. I'll queue up a laugh."

Molon sighed. If John stayed on *Star Wolf*, it was clear Molon's job description would include keeping his security chief and ship's doctor from killing each other. John was naive to be so quick to trust the Brothers, who thus far had proven extremely untrustworthy.

"Even giving Zebedee the benefit of the doubt," Molon reasoned, "Smythe served under Emperor Halberan, and an experienced carrier captain like that could easily have spent time fighting Prophane. He had to know what the VS inhibitors were, and removing them at least leaves the option open for her to attempt a jump."

"You might be right, captain," Voide said, her face tightening into a disappointed scowl. "I doubt the monks could have figured out how to disengage those Imp VS inhibitors anyway. Had to be Smythe's men. GalSec was playing with prototypes years ago. I guess they got a working model. At least we know what they look like for next time."

"I wish we still had them," Molon said, shaking his head. "I'd love Dub to give them a good once over. Your ability to teleport has gotten us out of more than a few messes. If there is tech that can take away that ace in the hole, I'd sure feel better knowing how it works and how to break it."

"Fancy bracelets or not," Voide replied, "it looks like we are back to the brute force method for busting out of here."

"I hate to burst your bubble when you are so looking forward to rampage," John replied, "but your idea of smashing down the doors won't work."

"Oh, yeah?" Voide said, squaring off with John as though he had just challenged her to a fight. Hands at her sides, balled into fists, she leaned in closer to his face. "Why not?"

"Because," John said with a smug smirk showing he was not intimidated as he leaned back into Voide almost touching nose to nose. "Sickbay doors on most ships are sealed with hardened screens built into the walls and doors. It prevents viruses and radiation from escaping in quarantine situations."

"John is right," Molon added. "Even our dinky little sickbay on *Star Wolf* is fitted with hardened quarantine screens."

"It looks like we aren't going anywher," John said, renewing a scowl at Voide. "So, can I safely lie down on my bunk again, or should I expect another friendly-fire ambush?"

"Oh, stop whining," Voide snapped. "For dreck's sake, you cut apart bodies and put them back together again but a little horseplay puts you in a dither? I thought hermit-worlders were supposed to be tough, pioneer types. You're more like a pampered core-worlder."

"That's enough, you two," Molon snapped. "It looks like we aren't breaking out of here forcibly, so we had best put our energy on figuring out plan B."

"I thought smashing down the doors was plan B," John said.

"Well, plan C then," Molon answered.

A loud thud sounded from outside the sickbay doors. Voide covered the distance in the blink of an eye and peered through the small square windows. The guards outside sickbay as well as the two next door outside the CCB were on the ground, clutching their heads and writhing. Whatever was assailing them lasted less than a minute before all four were still.

"What is it?" Molon asked.

"No idea, but our chaperones just took a nap," Voide answered.

"What?" Molon and John replied in unison.

Any further discussion was circumvented as the locks disengaged on the sickbay doors. Voide jumped back, dropping into a fighting crouch, prepared for whatever new threat was upon them. The doors flung open and in walked Dub. The twisted grin on Dub's mutated visage was a welcome sight.

"Hiya, Cap, Voide, Doc. You ready to check out of this place, or you sticking around for dinner? I hear they might have pudding."

"Dub?" Molon said, scrunching his muzzle up as he puzzled over his chief engineer's unexpected appearance. "How did you—"

"No time to explain, Cap. There is supposed to be a critical-care-bay around here somewhere where they are holding Mel and Cowboy."

"That's right next door," John interjected.

"Well let's grab them and go. We got a lot that needs doing before we can separate from *Hornet's Nest*, and I have no idea how long these wags will be out."

John opened the door to the CCB and called to their crewmates.

"Mel, are you okay to get up?"

"I'm fine, John," Mel replied. "Are we leaving?"

"Apparently, and in a hurry. Bobby Lee, what about you?"

"Right as rain, Doc," Cowboy answered, almost leaping to his feet. "Let's roll."

John came back into the sickbay with one arm around Mel for extra support. Cowboy was in tow and other than being slightly pale, he seemed fit enough.

"Listen up," Molon ordered. "Everyone follow Dub, and stick close. Cowboy, Voide, and Dub, grab those combat rifles off the guards. I'll take the last one. Hand Mel and Doc two of their laser pistols. Stay sharp, and only fire if there is no other choice. I'd just as soon leave peacefully if we can."

"Should be a clear path back to *Star Wolf*, captain," Dub answered. "After that, it gets a bit sketchy."

Eighteen – Cast Off

Molon and company followed Dub through several twists and turns as they navigated *Hornet's Nest* between sickbay and the main docking port. They passed various members of the pocket carrier's crew in a condition similar to that of the guards outside sickbay. Lying strewn about the corridors, many of their hands still clutched their unconscious heads.

As Dub led them to a T intersection, he pulled up short and shouted around the corner.

"Chief Dubronski, incoming. I've got the captain and our missing crewmen in tow. Hold your fire."

Dub lowered his rifle and advanced around the corner. As Molon entered the intersecting corridor, he saw four of *Star Wolf's* security officers posted at an airlock a few meters down the passage. The ranking non-com was Master Gunnery Sergeant "Handsome" Hank Tibbs.

"Master Guns," Molon called out with a wolfish grin. "Your pretty face is a sight for sore eyes."

Tibbs smiled as he snapped a salute to his captain, which Molon promptly returned.

"They must've scrambled your brains good if this face is a pleasant sight," Tibbs replied. "Glad to have you back, Captain."

"Good to be back, but we aren't out of the woods yet. Hold your position here. We'll cast off as soon as possible."

"Aye, sir," Tibbs answered and nodded to his men to clear a path through the airlock before resuming their ready alert positions.

Beyond the airlock, a mobile, configurable corridor snaked around into a U curve. Once they wound their way around the tubing and entered *Star Wolf's* port side airlock they quickly made their way through the half-empty barracks amid welcoming greetings from some of the marines housed there.

"Captain?" said Bobby Lee once they had entered the barracks.

"Yeah, Cowboy, what is it?"

233

"If you don't mind, sir, I'll rejoin my unit. I'm feeling better and am anxious to get back to work."

Molon looked to Voide who was in charge of the security forces.

"If Doc says you are cleared, it is fine with me," she responded.

"He should be okay," John answered. "I'd stay away from anything too strenuous until that shoulder fully heals, but you should be fine for light duty. Whatever else happened aboard *Hornet's Nest*, you guys got top of the line radiation treatment."

Cowboy headed for his bunk while the rest made their way toward the bridge. Upon entering, Molon noted Twitch had the bridge crew scrambling with pre-launch prep and systems checks. No need for worry or second guesses with Twitch in charge. You could guarantee that everything was by the book under her watchful eye.

"Molon," Mel said, "do you want me to take my post at the comms station? I too am feeling much better."

"No, Mel," Molon answered. "I want you with us for the briefing. As one of the senior officers, you will need to be part of whatever decisions there are going forward. Twitch," he called out to his executive officer, who was currently occupying the captain's chair.

"Aye sir?"

"You join us too. Everyone knows their jobs well enough to keep working for a bit. We've got a lot to cover and no idea how much time we have to cover it."

Twitch nodded and fell in behind Molon, Dub, John, Voide, and Mel as they entered the briefing room aft of the bridge.

Molon decided to forego the usual security sweep of the conference room in the interest of time. The others each took their seats, including the one oversized chair custom made to accommodate Dub's large frame.

"All right, Dub, Twitch," Molon said, "bring us up to speed."

Dub nodded in deference to Twitch's higher rank.

"No, Dub, you had the most contact with *Hornet's Nest*'s engineers. You also devised and executed the rescue of the captain. By all means please lead the briefing."

"Right," Dub began. "*Hornet's Nest*'s is one heck of a custom mod. She's got stacked launch bays designed for rapid deployment launches. No Humaniti ship on the books has anything close to that configuration. It's a brilliant idea actually. She also has a prototype VS drive that takes up about half the space of the standard Humaniti-made drives. I only caught a glimpse of the specs, but brother I'd love to see that thing in person."

"Smythe mentioned serving along the Hinterlands border. Maybe he made contact with a race we haven't seen yet that helped reconfigure the ship."

"Not reconfigure, mimic," Dub replied.

"Mimic?"

"Yeah. This ship looks on the outside like a *Hive*-class pocket carrier. Detail is spot on. But one glance at the inside and you'll know she isn't at all like any Humaniti ship design on the books. On top of everything else, she's a pocket carrier with a spinal mount neural weapon."

"Yeah," Molon agreed. "I was wondering about that. I've never heard of a spinal mount on a carrier."

"That's because according to everything I know about ship design and configuration, which is quite considerable, it should be impossible," Dub said, rubbing a mechanized glove-hand across his bald pate.

"Unusual, I get," Molon replied, "but smaller ships like destroyers and man-o-wars can have spinal mounts."

"But they don't need the space to store dozens of fighters and the power to prep, fuel, and maintain them. Even if one solves the space issue, which they have, it is the power draw that makes it impossible."

"How so," Molon asked, knowing they needed to get to the matter at hand but equally fascinated by how Smythe might have gotten ahold of such amazing technology.

"Most carriers have enough hangars to launch about twenty percent of their birds at once. That's why rapid deployments are so dangerous. Trying to launch five fighters one after another just amplifies exponentially the potential for something going wrong. *Hornet's Nest* doesn't do that. They have fifty separate launch hangars stacked all along the outer hull. They aren't using mechanical catapults either. This thing is rigged with some kind of gauss launchers in every bay. No moving parts to foul up, but a power draw that defies anything I can figure. I'm telling you, captain, I have no idea where this tech or design came from, but in all my years I've never seen anything like this."

"Look," Voide interjected, "can we stop drooling over their hardware and get onto the part where we get away without blowing ourselves up or ripping a hole in voidspace?"

"Patience, Miss Congeniality, I'm getting there," Dub

answered with what passed for a smile on his disfigured face. "When we were patching up *Star Wolf*'s systems and crew, I noticed they had rigged our hull with strange packages near the docking clamps. They tried to be sneaky about it, but I have sensors even Voide doesn't know about. Nothing happens on any ship I maintain without me knowing about it."

"We appreciate your diligence, Dub," Molon answered. "I'm guessing those were the explosives Smythe mentioned he had installed?"

"Yep. Directional plasmatic charges. If those docking clamps disengage without disarming them, they'll perforate *Star Wolf* like a flechette rifle through a paper doll."

"I take it you have a plan to make that not happen?" Molon quipped. Dub adopted an indignant look.

"What do you take me for, Cap, some half-wit dock hand?"

"Of course not, Dub."

"Well, it's a good thing that's exactly what those *Hornet's Nest* engineers took me for. Duh, big dumb malmorph help smart guys fix pretty ship," Dub said, mocking a slow-witted slur with that last line.

Molon laughed and John looked confused as Molon explained the comment to the puzzled doctor.

"Most people have little experience interacting with malmorphs. They assume physical deformities also mean mental impairment. This is not the first time Dub has played dumb to trick hostiles into underestimating him."

"Yep, well while they weren't looking I set my army of micro-drones to find and disarm the charges. The charges are inert now, with our would-be saboteurs none the wiser. I had my drones wire up fake signal emitters, so as far as *Hornet's Nest* knows, everything is still set to blow."

Molon was truly blessed to have found an engineer of Dub's talent looking for a billet. His malmorphsy kept most captains from considering him, but Molon had learned long ago not to judge by appearances.

"Solid work, chief," Molon said, lighting up in a grateful smile at Dub.

"Thanks, Cap," Dub answered. "That little trick put the ship out of immediate danger, but didn't put us back in possession of a captain, security chief, comms officer, or doctor. I hacked into their ship's systems to find where you were being held, which is when I found *Hornet's Nest*'s nifty blueprints. Unfortunately, the power specs were locked down tighter than a bull's butt during fly season, but the info on your location wasn't classified."

"So you found us," Molon said, "but how in the galaxy did you take out the *Hornet's Nest* crew without affecting us?"

"Ah, the wonders of modern engineering," Dub replied. "Capital ship sickbays are equipped with hardened screening in the walls for quarantine purposes."

"See, I told you," John interjected, a smug smile on his face roughly aimed in Voide's direction.

"Hardened screens protect against neural weapons," Dub added.

Molon was still puzzled.

"Uh, last time I checked," Molon said, scratching his head and wondering where Dub was going with this. "*Star Wolf* isn't outfitted with neural weapons."

"*Star Wolf* isn't," Dub said, giving Molon a wide, mutant grin. "But *Hornet's Nest* is."

A lupine grin mirroring Dub's crept across Molon's snout as what Dub had done dawned on him.

"You turned their own weapons against them?" John asked.

"Yep," Dub said with a wink in John's direction. "I set up a feedback malfunction in their spinal mount which dumped a neural pulse field down the length of her. Not quite as effective as being hit by the actual weapon, but with no one aboard expecting an attack, it was effective enough."

"Fantastic!" John exhorted.

"Not bad for a critically deformed mutant, huh Doc?"

"You just earned a feature spot in that research paper, Dub!" John replied with a laugh.

"Great work, Dub," Molon said. "Now, we can detach *Star Wolf* from *Hornet's Nest* and be on our way."

"*No, you cannot, captain,*" came a voice across the loudspeaker in the conference room. "*Captain Smythe anticipated you might desire to leave early, so he put the strongest encryption at his disposal on the overrides for the docking clamps.*"

"What the...?" Voide interjected and grabbed her security scanner and began sweeping the room. Molon's superior Lubanian hearing already recognized the voice even with the transmission distortion.

"Brother Martin?" Molon answered the disembodied voice, mentally biting himself for foregoing the customary security sweep. "I thought you might be taking an afternoon nap with the rest of your shipmates."

"*Yes, quite a clever plan, that. It might have worked*

237

perfectly, but unfortunately for you I have a little secret of my own."

"You are a psionic," Mel stated, matter-of-factly.

"*Very perceptive. I'm guessing I am addressing the Fei officer from the CCB?*"

"It is obvious," Mel replied, ignoring Brother Martin's request for identification. "If Dub used a neural weapon against the crew, unless you were somehow shielded, you must have your own psionic defenses."

"I've found the bug, Molon," Voide interrupted before Brother Martin could respond. Her scanner flashed rapidly above the far end of the conference table. "Do you want me to destroy it?"

"*That would be unadvisable,*" Brother Martin answered. "*At least for the moment. While my tap-in to your ship's conference room comms system allows me to talk to you, I'm afraid if you disable the listening device we placed there then it will become a one-sided conversation.*"

"Leave it for now, Voide," Molon ordered. "So what do you want, Martin? We've not harmed your crew. We just want to leave peacefully."

"*Brother Martin, if you please, captain, and I believe you already know what we want. Turn over Dr. Elena Salzmann's research and we can discuss your peaceful departure.*"

"Nice try, dreckball," Voide snapped. "Zebedee and Smythe already said we aren't going anywhere now that we know your plans. The only reason we are still alive is you don't have your hands on what you are after yet. As soon as you do, Smythe will be quick to dispose of his inconvenient guests."

"Voide has a point," Molon added. "If you force my hand, I will fire up *Star Wolf*'s weapons systems and blast ourselves free, leaving large holes in the hull that stands between you and raw voidspace. So how about you release the docking clamps and let us go our separate ways?"

"*From our brief times together, captain, I am convinced you are a moral sophont. I sincerely doubt you would murder an entire ship's crew when we have treated you well and have not harmed a single one of your crewmen. We are not murderers, captain, and neither are you. I am afraid I must call your bluff.*"

Molon pounded a fist on the table. Whether or not he believed the Brothers of the Lion would not kill them, Brother Martin was right. Molon was bluffing. He would have to find another way.

"Voide, destroy that bug and have your security teams

sweep the ship for any others. Dub, secure all ships systems immediately and make sure we are cut off from any remote access coming from *Hornet's Nest*."

"Aye, sir" they said in unison.

Voide gleefully crushed the listening device and started tapping orders into her wrist comm unit. Dub's NID snaked its way to jack into the conference table console while his fingers furiously pounded away at the keyboard of the terminal.

"So, Molon," Twitch said with a compassionate look. "What now?"

"I have no idea, but if we don't do something soon, *Hornet's Nest*'s crew is going to wake up from nap time, and we are going to have more trouble than we know what to do with."

"Captain," John said, tentatively. "I have an idea, but I doubt you are going to like it."

"Right now, Doc, I'll take all the ideas I can get."

Nineteen – Clean Break

John recoiled. He had expected resistance, but found himself on the receiving end of far more than he had anticipated as Voide shouted at him across the conference table.

"Are you insane?"

"Probably, but still," John replied. "It makes perfect sense. I read up on Prophane physiology after our trip together on Tede. Besides their own bodies, Prophane can force a certain amount of matter to transition with them when they phase into voidspace. That's how your clothing, weapons, breathers, etc. go back and forth."

"You are an idiot," Voide grumbled. "I already told you, I phase to realspace and I'm lost in space, adrift forever, you stupid pale. Do you not get that, or are you trying to get me killed?"

"Just hear me out," John answered as the rest of the senior officers watched this verbal sparring match with silent interest. "According to the research, they have been attempting experiments with Pariahs forcing objects into voidspace without actually transitioning themselves. It's like a space flight where you check your luggage but you don't actually board the ship."

"You are deranged. We are not talking about booking a berth on a spacer, we are talking about a biological function that is like a reflex for me. I don't have that kind of precise control over it. It would be like me asking you to will your own heart to stop. Could you pull that off?"

John scratched his head wondering if she were being serious or just baiting him again.

"Possibly, I suppose, with enough incentive and practice. But even if I could not stop it completely, there are verifiable studies where humans have been able to slow down or speed up their heart rate purely by willing it. Others have been able to control other involuntary biological functions like body temperature and blood pressure. Besides, the studies say other

240

Pariahs have had some limited success in doing this. I can talk you through it."

Voide stood up, took a double-handed grip on the edge of the table, and leaned in John's direction as though she were seconds from pouncing on him.

"So you are going to employ your vast experience with personally phasing into and out of voidspace to talk me through it, huh?"

John ran his fingers through his hair as he and Voide stood locked in a mutual stare. John knew he had to keep his cool if he was going to get through to her. Without one of her more respected peers weighing in to break the stalemate, John knew he would never convince Voide to even give it a try.

"Voide may be right," Twitch added. "This is a heck of a gamble. Can't we just use tools to sever the connection with their airlock and break free?"

"It's not that simple," Dub answered. "Theoretically I could use a fusion torch to cut off the end of the docking cuff completely, but that would take a couple of hours. Those cuffs are built to withstand battle damage from ship weapons, radiation, and the vacuum of space while maintaining pressure. It would also mean whoever was doing the cutting would be exposed to raw voidspace as they completed the cut. Enviro-suits have never been tested in raw voidspace. No idea how they would hold up under extended exposure. Voide is the only one we know who might be able to do this work and survive."

"That sounds like a less insane option than what this idiot pale is proposing," Voide replied.

"Maybe not," Molon added. "Training you to use the fusion torch equipment is one thing, but we have no idea how long *Hornet's Nest*'s crew is going to be out. The last thing we need is having to somehow repel a boarding party while you are trying to cut us free. You'd be an open target out there."

"They'd be no more able to sustain raw voidspace than our crew would. Once I start cutting, that'd be my protection."

"Just because we wouldn't risk field testing vac-suits against raw voidspace doesn't mean they wouldn't. Besides, they could set up remote weaponry on their end, or just say forget the whole thing and use ship's weapons to blast *Star Wolf*. No, whatever we do needs to be quick and as safe as we can make it."

"That's why my plan is better," John said, seizing the moment. "I could talk her through this fairly quickly. We could break free, bring Voide back inside our airlock, and be off

241

before anyone besides Brother Martin wakes up."

Mel frowned and twitched nervously.

"There may be another problem," Mel said.

"Such as?" John asked.

"If Brother Martin is a psionic," said the blue-skinned Fei comms officer, "it is unlikely that his abilities are limited to defense. He may have a way to mentally attack anyone trying to sever the connection between the ships."

"Great," Molon grumbled. "We know the PI Marines had psi-shielded helmets, but it is doubtful we could board *Hornet's Nest* and raid their armor lockers for a psi-shielded helmet before they start waking up from their nap."

"I could do it," Mel replied.

John swallowed hard at the idea of Mel putting herself into further danger.

"Do what?" he asked.

"I could shield her. I would need to be close, and would have to have line of sight, but if I was inside the airlock while Voide was working outside, I believe I could keep her safe."

"Are your abilities stronger than Brother Martin's?" John asked.

"I have no idea how powerful a psionic Brother Martin is, but I am confident my abilities should be sufficient to at least buy Voide time to do her work."

"Thanks for the offer, powder-puff," Voide snapped. "But everyone seems to be forgetting this whole plan revolves around some hermit-world pale talking me through something I am not sure is even possible and that he has only read about. That kind of renders this plan useless, don't you think?"

John swallowed hard, remembering Molon's warning about pushing Voide too far, but the time had come to raise the bet or fold his hand. If they didn't break free, a lot more than John's life would be in danger.

"What's the matter, Voide? Are you afraid to try? Or is it the possibility I might be right that's really eating you?"

The other bridge officers drew a collective breath as Molon and Twitch tensed, presumably preparing to intercept Voide if she leapt to rip out John's throat. No rage-filled attack came from the security chief. Instead, a slow smile crept across her face, bearing her extended canines in a feral grin.

"You've got guts, pale," she said to John. "Heck of a gamble going the one place you knew would get my full and undivided attention. If you are that willing to risk your own life to talk me into this plan, I guess I've got nothing to lose giving it my best effort. If it fails, that'll save me the trouble of killing you. If it works, that'll either balance the books or I'll decide to kill you anyway. So, Doc. What do I need to do?"

*****

Voide adjusted her breathing mask and double-checked the security cable anchoring her to the frame of *Star Wolf*'s airlock. Dub had removed four access panels to expose the locked docking clamps attaching the ship to *Hornet's Nest*'s docking sleeve. Just beyond the airlock door, safely inside *Star Wolf*, were Mel and John. Voide spoke into the communicator built into her breathing mask.

"*Okay, pale, what now?*"

"*Voide,*" John's voice came back across the comms. "*You need to go to the first access panel, place your hands on the docking clamp, and close your eyes.*"

"*What?*" she snapped. "*Am I phasing or meditating? Can we cut the hocus-pocus and just tell me what I need to do?*"

"*Look,*" John said, his exasperation clear even through the comm system. "*You can argue with me every step of the way, in which case Hornet's Nest's crew will wake up and blast you to atoms before we get through this or you can just trust me. According to the studies, closing your eyes will help you visualize. You are doing something new here. If you use your normal senses it will only confuse and impede you.*"

"*Please, Voide, listen to John,*" came Mel's soft voice.

"*Stow it, powder-puff!*" Voide snapped. "*You just keep Brother Martin from frying my egg. That's your job.*"

Voide had instructed her security teams to seal the far end of the docking umbilical and plant a remote, motion sensing blaster station to guard the door. It was unlikely any physical breach would be coming this way without her knowing about it, but she had never trusted psionics. She didn't understand their abilities, and in her experience killing things one didn't understand was generally the safest bet.

She hadn't gotten to know Mel very well. The soft-spoken, overly empathic comms officer wasn't exactly her type of person. Still, Fei were known to have some psionic abilities, and what she had seen from Mel indicated she might have more ability than anyone suspected. Voide could only hope whatever was going on in that blue head of Mel's was stronger than whatever Brother Martin had worked so hard to keep hidden.

Either way, the clock was ticking and they needed to break free of *Hornet's Nest* soon or all that wouldn't matter anyway. She moved to the access panel, reached out to touch the docking clamp, and closed her eyes.

"*Okay, Doc, what next? You gonna lead me in a chant?*"

"*Knock it off, Voide. When you phase into voidspace, what are you normally thinking when you do it?*"

"*Nothing. I told you. It's like a reflex.*"

"*Work with me. When you phase, your feet are touching the floor, your body is touching your clothing, and if you have anything in your hand, that goes with you as well. So how do you manage to take some things with you but not the floor or the walls or some part of the ship?*"

Voide didn't like this analysis session. Still, if she was going to do this, she was going to have to follow John's lead. If others had done it, she could too. She cleared her mind and prepared as if she was going to voidspace jump. She visualized the process in her mind, slowing it down and examining it as if she were watching a holovid.

"*I don't know,*" she replied. "*I guess I just see it like a doorway in my mind and I step through. What I bring with me comes, but what I leave behind stays.*"

"*Exactly!*" John exclaimed, his excitement tangible even through the transmission. "*And when you come back to realspace, it is the same, right?*"

"*Yeah, so?*"

"*So, I want you to visualize that doorway back to realspace. Only I don't want you to step through it. I want you to envision pushing the end of the docking clamp you are touching through the door.*"

Voide began to lose control of her calm. She could feel frustration rising within. This stupid pale who rarely went into interstellar space was trying to coach her through a fundamental alteration of a voidspace jump. What did he know about anything?

"*I don't know how to do that!*"

"*Yes, you do,*" John argued. "*It is exactly what you have done your whole life since you started phasing. You just didn't think about doing it. You have always done it automatically, but this time you need to do it deliberately. It's like breathing. You do it automatically, but you can control it when you focus on it.*"

Voide exhaled and then took a deep breath. She envisioned the dark sliver of a hole into realspace forming within the swirling, comforting patterns of voidspace. Although she could not see voidspace from inside the docking umbilical, she knew and could feel the familiar environment all around her. She recoiled, and opened her eyes.

"*Wait! If I do this, I am going to rip a hole in this*

244

umbilical. It will expose everything inside to raw voidspace."

"Yes," John said with none of the stress in his voice that had just filled her own. *"Which is why we have already depressurized the umbilical and everyone whose biology is not equipped to survive raw voidspace is on this side of the airlock door. Even once we tear away from Hornet's Nest, you will be fine. You are tethered to the ship. Dub has fired up the voidspace drives into standby mode. Once we are free, he will extend the VS field around you so we can open the airlock and bring you back inside. We already talked about this on the way to the airlock, remember?"*

Voide had a vague recollection of the conversation, but had been more concerned with doing the impossible and with whether or not Mel would be able to protect her from Brother Martin, than with grasping their game plan fully.

"Yeah, I suppose so."

"Then, focus. Break the first clamp."

Voide once again closed her eyes and envisioned a dark sliver of realspace forming in the fabric of voidspace just outside the ship. She tried to envision breaking off the piece of the ship she was touching, but it would not separate. Straining and pushing with all her muscles, her gray skin erupted with sweat, but to no avail.

"I can't do it!" she growled through the comms, the physical strain in her limbs carrying through her voice. *"It's too big, I can't move it."*

"Stop trying to physically rip the ship apart, Voide. You aren't that strong. This is a mental exercise, not a physical one. Focus on sending the end of the docking clamp through to realspace."

Suddenly, something clicked in Voide's mind. Instead of trying to force a piece of the ship through the doorway, she began bending the doorway into realspace. She used her mind to shape the portal into a convex lens. Slowly, with as much control as she could manage, she eased the curving edge of the lens onto the end of the docking clamp engulfing it.

"I've got it," she announced, keeping her eyes closed and her mind focused on the open doorway into realspace. *"The end of the clamp is through. Now what?"*

"Now close the door," came John's reply through the comms.

Voide visualized sealing the portal and bisecting the docking clamp. There was a violent buckling as the end of the docking clamp was ripped out of voidspace and sent off into realspace. Had the umbilical not already been vented of all atmosphere, she imagined the sound of rending metal would have been deafening. She opened her eyes to see before her, through the access panel, a tiny window into the swirling, colorful cloud of voidspace.

"*Ha-ha! You did it!*" John yelled into the comm system loudly enough to leave a ringing in Voide's ears. "I knew you could!"

"*Yeah,*" Voide replied. "*Let's hold off the parades and valor medals until I get the other three loose and come out of this alive, okay? Posthumously is not my favorite way to celebrate a victory.*"

"*You are such a cynic,*" John said.

The smile that doubtlessly rested on his smug, sallow face came beaming through his voice. Maybe this pale wasn't so bad after all. If they lived through this, Voide would have to cut him some slack, at least as much as she cut anyone else.

Voide moved to the next clamp ninety-degrees along the circumference of the umbilical from the now-missing one. Colorful wisps of voidspace wafted through the opening she had just made, and danced like prismatic serpents exploring the interior of the umbilical.

"*Okay, Voide. Three more times and we will be free. Do it just like the last time.*"

"*Really, Doc,*" Voide responded, unable to resist taunting his simple, hermit-worldly way. "*I thought I might try something different each time just to keep it interesting.*"

The quip went unanswered as Mel's voice broke through the comm channel.

"*He's here.*"

"*Who's where?*" John asked.

"*Brother Martin. He must have detected we have some way of breaking free of the docking clamps. He is at the Hornet's Nest's airlock. He is trying to repressurize the umbilical.*"

"*Hah,*" Voide whooped. "*Good luck with that. Given the hole I just opened, that pocket carrier would have to have enough atmo to pressurize all of voidspace.*"

"*He just figured that out,*" Mel added.

"*How do you know that?*" John asked. "*Are you in his head?*"

"*It doesn't matter,*" Voide interrupted before Mel could answer. "*He comes through that airlock door, our remote blaster turret will depressurize him.*"

"*Just get those other clamps loose,*" John said. "*Once we are away, it won't matter.*"

Voide tamped down the feeling inside her that wanted to rush to the end of the umbilical and rip into Brother Martin. Combat was hardwired into Prophane, but through the years she had learned to suppress those urges when a non-combat solution was more prudent. Right now she had to get those other docking clamps loose before the fanatical monk found a way to stop them.

Voide closed her eyes and reached out to the next docking clamp. She once again visualized a dark sliver of realspace forming and bowing into a curve. Suddenly, a scream erupted from her, slipping voicelessly into the airless void of the umbilical as an intense bolt of pain shot through her skull like a blaster bolt between her eyes.

"*Voide, what's wrong?*" John asked.

She hadn't keyed her comms channel, so he must have seen through the airlock viewing panel as she grabbed her head in both hands, her body shaking in violent convulsions.

"*It's Brother Martin,*" Mel's voice came across the comms, somehow distant and wispy to Voide's ears.

"*Well, help her,*" Voide heard John's voice say just before she slipped into unconsciousness from the pain.

"*Voide! Can you hear me? Snap out of it!*" was the next sound Voide heard. Her head throbbed, but the intense pain was gone. She was still floating in the umbilical but had no idea if a minute or an hour had passed.

"*What happened?*" she whispered weakly into the comms.

"*Brother Martin attacked you,*" John replied. "*He knows he can't breach the airlock safely, especially with the umbilical now venting to voidspace. He is trying to shut down your mind to keep you from completing the task.*"

"*And where is powder-puff?*" Voide snapped, suddenly feeling it was a coin toss as to who she wanted to disembowel more, Brother Martin or Mel. "*Isn't she supposed to be running interference?*"

"*Mel is shielding you, but Martin's psionic ability must be quite strong. She is showing the strain here, Voide, and I don't know how much longer she can hold him off. You have to hurry. We are out of time.*"

"*It figures.*"

Voide shook her head and let her blood rage seep in and fill her with energy and determination. She might not be able to rip Brother Martin's throat out, but she could see to it that his attacks against her were an ultimate failure. She approached the next clamp, closed her eyes and repeated the earlier process.

The umbilical shuddered and strained against the burden of holding with half its clamps gone. The remaining two clung on doggedly, like a pair of snake fangs that refused to release its prey.

She felt Mel's protective efforts like a cushion of peace around her mind, but the pain in her head was starting to push through. It was only a dull throbbing now rather than the sharp pain which had robbed her of consciousness minutes earlier. Still, it was growing more intense every moment as she felt Mel's protection slipping and Martin's attacks rallying forth.

Voide approached the third clamp and released her rage almost fully. She kept only the most tenuous grasp on her control, but let her fury rise to drown out the growing pain. It was everything Voide could do to focus on forming the doorway a third time and bending it to intersect with the clamp. She only entertained for a moment the idea of forcing the doorway toward the far end of the umbilical and sending Brother Martin and a large section of *Hornet's Nest* through to realspace instead.

Her restraint won out and the third clamp was violently ripped from the ship and sent hurtling through to realspace. The one remaining clamp was unable to maintain its hold on *Star Wolf*, and the umbilical tore free gratingly. The two ships drifted apart.

Voide dangled like a fish on a line in the vast, kaleidoscopic expanse of voidspace. She never got over how beautiful it was. Her shipmates had only really seen it through digital recreation on viewscreens, but that paled in comparison to the glory of raw voidspace.

She was at the end of her tether, being dragged behind the bulk of *Star Wolf*'s hull as it rapidly withdrew from *Hornet's Nest*. One final shot of pain hit like a punch between her eyes before Brother Martin ceased his assault. She felt Mel's comforting cushion of defense collapse.

"*You did it, Voide!*" John's exuberance rang in her ears. "*I knew you could!*"

"*Yeah, yeah, Doc. How about you just reel me in. You can break your arm patting yourself on the back later.*"

"*Cynic,*" came across the comms as Voide felt the retraction system on her tether engage, drawing her back toward the lip of the airlock.

Twenty – Advance or Retreat?

Molon Hawkins looked into the faces of the assembled senior officers around the conference table. Dub was distracted, tapping commands to his engineering team via his mobile tablet. Twitch fidgeted. Molon knew his XO would rather be on the bridge overseeing operations than sitting around talking. John beamed an unquenchable smile, elated that his plan had worked and freed them from the grasp of the *Hornet's Nest*. Mel looked exhausted after her psionic battle with Brother Martin. Finally, Voide was clenching and unclenching her fists. Molon had seen this too often and knew the Prophane was fighting an inner battle with her own rage as challenging as any physical fight had ever been. The crew had been through a lot, but Molon was grateful he had such a competent and resilient group of command officers to depend on.

"Well," Molon began. "Where do we go from here? Dub should have the VS drive fully calibrated in the next few minutes, so we need to figure out what direction to point ourselves. Thoughts?"

"As soon as the VS drive is online, we will scan and beeline for the closest exit point," Twitch replied. "Once we know where we are, then we can figure out where we are going."

"How far do you think *Hornet's Nest* made it towing us?" Molon asked. "We could be halfway to anywhere by now."

"Not really," Twitch replied. "I did some preliminary navigational scans while we were waiting for everything to unfold with the separation. It looks like *Hornet's Nest* was folding voidspace and gearing up for a long jump, which means we may not have moved far yet, if at all. Unless they did some quick jumps before we regained control of *Star Wolf*, we are likely to dump back out into the Hatacks system."

"What long-distance jump points are there out of Hatacks?" Voide asked. "If they were gearing up for a big jump, they weren't heading to Hececcrir or Corespoun."

"I had Warbird run the charts," Twitch answered. "I can't

249

imagine the Faithful monks were going into Empire, Dawnstar, or Imperium space, and the only long jump anywhere near Theocracy space is to the Cappadocia sector, into a system there called Osvec."

"There's a charted jump point to Cappadocia sector from Hatacks? Is Osvec on the Theocracy side of Cappadocia or the PI controlled side?" Molon asked.

"Theocracy side," Twitch confirmed.

"Really? Is that a back-door into Theocracy space?" Molon inquired.

"Doubtful," Twitch replied with a shake of her head, "given it is a known and charted jump point. According to our latest system data, it is a major military world with a Theocracy naval base. The voidspace exit is likely mined, but the monks may have a minefield map and safe passage codes. After all, they are supposed to be allied with the Theocracy, right?"

"Planned xenocide notwithstanding," Voide muttered.

Aside from a raised eyebrow from Twitch, Voide's comment drew no reaction. Perhaps those who didn't know the context were too busy with their minds elsewhere. Molon noticed John fidgeting and looking as if he had just thought of something, but his twitching had started before Voide's remark, so was likely unrelated.

"Something about Cappadocia or Osvec ring any bells, Doc?" Molon asked.

"Maybe," John replied. "I told you the monks relocated their base away from Tede. I remember hearing through the grapevine that their new base was somewhere in the Cappadocia sector."

"Coincidence?" Molon smiled at his officers.

"I don't believe in coincidence," Voide replied.

"That's gotta be where they were taking us," John added. "If they got back to their hidey-hole, they could take their time scouring *Star Wolf* and the crew for Elena's research."

Molon cringed, realizing Mel had not been read in on the situation with Elena's research. The blue-skinned comms officer hadn't looked surprised. Had she been fishing around in John's mind? Molon knew having a psionic on board was a risk, and not knowing the extent of Mel's abilities put Twitch ill at ease. He only hoped he was right about Mel. If she did break as Twitch predicted, then given Mel's psionic abilities the damage could be far greater than Molon imagined.

"If we do dump back into Hatacks," Voide said, "and assuming *Revenge* and her VDE-equipped Dawnstar fighter friends aren't still drifting about, I guess we make for the jump point to Tede?"

"No!" John interjected.

"No?" Voide replied, raising an eyebrow.

"I hired *Star Wolf* to take me back to Ratuen."

An uneasy tension filled the briefing room. All eyes turned to see how Voide would respond to John's challenge.

"Are you insane?" she snapped. "Or have you been in a walking coma the past few days? Please tell me after all that has happened you don't seriously believe there is anything waiting on Ratuen other than another PI ambush."

John fidgeted and gazed at the floor for a brief moment, but then raised his gaze to lock eyes with the security chief.

"Look, I'm sorry for all the trouble we encountered, but Molon said this was a merc crew and that trouble came with the job—a job that is not complete yet. If there is even a hope Elena is still alive, no matter how remote, I will comb every inch of that facility of Ratuen until I know for sure."

Molon scratched his chin fur as a heated cacophony of discussion broke out among the senior officers. He let it go on for a moment or two, but then brought it to a jarring end with an open-handed slap of the conference table. Every officer at the table jumped, dropped into silence, and turned their full attention to their captain.

"If squabble-time is over, then I got something to say, as captain of this tub. We've taken a job, no doubt, but the parameters have changed. Breaking into a remote Dawnstar detention facility is one job—a completely different job to flying into the face of a PI cruiser under the command of GalSec. Not to mention we get to do all that while dodging a fanatical sect of Theocracy monks who have some kind of tricked-out pocket carrier armed with neural weapons, and who possess a rabbit-hole map of the sector we have to traverse en route."

"Not to mention—"

"Hold your peace, Twitch. I'm not done yet," Molon said, cutting her off in mid-sentence.

Molon felt a twinge of regret as soon as he had snapped at his executive officer. Twitch, for her part, folded her hands, dropped into a respectful silence, and shot Molon a glare that told him he was in for an earful later. He let out a sigh before continuing.

"We're also low on supplies, in need of repairs, and don't have the credits to make payroll at the end of the month without a paying gig. The Brothers stiffed us on the Salzmann contract, and if we abandon the job John has hired us for, he is under no obligation to even reimburse us for the fuel we have used. Even if we made it back to Tede and hit the jump to Furi, there's no guarantee of a contract there."

"So that's it," John asked. "You are giving up?"

"I didn't say that."

"Well, what are you saying?"

"I'm saying, Doctor, that given the odds we are facing, I'm inclined to cut our losses and trust to luck in finding a new gig before we go bust."

"And what about me?" John asked.

"We could drop you off on Tede or Furi as you please."

"I thought you weren't giving up?"

Molon took a deep breath and bit back his desire to snap at the doctor. John was a civilian and not used to following orders or respecting the chain of command. Molon had no idea if John would even consider sticking around after this trip, but if so, Molon would have to have some of the military crew run John through a makeshift basic training camp. A civilian on board was a breath of fresh air, but too much of anything could kill you.

"I said I am *inclined* to cut our losses, but I will leave it to a vote from the senior officers. It may be my ship, but it will be each of you putting your and your team's lives on the line, so I won't make this decision unilaterally. What will it be—forward to Ratuen, or back to Tede?"

"Forward," John exclaimed without hesitation.

"He's the patron," Voide objected. "He doesn't get a vote."

"He's also our acting Chief Medical Officer," Molon replied. "So as a senior officer, his vote is counted."

"And countered," Voide said. "Back. I told you this was a trap from the beginning, and moving further into Dawnstar territory with two different enemy forces pursuing us is insanity."

"Since when is doing something insane an issue for you?" John riposted.

"Look," Voide said, locking her yellow eyes firmly on John. "I'm all for a good fight, but *Star Wolf* one-on-one is not a match for *Revenge* or *Hornet's Nest*. That's not bravery, it is suicide."

"I've got to agree with Voide on this one, Molon," Twitch said, her voice more emphatic than normal. Clearly she was still a bit steamed at being cut off earlier.

"I'm sorry, John," Twitch continued, softening her tone toward the doctor. "I know you want to do all you can to hope against hope your wife is still somehow alive, but this stinks to high heaven as a setup. You've been duped, and the wisest

252

course is to get back to Theocracy space and regroup. Once things cool down there may be a way to investigate further, but now is not the time."

"Sorry, XO," Dub chimed in, shaking his head at Twitch's assessment. "I gotta go with John on this. Dr. Elena Salzmann was one of the few people in the galaxy that cared enough about malmorphs to even look for a cure. You all may be used to me just being a little different, but I'm telling you, I've got it good. Having been to malmorph colonies on several worlds, many are barely even recognizable as sophonts. They are in constant pain, and their enhancements aren't even useable given the severity of their physical deformities. If there is even a sliver of a chance at recovering Dr. Elena Salzmann and having her continue her work, we gotta give it a shot. This is bigger than John or even *Star Wolf.*"

"That's two and two," Molon said, folding his furry hands in front of him and rocking back in his chair. "Looks like the deciding vote is yours, Mel."

The waifish, blue-skinned comms officer looked as if she might wilt beneath the sweltering gazes of her crewmates. She cleared her throat and spoke out in her normal, soft voice.

"I have no desire to die or to see any more crewmates give their lives."

John exhaled and slumped in his chair.

"However," Mel continued, "whether or not there is any hope of recovering Elena, John deserves the chance for that closure. He has hired *Star Wolf* for a difficult job, but heading into Ratuen beneath the noses of the Provisional Imperium, Dawnstar, and the Brothers of the Lion is no more dangerous than flying into an Alpha Pack garrison and liberating a Fei terraforming colony. Had *Star Wolf* second-guessed that job, I would not be here today."

Twitch and Voide, both of whom had been part of the crew when Molon led the raid on Tetoyl where they had liberated Mel and Bob, exchanged knowing glances. They might have voted against going forward, but Mel's argument hit home. Molon could see it on their faces. Nay votes notwithstanding, Molon felt Mel had united the command crew on the decision. He only hoped the change of heart was their own and not "assisted" by Mel in any way beyond her persuasive appeal.

"I have never known this crew or its captain to give up on doing the right thing just because the odds were against us," Mel continued. "Let us give John and Elena that chance if we can."

John jumped from his seat, pulled Mel out of her chair,

253

and picked her up in an engulfing hug, twirling her around in a circle. Mel's powder blue complexion flushed a bright violet.

"John," Molon interrupted the doctor's display of exhuberance. "Protocol prohibits hugging and spinning senior officers. Could you kindly return my comms officer to the deck?"

John placed Mel back on her feet in front of her chair, but the smile those two shared was echoed by a grisly grin from Dub.

"Well, it's settled then. Dub, get us out of voidspace as soon as possible and Twitch, once you get our bearings, if we are indeed in Hatacks, lay in a course for the rabbit hole to Ratuen, best speed."

"Aye, sir," came the replies from both officers.

"Dismissed," Molon announced before anyone had a chance to extend the discussion.

He knew the right of it likely rested in Voide and Twitch's assessments, but was glad the decision had gone the way it had. He liked John, and he had never been one to shy away from a good fight. If it was blaze of glory time, so be it.

There was also clearly more of a mystery to unravel here. Someone had sent that message to John, either Elena or someone pretending to be her. The answer to that riddle lay on Ratuen. Ideally, with Molon's instincts and the experience of the crew, they could get to the bottom of it all with *Star Wolf's* hull intact.

At least, after all that had happened, pushing on to Ratuen should be the last thing the Brothers of the Lion or GalSec would expect. The element of surprise wasn't much, but it was something.

Twenty-One – Back to Ratuen

Molon sat nervously on *Star Wolf's* bridge as they drifted into a low orbit around Ratuen. The flash of lights marking the status and communication readouts coming across his screen at the captain's chair, and the buzz of bridge officers about their duties, as all felt distant as if he were viewing them through a dense fog. He was mentally engulfed, intent on digging out the root of his unease.

Things had gone smoothly, far too smoothly, since they had effected their escape from *Hornet's Nest*. They had emerged from voidspace back into the Hatacks system as Twitch had predicted. No sign of *Revenge* or of the VDE-equipped Dawnstar fighters had greeted their emergence.

Not even Hatacks system defense forces had been able to scramble before they left the system. The mapped jump point to Osvec which the Brothers of the Lion had dragged *Star Wolf* into was mere minutes away from the rabbit hole to Ratuen. With luck, their brief appearance and disappearance had looked like nothing more than a shadow or sensor glitch to the Hatacks system defense satellites. It was unlikely anyone had expected them to return to Hatacks, much less to be on an excursion deeper into Dawnstar space. Madness had its advantages.

A question still plagued Molon. If *Revenge* had not stayed in Hatacks, where had she gone? Had she somehow tracked and pursued *Hornet's Nest* into voidspace headed for the Osvec system? As far as Molon knew, the technology that could track a ship through voidspace didn't exist, but he understood GalSec well enough not to underestimate their capabilities. Would a lone Provisional Imperium cruiser really risk an incursion that deep into Theocracy space just to chase them? Doubtful.

Mark Russel had many qualities, but neither bravery nor foolishness made that list. He might have risked going to Tede if he thought he could intercept *Hornet's Nest* before Tede could scramble system defenses, but he was surely not reckless enough to take a lone cruiser against the Theocracy Naval base at Osvec.

It was far more likely Mark would have taken *Revenge* to the Dawnstar base on Hececcrir or pulled back across PI lines to their base on Corespoun. However, if Russel had anticipated *Star Wolf* returning to Ratuen, then they were in trouble.

So far, however, there had been no sign of the cruiser since they entered Ratuen. From previous visits, Molon knew there were no system defense forces stationed here. Why should there be? Dawnstar had located this prison facility on a tiny, desert world, the only even remotely habitable one out of the eight planets in this system. No gas giants, no asteroid belts, just seven balls of caustic seas, corrosive atmospheres, extreme temperatures, and general inhospitality, plus this one nearly waterless chunk of desert rock roughly half the size of Old Earth's moon. Ratuen's mainworld contained the Ratuen prison complex and, two-hundred kilometers away and across an impassably deep canyon that stretched for thousands of kilometers in both directions, there was a single city of fewer than a million people, built around the only freshwater lake on the planet. There was nothing here to defend, and very few places to hide in this system. If this was an ambush, Russel was going through a lot of effort at disguising it, and taking his time about springing it.

"XO, take us into tight proximity to the backside of that large planetary comms-satellite array. I want you close enough to swap paint with that thing, but don't touch it or set off any alarms."

"Aye, captain," Twitch replied and began maneuvering *Star Wolf* into the shadow of the satellite.

Twitch had her helm control interface plugged into the CID at the base of her skull, but its slow, sporadic flashing showed it was only providing her basic telemetry at the moment. She was not using her interface for piloting. In tense, time-critical situations Twitch could do so much more via the interface, when her sole focus was piloting the ship, but when the situation was unclear, Molon much preferred her full and interactive attention on the physical world. Flying into the unknown, Molon wanted every pair of eyes he could get focused on their situation. Twitch had an intuition and ability to read situations that even he couldn't match.

The starboard door to the bridge, closest to the sickbay and doctor's quarters, opened, and in strode John Salzmann. The doctor looked paler than usual, and may even have faded another shade or two as he observed the digitally created rendering of the Ratuen prison world on the bridge display screen.

"So here we are again," John said, flashing Molon an uncertain look.

"Home sweet home," Molon remarked with a grin. "I wasn't sure you would even recognize it from orbit. You were napping when we left last time."

"I haven't seen it," John replied, "other than poring over all your logs and everything I could find in *Star Wolf's* database about it, trying to get any idea where they might hide Elena."

"So, did you miss it?" Voide teased.

John scowled and his brow furrowed deeply.

"That is not even close to funny."

"Well, it was a little funny," Voide said, through an impish grin which exposed just the tips of her elongated canines.

Molon mused at how Voide could make even a playful smile look menacing. Given all that John had been through during his time here, joking about it probably wasn't the best idea. Molon knew Voide was just trying to lighten the mood and take away some of John's trepidation. Prophane empathy was a prickly thing for most humans to adapt to, but Molon knew Voide was actually trying to be positive, in her own, Pariah-esque style. Hopefully John would take it that way.

"So," John said to Molon, not responding to Voide's taunt. "How are we going to do this?"

Molon winced. John wasn't using "we" figuratively. There were downsides to having overly-enthusiastic civilians in the crew. With civvies, orders meant as much as a bucket of spit. On top of that, humans were the most stubborn race in the galaxy. Still, he had to run this mission in a manner that gave the best chance for success.

"As quickly and quietly as possible, I hope," Molon answered. "If they are running heavy, we haven't the manpower to storm the facility anyway. Voide and I will go in under disguise and stealth. I still have the Dawnstar guard vac-suit. We will give the place the once-over, scan for any signs of Elena, and get out, ideally while attracting as little attention as possible."

John spun to face Molon. The paleness that had hallmarked his features had vanished, to be replaced with a rising reddish hue. His face was a twisted grimace and his raised voice filled with the emphatic passion so endemic to heightened human emotions.

"You aren't *seriously* under the impression I am staying

behind on this, are you?"

There it was. Molon had expected this, but that didn't make dealing with the question any easier. John was a dilettante physician from a hermit-world—not a soldier, spy, or even trained scout. Babysitting him on this mission could change the outcome from in-and-out to dead-and-gone.

"John, listen—

"No, *you* listen," John snapped with uncustomary intensity. "I appreciate everything you have all risked to bring me here. Moreover, I know you are professionals who are very good at what you do. But there is no one in the universe more determined to get to the bottom of this than I am, and I won't risk anything being missed because the person most motivated to turn over every pebble on this planet in hopes of finding Elena was sitting in orbit."

Molon had been raised among humans. He'd seen them when they got like this. It was time to cut his losses. He wouldn't win this.

"Fine," Molon said, shaking his head. "But you have to know things could get ugly. There won't be any room for pacifists on this mission, Doc. Either you are willing to do whatever it takes, or you stay here. End of discussion."

John stood up straight, stuck out his chest, smoothed the front of his shirt, and looked Molon square in the eye as he responded.

"Then I suggest we get me fitted for body armor. I may not be much with firearms, but I can use a bow. If I'm not mistaken, Voide should be able to accommodate that request."

A choked scoff came from the security station. Molon and John broke their staring deadlock and turned toward Voide.

"Do you have something to say, Lieutenant Commander?" Molon probed.

"Yeah," Voide replied. "I say let him come. If everything goes haywire down there, we can use him as a body shield. Just make sure you pre-sign that payment authorization before we go dirtside, Doc. Hard to collect from a corpse."

"Yeah, and give you an excuse to put a bullet in my brain, psycho?" John replied, grinning at Voide's verbal sparring. "I don't think so. Just consider it extra incentive to get me out of there alive."

Molon rolled his eyes. At least they weren't trying to kill each other. Maybe John would be able to fit in with this crew of roughnecks after all. He was already adjusting to Voide's acerbic wit. If he could master that, the rest would be easy.

"If you two are done," Molon said, bringing the focus back

to the task at hand, "then let's get this over with. Hoot, keep those sensors tuned for max range and let me know if so much as a particle of space dust moves in a way it shouldn't. Twitch, keep the engines hot and be ready to get us out of here in a hurry if this thing goes all catawampus. Voide, John, you two with me."

"Aye, captain," came the replies.

Molon stood from his chair and strode off the bridge with Voide and John in tow. They took the lift to the second deck in silence. Instead of making the left turn toward the shuttle bay, he turned right toward the weapons locker.

"John, you probably didn't notice it before, because Dawnstar had artificial gravity operating in their facility, but Ratuen's gravity is very low. We're likely going to have to put down on the planet away from the complex and make our way on the surface. Using a bow and arrow in ultra-low-G is going to be challenging."

"Tede is a low-G world, Molon."

"Ratuen has only about one-quarter of even Tede's gravity. This place is more like a large asteroid than a planet."

"We also have asteroid bases and small inhabited moons in the Tede system. I've fired a bow on all of them. I assure you I am well-equipped to handle adjustments for variable gravity."

With this last, John flashed an odd smirk in Voide's direction. Her scowl in response showed she got the message. Molon assumed the exchange had something to do with their excursion on Tede, but whatever it was didn't seem to be an impediment to working together.

"Okay, then," Molon replied. "Voide, grab your bow and arrows and meet us in the shuttle bay. I'm going to get John into some body armor. You're planning on wearing your cat-suit I suppose?"

"Yep. You said quick and quiet, right?"

"I did."

"Okay, but this pale better not lose my bow. It's worth ten of him."

There was the barest hint of a smile on Voide's face. Was she being playful with John? The doctor's return smirk was less subtle.

"Don't sweat your gray brow, Princess Pick-a-fight," John remarked. "I'm rich, remember. We find Elena and I'll buy you a matching set of six."

Molon decided it was time to throw come cold water on their banter. The task ahead was serious and dangerous. Unlike himself and Voide, John was ill-equipped for mercenary work, so they all needed to be on their A-game if they were going to come out of this in one piece.

"Knock it off you two," Molon chided, "or just kiss and get it over with,"

He took perverse pleasure in the look of horror that flooded the faces of both his officers. Molon knew there were no romantic feelings between these two, but just planting the seed that their constant squabbling, playful as it might be, could be misconstrued should be enough to keep them quiet for a while and give him time to think. Voide jumped back into the lift to head for her quarters after firing a fuming look at Molon.

Punching his access code into the security panel by the armory, Molon led John inside. A large locker at the back was marked *Cpt. M. Hawkins*, whilst row upon row of lockers filled the middle section of the room. Along the rest of the walls were secured cages filled with all manner of weapons.

"Try that second locker on the left, John," Molon said, pointing to a locker with the label *Cpl. A. McGintis*. "We lost McGintis during *Revenge*'s boarding action. He was just about your size, so his body armor should fit well enough."

Molon moved to his locker and donned the boarding vac-suit he had commandeered on his last trip to Ratuen. He'd had Monkey replace the Dawnstar service patch with the ugly golden sunburst. It looked as official as when Molon had pulled it off the slain Dawnstar sergeant during his trip to rescue John.

Suited up, he walked around the corner of the row of lockers expecting to find John also dressed and ready. Instead, the doctor was standing still, staring pensively into McGintis's open locker.

"You all right, John?" Molon asked, wondering if the doctor was having second thoughts about the away mission. John started at the sound of Molon's voice, as if the doctor were coming out of a daydream.

"Yeah, I'm fine," John said slowly, not sounding completely convinced himself. "I was just thinking about the crewmen, like McGintis, who have already given everything on this mission. I never even met this man, yet he died because of me. Was I right to bring you all here? I mean if I hadn't hired you all, they'd still be alive."

"John," Molon said, placing a hand on the human's shoulder. "Death is a risk of the mercenary life. Every merc knows that. If it wasn't this mission, it would have been another. It is not your fault. It's a fact of life."

"I know that, on some level at least," John said, his eyes still slightly glassy. "There is something that puzzles me, though."

"What is it, John?"

"Dub told me that dying is the only way anyone has ever left *Star Wolf*. He told me that since you've been captain, not one person has gone looking for a better billet elsewhere. With all the changing lives aboard, it must be impossible to keep up with all the names."

Molon's heart slowed in his chest as he tightened his grip on John's shoulder. A flood of faces of those who had served with him threatened to overwhelm him. How many times had he ordered replacement locker nameplates? How often had he gathered personal effects, pulled names and patches off of uniforms, written those letters? But as he had just told John, it was a fact of life and part of being captain.

"I remember the names," Molon murmured in a far-away voice, as if only part of him were still standing there in the armory. "I remember every sophont who has served under me on *Star Wolf*. I wrote every condolence letter that accompanied a box of personal effects. I issued every final pay voucher bound for friends and family of those lost in the line of duty. Most times, aboard a merc ship, living or dying isn't a choice we get to make. Forgetting is. I choose to remember."

Thankfully John left it at that and began to put on McGintis' tight-fitting body armor. While it didn't cover every part of the body like a combat suit or Molon's boarding vac-suit, when combined with a tactical helmet it covered most of the vital areas.

"That fits snugly enough to go under a standard vac-suit if we need to vent atmo from the STS for any reason, and it should be light and mobile enough to let you move fast if it comes to that while keeping out most unwanted bullet or blaster holes."

"*Most?*" John said, grabbing the tac helmet from the locker and closing the door. "That's comforting."

"Ain't it though?" Molon laughed as he turned and led the way to the cargo bay.

Voide was already standing outside the STS with the bandolier containing her compressable bow and a hip quiver full of arrows in hand.

"I was wondering if you two stopped to take a nap before suiting up. Here," she said, tossing the bandolier to John. "Don't mess with the settings, and if you lose it I'll kill you."

"Yeah, yeah," he answered, slinging the bandolier around

his shoulders and taking the quiver of arrows from her. He affixed it expertly to his belt. "I bow hunt for sport, remember. I'm not going to break your toy."

"Shooting at dinner and shooting at sophonts are two very different things," Voide replied. "Dinner doesn't shoot back."

Molon noticed Voide's sword was slung over one shoulder and a long dagger was sheathed on one hip with a heavy blaster strapped to the other. She was wearing the same stealth suit she had on when she had accompanied John to his house on Tede. Over her other shoulder was slung a short-muzzled grenade launcher to accompany the bandolier of assorted grenades that crossed her torso, shoulder to hip.

"Have you already forgotten the part of the plan where I talked about quick and quiet?" Molon asked.

"I can do quiet," Voide smirked, tapping the hilt of her sword. "I'm also ready if things get loud."

Molon shook his head and boarded the STS. Having an untrained civilian like John along was unnerving. Civvies were unpredictable at best. Voide being on mission didn't exactly raise the predictability, but it certainly calmed his nerves. Her skills paid for her chaos and then some.

"Let's aim for quiet," Molon said, to Voide before taking the pilot's seat.

"Spoilsport," she snorted, and strapped herself in.
*****

Molon was grateful that the short STS flight to the surface was uneventful. Dub had remotely hacked the satellite array and given Molon the satellite scan pattern to avoid. There was a narrow window that could get them half a kilometer from the detention facility's perimeter fence. Given that the compound was the only thing worth watching on this desolate planet, it was as close as they would get.

As Molon piloted the STS down toward the surface, he squeezed the craft in between two sharply jutting mounds of rock. The extremely low gravity here meant the terrain was very uneven, and formations like yellowish-brown stalagmites jutted skyward like a field of stony grass. The small, relatively flat place where he had landed last time—when he had sought a sentry whose uniform he could steal before flying to the prison's docking bay—now hosted his STS for a second time. The high mounds would conceal the STS from being spotted from the surface, and this expanse of nothing between the prison complex and the canyon was not part of the satellite's coverage pattern. The rough landscape would give them ample cover, at least to the edge of the prison complex, where the surface had been razed smooth for several hundred yards around the prison proper.

As they exited to the surface, leaving the artificially generated gravity in the STS, their steps were floaty, with their higher-gravity accustomed muscles propelling them in great leaps. John adjusted quickly, but it took Voide and Molon several minutes longer. Suppressing their muscle-memory of how to walk in normal gravity, and shifting instead to the light touch and rolling glide required when navigating low-G, took some getting used to.

"Looks like I'm the expert for a change," John teased his cumbersome companions as Molon and Voide flailed about on their first few steps, trying to adjust to the gravity.

"I would think even you would take a bit of adjusting to this large a difference. I haven't felt gravity this light since we took a job on an asteroid mining colony."

"As I told you," John reminded him, "the Tede homeworld is the heaviest-G inhabited body in the Tede system. I may not be a spacer, but I get around quite a bit within my own system. I even had a high-G workout room in our home, which is why I was not tottering around in the heavier gravity aboard *Star Wolf* like Brother Zebedee was on *Hornet's Nest*."

"Feels like we could just jump to the prison in a bound or two," Voide interjected. "How in the world am I supposed to fight like this? I can barely walk without launching into orbit."

"You'll get used to it," John replied. "Just forget about stepping and glide. Walk more like you are dragging your feet and shuffling instead of trying to push against resistance. As for fighting, though, I don't know. That's outside my expertise."

"Once we reach the complex," Molon added, "it won't be an issue. The prison has artificial gravity generators that push around one-G."

"That's a relief," Voide replied. "At least we can breathe, even if just barely."

Molon understood what she meant. Few worlds had a breathable atmosphere at all, especially ones with gravity this low. Ratuen's atmosphere was thin, but it was enough to keep them from needing fully-sealed vac suits. The pull from the twin suns, two dwarf main sequence stars, one orange and the other red, had apparently worked together to keep Ratuen's mainworld from becoming tidal locked. Perhaps this rotation had kept the wispy atmosphere intact.

Molon hoped they wouldn't find themselves fighting outside the prison complex. The combined unfamiliar variables of ultra-low gravity and very thin atmosphere would put them at a severe disadvantage against anyone who had grown accustomed to life on Ratuen. By contrast, life support systems inside the complex would give them a much more familiar environment in which to carry out their mission.

Voide called for a halt just before they cleared the huge stone column on the prison side of the clearing which housed their STS. She strapped large black bracelets with small digital readouts and three control buttons onto each of their wrists. Molon recognized them as security scramblers.

"What are these for?" John asked, fumbling with the device.

"They will mask our image on video and conceal our heat signatures from the satellite and electronic surveillance," she explained. "They won't stop a live guard from spotting us, though, so be careful."

John continued toying with the device and poised a finger over one of the control buttons.

"Don't mess with it," Voide snapped. "It is already set."

"I was just curious."

"Curiosity gets stupid pales killed."

"I don't think that is how the old adage goes," John said, flashing Voide an annoyed scowl.

"What adage?" she replied, unable to hold back the slightest hint of a grin.

"Enough, you two," Molon snapped. "Save it for downtime. We have a lot of terrain to cross and the chronometer is running. The longer *Star Wolf* sits in orbit, the greater the chance she gets spotted."

They moved slowly and deliberately toward the prison complex. In between the towering landscape spires, they occasionally caught sight of a single, larger mound that was resting on a relatively flat plateau. Atop the mound was a large communications array aimed skyward toward the orbiting satellite behind which *Star Wolf* currently hovered. Keeping as low as possible while adjusting their airy steps to the terrain, they took advantage of the dry shrub-like trees and rocky spires littering the surface. The abundant cover was challenging to navigate, especially given Molon and Voide's relative unfamiliarity with maneuvering in ultra-low-G, but rounding a large stony outcropping they spotted a wire fence where cover ended and a flat plain began. As they approached this perimeter fence, Voide pulled out her security scanner and waved it over the surface of one section.

"The fence isn't electrified and doesn't appear to have any

current through it for continuity alarms. Should be safe to cut, captain."

Molon nodded and Voide pulled a small laser cutter from a zippered pouch on her suit. She made quick work of the fence, which was nothing more than a typical chain link constructed out of high-end material. Doubtless it would have proven impervious to typical low-tech metal cutters, but the laser glided through it easily. Soon a hole large enough to permit even Molon's bulk stood before them.

"The first patrol that spots this hole will sound the alarm," John commented.

"It's a chance we have to take," Molon answered. "Besides, people don't generally break into prison."

"Yeah, but you already blew it up once," Voide added. "Anybody with half a brain would upgrade security after that."

"Maybe even Dawnstar has equipment supply woes just like the rest of the galaxy," Molon answered. "I can't see some ratty, backwater prison complex as very high on their upgrade list. We may not have to fight our way out of this after all."

"Lucky us," Voide said, looking more than mildly disappointed.

The prison facility on Ratuen had been dug into a large, rocky hill sitting alone on an otherwise cleared plain. Defensively, it was ideal. There were only a few paths of approach, with easy visibility all around, if anyone cared to look. Molon hadn't spotted any thermal signatures outside the complex from the STS sensors, but that didn't mean there weren't windows or observation posts inside the hill. But there were no alarms or apparent activity yet, so it was doubtful they had been spotted.

Molon remembered from his previous visit that there was a single blind angle near the northwest corner. A sheer rock face limited approach directly from the northwest, but that had allowed him to get close enough last time to take out a patrol guard and steal his uniform. He had then been able to return to his STS and fly in like he belonged there. Unfortunately, this time they would be forced to go in on foot.

With Voide's bracelets protecting them from cameras and IR scanners, he was willing to gamble on not running into a live guard while crossing from the perimeter to the entrance on the west side. As they approached the path, however, Molon's spirits fell.

There had been a door on the west side, just north of the hangar bay, that led to the courtyard outside via a short, straight path. From this distance it looked like blast damage from the surprise he had left behind had at least partially melted the large metal door on that guard entrance.

"I'm betting that door doesn't work anymore," Molon grumbled. "We may have to chance the short climb to the hangar bay. As bad as that explosive wrecked the place, it will either be abandoned or it will be awash with people working on repairs."

"Um," John said, frowning. "Isn't being awash with people kind of the opposite of what we are wanting? What happened to quick and quiet?"

"Crowds and chaos are good for stealth," Voide answered before Molon could. "Repair crews, especially coming from elsewhere, mean nobody knows anyone."

"Yeah," Molon added. "When most everyone are strangers, new faces don't stand out."

"I'm thinking your faces are going to stand out," John said, nodding toward Molon and Voide.

"Nah," Voide said, turning on her disguise module on her stealth suit. Her gray skin faded to the human tone he had seen her use back on Tede. "Molon said Dawnstar used Lubanian security on this rock, and he already has one of their custom-made security vac-suits."

She popped on a pair of shaded lenses that shielded her yellow eyes from view. "See, now I'm a worthless pale, just like you."

"Okay, whatever" John said, ignoring her taunt and running his fingers through his hair before donning his tac-helmet. "Let's go."

The partly melted door entrance was a level below the hangar entry. Molon's acute hearing didn't pick up any noise of construction or commotion coming from the hangar bay. He tried the door but as he had suspected the melted metal had fused to the frame and made the entry impassible.

The climb to the hangar entrance was only about ten meters, and there were ample handholds and footholds. It was close enough to the complex's gravity generators, however, that they were approaching a standard one-G. In Ratuen's natural gravity, they could simply have jumped to the hangar entrance, but thanks to the generators, they would be forced to climb.

"You up to this, John?" Molon asked.

"Oh, yeah," John replied, "the climbing wall at my gym is a tougher climb than this, and I usually set the wall at point eight Gs. Null sweat."

"Do people in your gym shoot at you while you are climbing?" Voide quipped.

"It depends on whether or not I am paid up on my membership fees," John retorted, before turning and starting up the wall.

"Slow down there, Doc," Molon said, grabbing ahold of John's bandolier. "Might want to let Voide scout it first."

Voide harrumphed in John's direction before turning on her stealth mode and fading to little more than a transparent silhouette. She went up the wall and rolled into the lip of the hangar cave entrance quickly and silently.

"She must be part spider," John remarked.

"Among other things," Molon answered.

Voide's no-longer-transparent but still human-looking head poked over the edge of the hangar a few moments later. She called down to them in a loud whisper.

"All clear."

Molon and John followed Voide's path up the rock face easily enough. As they too rolled into the hangar, Molon gazed around to assess the carnage he had left behind on his last visit. The hangar was badly damaged from the bomb and currently abandoned. He quickly spotted why. The heavy metal hangar door leading to the rest of the complex was little more than a sheet of cooled slag set into the cave wall.

"Guess we have to find another way in," John said, his voice breaking slightly.

"We will, John," Molon said, patting the human on the shoulder. "Getting this far without being spotted was better than I had hoped for. Welcome to the mercenary life. Nothing is ever easy."

"It may be easier than you think," Voide added, having once again pulled out her scanner and wandered over toward the melted door. "Looks like no life-form readings anywhere nearby on the other side of this slagged door. My laser cutter may be enough to get us in."

"This is a heavy reinforced door," Molon said, furrowing his brow. "It will take hours to cut through that with a small laser cutter."

"You got somewhere else to be?" Voide snapped. "Besides, half this door is in that cooled slag plate on the floor there."

Molon noted where she was pointing. Indeed, it looked as if a puddle of the melted metal had spread out before the door. Its dull and charred surface did not rise more than a few centimeters above the hangar floor, but the flooring in the hangar was more rough-cut stone than any smooth flooring, so any number of pocks and crevasses might belie the true amount of melted metal below the plate.

"There is a good-sized thin spot where the old locking mechanism used to be," Voide continued. "I can cut a hole big enough for me to get in easily enough, and the pale if he wants to go. It'd be too tight for you, Molon, unless you shaved your fur and greased up really good."

"As much fun as that sounds," Molon quipped. "I think I'll pass. You get started on cutting this door. John, you play lookout near the cave mouth. The last thing you need is to get caught flat-footed by a patrol coming to check out all the noise in the hangar."

"Where are you going?" John asked.

"To find another way in. If I can find another access door, I can route through from the inside and meet you all on the other side of this door. I'm in uniform, so should blend in well enough."

With that, Molon scrambled back down the cliff face below the hangar bay and headed south toward the main entrance. If he intended to bluff his way in, the front door would be the least expected place for someone unauthorized to walk in. Go big or go home!

The front doors to the facility, on the south side of the hill, were locked down tight. The gate area showed no sign of activity, so blending in with a delivery or patrol was not going to be an option. However, from the other side of a single, clear panel on the west side of the vehicle-sized double doors, a young man in a Dawnstar security uniform stared out at Molon as he approached. The insignia on the man's uniform indicated a lowly private. Molon's own stolen combat vac-suit marked him as a sergeant. He hoped that was enough to carry his bluff.

"Private, open these doors," Molon shouted while still a few paces away, marching with intensity toward the doors as if he expected they would open quickly enough to prevent the need for this surly sergeant to even break stride.

The man blinked with uncertainty before issuing a calm response.

"Sergeant, did you forget your security card?"

"No," snapped Molon, as if that completely addressed any possible questions. Unfortunately, for the inquisitive private, it did not.

"I don't recognize you, are you one of the reinforcements from Hececcrir?"

Molon pulled off his tac helmet so his lupine snarl would have no impediment to communicating his displeasure.

"I'm from Hececcrir all right, but if they had transferred me to this crap pile of a planet, I'd have shot myself in the

268

head. I'm here with a SEC-COM for your CO."

"Oh, I see," the private answered, but before he could formulate another question, Molon took control of the exchange.

"Now you listen up, private. I just walked halfway around this glorified dung heap because it looks like someone has been using your hangar bay for testing tac-nukes. So, if you leave me standing in this dust bowl any longer, I'm gonna claw my way through that security glass, rip your pale head off, and take a dump down your neck. Do I make myself clear?"

The private went even paler than usual for humans. The man was clearly shaken and deliberating the best course. Suddenly, the young human's curiosity got the best of him and his brow furrowed as he spotted a possible hole in Molon's cover story.

"Why wouldn't Hececcrir just transmit the SEC-COM on an encoded message via a System Express ship?"

This private was smarter than most. That was most inconvenient. Time to push the limits and hope military discipline outweighed this private's intelligence and inquisitive nature.

"You want I should catch some rack time out here in the dirt while you dispatch a System Express jumper to ask the brass that question? I'm sure that'll make you real popular. Yep, bright career ahead of you, grunt."

"But—," the private started to interject, but Molon was already neck deep in this gambit and couldn't risk losing momentum. He cut the young man off as he continued his tirade, bringing his volume up to just below a full-on shout.

"And your boss will be thrilled he missed a critical SEC-COM because you decided to play twenty questions. I'll be sure to note your helpful inquisitiveness at your court martial. Maybe they can reference it on your tombstone as well."

That tipped the scales for the young private. Molon hadn't been sure this young man was going to cave. Fortunately, the military drills its recruits so harshly about following orders that an extra stripe or two was usually enough to make them more afraid of disobeying a superior than of any consequences of not adhering to boilerplate procedures. Following wrongful orders might land someone in hot water, but disobeying a lawful order during wartime was a capital offense. Since the Shattering, the entire Empire of Humaniti had been considered at war, and lawful vs. unlawful orders was a very gray area. The default choice in these situations was to err on the side of obeying a superior, which was exactly what Molon had counted on.

269

The private punched a button in the booth and Molon heard a loud clang of the electronic locks opening on the doors.

"Good choice, private," Molon said as he moved toward the heavy metal door now slightly ajar. "Now tell me, where can I find your CO?"

"I can escort you, sergeant," the young guard replied.

That was the last thing Molon needed. One time, just one time, couldn't things just go smoothly and according to plan? Molon didn't want to do anything drastic, but he was on the verge of this situation going pear shaped in a hurry. He moved inside the heavy metal door and spoke to the guardsman from the open, inside door to the guard post.

"You wanna add abandoning your post to your list of distinguished achievements, soldier? Just point me in the right direction. I'll find my way."

Molon released a subtle sigh as the young man nodded and began giving Molon directions to the warden's office. Fortunately, from the last couple of turns, Molon recognized part of the path he had taken on his previous visit. From there, he knew his way to the hangar. Molon suppressed a smile, relieved his bluff had worked...Until it didn't.

"I'll call ahead, sergeant, and let the warden know to expect you."

Poor kid. Too smart for his own good.

"Yes, you do that, private."

When the young man turned to access the comm panel at the security desk, Molon quickly grabbed him from behind, giving his neck a sharp twist. He heard the unmistakable sound of breaking bones just before the private collapsed in his arms like a rag doll.

"Sorry, kid," Molon said as he allowed the limp body of the dead private slump to the floor.

The young man had unfortunately picked the wrong place and time to be good at his job. Molon had no love of killing. The private was just a cog in the Dawnstar wheel. He wasn't responsible for any of this, and likely had no idea about any of the events that had led to his death today. Where had this kid come from? What turn of events in his life had brought him to this desolate place?

War was full of bad choices, and there had been no good choice to make here. If their cover was blown now, Molon, Voide, John, and possibly everyone aboard *Star Wolf* might be killed. Taking one life he didn't know to protect dozens he did—would these choices ever get easier? He hoped not.

Molon snaked his way through the passageways, following

the route the guard had laid out for him, to the point of getting to a familiar area. Molon focused his concentration on the route, shutting down stray thoughts in an attempt to cease deliberating about the young man whose life he had just taken. Why was this one sitting so uneasily on his conscience?

He had taken half a dozen lives in this very prison without a second thought when he rescued John. But those were nameless, faceless. This kid he had talked to—connected with, however briefly. How many young men just like this one had died while serving aboard *Star Wolf,* just from following Molon's orders? Unfortunately, he knew that number all too well. Maybe that's what made this one feel so different.

As he wound his way through the winding corridors of the Ratuen prison complex, Molon noted there was even less activity than during his last visit. How many prisoners did this ball of dirt house, anyway? He doubted they would leave anyone important here. Security this close to the border would be nearly impossible. For anyone worth hanging on to, Ratuen was likely just a staging area before they were shipped to a more central world with better defenses.

For the rest of the time, a place like this generally had one purpose—holding someone you wanted to deny was in your custody. That fit the profile for John and Elena Salzmann. Maybe the place was empty since Elena's death and John's escape. Molon hoped that was the reason for the inactivity and not that the complex's security forces were all poised somewhere waiting to ambush the intruders.

Molon passed only one Lubanian security guard en route to the hangar bay. The guard bore no rank insignia, indicating a raw recruit still in training. He gave Molon a cursory nod rather than a salute as he passed. Many of Dawnstar's security were from the private sector, with little to no military background. It was hard to get used to seeing uniforms without the discipline that generally accompanied ex-military, but that also meant they weren't as attuned to trouble as a battle-hardened vet would be. If Molon's team did end up having to blast their way out of this place, he'd rather face ten civvies than one experienced combat vet.

As Molon approached the hangar bay door, he noticed the telltale red glow from Voide's small cutting laser had completed three-hundred degrees of a circle about seventy centimeters in diameter.

"Cutting that a bit tight, aren't you Voide?" he called through the thin gap.

"Thought we were in a hurry," Voide replied. "Besides, I

can easily slip through this. If the pale can't fit, I guess he stays here."

"I'll fit just fine," came John's voice from farther away. "You just hurry up and get that hole made."

Within ten minutes the heated disc was hanging on by a thread of steel. The weight of it finally broke away from the rest of the door and it fell to the hangar bay floor with a deafening clang. A grating, metallic grind then echoed through the abandoned hangar as the heavy metal disc rolled unsteadily across the floor. Hitting a small imperfection tipped the rolling disc into an ever quickening heavy thrumming that resounded off the hangar bay walls before settling with a booming thud into deathly silence. The three companions stood motionless, listening for the sounds of alarms or of feet rushing down the corridor to investigate the cacophony.

"Well," John snapped as he jogged over from the hangar entrance. "If anyone didn't know we were here, they do now."

"Not necessarily," Molon answered. "These stone walls are thick, and the place is nearly deserted. Anyway, there is nothing to do about it now, so get in here and let's get moving. We'll check the cells first."

Voide's lithe form flowed through the opening like water. John took a bit more maneuvering, earning a few minor burns from the still-hot edges of the circle, and a scratch or two from places where Voide's cut had not been perfectly smooth. Voide drew her sword. John extended Voide's bow and nocked an arrow, ready to draw. Molon pulled his automag and attached a suppressor to the barrel.

The three slipped down the corridor toward the prison cells. The naked ceiling bulbs cast flickering shadows before and behind them. The light was enough to see, but the bulbs were spaced far enough apart to give plenty of hiding places to any would-be ambushers.

Molon was unaccustomed to being the loudest one on an away team. John was remarkably stealthy for a civvy, and Voide was, as always, silent as a shadow. Molon's combat vac-suit was not designed for stealth, and its sheer bulk made an inevitable *clack-clack* with each step. Footsteps in prison halls were not out of place, however, especially given any guard with an outside patrol route would be similarly attired.

There were only twenty cells in the place. All but two so far had been empty. One held an emaciated old man with a beard that appeared to have been cultivated for over a decade. Only a slight rise in his chest as he sat, slumped against the far wall, gave indication he was even alive. Alive or dead, however, he wasn't Elena Salzmann.

The other occupied cell had held a man in the tatters of a Dawnstar security uniform. The man had been beaten badly, and his breathing was erratic and labored. Molon doubted this man would even be capable of regaining consciousness. He bore marks of the less than gentle ministrations of a torturer. Molon had no doubt this man had suffered under the same inquisitor that had been at John and Elena when Molon had made his earlier rescue run. He wondered what he had done to earn the torturer's ire. Whatever his crime, he was beyond their help at this point, and was also not Elena Salzmann.

As they approached the last cell, John stopped moving. He breathed in shallow gasps, his bow dropping from the ready position to hang limply in his hand. The last unchecked cell door seemed to be holding John mesmerized, standing motionless in the corridor with his eyes locked upon it.

"You okay, John?" Molon asked.

"Yeah," John replied, shaking his head as if to free himself from the daze surrounding him. "It's just...that was our cell."

"I understand," Molon said, trying to comfort him.

Whether or not Elena was in their old cell, it was the last one to check. He silently motioned Voide forward. She slipped quickly to the last cell door and glanced through the small, barred window.

"It's empty," she announced in an elevated whisper.

John's brow wrinkled.

"Empty? But that's the last cell. She has to be here."

Molon sensed John was on the verge of a humanesque emotional outburst. Which was precisely why Molon had wanted John to remain on the ship. If the doctor lost it here, it could get them all killed. He had to try and defuse the situation.

"John, we knew this was a longshot. She's gone, and we need to leave before we are detected. Quick and quiet, remember?"

Molon had never seen a look like the one now on the face of the human doctor. There was a dark determination in his eyes that ran contrary to everything Molon had known about this normally good-hearted Faithful.

"I'm not leaving until I look in the eyes of our torturer and ask him if Elena is dead."

"You don't think he will lie?" snapped Voide.

"I'll know if he does," John replied.

While not the emotional outburst Molon had feared, he was not sure this sudden dark determination was any better.

273

Sneaking around an almost empty detention facility was one thing, but deliberately confronting the inquisitor was something else altogether. He had no idea where to find the torturer, but if he couldn't sway John from this course, he at least knew someone who could tell them where to find the inquisitor. It would be an even worse idea than confronting the torturer, but there was no other way.

"Fine," Molon answered. "The front gate guard told me where the warden's office is. We find the warden, he'll know where to find his pet inquisitor."

Twenty-Two – Inquisitor

Molon, John, and Voide carefully picked their way down the deserted halls toward the warden's office. Luck had held so far. Molon alone and in uniform might go unnoticed by a passing guard. Voide, even with her human-tinted skin, bearing a sword, and John armed with a bow and arrow would be a bit harder to ignore.

Molon raised a fist, giving the signal for hold position as they approached the last corner before the warden's office. Voide grabbed John and pulled him back before he could walk forward in plain sight around the bend. Of course, the civvy wouldn't know military hand signals. Voide's vigilance had prevented disaster.

Molon nodded at Voide who turned on her suit's stealth mode, fading from view. Her shimmering silhouette peeked around the corner before she drew back and decloaked. She held up two fingers and made the sign for armed targets. Molon crouched and motioned John and Voide to draw in close for a whispered huddle.

"Low and slow?" Voide whispered.

"No," Molon replied, shaking his head. "Too risky. Besides, you are the only stealth asset we have."

"Well, you have the uniform," Voide noted. "You going in loud and proud?"

"That's the best play, I think. But you shadow in there quick to help, or things are likely to go all Charlie Foxtrot, fast."

Voide nodded. John just looked confused. This was another disadvantage to working with a civilian. All the things military or security-trained folks took for granted were like a new language to John.

"I'm going in like I belong here," Molon explained in a low whisper to the puzzled doctor. "Voide is going to stealth her way into position near the other guard while they are focused on my approach. Once I get close enough to take out at least one guard quickly, Voide is going to quickly take the other out so we can make as little noise as possible."

"Yeah," Voide whispered, with a mischievous grin on her face. "If we don't take them down quickly and quietly enough, we are going to be in a real cluster—

"Ahem," Molon interrupted as quietly as possible.

He emphasized his annoyance with a grab of Voide's forearm. He knew she was trying to offend John's Faithful sensibilities, but now wasn't the time for such shenanigans.

"We'll be in a real soup sandwich," Molon added, using much tamer military vernacular to explain what a Charlie Foxtrot situation was. "That is what Voide was trying to say, if you catch the meaning."

"Gotcha," John whispered, nodding. "I actually caught it before. Don't worry about Voide shaking me up with foul language, captain. I've patched up spacers, soldiers, sailors, miners, farmers, and truckers. I seriously doubt gray-face here could utter any profanity I haven't heard before."

"I'll take that bet," Voide snarked.

"You two can play at swapping swears later. Right now we've got work to do," Molon snapped in a stern whisper.

He rose to his feet and strode confidently around the corner as Voide reactivated her stealth field and followed a few steps behind. Still holding his automag, Molon walked with his empty hand grasping his wrist, keeping his arms behind him as if he were out for a casual stroll. He approached the two guards standing outside the warden's office. The pair reached for their sidearms, but relaxed as Molon's Dawnstar vac-suit uniform complete with sergeant markings came into clear view.

"Good morning, sergeant, can I help you?" one guard said with a nod instead of a salute. Another civvy. Molon noted neither wore rank insignias. Rent-a-guards, probably replacement recruits for the guards he had killed while extracting John. Excellent.

"I'm here from Hececcrir with an urgent SEC-COM for the warden. I was told I would find him in his office."

"Yes, sergeant. I'll announce you."

"That won't be necessary," Molon said as he pulled the automag from behind him and fired a silenced round into the guard's forehead. His other hand shot forward and grabbed the man by the collar before he could fall, easing him slowly to the floor.

In the same instant Molon had fired his pistol, a blood-covered projection in the shape of a blade emerged from the chest of the second startled guard. The man hung there, bleeding, suspended on Voide's invisible sword. Voide turned off her stealth field as she pulled the blade out of the back of

276

the now dead security officer and also eased him to the ground.

"Quick and quiet," she said. "Now let's facilitate Doc's chat with the inquisitor and get off this dirtball before someone worth fighting shows up, huh?"

Molon nodded and the three burst into the warden's office, with Molon and Voide dragging their respective guard corpses inside and out of sight. There, sitting with his feet propped up on the desk, was the porcine torturer. To say the man was surprised would be a massive understatement. He looked more like someone desperately trying to thrash themselves awake from a nightmare.

"Wh-who are you? What have you done to the guards? This is my office, how dare you barge in?"

"You don't remember me?" John growled. "Well, let me refresh your memory."

Before Molon could move, John dropped Voide's bow and launched himself across the room toward the torturer. He had the man laid out on his desk and was about to deliver the fifth punch to the man's face by the time Molon and Voide could pull him off the warden inquisitor.

Molon had never seen John like this. He was like a man possessed. Rage and grief together was a potent draught, capable of pushing even a Faithful into the depths of madness.

"John, enough!" Molon said. "Are you here for answers or revenge?"

"A bit of both is always nice," Voide quipped.

"Stow it, Voide," Molon growled.

Suddenly, a calm demeanor more befitting the Faithful doctor replaced the violent rage that had just controlled him. He stepped back from the groaning, beaten torturer lying half senseless on the desk. John gazed at his bloodied knuckles as if he were trying to figure out who they belonged to.

"I'm...I'm sorry," John mumbled. "I don't know what came over me."

"It's all right, John," Molon said, placing a hand on John's shoulder. "After all you've been through, who could blame you."

"No," John shook his head. "That's not who I am. These hands heal, they don't harm. I took an oath."

Voide pulled the moaning warden from his desk, dumping him into his desk chair. She pulled several sets of manacles hanging from pegs on the wall, and used them to secure the warden to his seat. Voide had no stake in the fate of this man, but Molon knew her well enough to recognize her inner fight against the bloodlust which battle and blood-scent invariably awoke in her.

John stood a couple of feet from the warden, his gaze panning between his bloody hands and the warden's battered face, as if trying to fit two jigsaw puzzle pieces together whose edges didn't match up.

Molon mused at how different his two companions were. Voide was on a knife's edge for lack of sufficient violence, while John was broken and haunted over the smallest taste he had delivered to his former torturer. Molon fell somewhere in between.

Turning to the warden, Molon delivered an open-handed slap to get the man's attention. Removing his tac-helmet, he drew his muzzle within an inch of the warden's nose, pulling his lips back over his canines and letting a low growl from his throat underscore his words.

"I wonder if you can take it as well as you dish it out, torturer. I tell you what—you lie, delay, or even think about giving a remotely evasive answer, and I promise you we are going to find out. I'll peel the skin off you one tiny bite-sized piece at a time and snack on it while you watch."

Right on cue, Voide removed her own eyewear, revealing her bright, yellow eyes. She tapped the switch on her wristband to turn off her human skin tone camouflage and let her full, Prophane-gray epidermis shine through. She drew in close, putting her face right next to Molon's muzzle, staring deeply into the jailor's eyes.

"And then it's my turn," she said, baring her own vampiric fangs as the man trembled where he sat. "And I won't stop at the skin."

A dark spot began to grow at the front of the man's trousers. Warm yellow liquid seeped off the wooden chair and began to drip on the floor. Typical, Molon thought. The most ruthless of men, when they were in power, often turned into weak cowards when someone else had the upper hand.

"What do you want to know?" the man said, his voice somewhere between a whimper and a weep. "I don't know anything. I'm just a warden of an empty prison."

"It is not completely empty," John said, snapping out of his stupor and pulling Molon and Voide back away from the prisoner. "Who is the old man?"

"I don't know!" the warden insisted. "Just some Faithful dissident. He was here when I got here five years ago. Word is he was caught in a place he wasn't supposed to be shortly after the Shattering. He's been here forgotten ever since. I tried asking about him once I arrived, but never got an answer, so here he sits until someone tells me what to do with him."

"And the prisoner who used to be a guard?" Molon asked. "What was his offense?"

A sudden recognition flared into the jailor's eyes and for a brief moment indignation overcame his fear.

"You are the one! You were the Lubanian that broke out the doctor and blew up my hangar."

"That's right," Molon said, "and this fine gentleman who introduced himself with his fists was that doctor. Maybe you didn't recognize him without his face all bashed in."

"I-I was only doing my job," the warden replied, his voice cracking and wavering with fear.

"And his job is being a doctor," Molon continued. "I bet he knows all kinds of ways to hurt you without killing you, and my gray-skinned friend here just loves to try new things. So answer the question. Why are you torturing your own guard."

"Blame yourself," the warden snapped. "He was the lead guard in the interrogation chamber when you showed up. Imbecile didn't even realize you weren't one of our Lubanians. He's been making restitution for his lack of attentiveness."

"And what about the woman?" John pleaded, shaking the jailor in his chair. "Where is she?"

"What woman are you talking about?" the warden replied. "We only have the two prisoners here."

Voide pulled her dagger and put it to the warden's throat. She grabbed him by the nape of his neck, his lack of hair denying any better handhold, and pressed the blade to his skin just hard enough to draw a trickle of blood from beneath the sharpened steel.

"Did you hear that little warble in his voice?" Voide asked no one in particular, never turning her intense stare from the bound jailor. "He's lying! Where is the woman, pale? Tell me while you still have a throat."

"The woman who was with me," John added. "The one whose throat you cut, where is she?"

"Dead," the warden answered, his eyes flashing back and forth between Voide and John.

"Liar!" Voide exclaimed and drove her blade a fraction of a millimeter deeper.

"Where is her body?" John asked, desperation filling his voice. "If she is dead, then where did you put her remains?"

"The incinerator, where they all go. Lazy guards never clean the thing, so if you want to sort her ashes from the hundreds of others in there, be my guest."

Molon knew they were running out of time. Even a nearly

empty prison had to have dozens of guards. How long before the perimeter fence hole was noticed, or the front gate guard's body, or the two bloodstains they had left spattering the walls outside the warden's office?

"John, we've got to get out of here," Molon urged turning toward the door. "Voide, cut his throat and let's move out."

"No!" John objected. "We are not going to murder this man."

Molon turned back to stare at John. Voide had pulled her knife away from the warden and looked as if she were debating sticking John with it.

"Are you crazy?" Voide snapped. "We've just killed two people getting you in here."

"Three," Molon interjected, thinking about the young private at the main gate.

"Three, then," Voide continued. "So what's one more body, especially when it belongs to a stinking torturer?"

"The others were armed enemy combatants," John answered. "Taken by surprise, no doubt, but armed enemies nonetheless. This man is tied to a chair. Killing him would not be a casualty of war but murder, plain and simple. I won't be a party to it, and neither will you if you expect to get paid."

Voide spun toward John, dropped her knife on the desk, and pulled her sword halfway out of its sheath. She took a step toward him before Molon held up a hand which checked her advance.

"Drecking frags, Molon," Voide spat a vitriolic response, never taking her gaze off John but fully sheathing her sword and picking up her dagger once again, also returning it to its sheath. "I *told* you bringing this civvy pale along was just asking for trouble. So what, Doc, you plan on hauling this overweight pig back to Tede to stand trial or something?"

"No," John answered, calmly. "We are going to leave him tied up right here."

"John," Molon said, clenching his jaw. "We can't just leave him. Either kill him or take him, but we've gotta pick one right now. If that alarm sounds none of us is leaving alive."

"I will not kill him," John answered, folding his arms defiantly. "The Lion of Judah says to bless those who curse you. Perhaps this man will realize he owes his life to God and will change his ways. Besides, we can't take him."

"Why not?" Molon asked.

"We are going to have our hands full."

"Full of what?" Voide said, clenching her fists as if she were fighting back the urge to punch John.

"An old man and an unconscious guard," John answered.

Voide kicked the side of the warden's desk and began sputtering and swearing under her breath. Even Molon shook his head and ran his hand through the fur on the top of his head and back of his neck.

"You really are crazy," Molon said. "You're going to risk our lives to rescue two people you don't even know? Need I remind you one of those people stood and watched while this twisted freak murdered your wife?"

"So did you," John replied.

There had not been so much as a hint of anger or condemnation in John's voice when he delivered that verbal blow, but Molon could not remember a punch to the gut ever hurting that much. That settled it. John was the patron for this assignment, and he gave the orders. If he wanted to let this inquisitor live and rescue two strangers, then that's what they were going to do.

"Molon?" Voide asked.

"Stand down, Lieutenant Commander. We have our orders. The guy paying the bills wants a rescue, we launch a rescue. Gag that pig so he doesn't yell and make sure his bonds are secure. Grab the security card off his belt and let's move. The quicker we nab the prisoners, the quicker we can get off this rock."

They encountered no guards and no obvious alarms sounded on their way back to the cells. Molon couldn't help but feel they had far overstayed their welcome. Every second increased their likelihood of being discovered and, even with only a skeleton crew of guards manning the facility, they would be hard pressed to fight their way out with a non-combatant doctor and two helpless prisoners in tow.

When they got to the prisoners, the old man was conscious but could barely walk. Voide refused to help at all other than being ready to clear any resistance. She was in a seething mood, holding the grenade launcher loaded and ready in her hands. Molon knew that at that moment, if she could fire one down John's throat, she would. What they were doing had to be rubbing every nerve in her Prophane body the wrong way.

John had returned the bow to its folded position and snapped it back into the bandolier so his hands were free to help the old man. The guard was unconscious. After John had examined him and determined there were no life-threatening injuries that would prevent him from being moved, Molon took the job of carrying the man over his left shoulder while keeping his automag in his free right hand.

281

There would be no way to squeeze the two prisoners easily through the small opening in the shuttle bay door. Even if they could, it would mean trying to navigate two nearly immobile prisoners down the cliff face below the bay exit. That left them only the front doors as a viable exit. If any alarm sounded, Dawnstar forces could easily form a defensive barricade at the front gates. That would bring this little rescue attempt to a sudden and violent end.

They were almost to the front exit when the PA system in the complex came on. Playing over the loudspeakers was an all-too-familiar message.

"John, I...I don't know if you will hear this, but I found a way to uplink to the...to the System Express boat in orbit. I looked for you when the explosions freed me. You weren't in our cell. I...I don't know how long I can stay hidden. I'm afraid, John...If you get this message, please come find me. I'm alive, John. I'm waiting for you."

John stopped in his tracks, nearly letting the old man fall to the floor.

"It's a trick, John. The jailor probably got free and played the message to lure us back. She's gone and we have to go."

As if in answer, a klaxon sounded throughout the complex. Red warning lights flashed an alert.

"No, Molon. This message had more to it than the one we received. She said she was alive. She said she was waiting. She's here, Molon."

"The rest of the message was exactly the same, John, word for word. They just cut off the one they sent via the System Express jumper. They are taunting you to draw us back into an ambush. We have to get out of here now!"

Voide slapped John across the face hard enough to draw a deep flush of red to his cheek. He staggered back and it was the old man who steadied the doctor.

"Snap out of it pale," Voide said, seething. "We are leaving now. Payday isn't worth spit if we are dead, so come with us or stay on your own."

"You are right," John said, moving himself and the old man he was half carrying toward the exit. "Elena isn't here."

A pitched battle rolled along their path back to the STS. Small squads of Dawnstar guards harried them from defensive positions. They had little trouble fending off the advances, but Molon felt this was likely just a delaying tactic. Their real challenge was likely to come once they reached the STS, if Dawnstar had not already destroyed it.

Voide had spent half her grenades and Molon had emptied

282

four magazines from his automag to clear the path back to the STS. The defense forces for the prison complex only seemed to be advancing at about the same pace as the escapees. However, someone had radioed ahead to the settlement for help. Near the STS were two hovercars marked as local law enforcement. Eight members of the Ratuen constabulary had arrayed themselves behind cover, and their hovercars flanked the path through the spires hiding the STS. Molon and company ducked behind a spire just out of line of sight of the defenders.

"We're fragged," Voide growled.

"Maybe not," Molon replied. "These are local yokels. I doubt they have anything capable of breaching or blowing the STS, so our ride home is probably secure. Looks like these guys may have some light slug throwers, maybe shotguns."

Voide harrumphed.

"This is still a Dawnstar planet. For all we know, these techno-hicks might be packing plasma pistols."

"It's a Dawnstar planet on the butt-end of Dawnstar space. I seriously doubt the local flatfoots are going to be better armed than the detention facility guards."

"In that case...," Voide said as she dived from their cover.

Before Molon or John could react, the dull *thump* of the grenade launcher sounded twice in a row, separated by the sliding click indicating the chambering of a new grenade round. Molon snapped his last fresh magazine into his automag and stepped from cover just as the two hovercars erupted in metal-rending fireballs. The explosion sent the local police officers not caught in the initial blast scrambling for a place to hide from the artillery barrage.

John scrambled behind Molon, half leading, half dragging the older prisoner. Molon carried the still unconscious guard, but had already determined the man would be a body shield if things got too hot. He fired a couple of rounds off in the direction of the fleeing constables, which only served to intensify their desire to go farther and faster in any direction away from the escapees. Voide's pyrotechnics had robbed these locals of any will to fight. Molon doubted the border-worlders had seen anything more exciting than a rambunctious drunk since settling this dusty rock.

Reaching the STS without any further conflict or pursuit, Molon tapped in the access codes that opened the boarding hatch. After quickly scrambling to get their prisoners secured, Voide turned to John.

"Since you brought along extra guests and this STS only seats four," she said, "then I guess you get to hang on and

283

stand for the trip back to *Star Wolf.*"

"Fine by me," John replied, grabbing the webbing attached to one bulkhead and bracing himself.

Molon cleared the flight systems and Voide dropped into the co-pilot's seat, scanning sensors for any indication of serious pursuit. The small arms of the local police couldn't penetrate the STS, but if they had bigger guns somewhere, or even a defense force, the unarmed STS might be in trouble. They lifted off and began the ascent back toward *Star Wolf.* Molon called ahead on a secured comm frequency.

"Twitch, we're coming in hot. Keep your eyes peeled for any hostiles behind or from the system. As soon as we're aboard, get us into voidspace ASAP."

"Destination, captain?" came Twitch's reply.

"Mission here was a bust, but whatever else we owe a warning to Enoch and the Theocracy about what the Brothers of the Lion are planning. Get us onto the rabbit trail to Hatacks. There's a system jump from there to Furi and from Furi to Hiped, the Theocracy main base which the Faithful call Haven. That's our destination."

"Aye, captain," Twitch replied. "Cargo bay doors open and ready to receive you."

Molon thought out the plan ahead. He reasoned that John's voucher should be good anywhere in Theocracy space. They could provision and restock at Furi, picking up recruits to replace the full crew compliment, and could hopefully pick up temporary access codes from Furi's government to get past the system security net at Hiped. Whether John agreed with Molon's decision or not the doctor was along for the ride on this one, at least until after Molon got word to Enoch about the Brothers of the Lion and their weapon research. At least the Angelicum Host would have time to prepare, and hopefully Enoch could negotiate with the fanatical monks. What happened after that was anybody's guess.

"John?" Molon asked, hoping he wouldn't get too much resistance from the doctor about their next plans. "About our payday..."

But John was still locked somewhere deep within his own mind. The doctor stared blankly at the wall panel beside him, unaware of anything or anyone else around him. Molon doubted John was going to be fully himself again anytime soon.

Twenty-Three – Revenge

The jump point to Furi was on the opposite side of the Hatacks mainworld from the rabbit hole they had found to Ratuen, and from the jump point to Tede. This stretch of space was the most critical part of the run, so Molon had his senior officers on the bridge stations. They had been lucky to escape *Revenge* once, but if the cruiser was in the Hatacks system and poised to intercept them, there would be little hope of getting away a second time.

As the frame of normal space grew from the swirling, colorful chaos of voidspace and drew close on the view screen, the bridge crew was prepped and ready to make a dash for the Furi jump point. Should anything go wrong that might prevent them from reaching that jump point, plan B was to beeline for the jump point to Tede instead. Molon felt they had plans for the most likely contingencies. But as *Star Wolf* transitioned out of voidspace and into the Hatacks system, those plans vanished in an instant.

Alarm klaxons and warning lights flashed throughout the bridge. Navigation, weapons, and helm were scrambling for an updated sit-rep.

"What's our status, Hoot?" Molon called to the senior sensors officer.

"Four Dawnstar VDE-equipped fighters just closed the door behind us. Another four are sitting at the jump point to Tede."

"Voide, can you take them out?"

"Doubtful, captain. They are flying evasive. They are also pumping some kind of ECM transmitters. I can't get missile or targeting locks. We could fly around in circles taking pot-shots, but with four of them, we aren't accessing those jump points unless they break pattern and pursue us."

"Well," Molon said, "it's a good thing we were heading for Furi."

"You realize they are herding us, right?" Twitch responded.

285

"Really?" Molon said, his scowl showing his annoyance at his XO for emphasizing the reality he was trying not to dwell on. "Thanks for the heads up."

"Don't get snarky," Twitch added. "I'm just saying if the Furi jump point is where they seem to be herding us, maybe we ought to go elsewhere."

"Nowhere else to go, Twitch. Unless someone knows of another out, Furi is our best exit. We just need to be ready for whatever gauntlet we have to run to get there."

"Voide," Molon barked toward the weapons station. "If any of those fighters start following us, all bets are off. We go full offensive and light them up."

"A girl can hope," Voide replied.

"In the meantime, get your best people on trying to counteract those ECM transmitters. If it comes to a shooting match, I'd like to hit something."

"On it," Voide replied and began issuing commands through her security console to her teams elsewhere on the ship.

"Twitch, how long at max speed to reach the Furi jump point?"

The control module which was plugged into Twitch's CID flashed furiously for a few seconds. Doubtless it was running hundreds of simulations and calculations simultaneously to arrive at the best option.

"Six and a half hours, current course," Twitch answered a few seconds later as the flashing on the control module slowed. "If uninterrupted."

"No joy on uninterrupted, boss," Hoot announced. "I have *Revenge* pulling out of orbit around Hatacks mainworld and heading for the Furi jump point. Looks like they want to party."

"We're faster than they are," Molon replied. "Can't we outrun them?"

"Negative," replied Twitch. "They have the angle on us. By my calculations, they will reach intercept range twenty minutes before we reach the jump point."

"Options?" Molon asked.

"I just ran seventy-three theoretical approaches," Twitch replied, her CID mounted control module once again flashing furiously. "We can't overcome the relative positions. Best I can do is to get us ten minutes away from the Furi jump point when we pull into range of *Revenge*'s big guns."

"That's something," Molon said.

"Won't help," Voide replied.

"Why not?" Molon answered. "We might find a way to

slow them enough to make up ten minutes."

"They could dump a whole grid of assault shuttles in between us and the jump point before we get near it. If they put the cruiser right in front of the entrance, they might even be close enough to use the tractor beams on us even without boarding shuttles."

"Voide's right," Twitch acknowledged. "Whether they decide to blast us or board us, we can't get past them before it happens."

Molon pounded a fist on the arm of his captain's chair, retaining the presence of mind to avoid the controls. It galled him to be herded, but there was little choice. They could just pick a direction and head to open space in the hopes of finding a rabbit hole to crawl in, but there would be no way to know where it would come out. No, as much as it irked him, forward through the trap was the only way. But he was not about to just meekly follow the path Russel had laid out for them. Molon had a few tricks up his sleeve yet.

"We have six hours to figure something out. Senior staff bring me your ideas in one hour, briefing room. Boom-Boom," Molon said, turning to the engineering officer. "Tell Dub I want every engineer puzzling through how to get me enough speed to make up those ten minutes, and a few more, before that briefing."

"Aye, sir," Boom-Boom answered.

"The rest of you, call me if anything changes. I'll be in my quarters working up contingencies. Twitch has the conn."
*****

Necessity and purpose had pulled John out of his stupor. There would be time to figure out what exactly had happened after he left Ratuen, but for now his attention was needed aboard *Star Wolf*. He had checked and rechecked the sickbay supplies. Everything was as ready as it was going to get, but even with the security teams bringing in two extra beds and moving his desk and examination space to his quarters, four beds weren't going to be enough if this encounter with *Revenge* went anything like the last one. John even had the crew convert the auxiliary space outside the elevator on this deck to set up four more beds. Those would be useless for intensive care, but could serve as a triage station or as a place for less critical cases. Beyond that, John could only hope Molon found a way to keep them out of any major battles. In the meantime, all there was to do was wait.

Even John's personal quarters were overcrowded. He'd had security install a set of bunks in his chambers for the two refugees from Ratuen. The guard's condition was stabilized, but he had not yet regained consciousness. The old man was awake, but was just this side of catatonic. He would eat and sleep, but beyond that he met any attempts to engage him with an empty stare. It was almost like whoever he had once been, wasn't there anymore.

John had hoped he might be able to save these two. That somehow his intercession would spare them any further torment from the man who had tortured John and killed Elena. Now, however, time was running out for all of them.

The door to the cramped sickbay opened and in walked Mel. He wasn't sure whether to be excited or terrified at her visit. The earlier episodes of overwhelming, inexplicable emotion around her had not recurred recently, but then again he had made it a point to heed Molon's advice and keep his distance as much as possible. This was the first time they had been alone together since they were aboard *Hornet's Nest.*

"Hey, you," John greeted her as casually as he could manage.

"Hello, John," she answered.

Mel's sweet smile failed to cover the deep pool of emotion swirling in her eyes. John couldn't help but feel that she might be just as fearful and unsure around him as he was around her.

"How are you feeling?" John asked, trying to build a layer of cordiality on top of the foundation of tension filling the air.

"Much better," Mel replied. "But Molon wanted you to make certain there are no after-effects of the radiation still in my system before things get crazy."

"Well," John answered, patting the other end of the extra bunk he was sitting on, "since they moved out my examination station, why don't you have a seat and I will check you out...um...medically I mean."

Mel smiled and moved to the bunk as John grabbed a portable cellular scanner and calibrated it for Fei physiology. He set it to detect any residual effects of the radiation rounds.

"I, uh..." John started, fishing for the right words as he waved the medical scanner over Mel. "I wanted to thank you for your vote."

"My vote?" Mel asked, raising an eyebrow.

"Regarding the mission, I mean. Without you I would never have gotten the chance to see for myself that Elena was not still alive on Ratuen."

"You deserved closure, John. It was the right thing."

"You think so?" John replied, shaking his head. "If I hadn't dragged *Star Wolf* back to Ratuen, we wouldn't all be about to

288

die. So maybe not so right after all, I suppose."

"Everyone dies, John," Mel said, looking deeply into his eyes. "But to live in pain is much worse. I am sorry for your loss, but there is an old Fei proverb that says, '*shared pain is reduced, shared joy is magnified*'."

John turned away and stared at the wall, blinking desperately against the tears threatening to well up in his eyes. Emotions were threatening to overwhelm him once again, but they weren't coming from Mel. He wasn't sure he had the capacity to rediscover what life meant without Elena.

"Honestly, Mel, even if we live through this, I am not sure I will ever know joy again."

Mel placed her hand on his. Her powder blue skin was cool, but the emotions which flooded into him were warm and peaceful. His own torrent of anger, guilt, and sorrow subsided under Mel's gentle touch.

"You will, John. It will just take time."

He could not fathom why he believed her, but he did.

"Then I had better get started," he answered with a smile as he finished the medical scans. "We have about five and a half hours left to live. The good news is, you will get to die in perfect health, Lieutenant."

Mel smiled warmly, apparently unbothered by John's dark attempt at humor. She stood and walked slowly out of the sickbay. John noticed his normally rock-steady hands trembling slightly. He labored to breathe. He could hear his heart pounding in his ears amid the silence of the empty sickbay. His tongue felt thick in his mouth.

These symptoms matched no physical ailment. He grasped his head in his hands and took hold of two handfuls of his golden hair. He wanted to pull it out by the roots. He wanted to scream. He wanted to sleep...He had no idea what he wanted.

Elena was gone, but she had been the love of his life. How could he feel anything for Mel this soon? Was this some effect of Mel's psionics, or were these feelings from within himself?

John had no idea how to work his way through this tangle of emotions. The upside was, he was fairly certain they would all be dead in a few hours anyway, so he wouldn't have to live with this emotional labyrinth for very long. That was some comfort, wasn't it?

Twenty-Four – Spider's Web

Molon's lips drew back over his canines in a wolfish grin as he assessed the tactical and navigational displays which plotted the relative positions of *Star Wolf* and *Revenge*. They were going to make it!

Dub had found a way to overdrive the ion-fusion engines that were *Star Wolf's* main propulsion in real space. The overdrive Dub had rigged was risky and potentially unstable, but would put them at the voidspace entry point to Furi twenty minutes ahead of *Revenge*. They might, at worst, have to dodge a few boarding shuttles, but no VDE-equipped fighters were anywhere to be seen ahead, and none had followed from where they entered Hatacks, so nothing stood between them and freedom other than open space and possibly a few evasive maneuvers.

The fuel cost of Dub's rigged-up overburn was tremendous. They would expend nearly all their reserves to beat the cruiser to the jump point. It would be enough, though. The voidspace drives had their own separate, self-contained fission-fusion reactors and drew no fuel from the main ship systems. They would only need enough ion-fusion fuel to power the real space drives enough during their voidspace transition in order to keep minimal ship systems functioning. That was miniscule compared to the fuel used in real space propulsion. The Furi system had several gas giants they could skim for raw ion-fusion materials, and *Star Wolf's* internal fuel refining systems would produce plenty of ion-fusion fuel during the next voidspace jump to Hiped.

Dub had laid out all these facts to him in the briefing, but Molon still had a nervous knot in his stomach. He had never before dipped this deeply into his fuel reserves. In space anything could happen, and when it came to critical supplies, it was much better to have them and not need them, than to need them and not have them. This time, however, given the alternative, pushing the limits was by far the better choice. Gambling against some random, catastrophic, unforeseen system failure gave way better odds than going one-on-one against a Provisional Imperium cruiser. Still, Molon wanted to be prepared for anything. He even had Dub relieve Boom-Boom at the bridge engineering station.

Thus far, *Revenge* had not even launched shuttles. Surely *Revenge*'s officers would know *Star Wolf* had made up time and distance on them. Shuttles or fighters might be able to block *Star Wolf* long enough to draw *Revenge* into weapons range. Yet they had not deployed either. While that meant *Star Wolf* wouldn't have to fly evasively to gain the entry point to voidspace, it also meant that this time *Revenge* was no longer interested in capture. They were flying full bore on an intercept course, with the only offensive option on the table being their big guns. Fortunately, *Revenge* wasn't equipped with a spinal mount, or they would already be within range. Even without a spinal mount, however, the guns on *Revenge* wouldn't even need to warm up in order to blast *Star Wolf* into scrap.

The fact remained that *Star Wolf* would be at the entry point and into voidspace before *Revenge*'s guns could reach them. Unless that cruiser had some prototype weapon that could hit them from this distance, *Star Wolf* would get away. Molon's luck was never this good. Something was deeply wrong.

"We are drawing close to the entry point, captain," Twitch announced. "Voidspace entry in six minutes."

This was not possible. Russel was no ship commander, but he wasn't an idiot either. Molon had missed something, but he couldn't put his finger on what.

"Great news, Twitch," he said, choosing encouragement rather than sowing his own seeds of doubt among the crew. Maybe they really had just caught a break for a change. "Thanks to Dub for rigging our engines to get us here ahead of *Revenge*."

"Don't thank me just yet, Cap," Dub replied. "Honestly I'm amazed this rig hasn't blown up yet."

Molon glanced to his right toward the engineering station where a yellow warning light flashed ominously. Dub's mechanical hands were flying furiously over the engineering panel, but the look on his malmorphed face and the sweat pouring down Dub's face caused Molon's stomach to draw up in a knot.

"We miscalculate on the fuel, Dub?" Molon guessed, trying to keep a calm in his voice that he didn't feel in his chest.

"I wish," Dub replied. "Still have fuel but we're losing speed."

"Losing speed?" Molon said. "Why?"

"Dunno," Dub replied, not looking up from his mechanical glove hands flying around the engineering station controls. "Something is interfering with the engines and dragging our speed down fast. It's not a mechanical issue. It's like something outside has latched onto us."

Was that it? Was *Revenge* equipped with some kind of extreme-range tractor beam? All Molon knew about the technology said it wasn't possible, but then again, prior to the discovery of voidspace, galaxy-spanning travel wasn't possible either. He gripped the arms of his captain's chair with an intensity intended to drain all the anxiety out of his voice. He wasn't sure it completely worked.

"Dub, figure it out fast. We're still five minutes from the entry point and *Revenge* will be in gun range in twenty minutes."

"Nineteen," Hoot interjected.

Molon repressed a snarl.

"Nineteen then," Molon corrected. "If that cruiser gets into weapons range, one minute one way or the other won't make much difference."

"I have an answer, Cap," Dub said. "But it doesn't make sense."

"What is it, Dub?" Molon asked.

"We are getting heavy propulsion drag from anti-phase bands but we're nowhere near a nebula. There's no reason to encounter anti-phase bands in open space."

Molon knew the reason. The knot in his stomach turned to stone and his eyes went wide.

"Pirates!" exclaimed Molon, Twitch, and Voide in unison, startling the rest of the bridge crew with the sudden simultaneous outburst.

"Winner-winner-chicken-dinner," Hoot announced from the sensor station. "We have a three-way tie for the correct answer. Three *Corsair* class corvettes just dropped camo-screens. They are right on top of us. Picking up some type of energy field being emitted between them."

"Yeah," Molon answered. "That'd be an anti-phase net. Anti-phase emitters are older Lubanian tech, mostly abandoned due to their huge power drain and sensor interference. Some pirates still use it to hold and stabilize ships for boarding."

"Molon," Mel announced. "I am receiving an inbound hail."

"Fantastic," Molon replied. "Put it on screen so I can tell

these imbeciles that their phase nets have left them blind to the PI cruiser bearing down on them. They chose a bad day to pick a fight."

"Yes, Molon," Mel replied and began setting up the communications link with the pirates.

"In the meantime, Dub," Molon continued, "raise and harden our screens. The last thing we need is for some trigger-happy brigand to blow holes in us this close to the exit door."

"Aye, Cap," Dub replied.

"Voide, sound the alarm and prep for depressurization. We vent atmo in five minutes."

"On it," Voide answered.

Molon and the rest of the deck crew reached into the storage compartments below their stations and began to pull on the emergency vac-suits stored there. The warning klaxon and flashing lights announced the impending depressurization throughout the ship. Once Mel had sealed her vac-suit helmet into place, she moved the controls on her comm station and sent the incoming hail to the bridge screens.

As soon as the face from the incoming communiqué appeared on the viewscreen, any hope Molon had of reasoning or threatening their way out of this vanished. He heard the deep, reflexive breath come across the suit comms from Twitch and a simultaneous low growl from Voide. Molon closed his eyes and ground his teeth together hard enough to hurt. The odds against this were astronomical. Of all the pirates in the galaxy, why him?

"I thought I recognized my ship," said the swarthy man whose pierced, studded, scarred, and bejeweled face filled the viewscreen. "Lobo, you pirate, how nice of you to finally return it to me."

"Razdi Chadra," Molon growled. "I wish I could say it was good to see you again, but I'm afraid I would choke to death on a lie that big."

Chadra, who was not in any type of vac-suit, laughed aloud as he fiddled with a ribbon tied to one of the silvery rings piercing his right cheek.

"Aw, come on Lobo, don't be that way. No need to hold a grudge. I don't. I moved against you, you moved against me, it's the pirate way. All that's plasma through the vents."

"Very gracious, Razdi," Molon said. "But you don't seem to understand the situation."

"I'll make you a deal, Lobo," Chadra continued talking as if he had not heard Molon at all. "You hand over my ship and I'll even give you your pick of one of these nice corvettes. Of

293

course a corvette only holds a crew of six, but you pick the five friends you like the best and I promise not to kill the rest you have to leave behind, as long as they agree to keep doing their jobs under their new captain. I'm feeling so magnanimous that I may even let you keep your tail in the bargain."

"As generous as that sounds, Chadra, I'm afraid I must decline. You see, if you would drop those sensor-blinding anti-phase nets, you'd see that in about fifteen minutes you will have to haggle with a *Nova* class PI cruiser over possession of *Star Wolf*. And given who commands that vessel, I doubt he's in the mood to negotiate."

The pirate captain let loose a raucous belly laugh, slapping the arms of his captain's chair and blinking back tears of laughter.

"Lobo, you were such an accomplished liar, once upon a time. At least your lies to me were feasible. You expect me to believe an Imp cruiser is approaching a jump point to a system housing a Theocracy naval base? Why would they?"

Chadra's face suddenly went somber and his tone changed from mocking to threatening. Molon knew the pirate king was subject to severe mood swings, and when they swung to the darker end of the spectrum, no good ever came of it.

"That you would resort to such a ridiculous fabrication," Chadra continued, his dark eyes fixing intently on Molon, "shows me you have no plans to be reasonable."

Chadra gave a nod to someone off-screen. *Star Wolf* began to shimmy slightly under the impact of weapons bombardment from the pirate ships.

"Hardened screens holding, captain," Dub announced from the engineering station. "Negligible effect."

"Oh ho!" Chadra announced, his eyes widening and a wicked grin returning to his face. "I see you've done an upgrade or two to my ship since you stole her from me. I don't recall her having hardened screens."

"Yeah, the galaxy is a dangerous place," Molon answered.

"So I've heard," replied Chadra. "But now I'm very puzzled, Lobo."

"Sorry to hear that," Molon answered. "You are usually so well informed."

The snarl on Chadra's face showed Molon his little jibe had hit home. Molon, Twitch, and, unbeknownst to all of them even Voide, had been working undercover on Chadra's ship without him ever having figured it out.

"You see," Chadra continued, clearly not wanting to acknowledge Molon's taunt. "Your fixed forward pulse lasers

294

are useless while you are trapped in the anti-phase net. They also affect targeting systems rendering your missiles harmless. But *Star Wolf* has perfectly functional and targetable phase cannon batteries. Those could fairly readily chase off three measly corvettes, yet there they sit, unpowered. So if you truly have a cruiser after you, and you have weapons to fight back with, why are you just sitting there like a fly in a spider's web?"

Running the hardened shields was going to put them at enough risk of running out of fuel before Furi. If Molon was right, they might have enough to keep the shields up until *Revenge* was close enough to chase off the pirates. Unfortunately, if Russel was intent on destroying them this time, they would only have traded one executioner for another. But there was still that nagging doubt. Why had Russel not deployed shuttles or fighters? Had he known about Chadra? Were they working together?

Molon scrambled to think of a way to get them away from Chadra before *Revenge* drew in range, all without expending the last bit of their fuel reserves that would leave them without life-support systems before they reached Furi. Maybe he could taunt Chadra into a mistake.

"Maybe I just missed chatting with you, Razdi," Molon said, his voice dripping with sarcasm. "You were always such pleasant company. Or maybe I just want to see the look on your face when that cruiser gets here and starts swatting your little gnat corvettes. You see, it's Mark Russel running that cruiser. Ask yourself, Razdi, which of us do you think that glory hound will be more intent on capturing, a notorious pirate lord or some nameless Lubanian merc captain. You might want to get while the getting is good."

Molon noted the pirate captain had still not depressurized or donned a vac-suit. On ships as small as corvettes, any hit that could breach the hull was likely to do catastrophic damage to the ship itself. That was why ships smaller than destroyers were rarely even built with depressurization capabilities. Apparently Chadra's current vessel was no exception.

"Hmm," Chadra replied, rubbing his chin. "That's unlikely, my old friend. I'm no military expert, but I don't think they put GalSec spooks in charge of navy ships. No, I'm thinking the only reason you haven't powered your plasma cannons is that you have a fuel problem. Those cannons take a good bit of energy to fire. No gas giants in this system, so I'm betting if I just hold you here long enough, with you burning energy on life-support and keeping those hardened screens up, you are going to power down very soon."

295

"You are going to realize your mistake in about twelve minutes, Razdi. Seriously, if you have any visual capabilities in those crates not affected by your anti-phase emitters, look toward the Hatacks homeworld and you will see the *ICR Revenge* running full speed right at us."

Chadra shook his head and began to thrum his fingers on the arm of his command chair as he considered Molon's words. Molon could see a hint of doubt in his eyes. That hint of doubt told Molon Chadra likely wasn't working with Russel, but that was not to say he wasn't working for Russel. GalSec was very good at directing the actions of others like chess pieces; pawns who thought they were acting on their own. Having been a GalSec pawn at one time, Molon almost felt sorry for Chadra. Almost.

"Lobo," Chadra said, breaking his nervous and contemplative silence. "I'm going to have to call your bluff. Looks like I will be getting my old ship back today after all, but making me wait is definitely going to cost you that tail."

Razdi Chadra did not realized he was so right and so wrong all at the same time. He had rightly guessed *Star Wolf*'s fuel dilemma. Molon could keep the hardened screens up for several more minutes without jeopardizing their needed fuel to reach Furi, but if he fired up the phase cannons to break free from Chadra, they wouldn't have enough to keep ship's systems powered for the long voidspace journey. However, Chadra wasn't getting his ship back today. In about ten more minutes, his corvettes would begin vaporizing under the fire of *Revenge*'s guns. Then it would be *Star Wolf*'s turn.

Twenty-Five – Called Bluffs

Molon took a deep breath as a warning alarm sounded from the sensor station.

"*Revenge* has just joined the dance," announced *Star Wolf*'s sensor officer, Jerry "Hoot" Barundi. "She is now in weapons range."

There was no more strategy. Molon's brainstorming at this point was reduced to wishful thinking. *Revenge* had still not deployed shuttles, so if she chose to fire at the pirates first, and did it out here at maximum range, maybe they could still break free and beat the cruiser to the jump point. If Admiral Starling had deeper knowledge of pirate tactics, though, he might well have figured out *Star Wolf* was stationary because it was trapped in an anti-phase net. If he also knew that would make the corvettes blind at long range, he would wait until he was close enough to destroy the corvettes and still nab or destroy *Star Wolf*.

"Dub, you keep those engines ready to haul hull toward that jump point the minute that net drops."

"If it drops before we are vaporized," Voide said.

"Always sunshine and rainbows with you, ain't it darlin'?" Dub chided.

"Twitch, keep that course locked and loaded," Molon said, clenching his jaw to bite back a retort to Voide's pessimism.

"Aye, sir."

"Hoot," Molon said, turning his attention back to the sensor officer.

"Yeah, boss?"

"Extrapolate a virtual model of what's going on outside and put it on the display screen? I can't stand sitting here blind."

"One 3-D color-coded tactical holovid simulation with surround sound coming up," Hoot replied.

A few moments later, a panorama of deep space appeared, with a digital rendering of the three pirate corvettes, *Revenge* closing in, and *Star Wolf* sitting dead in space like a bug caught between the ground and a boot. A shimmering disc, tantalizingly close, represented the location of the invisible voidspace entrance that would lead them to the Furi system and freedom.

The giant cruiser had drawn close enough to dwarf the four smaller ships in its path when suddenly a barrage of fiery fingers erupted from the plasma cannon arrays in *Revenge*'s forward firing arc, pulverizing one of the corvettes and dismantling the anti-phase net. The other two corvettes quickly peeled off toward the voidspace entrance as *Star Wolf*'s own engines leapt to life.

"Incoming hail, Molon," Mel announced.

So who was calling—Mark Russel to gloat or Razdi Chadra to curse?

"On screen, Mel."

Chadra's face filled the front wall of the bridge, but it wasn't smirking or smug anymore.

"Guess you were telling the truth after all, Lobo. Here's hoping Russel hates you more than he hates me. We'll meet again, and I will have my ship back."

The signal ended as the remaining two speedy corvettes began evasive maneuvers as they punched in maximum thrust toward the voidspace entrance point. Furi would be no haven for pirates, but Molon knew Chadra well enough to know he would have more than a few fake transponder beacons aboard ready to pretend like he belonged there.

"Sorry, cap," Dub said as the familiar shimmy from overstrained engines shook the ship. "We're caught."

Starling was no fool. He had waited to fire on the pirates until he had *Star Wolf* in tractor beam range. While Molon was grateful Russel hadn't simply destroyed *Star Wolf*, now they were back in the hands of the Provisional Imperium, and worse yet, the hands of GalSec.

"Shut down propulsion and the screens, Dub. Save whatever fuel we have left."

"You got it, Cap."

"Déjà vu," Twitch quipped.

"Yeah," Molon said, biting back a laugh. "We've seen this holovid before, haven't we? Two will get you ten that *Hornet's Nest* is about to make an appearance and spring us any minute now."

"No bet," Twitch replied. "Although even if they did show up, Admiral Starling isn't going to let himself get sucker-punched again. We're cooked this time."

"I don't know," Molon replied, trying to muster something

hopeful to say. "Russel has to know we had nothing to do with last time. Maybe Voide can still salvage things with him."

"Don't count on it," Voide replied. "Mark was fishing for me to sell you guys out to save myself when the Brothers showed up. Whatever negotiating opportunities there were disappeared when we did. No matter. I've always preferred fighting to talking anyway. More entertaining."

Voide cracked her knuckles and then stretched her neck from side to side as if warming up for a sparring match. Molon admired her spirit, but even if every person on their crew were as skilled in combat as Voide was, they were so hopelessly outnumbered and outgunned by *Revenge* that it wouldn't make a difference.

"Molon, I have an incoming hail from *Revenge*," Mel announced.

"Of course you do," Molon said with a sigh. "Time to face the music. On screen."

Mark Russel's face filled the viewscreen, with Senior Special Interrogator Simmons standing stiffly in the background. Mark exuded what looked to be a forced and condescending smile.

"Captain Hawkins, Yasu," Russel said, briefly turning his gaze to address Voide before returning his attention to Molon. "Since our earlier discussions were interrupted, I have had a chance to examine *Star Wolf*'s logs in great detail. Here's how this is going to work, captain."

"I'm listening," Molon said, bracing for what was doubtless to be a set of ridiculous demands.

"We have your ship monitored through sensors scanning every square inch. Anyone so much as goes near a weapons control room or even a small arms locker, I destroy your ship. You fail to comply completely with what I am about to tell you, I destroy your ship. If another ship, even one that has nothing to do with you, drops out of voidspace anywhere near us—"

"You'll destroy my ship. I get it. What do you want, Mark?"

"You will dock with *Revenge*. You and your senior officers, including Dr. John Salzmann, will board *Revenge* unarmed and unarmored. Everyone else on board has ten minutes to return to their quarters and remain there. We see anyone moving anywhere other than toward crew quarters—"

"You've made that abundantly clear, Mark," Molon said, taking at least a little satisfaction at cutting that smug prig off in mid-sentence. "But what does this have to do with my Chief Medical Officer? He's not a command officer, so any decision we need to reach will not benefit from his input."

"Molon," Russel answered as his face changed into a mix of condescension and frustration. "Do you think my promotion came with a lobotomy?"

"GalSec does things differently," Molon quipped. "Anything is possible I suppose."

"We all know this has everything to do with Dr. Salzmann," Russel continued, ignoring Molon's taunt. "Why, he may be the most valuable person in the galaxy right now. So, hurry along before my friend Simmons takes over. I don't think that would end pleasantly for anyone...except Simmons."

*****

John lagged a couple of steps behind his crewmates, who in turn were following the single, unarmed crewman sent by Admiral Starling to guide them to the meeting room. The man was dressed in the military garb of the Provisional Imperium, a typical Empire Navy crewman utterly unspectacular in every way. His rank of Spaceman Second Class showed that little consideration was being given to *Star Wolf*'s command officers whom he was escorting. Russel had not even sent a proper honor guard, just a lowly messenger.

The man seemed unconcerned about any hostility toward him, either because he was too dim to feel threatened or because Starling had assured the man that there would be no trouble from the command crew while *Star Wolf* sat in the shadow of *Revenge*'s massive firepower.

John couldn't help but admire the way Molon led the away team with a firm determination in his step. While the instructions had been given that they were all to arrive unarmed, Molon couldn't exactly leave his Lubanian physiology behind. He had natural weaponry wherever he went, in the form of teeth and claws. However, John had been reading up on Lubanians, and knew those were weapons of last resort and would be no more dignified for a Lubanian to employ than if a human were to dive into a fight biting and scratching.

John shook his head as he noted how Voide swaggered, fists clenched, as though she were marching to battle. Demands that the command crew be unarmed notwithstanding, John recognized Voide's stealth suit and the control armband she was wearing. To the casual observer, she was complying with orders, but he suspected that Voide might be bringing more than advertised to this party.

John also glanced at the large malmorph engineer. Dub's mechanical hands were legitimately weapons by themselves. It could be argued that they were a part of what made *Star Wolf*'s

300

chief engineer functional. It was doubtful *Revenge*'s security would give Dub's prosthetics more than a cursory glance. Even if they did remove the mechanized hands, however, Dub's malmorphsy gave him the physical strength of several men. Dub would be a tough customer in a fight, armed or not.

Mel looked the least threatening, but John knew better. Fei psionic abilities were beyond the scope of his knowledge, but what he himself had encountered bore witness that Mel was anything but defenseless. Could she actually use her abilities in an offensive attack? John didn't know, but he expected that if things got ugly, whatever cruiser crewman was closest to the blue-skinned Fei might become overwhelmed with the idea that attacking his crewmates might be the best way to please the lovely alien girl.

Twitch, *Star Wolf*'s executive officer, seemed an unarmed, normal human. From what John had learned of her service record during his time aboard *Star Wolf*, she was a capable fighter with a head for tactics and as much field experience as any officer aboard. One did not survive several tours of duty with the Imperial Scouts, surveying wild planets and investigating subversive organizations, without knowing how to get oneself out of a scrap or two.

Suddenly a sobering fact dawned on John. Out of all of the *Star Wolf*'s command officers, he was the least likely to survive this meeting if anything went wrong. He wasn't a combatant. He had no real field experience doing anything dangerous at all. Diplomacy wasn't even in his purview. In fact, unless a spontaneous card game broke out, his only real contribution would be patching others up so they could continue the fight.

But he knew that wasn't why he was along on this ride.

John fingered the small cube that hung on a cord around his neck, hidden from view by the collar of his shirt. This was what it was all about. Would his crewmates, the ones who knew of the datacube at least, turn him over to save themselves? If they did not, could John honestly stand by in silent defiance as his newfound shipmates were tortured or killed for his secret? His life with Elena on Tede was a lifetime ago and a million light-years away.

Elena...

The unarmed crewman opened the door to a meeting room and then turned away, presumably to return to whatever his normal duties entailed when not escorting enemy officers through *Revenge*'s corridors.

The large conference room looked far more spacious and accommodating than John had seen aboard any ship. It was worthy of comparison to some of the finest boardrooms he had encountered at any planet-bound corporate headquarters. Awaiting the *Star Wolf* contingent were the two GalSec agents, Deputy Director of Intelligence Mark Russel and Senior Special Interrogator Simmons. An older man in a sharp, medal-adorned Provisional Imperium military uniform was also seated with the GalSec agents at one end of the large table. John suspected this was the commanding officer of the cruiser, Admiral Starling.

The last person seated with the others John had not seen before. He was dressed in a white, high-collared jacket typical of practicing physicians or medical researchers. His red hair and green eyes gave the impression of a fairly young man, but more than a few wrinkles, as well as him being seated at the table with the GalSec leaders and the ship's Admiral, proved that this man was someone in authority. He bore no military insignias of any kind, but the universal Humaniti medical symbol dating back to ancient Earth, the caduceus, was emblazoned in gold thread over his left breast pocket.

Had it just been these four men, John might have thought the *Star Wolf* command officers more than a match for their hosts. Unfortunately, they were not alone. Scattered around the edges of the room stood half a dozen security officers, dressed in GalSec black, heavily armed and looking extremely unhappy, or possibly, in John's expert medical opinion, more than mildly constipated. That is, all save one.

One of the six security officers, the only female, bore the rank insignia of a sergeant, making her the ranking non-com of the security team in the room. Her face seemed not only calm but even kind. Despite this one ray of positivity, John found it unsettling that the security team was comprised of GalSec agents rather than the expected PI Navy security.

"Is it normal for security to be GalSec rather than PI Navy?" John whispered to Molon.

"It's not normal for GalSec to be aboard a Navy ship at all," Molon replied. "I'm guessing the security detail has to do with trust issues."

"GalSec doesn't trust the PI Navy?" John asked, raising an eyebrow.

"GalSec doesn't trust anyone," Molon answered.

John could have sworn he caught just the briefest glimpse of a smile from the female sergeant as his eyes met hers. This was not a condescending smile, nor did it seem smug and patronizing. There was a genuine compassion in her face, though she quickly turned it back to an eyes-forward expressionless attitude of disciplined attention.

Her pale skin, bright blue eyes, and jet black hair accented her soft, lovely features. John couldn't help but think that she would look more at home as a starlet in some holovid than the drab, ebony garb of a GalSec security officer. His musings were cut short by Mark Russel.

"Captain Hawkins, if you and your crew would please take a seat, we can get started," said Russel. "I'm anxious to conclude our business before any more unexpected surprises arise. I found the premature interruption of our last meeting quite inconvenient."

"I would have hoped some of you all found it educational," Voide growled. "Maybe next time someone tells you to roll a ship, you will listen."

The admiral flushed at Voide's comment, but kept silent. John was amused that Voide wasn't only good at getting under his own skin. It seemed that she employed her gift universally.

"Yasu," Russel replied. "You can't blame Admiral Starling. You must admit, the timing of that pocket carrier's arrival was rather suspicious. Nonetheless, that is irrelevant to the discussion at hand. Shall we continue?"

Russel motioned toward the opposite end of the conference table from where he and his compatriots were seated. *Star Wolf*'s five command officers, plus John, took their seats at the end of the large, oval table. To John, the scene looked almost comical, like a B-rate holovid set on ancient earth where a royal couple was seated for dinner at opposite ends of a huge banquet table. Whether for intimidation purposes or simply to put a cautious distance between *Star Wolf*'s officers and himself, Russel had controlled the setting masterfully.

"Let me be blunt," Russel continued. "Since your untimely departure from *Revenge*, we finished decrypting our copy of *Star Wolf*'s logs. We know you broke Dr. Salzmann out of Ratuen. We know you returned to Tede. Finally, we know you are in possession of Dr. Elena Salzmann's malmorphsy research."

John tensed. He caught himself as he subconsciously started to reach for the hidden necklace that held Elena's datacube. Fortunately John's hand had not risen more than a couple of inches off his lap and he forced it to return there. Were they just fishing, or did they know?

"You are right," Molon said.

John's stomach jumped to his throat. Was this it? Was Molon about to sell him out? The ramifications of Molon's admission zipped through John's mind. He was a gambler, though, and no matter what happened, he needed to not tip his hand. If Molon was going to sell him out, he would have done it before now. John needed to stay calm and be ready to back Molon's play, whatever it was.

"We did break Dr. Salzmann out of Ratuen," Molon continued. "A breakout necessitated by Dawnstar's unlawful intrusion onto a Theocracy world and illegal abduction of Drs. John and Elena Salzmann."

"So you admit your crimes against the Dawnstar Technocracy?" Russel replied, raising an eyebrow.

"I admit to a rescue mission across factional lines during wartime," Molon countered, his ears twitching forward as he focused his gaze intently on Russel.

"Ah," Admiral Starling interjected. "But you are not soldiers of the Theocracy. Therefore your actions are not protected under the Humaniti Articles of Warfare. You are pirates according to Empire law."

Starling paused, stroking his chin that hung beneath a slowly-spreading smile.

"Unless, of course," he continued, "you have a letter of marque authorizing you to act on behalf of the Theocracy. Do you have such a letter?"

Molon's ears flattened against his head as his brow furrowed and his whiskers twitched. He made no immediate reply.

"Ah," Starling added. "I thought as much."

Admiral Starling smirked like a cat that had cornered a mouse, but Russel simply folded his hands and smiled, relishing what he obviously perceived as a verbal victory.

To John's surprise, it was Twitch, not Molon, who broke the silence. Her matter-of-fact tone and military demeanor wiped the smug looks off the faces of the admiral and GalSec deputy director alike.

"We are an unaligned mercenary vessel with authorized Articles of Operation issued by both the Provisional Imperium and the Theocracy of the Faithful. We accepted a contract while on a Theocratically controlled world. Confidential contracts are often initiated anonymously, and given the nature of the mission we acted in good faith that this was a lawful contract sanctioned by the Theocracy."

"And was it?" Starling asked, his smile a bit too smug.

As a gambler, John knew it was foolish to call a bluff by asking a question one didn't know the answer to. He suspected Admiral Starling knew this as well.

"No," Twitch admitted. "But it was not until after we had completed the contract that we learned the anonymous issuer of the contract was not, in fact, the Theocratic government, but rather an interested third party."

"Well," Starling replied. "I fail to see how that helps your case."

"Then let me educate you," Twitch responded, drawing an indignant scowl from the admiral. "Given the anonymity of the contract, and the fact that we will testify under oath that we acted in good faith under the presumption this was a sanctioned mission for the Theocracy to rescue two of its citizens unlawfully abducted from a sovereign Theocracy-controlled world, article sixteen sub-section two under the 'Fog of War' provisions, it cannot be proven we were acting solely for personal gain or with criminal intent. Therefore you cannot legally bring piracy charges against *Star Wolf* or her crew."

"You know your Humaniti Council law, commander," Senior Interrogator Simmons interjected. No emotion whatsoever graced his monotone voice. "Yet you freely admit you were not operating under a contract for the Theocracy."

"That is correct," Twitch replied, "and as I noted, irrelevant."

"You further claim," Simmons continued, ignoring her objection, "to have independent operator licenses with the Provisional Imperium and the Theocracy."

"That is correct," Twitch replied.

"Unfortunately," Simmons continued, steepling his fingers. "You have no Articles of Operation agreement with the Dawnstar Technocracy."

"That is correct," Twitch acknowledged.

"Thus, you entered Dawnstar space illegally. This is a fact, even if you could make a good faith case that you believed your employer to be the Theocracy of the Faithful."

Twitch nodded, locking her gaze on Senior Special Interrogator Simmons. She sat up even straighter in her chair as she addressed the accusation leveled at her.

"While ordinarily that might be true, under article sixty-seven, subsection four of the Unaligned Forces Operational Agreement, I quote, 'A mercenary vessel with a secured, validated contract agreement may engage in recovery actions for persons or property pursuant to an unlawful act carried out by any of the officially recognized Humaniti factions.' The kidnapping of the Salzmanns was an illegal act by Dawnstar against civilian targets, thereby legitimizing *Star Wolf*'s rescue operation regardless of the identity of our employer. I'm sure

Captain Hawkins will be happy to produce the contract records to prove we were under a confirmed, validated contract at the time we entered Dawnstar space. Now if there will be nothing else, gentlemen, we will take our leave."

Twitch stood as if a staff meeting had just concluded and it was time to get back to real work.

"Sit down, commander!" Russel ordered, his face flushing red and his voice losing the smug calm that had marked his earlier conduct in the meeting. "We are far from finished here. Even if the story concerning your initial incursion checks out, there is still the matter of *Star Wolf*'s actions on Ratuen to settle. Can blowing up an STS and a docking facility rightly be defined as a 'recovery action'? I believe that firmly crosses the line into terrorism."

Twitch, unrattled, held her head high as she retook her seat. Molon patted her arm reassuringly as he leaned over and whispered to her.

"Whatever else happens, that was beautiful! Say you will marry me."

"Sorry, captain," Twitch grinned. "I prefer my men clean-shaven, and you'd just look silly without fur."

Both laughed quietly to each other. Russel's face reddened even more, and it looked like one vein in his forehead might rupture. John suspected the GalSec deputy director was unaccustomed to having those under his thumb enjoy a moment of amusement at his expense.

"Captain Hawkins," Russel said, flustered and struggling to regain his former composure. "Explain for me in detail what happened on your visit to Ratuen when you effected the escape of Dr. John Salzmann."

"I'd be glad to," Molon replied as he leaned forward and placed his forearms on the table. "After the warden of Ratuen murdered an illegally-abducted Theocracy citizen, Dr. Elena Salzmann, I utilized whatever means necessary to preserve my life and the life of the remaining abductee, Dr. John Salzmann."

"Whatever means necessarily including a tactical nuclear explosion," Russel quipped.

"Technically it was a simple blastiplast explosion, but when that reacted with the STS's propulsion fuel, it cascaded into a tac-nuke. Anyway, we escaped Ratuen and I returned Dr. Salzmann to his home planet of Tede. He returned to find his home and all his possessions burned up in a house fire. With his wife gone, his home destroyed, and nothing to return to, he decided to sign on with *Star Wolf* as chief medical officer."

"Nothing to return to?" Simmons asked, his voice rising with the inquiry. "I assume you mean nothing other than a multi-billion-dollar interstellar pharmaceuticals company."

John figured this was as good a time as any to speak for himself, as long as the focus was on him and far away from Elena's research.

"Salzmann Pharmaceuticals has a very competent board of directors. Fortunately, my physical presence is unnecessary for my company to continue to function. The qualified people in my employ have general directives to guide routine operations, and my attorneys are more than capable of handling any urgent decisions that arise in the event I am unreachable."

"I'm sure that is immensely comforting to your shareholders, doctor," Simmons replied, sarcasm dripping from his voice. "And then, after you escaped captivity, you had an epiphany that your existence as an over-privileged wastrel was unfulfilling. To alleviate your growing wanderlust, you decided to risk life and limb as an interstellar mercenary? Is that what you seriously expect us to believe?"

"I was grateful for my rescue," John responded, his throat tightening a bit under the weight of Simmon's scathing sarcasm. "*Star Wolf* was without a chief medical officer, so I decided to fill that role while they looked for one."

"And what about your wife's research, doctor? Where is that now?" Simmons smiled ever so slightly as if, having baited John into joining the conversation, he might now draw the noose to capture his prey.

John's mind reeled. He mentally kicked himself for jumping into the conversation at all. Now he was back on the hook with the subject of Elena's research leaving him wriggling for a way out. Molon did not leave him dangling long, however, as the Lubanian captain once again came to his rescue and assumed the role of spokesperson for *Star Wolf.*

"As far as whatever research you are referencing, we cannot speak to that. Our best guess is that whatever you are looking for was a casualty of the fire that destroyed the Salzmanns' home."

The two GalSec agents and Admiral Starling huddled together at the far end of the table, whispering back and forth. Simmons was pointing to a datapad in front of them. After a nod from Russel, the men sat straight in their chairs once again.

"You are denying that *Star Wolf* personnel entered the Salzmann home prior to the fire?" Simmons inquired, raising an eyebrow and locking his icy stare on Molon.

John shifted uncomfortably in his chair with the questioning from Senior Interrogator Simmons. He had seen that man take down Voide in hand-to-hand combat like she was little more than a rag-doll. Molon also seemed more than apprehensive about Simmons. Twitch may have won them a point or two, but this meeting had taken a grave turn when control of the interrogation shifted from Russel to Simmons.

Before Molon could answer the question, Voide interjected. John noted the icy calm that had overtaken *Star Wolf*'s security chief.

"When I escorted Dr. Salzmann to his home on Tede to pick up some personal belongings, we discovered the Salzmanns' home had been set ablaze. We were unable to enter the home before it burned to the ground. Failing to gain entry and suspecting that whoever had started the fire might still be nearby posing a threat, I urged Dr. Salzmann to get back into our vehicle, after which we returned to *Star Wolf*."

"I'm terribly sorry," said Senior Interrogator Simmons, his deadpan face revealing little of what was coming next. "Your account is discordant with the facts on a number of points.

"First off, you, being non-human, would not have been allowed outside Tede's starport. Tede is a xenophobic hermit-world with strict laws concerning non-human sophonts."

"I know," Voide answered. "When I accompanied Dr. Salzmann I was disguised as a human."

"I see," Simmons said, nodding. Leaning in toward them, he slowly added, "It seems while your executive officer made quite the case for how lawfully *Star Wolf* acted in its Ratuen insurgence, you now willfully admit to violating a sovereign Theocracy world's immigration and inter-species interaction laws. While we have no authority to enforce the law of Theocratic worlds, your testimony amply demonstrates that legality of action is an ambiguous concept where *Star Wolf* is concerned."

John's eyes went wide. He knew enough about Voide to expect Simmons's taunts would have the Prophane's blood boiling. To John's surprise, only the sound of the arms of her chair taking much more than their expected tension stresses gave indication of the difficulty in maintaining her restraint. Otherwise, the chief security officer kept her head as Simmons continued.

"Secondly, according to our sources on Tede, the Salzmann home was perfectly sound when you arrived."

"Your sources are incorrect," Voide said, her caged fury clearly pushing against the calm of her response like a thoroughbred waiting to burst out of the starting gate.

"I highly doubt that," Simmons continued. "We have incontrovertible evidence that you removed the aforementioned research before torching the house yourselves to cover your tracks.

"And finally," Simmons said, turning his attention away from Voide and back toward Molon. "There is the whole matter of your return to Ratuen."

"I'm not sure what you mean," Molon replied.

"What I mean is that if one has been illegally abducted, one generally does not break back into prison. Yet forces under your command, Captain Hawkins, carried out not just the one, but also a second terrorist attack against a world and facility under the control of the Dawnstar Technocracy. While your well-spoken executive officer might be able to wiggle a way around charges for the first attack, I am afraid your return to Ratuen, and murderous actions while there, are not covered under your initial contract. Given that Ratuen is a sovereign Dawnstar world, and given Dawnstar's alliance with the Provisional Imperium, this is a case of high treason and thus a capital offense."

John gave a quiet gasp as Molon stared silently at the interrogator, his ears flattened against his skull, likely unconsciously. John surmised that the same thing was going through Molon's mind as was going through his own. They had left Ratuen and proceeded straight to Hatacks. FTL communications didn't exist. How had Simmons possibly gotten word about their most recent visit to Ratuen before *Star Wolf* arrived?

"Ah, I see you didn't expect me to know about that yet," Simmons added. "Yes, we have a mapped route between Hatacks and Ratuen that cuts several hours off the rabbit trail you uncovered. So your return to Ratuen and your unprovoked, murderous actions against Dawnstar citizens contradict this fanciful abduction story, don't you see?"

The smug, matter-of-fact manner of the GalSec interrogator sent chills down John's back. It was almost like this man was not even fully human. Still, his calloused twisting of the facts was more than John could continue to stomach in silence.

"You rotten liar! Dawnstar did kidnap us, and that pig of a warden murdered Elena in cold blood in front of my eyes. You are right; I hired *Star Wolf* to take me back to Ratuen, because you lousy spooks, or someone you know of, faked a message to trick me into believing Elena was still alive. If there is any crime on our part, it rests on me and me alone. Let *Star Wolf*'s crew go and you can carry out your capital punishment on me, if that's to be the way of it."

Simmons's impassive face actually cracked a smile. John was not sure it was an improvement over his stone-faced coldness.

"I'm sorry if my amusement appears rude, doctor," Simmons replied. "I am afraid I could not control myself in light of your response. You see, you almost made it sound as if you had a say in the matter."

Russel and Starling started to laugh at the unexpected quip from Simmons before Twitch's firm, commanding voice cut their mirth short.

"Actually, Senior Special Interrogator Simmons, legally we were still under lawful contract, albeit not the same contract. This second incursion was under contract directly with Dr. John Salzmann. Given that Salzmann Pharmaceuticals has standing contracts with the Theocracy government, there is precedent upon which to argue an implied limited agency between Salzmann Pharmaceuticals and the Theocracy. As CEO, Dr. John Salzmann has rights of action under that limited agency. Given his belief, based on compelling physical evidence, that Dr. Elena Salzmann could still be alive, the return to Ratuen would still legally be considered a 'recovery action' by extended agency."

John deeply appreciated the commander's arguments on his behalf. Molon had shared with him that during their time together in the Imperial Scouts, getting them into trouble was his job while getting them out had been Twitch's. John was beginning to understand what Molon meant by that.

Unfortunately, John doubted that Twitch's legal grandstanding would avail much. For all their pretext of authority and decorum, this was a glorified blackmail session, not a legitimate court of inquiry. John was convinced he would not leave *Revenge* alive. The best he could hope for was to try and negotiate for the lives of the *Star Wolf* crew, who had risked so much already on his behalf.

After several tense moments while those at the head of the table whispered amongst themselves regarding Twitch's statements, Mark Russel turned toward John.

"Dr. Salzmann, despite Commander Richardson's deft and articulate defense, you and I both know the truth of the allegations made against *Star Wolf* and her crew. Whatever limited agency may actually exist between Salzmann Pharmaceuticals and the Theocracy, it can in no way be reasonably extended to include espionage, acts of terrorism, and wanton destruction of Dawnstar property. However, I am so moved by your impassioned plea and willingness to surrender your life on behalf of your friends that I feel obligated to respond to your petition."

John felt his heart drop at the condescending tone in Russel's voice. Whatever he was about to propose, it definitely did not stem from respect or compassion.

"I will make you a one-time offer that is going to expire in about sixty seconds. You hand over your wife's research notes to us, and I will drop all charges against you and against *Star Wolf*'s crew."

"Then I suppose we just get to fly away free?" John asked, curling his lip derisively.

"Quite so," Russel continued. "We will escort *Star Wolf* to the jump point to either Tede or Furi, whichever you prefer. You will be allowed to leave, provided you promise never to return to Dawnstar or Provisional Imperium space. Unfortunately, I will be forced to issue a revocation of *Star Wolf*'s authorized Articles of Operation for Provisional Imperium contracts, but I am certain your captain would admit this is a small price to pay in exchange for your lives and freedom.

"Should you, however, refuse this generous and lenient offer, I will execute every single member of *Star Wolf*'s crew for engaging in acts of terrorism, piracy, and treason, saving you for last so that you can watch as each life is extinguished due to your recalcitrance. It's your choice, doctor, but choose quickly. My patience is expended."

John took a deep, slow breath. His heart fluttered in his chest. Part of him wanted to search the faces of his companions for guidance, but he dared not look for fear of the condemnation or accusations he might find lurking behind their eyes.

If he complied with Russel's ultimatum, billions upon billions might die in an insidious genocide. Who knew how far the Provisional Imperium would go if it developed a genetically selective bioweapon? Refusing to comply meant an immediate death sentence for a crew full of sophonts whose only crime was trying to save John's life.

Even with that, the choice was not nearly so clear cut. With all Molon had shared about GalSec, there was nothing that gave John the slightest assurance that Russel would keep his word even if John handed over Elena's datacube.

John's gambling instincts told him he was holding a losing

hand. When a gambler is into the pot too deeply to fold, holding losing cards, and facing an opponent who appeared to be sitting strong, a half-hearted bluff would accomplish nothing. There was only one move—all in!

"I can't help you, Deputy Director Russel," John said, looking straight into Russel's eye and doing his best to show the steely resolve of a man with nothing to lose. "So you do what you have to do. I swear by the Lion, I don't have Elena's research to give to you."

John kept his external composure, but his stomach fluttered. He knew he was lying, but lying to protect the lives of others was a gray area. After all, in the Bible wasn't Rahab the prostitute praised for lying to protect the Hebrew spies? And didn't God Himself instruct Samuel not to tell Saul the whole truth about his intention to anoint David as the new king? While he did have Elena's datacube, he certainly did not have data he could rightly hand over to genocidal maniacs. At least that much was true.

"That is most unfortunate," Russel replied, a sardonic smile crossing his face.

"I'm sorry," John replied. "It is not a choice."

That much, in John's mind, was true enough.

Russel rubbed his face and ran his fingers back through his hair in frustration.

"I had hoped to avoid this," Russel said, nodding toward the silent, ginger-haired man in the medical coat seated next to him. "But perhaps my colleague here, Dr. Rickham, is correct. There is only one thing that will change your mind."

Russel tapped the controls on the table's build in comm unit.

"Send in our guest."

Momentarily the doors behind where Russel was seated opened. John's breath caught in his throat. His ears rang and his hands went cold. John blinked his eyes furiously to batter back the tears as he fought the swooning light-headedness that threatened to rob him of consciousness. There before him stood...

Elena?

Twenty-Six – Shattering

The room rested in silence for what seemed to John like an eternity. There she stood, not ten meters from him. His brow sweating, hands quivering, and stomach churning, John fought against the swirling vertigo threatening to rob him of consciousness as he rose slowly from his seat.

"Elena?...How?...What?"

Part of him wanted to rush to the image of his late wife standing before him. Something deep in his mind, however, sounded alarm bells. He leaned slightly on the conference table with one hand to steady himself as he fought the urge to collapse.

"I'm sorry, John," said the apparition bearing the face of his beloved Elena. "It was never supposed to play out like this. You should be back on Tede, safe and starting a new life without me. Dr. Rickham was right, though," she said, nodding toward the white-coated figure seated next to Russel. "After examining your psychological profile, he predicted that once everything had gone this far off track, you would never stop unless I showed myself and explained things to you."

"John," Molon said, taking a grip on his arm. "This can't really be Elena. It's some kind of clone or copy made to look like her."

"But..." John argued, hope and denial fighting for control of his mind.

"We both saw Elena die," Molon said, squeezing John's arm even tighter. "Whatever slick game GalSec is playing at, don't fall for it."

"I'd guess an android," Dub added, rubbing his chin with his mechanized glove-hand as if he were looking over a new engine prototype. "Those cover artists can do wonders. With a holo and a few hours, they can make a 'droid look like anyone."

"Shut your mouth, Lubanian," Elena shrieked at Molon. "This is *your* fault! If you hadn't shown up and pulled John out before we were finished, none of this would have been necessary. John would have been returned to Tede and moved

313

on with his life. Meanwhile, my research would already be helping to put us back on the road to peace and reunification of the Empire of Humaniti."

John wavered slightly, shaking his head in a continuous series of miniscule motions that looked like a motor function glitch in an android. His mind reeled, trying to process the reality of all he saw and heard.

"Dr. Rickham?" John asked, finally snapping out of his denial loop and looking up toward the ginger-haired physician.

"Yes, Dr. Salzmann?"

"Do you carry a portable bioscanner?"

"Well," Rickham laughed, "I can't say as head of a research division I have much use for it nowadays, but yeah, I still carry one. Old habits are hard to break."

"I understand," John said, walking toward the far end of the table and feeling like he was watching himself from somewhere else. "Might I borrow it, please?"

The armed guards around the perimeter of the room raised their weapons as John moved toward the head of the table. He didn't break stride. Somewhere deep inside he hoped one of them would pull a trigger and wake him from what most certainly was the most disturbing nightmare he had ever dreamed.

"Stand down," Admiral Starling ordered. "Dr. Salzmann poses no threat."

The security officers complied, but John only caught the lowering of their weapons out of the corner of his eye. He was walking toward Rickham, but he could not take his eyes off the visage of Elena. If this was a fake, they had her copied exactly, from the tiny freckle below her left eye, to the way she inhaled much more quickly than she exhaled when she was nervous. Even the tiny dimples in her smile were perfect. But how?

John took the bioscanner from Rickham's outstretched hand. It was an old Lifetex model 600. Those things were outdated and being replaced when John was still in his residency. He looked it over, and from what he could remember everything was distantly familiar. As far as John could tell, the device was genuine.

"Dub," he called back to *Star Wolf*'s chief engineer. "Could you come look at this for me, please?"

Weapons again rose to ready when the huge malmorph stood from his seat and lumbered toward the head of the table. Their other hosts remained seated, but Simmons stood up and interposed himself between his cohorts at the head of the table, and John and Dub. Starling motioned again for the guards to lower their weapons, but there was a look of apprehension in the admiral's eyes at the sheer size of Chief Dubronski. Simmons showed no such concern.

John had calculated this move very carefully. If this was a real scanner, and the scans gave any indication this was not Elena, he wanted someone from *Star Wolf* at this end of the table with him. Dub was the only one he could think of an excuse to get here, though.

"Dub, can you examine this scanner and tell me if it is what it appears to be, or if it has been tampered with in any way? Is there anything that would give you reason to believe it is not an ordinary portable bioscanner?"

Dub grasped the device gingerly in his mechanical hand-gloves. He eyed it carefully for a few minutes and did some cursory diagnostics using the device's built in systems.

"Looks right to me, Doc," Dub answered. "This thing is at least three decades old, though. Hardly see one of these anymore. If they were going to fake something, it would be a lot easier to reprogram one of the newer models. If I remember right from my days as a junker, these Lifetex 600's barely had enough memory to do what they were built to do, much less anything else."

"I told you," Dr. Rickham smiled sheepishly. "I have been doing R&D since I was in my twenties. Kept that thing mostly out of sentimental value and habit. It was my father's. I don't really practice medicine anymore, so there was no need to get an updated bioscanner."

John turned toward the putative Elena and raised the bioscanner. He set it for a complete physio-genetic snapshot scan. That setting was generally used for detecting mutational anomalies in victims of prolonged radiation exposure. John, however, knew Elena's physical and genetic scan patterns as well as he knew his own face in the mirror. He had been her physician for years and could picture her scans clearly enough to have drawn them by hand.

Once the combination scan was complete, John plugged the Lifetex unit into the data port at one of the table's built-in terminal stations. The data was quickly converted and displayed in full graphic and numerical formats on the screen in front of him. Dizziness swam through his mind as John dropped into the empty chair at the table.

"This *is* Elena," he announced loudly enough for all to hear.

For a few moments, all he could do was sit there, staring at the scans and shaking his head. It defied all logic and reason.

315

John's own mind was reeling. Had he imagined her death? Had he been drugged into believing it? If so, how did that explain Molon seeing it as well? John cleared his throat and struggled to once again find his voice.

"I don't understand how, but she *is* my wife."

"Whoa, Doc," Molon interjected from the far end of the table. "Wouldn't a clone also register as biologically identical?"

"Yes and no."

John looked up from the scan results to face Molon.

"The DNA of a clone would read the same, but not the experiential physiological markers. A DNA sample can only take a cellular snapshot of what a person was ideally, biologically designed to be. It can't capture the physical, non-genetic changes that happen after a person is fully formed."

"So you're saying," Molon asked, "that this scan can tell you her life story?"

"Sort of," John mused, still mulling through things in his mind as he rattled off a textbook explanation as if he were giving a genetics lecture. "A person's white blood cells, immunological profile, bone structure, cellular degradation, all add up to a genetic fingerprint of a person's life that goes beyond their genetics. Two clones, or even two identical twins, that had lived for a number of years in different places would be distinguishable by their physiological biometric markers.

"For example, I can see the Rumisian fever Elena caught when she was twelve, the elbow she fractured at sixteen while ice skating, the deep-tissue chemical burn she got from her lab partner, me, goofing off during an experiment in college. The slightly degraded retinas from too many years staring at display screens, the hair degradation from a few too many trips to the salon, the microscopic respiratory scarring from sandstorms in Tede's western desert where we lived for a few years. It is all here. Without question, this *is* Elena."

John finally caught up with his own mental processing. He leapt out of the chair and rushed to his wife, hugging her with all his strength. He never thought he would hold her again. Now he never wanted to let go.

"John," Elena rasped, "you are crushing me. Please, darling, let me go so I can explain."

Fighting against every instinct he had not to let go, John released Elena, but did not take more than half a step back from her. He finally noticed, poking out from beneath the decorative silk scarf she wore around her neck, the edges of a wicked-looking scar across her throat. Doubtless that was the work of the torturer on Ratuen. What had they done to her mind that she would forget the atrocities they suffered on Ratuen and stand here willingly beside these people who allied themselves with the Dawnstar forces who masterminded their abduction?

He had to get her away from them and cleanse whatever drugs or devices they doubtlessly were using to control her. Already his mind was spinning through how he and the *Star Wolf* crew could rescue Elena and get away from *Revenge* without losing anyone else. He came up empty on ideas.

"I never wanted to hurt you, John," Elena said to him with that sad little frown that said she had bad news to share. "Don't you see? Dawnstar agreed to fully fund my work on a cure for malmorphsy as long as I share all results and work in conjunction with their head of biomedical research, Dr. Rickham."

John's brow furrowed. What was she saying? This Rickham was not with the Provisional Imperium but was head of research for the very people who had abducted them?

"But Elena, they tortured us."

"I know, John."

"They made me think they had murdered you."

"Yes, dear. That was unfortunate."

Unfortunate? What had they done to his dear Elena's mind? She was clearly delusional, or possibly mind-controlled. John had to find a way to break her free, had to get her away from these animals.

"Let me explain," Elena continued. "If they had contacted me through normal channels, we could have talked this all out. The abduction was admittedly a misguided idea, but that was because they had no understanding that our goals were aligned."

"Aligned? What do you mean?"

"One night while we were still on Ratuen, they drugged you to keep you under and pulled me out for a discussion. They whisked us off planet before I knew what was happening. Then, en route to Ratuen, they explained what they wanted. Initially they were threatening to kill you if I didn't cooperate, but once they laid it all out, I realized we wanted the same thing."

"Elena, something is wrong with you. I don't know what they told you, but these people are planning violence on a massive scale."

"I know, dear."

John's chest tightened. Spots appeared at the edges of his vision and it was everything he could do to stay focused. She clearly did not know what she was saying.

"Once we came to terms about my research," Elena continued, forcing John to focus. "I knew you would never agree. You have always been such a gentle soul, John. I told them we had to find a way to keep you out of it. We agreed that they would kill me, or at least make it look that way, and then return you to Tede none the wiser. I would accompany them back to Tede and grab my research before you were released, and all would be well."

"All would be well?" John's mind volleyed between confusion and rage. "They slit your throat in front of me?"

"I know, John," Elena replied. "It was never supposed to go that far, but the inquisitor on Ratuen has a flair for the theatrical. He performed his duty a bit overzealously. I'm sorry about that, John. I can't imagine the trauma that must have put you through."

John swallowed hard. They had to have her on some mind-altering drugs. This was not his Elena. So cold, so callous. Or maybe this was one of those high-tech mind-controlling implants he had heard about at the last government medical conference on Furi. She couldn't know what she was saying or how dangerous these people truly were. It was going to be up to him to save her from herself.

"Elena, do you have any idea why they want your research? They plan to develop a bioweapon the likes of which the Daemi used to cause malmorphsy in the first place. Once the Provisional Imperium can produce biologically targeted weaponry, who's to say they will stop at beating back the Prophane? What would stop them from taking out the Lubanians helping the New Empire, or the Fei helping the Theocracy? There wouldn't be a non-human sophont in the galaxy safe from Zarsus and his minions."

"I know, John. I know."

John couldn't breathe. To hear such casual assent to galactic-scale genocide coming from Elena, the most compassionate and merciful person he had ever known, was the epitome of cognitive dissonance. He didn't care what the bioscans showed, this was not Elena. Not the Elena he knew anyway.

"John, do you love me?" Elena asked, clearly seeing the shock and horror in John's face.

"I did..."

John's response was out of his mouth before he even realized he had said it. The scathing implication of his answer clearly cut Elena deeply. Her eyes glassed, and her lip quivered

318

slightly as she continued.

"Do you trust me, John?"

"How can I, Elena? You clearly are not in your right mind."

"I assure you, John, I am."

"You are not! You just admitted agreeing to cooperate in a project that could destroy countless billions of non-human sophonts throughout the galaxy? I'm not sure I even know you, much less trust you."

"Non-human sophonts?" Elena said, raising an eyebrow. "I see you've been through alien indoctrination training since you took up with the dog-man and his collection of alien freaks. Since when do you care about aliens, John?"

John reeled. He had never heard such invective from Elena before. What twisted device or drug had they used to warp his sweet Elena so thoroughly?

"Elena, why are you talking like that? You are a doctor."

Elena grabbed John's arms and shook him as if she were scolding a child. The fire in her eyes was like nothing John had ever seen from her before.

"I'm a *human* doctor, John. Why do you think I chose to remain on Tede? I was offered dozens of positions on integrated worlds, but I chose to stay sequestered on that backwater mudball, where at least I would be with my own kind and not surrounded by alien freaks. I thought you understood that. Isn't that why you stayed?"

Who was this person? Pieces of memories began to fall into place. Elena had always focused on human research, and often voiced dissent about Dawnstar bringing her "alien" DNA to work with. As soon as she was out of her residency she had let her non-human certifications lapse, but John had always assumed that was due to her research focus and their life on Tede, a humans-only hermit-world. John had let his own lapse for similar reasons. How could he have been married to Elena for twenty-three years and never have seen this side of her? Was love truly that blind?

"I stayed on Tede because that was where my parents' company was," John replied, frustrated confusion rising in his tone. "That was where you were. Everything that mattered to me was on Tede."

"Exactly! Including a government willing to keep Tede as a human colony. That's what the Provisional Imperium and Dawnstar are promising, John. They want to clear out the enemies of Humaniti and restore the Empire to the unity it once had. The human empire, John."

"But we are Faithful!" John shouted, shrugging off Elena's

319

grip on his arms and taking a half-step away from her. "If you were okay with your work being used for making a weapon, why not turn it over to the Brothers of the Lion instead of the Provisional Imperium and Dawnstar?"

"I am a Faithful," Elena replied with much more calm than John had managed to maintain. "But our shepherds have gone astray. Enoch made a pact with those blue-skinned freaks, the Fei. He doesn't care about the restoration of Humaniti."

John balled his hands into fists knowing Mel had just heard this hateful invective. He had never struck Elena in their entire marriage, no matter how drunk or angry he was. Now he fought against the impulse to break that streak.

"The Creator put the Angelicum there to serve humans," Elena continued. "The Daemi are fallen, but ultimately still part of God's plan for Humaniti. The Brothers are not only willing to spare those blue abominations, but are also looking to destroy the very servants our Creator gave us. The Provisional Imperium has returned the wayward Daemi to the service of Humaniti. The Brothers would have them destroyed. The choice of who to work with is clear, John."

John turned away from Elena. He spared as subtle a glance in Mel's direction as he dared, but she was too far away. He couldn't get a good read on how deeply Elena's invective had affected her. Rage boiled inside him, but he wasn't sure if it was directed more at the forces that had lured Elena down this dark path or at Elena herself for speaking so cruelly about Mel's people.

"No, Elena," John said, shaking his head and turning back toward her. "This isn't what the Lion of Judah would have us do."

Elena reached for John to take his hand but he recoiled as if she were a deadly serpent. Part of him wanted to run from this room, part just wanted to wake up from this impossible nightmare, part wanted to beat to death this twisted doppelganger pretending to be his sweet Elena, and part just prayed for some impossible rescue to deliver them once again from the hands of Russel and the imposing cruiser *Revenge*.

"John," Elena pleaded. "Just give me my research. I know you have it. I had a signal trigger set into our closet safe. I compared the time stamp on the signal to the alarm system reports on the house fire. I know you accessed it before our home was destroyed."

John's gaze focused on the floor before his feet. He wanted to throw up. He answered without meeting her gaze.

"Even if I did have it, why would I give it to you, knowing

what you intend to do with it?"

"It is simple, John. I never wanted to drag you into any of this. I still love you. I have told Deputy Director Russel that I would only continue to work with them if he agreed to free you and your friends."

John looked up into Elena's eyes. Behind the glassy, half-formed tears there, John saw sincerity.

"And you believe him?" John asked, hoping she would realize the naiveté of what she was saying.

"John, listen to me" Elena said in a forced and desperate whisper. "Please be reasonable. If you don't hand over the research, they will pull your ship apart bit by bit and kill each one of the crew to find it. If they have to do it that way, John, not even my life is guaranteed."

"Good," John snapped, instantly regretting it as soon as the word was out of his mouth. Elena looked as if he had punched her.

"John, please," Elena pleaded, her eyes flitting nervously between Simmons and John. "I can recreate all the research on that datacube, but it took me two decades to accumulate it. Starting over would be a huge setback to our timeline. You can't stop it, John, but you can save yourself."

"For the moment, at least," John snapped.

"The work will continue no matter what you do, but only you can decide whether or not you and your friends die here today."

John's heart sank. He knew if it came to a fight, *Star Wolf's* officers were unarmed, well mostly at least. Once they were dead, their bodies would be searched and Elena would immediately recognize her datacube on John's necklace. They would have died for nothing and it would all be his fault. He was out of options. There was only one play left to make. He raised his gaze and fixed his eyes on Elena's.

"You swear as the Lion of Judah is your witness you will refuse to work with them if they don't let *Star Wolf* and its entire crew go free?"

"I do," Elena answered, giving John a reassuring smile. "I swear it by the Lion of Judah and by our love and marriage. I know you can't walk this road with me, so I will let you go. Find happiness, my love, and know your friends will live today because of you."

John reached for his shirt collar and pulled out the necklace attached to the datacube from its hiding place beneath the collar of his shirt.

"No, John," Mel shouted. "They will kill every one of us

321

eventually. They will destroy my race, Voide's race, Molon's race. Do not do this, John."

"I'm sorry, Mel," John said without taking his eyes off his wife. "Elena is right. If they are determined to pursue this course, I can't stop it. But I can stop them from killing us all today."

"I don't think so, bud," Dub said.

Quicker than lightning the huge malmorph's mechanical hand-glove shot out and grabbed the datacube pendant from John's hand. He slammed his two metallic appendages together with the small, fragile cube in between, grinding the datacube to dust before the stunned gaze of all present.

"What have you done?" Elena shrieked.

Twenty-Seven – Guardian Angel

"Kill that man!" Simmons ordered.

The GalSec security officers bordering the room raised their weapons and aimed them in Dub's direction. John jumped in front of the chief engineer, extending his arms and holding his hands, palms outward, as if interposing his markedly smaller physique would somehow stop the blasters from firing. In the split second it took him to make that maneuver, there had been no time to consider the futility of it.

"Wait!" John shouted. "Elena, you promised."

"Stand down," Mark Russel ordered.

The security officers lowered their weapons slightly and held their fire as they looked back and forth between the two ranking GalSec officers. It was clear they were unsure whose command to obey. John was mentally rooting for Russel.

Elena just stood there, taking no notice of John or his plea. She gawked silently at the crumbled fragments of her datacube lying on the floor at her feet. She stood there, shaking her head slightly as if by sheer force of denial she could reassemble the destroyed datacube.

"But why?" she finally muttered, raising her gaze in Dub's direction. "You are a human malmorph. That datacube contained research that could have put me mere months away from a cure for you and others like you."

Dub spread his hands in front of him in a gesture of apology.

"I'm sorry, ma'am" Dub replied. "Sure, some part of me might want to be like everyone else. I do think about it sometimes. But nothing is worth what that cure would cost."

The calm pleading fled her face as a flush of rage rose in her cheeks. Her eyes narrowed and a scowl replaced the blank look of confusion that had graced her face just moments before.

"It would cost you nothing!" Elena snapped. "I want to help people like you. I'm not trying to turn a profit."

Dub shook his large head. John couldn't tell if the look in

323

his eyes was sadness or pity.

"You really don't get it, do you?" Dub answered, pointing a mechanical-glove finger in Elena's direction. "What these people are planning goes far beyond genocide. They are planning xenocide."

"Why do you care?" Elena replied, throwing her arms wide in frustration as if to emphasize the question. "They're aliens, you're human!"

Dub's hands balled into fists. The security forces raised their weapons slightly, but the large engineer exhibited wisdom enough to lower his fists to his sides.

"I'm sorry John has to hear me say this, you being his wife and all," Dub said through gritted teeth. "But I know a whole lot of those you call 'aliens', any one of whom is worth ten thousand humans like you. It ain't the shape or color a person is that makes their life worth saving. It only matters what they do with the life they've been given."

Dub and Elena were locked in an intense stare. Tension in the room was at a flashpoint, and John feared that any second something was going to be the spark that set the room ablaze. John was no diplomat, but maybe he was adept enough at selling a bluff to salvage this situation somehow.

"So what now?" John probed, testing the waters.

His eyes were locked on Elena but John knew full well she had little influence any longer. Their fate was in Russel's hands.

"Our agreement with your wife," Russel replied, clearly choking back his own rage at Dub's defiant act, "was your lives in exchange for Elena's data. Your crewmate just destroyed the data. You are an educated man, doctor; what do you think happens next?"

John turned to face the deputy director. There was no longer any smug look of superiority or catty grin remaining on Russel's face. While John deep down believed Dub did the right thing, the cost of his defiance would likely result in an execution order for *Star Wolf*'s crew.

"Wait!" Elena interjected.

All eyes fixed on Elena as she turned to face Russel. John heard a passion and desperation in her voice. He knew that tone. It was the one she used in debates in medical school when she saw a possibility others had missed and was about to spring it on them. John silently prayed that whatever oration she was about to drop on Russel worked in their favor.

"I am still the best qualified geneticist you have when it comes to malmorphsy. Dawnstar must have all my pre-

Shattering reports filed away somewhere. We can start with those and I can rebuild my data. I will continue to lead your research project provided you let John and his friends go free."

The look on Russel's face was hard enough to shatter diamond. He slowly closed and opened his eyes as if trying to rein in an outburst of fury at Elena's defiance.

"And should I decide to do otherwise?" Russel asked.

"Otherwise," Elena replied through a smug grin. "I wish you luck with the dead-ends Dr. Rickham has been stumbling into for years. He's a brilliant man, truly, but he just can't grasp the delicate complexity of the malmorphsy genetic matrix. You can't blame him, though. There aren't a handful of human researchers in the whole galaxy that can...besides me, of course."

"Are you threatening me, Dr. Salzmann?" Russel said to Elena.

"If you force my hand," she replied, straightening herself and locking eyes with the imposing deputy director. "Or if you kill me for forcing yours, I wish you luck finding that needle in a few trillion haystacks. Destruction of this data will delay us, but otherwise it changes nothing."

John loathed the truth he had discovered about Elena, but the woman arguing their case now before the GalSec director was the brilliant, amazing woman he had fallen in love with. How could one person hold so much light and yet so much darkness at the same time?

Russel pounded the table. His voice raised and his face reddened as he wagged a finger at Elena.

"Do you think I will be swayed by this emotional tripe? This mutant has set our timetable back years, possibly decades. Despite your smug assurances to the contrary, this changes quite a number of things. The Prophane are encroaching daily. Resources are depleting, fighting a multi-front war. The Provisional Imperium may not survive this delay. This defiance cannot go unpunished!"

"Really, Mark?" Voide interjected, rising from her seat and drawing the barrels of the two nearest security officers in her direction. "What if it had been me who destroyed the data? Would you still be so hell-bent on an execution?"

"It wasn't you," Russel tersely replied.

"There is no difference, Mark," Voide continued. "If you mean to kill Dub, you are going to have to kill me along with the rest of *Star Wolf*'s crew. You don't murder one of ours and expect us to walk away."

"One of yours, Yasu?" Mark said, his voice dripping with

incredulity. He swept his arm to indicate the other *Star Wolf* officers around Voide. "Is that how you really see them? These people keep you around as a pet because you can fight. You're their guard dog, nothing more. They don't love you, I do. I know you had nothing to do with this. Join me now; you don't have to die."

"I'm afraid you are wrong, Russel," Molon interrupted. "Voide is capable of a lot of things, but switching sides to save herself ain't one of them. If you knew her half as well as you pretend to, you'd know that."

"So you know her better than I do?" Russel snapped.

"She is part of my crew, and I know my crew. If you execute one of them, the rest wouldn't obey an order to stand down even if I gave one. Which, by the way, I wouldn't."

Russel folded his hands and closed his eyes. He took a deep breath and slowly exhaled before opening them again. An eerie calm flowed from him that left John feeling anything but comforted.

"Simmons, proceed with our original plan. Escort our guests back to their ship and allow them to enter the jump point to Furi."

Simmons nodded, silently.

"Elena, I trust that will suffice?" Russel said, turning toward her. "Now, you and Dr. Rickham return to the lab, you have work to do."

John wasn't convinced. Desperate for some security beyond Mark Russel's word they were being set free, he fought his revulsion and reached out for Elena's hand.

"Why don't you come see us off, Elena? I can't agree with what you are doing, but we are still husband and wife. At least we can say a proper goodbye."

The faked emotion almost stuck in John's throat. Nothing in Elena's feelings for him had changed. She still loved him. What had changed was John's heart when she revealed her dark hatred of non-humans. Could he ever love her again, knowing now who she truly was?

He certainly didn't feel it at the moment, but there were so many things going on inside, he would need a lot of alone time to sort through it all. Elena's good will was the only thing standing between *Star Wolf*'s crew and execution. Russel couldn't afford to jeopardize that cooperation by breaking his promise to spare John and his crewmates. Elena personally witnessing their departure was the best insurance John could think of to leverage that.

"You can say goodbye now," Simmons said, cutting off

John's play. The icy monotone from Simmons left the meaning behind his words highly open to interpretation.

"Two security officers," Simmons added, addressing the kind-faced GalSec security sergeant. "See Dr. Salzmann and Dr. Rickham back to the lab immediately. The rest of you, come with me."

The female GalSec sergeant pointed to two of the other security personnel and used a hand signal to direct them toward the doctors. She then motioned for the remaining three officers to form up around her and Simmons.

"John, I..." Elena said, her voice wavering.

Elena's eyes darted between him and Russel. John could count on one hand the number of times he had ever seen Elena look unsure of herself. This was one. He saw his ploy for security slipping away in the face of Simmons's icy impassiveness. His mind quickly scrambled for a backup plan as the security officer pulled Elena's hand out of his and gave her a semi-gentle push toward the exit door.

"I will send you a message via System Express as soon as I get back to Tede," John said as the security officers ushered the doctors out of the briefing room. "I'll send you a picture of me at the place I took you on our first anniversary. Then you will know we got back safely."

"I'll wait for it, John. If you can ever bring yourself to understand what I am doing, come join me. I will be waiting for you. I will always love you."

John felt nauseated leading Elena on like this. His heart rent. It was like he had never truly knowns his wife at all. He barely recognized her now, knowing this secret hatred for non-humans she had hidden from him all this time. Yet her affection for him, her belief that some way, somehow they might be together again was genuine. John could only hope that the prospect of Elena not receiving his 'arrived safely' message would be enough of a deterrent to any nefarious plans Russel might have in mind.

Simmons shook John from his speculation as he roughly spun John away from the door through which Elena and Dr. Rickham had just departed, and pointed him toward the doorway through which *Star Wolf*'s crew had entered.

Russel and Rear Admiral Starling stood and left through a third door without another word. The puzzled look on the faces of his crewmates told John he wasn't alone in finding the suddenness of their exit odd. John wasn't sure what he was expecting—certainly not a fanfare and parade. Still, Russel's final look back over his shoulder as he glanced at Voide was concerning. There was regret in his eyes.

"If you would all be so kind as to follow me," Simmons said with frosty formality.

Simmons gave a knowing nod to the GalSec sergeant, and then exited without so much as a backward glance to assure compliance. The security officers, however, motioned with their weapons, demonstrating that following Simmons was not merely the polite request it mimicked.

Dub and John were farthest from the door, so were the last to make their way out of the conference room. That also put them closest to the security officers. The GalSec security sergeant's bright blue eyes locked in with John's.

"It is going to be all right," she said softly to him as they exited.

"So what's with your new girlfriend?" Dub whispered to John as they followed the other officers down the corridor.

"Beats me," John replied. "I've never seen her before in my life. At least she seems to be the one person on this ship not looking to shove us out an airlock."

"Don't jump to conclusions," Dub replied. "Remember an Ormathi sand rabbit looks cute and cuddly too, right up until it rips your throat out."

"You know, you should hire out as a motivational speaker," John quipped, trying to lighten the mood of the ominous procession. "You have a rare gift."

"I'll give that some thought," Dub grinned, "if we live long enough."

"Yep, a true gift," John repeated.

"Speaking of threats to our life," Dub said, nodding toward Simmons. "I don't trust that dark-haired short-stack. I'm going to ease up front with Cap in case things go sideways."

"Be careful, Dub," John replied. "I've seen that 'short-stack' toss Voide around like she was a toddler. Simmons is dangerous."

"So am I, pal. I just look cute and cuddly to the untrained eye."

"Like an Ormathi sand rabbit?"

"Exactly!" Dub said with a wink.

John smiled as the huge malmorph quickened his pace to catch up with Molon at the front of the group. He liked Dub's twisted sense of humor, but he doubted the chief engineer's own mother could call him 'cute' and keep a straight face. On the other hand, while malmorphsy might have disfigured Dub's exterior, inside *Star Wolf*'s chief engineer was one of the most unsullied spirits John had ever encountered.

As Dub moved forward, John noticed Mel dropping back to walk beside him. He wasn't sure he was ready to deal with all the emotional baggage that went with his complicated friendship with the Fei communications officer right now. Still, he found her proximity comforting amidst all this chaos.

"Are you all right, John?" Mel asked.

"Ask me again once we are back aboard *Star Wolf* and safely in voidspace en route to Furi," John replied.

Fortunately Mel didn't press the issue, and they continued making their way behind Simmons. Two of the security officers moved partway up the line, to take a position in front of John and Mel, but behind Voide and Twitch. Close on Simmons's heels ahead of them all were Molon and Dub. The inexplicably friendly female GalSec sergeant and one other officer brought up the rear.

As Simmons strode past a T-intersection with a corridor branching off to the right, Dub grabbed Molon's arm and stopped the procession.

"Are you lost, shorty?" Dub said, addressing Simmons. "The hangar where *Star Wolf* is docked is this way."

Dub pointed down the branching corridor Simmons had just passed.

"We aren't going that way," Simmons replied, as if that answer sufficiently addressed Dub's question.

"Then where are we going?" Molon asked.

John could see, even from the back of the group, the hackles on Molon's neck stand up on edge as the captain's ears angled forward. The barest hint of the tips of his canines protruded from the edge of his subtly curling lip.

Voide too had dipped slightly into a crouch, her gaze fixed on Simmons rather than the security officer immediately behind her. Twitch, however, had already turned to face the guard closest to her. Intensity filled the air as the security forces sensed the tension escalation playing out before them. *Star Wolf*'s senior officers stood, tense and silent, as they waited for Simmon's answer.

"Fine," Simmons said, leaning his head from side to side, cracking his neck as if warming up for a workout. "I was planning to lead you all to another airlock where I was going to depressurize it before dumping you into deep space. Then I was going to instruct *Revenge*'s crew to cut *Star Wolf* loose and blast it to scrap. But now you've gone and ruined the surprise."

The GalSec senior interrogator took no other action, but just stood staring at Molon, awaiting a reaction. Even the security officers looked around as if trying to figure out if

Simmons was being serious or sarcastic.

After a tense moment or two, with both sides coiled and ready to spring into action, Simmons broke the awkward silence.

"Unfortunately, you are too clever for your own good. Fire!"

Before the order was even out of his mouth, Simmons had leveled a blurringly-fast sideways swipe with his left arm, delivering a vicious chop to Molon's chest. The large Lubanian yelped as the powerful blow sent him flying down the side corridor. John could not imagine how the short-statured GalSec interrogator wielded that much power, but it shed some light on how easily he had bested Voide in their first encounter.

The next few seconds exploded with such fast action that John could barely process all that was going on around him. Dub dropped a massive overhand blow aimed at Simmons's head, swinging his metallic glove-hand like a sledgehammer driving a spike. Voide, at that same moment, uncoiled like a striking viper, launching her body straight at Simmons, ignoring the GalSec security officer next to her whose weapon was trained on the springing Pariah.

It was not just Simmons who was a target. Before the hapless trooper who had been assigned to Twitch could even pull the trigger, *Star Wolf*'s executive officer had redirected the security officer's blaster barrel toward the ceiling of the corridor and was wrestling with him for control of the weapon. She hooked a leg behind his and used her leverage to force the soldier off balance, slamming him into the corridor wall, making him choose between controlling his weapon or remaining on his feet. He released the weapon and flailed his arms against the wall and against Twitch, scrambling for balance.

Beside John, Mel had already turned and touched the trigger-hand of the security officer closest to her. She used no physical force, but simply spoke softly.

"Everything is under control. Your legs are very tired. It will be okay if you just sit down and take a rest, right now."

The trooper's knees buckled and his grip on his weapon loosened as the man slumped to the floor. He sat, cross-legged, smiling and holding Mel's hand as he watched the drama unfolding around him.

John was amazed at *Star Wolf*'s senior officers. They were good, and fast, but they were also outnumbered. John could only watch helplessly as the guard who Voide had ignored in order to launch herself at Simmons, leveled his blaster rifle at

Dub's back. Simmons, in the meanwhile, had caught Dub's massive overhand blow with his right hand, stopping it cold. The GalSec interrogator twisted Dub's arm, forcing the giant man to his knees to keep his arm from breaking. Molon had told John how much stronger Dub was than a normal human, and Dub had admitted as much. But Simmons handled the huge malmorph as though he were a parent controlling a misbehaving toddler.

Without ever breaking his concentration on Dub, Simmons also lashed out with his left hand and caught Voide in midair, grabbing her by the shoulder and flinging her aside. The security chief's bodily trajectory was deflected sideways, slamming her hard into the corner of the corridor wall. John was certain he heard the sound of bones crunching as Voide's shoulder impacted the corner, but her face held no sign of pain; only fearsome rage.

John was too far away to do anything about the security officer leveling a weapon at Dub, but there was one he could reach. The kindly female sergeant was standing directly behind John. He might not be much use in a fight, but at least he might be able to keep her distracted until one of his crewmates could help.

John gasped as he spun to face the female security sergeant. There before him was the kind-faced woman who had smiled at him and assured him everything would be okay. Yet now, behind her back extended large silvery, translucent, gossamer wings. They were magnificent: glowing representations of wings such as had graced the imagination of man long before the Angelicum's existence as a race had become common knowledge.

The wings were clearly immaterial, some type of manifestation of energy emanating from the female sergeant. They pulsed with power as she extended her left hand in front of her, palm outward.

"Sleep," the woman said, in a soft but commanding tone.

John heard bodies dropping to the floor behind him. He felt something like a light breeze pass over him at her voiced command, but somehow her power had not affected him. Glancing over, John saw that not only the guard who had been about to shoot Dub in the back, but even the one wrestling with Twitch, and the man who had been holding Mel's hand, were all now lying on the deck, their eyes closed with peaceful expressions on their faces. All of *Star Wolf*'s crew were still awake, but so was Simmons.

"You filthy Malak spy," Simmons said, his face filling with

331

more emotion than John ever recalled seeing from the normally impassive interrogator. "You've been a snake in our midst all this time?"

When the Angelicum did not answer, Simmons gave Dub's arm an odd twist that brought the huge malmorph to his feet. Simmons grabbed the front of Dub's shirt and executed a hip toss that sent the larger man flying, landing on his back with a huge grunt further down the corridor. Now only John and Twitch stood between Simmons and this mysterious undercover angel.

"Well, Malak," Simmons said, using the term John knew was the highest biological caste of Angelicum. "You may have infiltrated GalSec and hid your nature all this time, but your petty mind games won't work on me."

Simmons tapped his temple with a forefinger, a never-before-seen malicious grin creeping widely across his normally expressionless features.

"I've got protection from your parlor tricks. You have no idea the money GalSec invested to prepare me for this. After all these years, I finally get my hands on a bona fide angel. This will be priceless."

John saw Twitch ready the blaster rifle she had wrested from the security trooper. Before she could even bring it to bear, however, Simmons moved with unbelievable celerity, grabbing Twitch by the throat and slamming her head hard against the corridor wall. John again heard the sickening crunch of bones breaking as the XO slid, unconscious, down the wall leaving a vertical streak of blood behind as a testimony to the viciousness of Simmon's strike. She lay on the floor, a strange sound coming from her as she labored to breathe.

John saw Molon, grasping his chest with one hand, stagger around the corner of the side corridor just as Twitch slumped to the floor.

"Twitch!" Molon growled out, his fangs now fully bared and his eyes fixed with deadly intent on Simmons's back.

John knew he was the least capable person to stop Simmons, but if anything could be done for Twitch, he was her only hope. Ignoring the advancing GalSec interrogator, John rushed to Twitch's limp body and gingerly began to triage the extent of her injury. She was still breathing, but just barely and most erratically.

John suspected a laryngeal fracture, but it seemed more than that. Simmons had grabbed her by the throat, but the crushing force with which he had slammed her into the bulkhead lent itself to a host of possibilities, none of which were good news.

A concussion was guaranteed, but likely a hematoma as well, given the force with which her head had impacted the wall. The most troubling, however, was the fact that even with her labored breathing, Twitch's body was completely limp. With Simmons's obviously augmented strength, a C5 or C6 spinal injury was highly likely. Twitch's diaphragm was struggling to compensate for her non-responsive breathing muscles, but even if her larynx wasn't crushed, a spinal injury that high might mean Twitch could suffocate or suffer brain damage from oxygen deprivation if he didn't get her to a ventilator soon. He hadn't brought his medical kit along for this meeting, but even if he had, Twitch was going to need to get to a real medical bay immediately or she would be beyond anyone's help.

Meanwhile, Voide had scrambled back to her feet, her left arm clutching her right shoulder as she and Molon, despite their injuries, stumbled like animated corpses down the corridor toward Simmons. Dub had just begun to roll over and try to regain his footing farther down the corridor. Landing that hard had to have knocked the breath out of him at the very least.

Mel darted over to where John was kneeling beside Twitch.

"Can I help, John?"

"She's badly hurt, Mel. I need to stabilize her, but if I don't get her to a sickbay very soon, she's not going to make it."

"What can I do?" Mel asked.

"We have to secure her neck as much as possible, and I might need to open her airway. Do you have a knife?"

"No, but he does," she said, grabbing a combat blade from its sheath hanging from the downed security officer's waist.

Mel handed John the blade and he began to cut strips from the fallen guard's uniform. Using the blaster rifle as a makeshift neck board, John bound Twitch's head as securely as he could to it.

"John, what else can we do?" Mel asked, the pleading tone evident in her voice.

"Nothing until we can move. She's struggling to breathe, but as long as air is coming and going I don't want to perform a field tracheotomy if we can avoid it. Besides I don't even have a fitting tube to use. We just need to pray someone can take this Simmons guy out soon. Twitch isn't going to last long lying here."

Mel stood up silently and joined Voide and Molon to turn

333

on Simmons. John wondered if the gentle Fei and the other two injured officers had any hope of triumphing over the clearly-augmented GalSec interrogator.

"Please stay back," their Angelicum defender said to Molon and Voide, who continued to advance on Simmons. "You cannot defeat this man. He will kill you. Leave him to me."

"Hah," Simmons scoffed loudly. "Leave me to you?"

Once again the augmented GalSec officer's voice revealed a more volatile and emotional state than his norm. It was as if something that had been buried deep within Simmons had suddenly been released, transforming the normally emotionless man into a volatile killing machine.

"You have no idea who or what I am, do you, Malak?" Simmons raged.

"Should I?" the faux sergeant answered.

"Well, you weren't the Angelicum that ripped me apart and left me for dead. That was one of those six-winged Seravim freaks. Unfortunately for you, I didn't die. GalSec kept me alive and offered me the chance to join Project Firelake. I was rebuilt, upgraded, and augmented for one purpose: to fight you and your kind."

As Simmons advanced on the Malak, fists balled and at the ready, the Angelicum only shook her head in disappointment, her translucent wings pulsing darker and more slowly.

"You have traded the gifts of the Creator for human technology," the Malak answered. "Despite what you think, you have not made yourself stronger. You have exchanged the perfected image of God for the flawed inventions of man."

Simmons laughed as a twisted grimace replaced the mocking rage on his face. He increased his pace and spat his final words as he closed the last few steps between himself and the Malak with blinding speed.

"You know, the heads of Project Firelake aren't sure if it is actually possible to kill your kind, but I am willing to give it my best effort."

Simmons reached the Angelicum agent and launched into a flurry of blows almost too fast for the eye to track. Attack after attack from Simmons was blocked and countered, the Malak's wings pulsing from bluish-white to gleaming silver, with each clash sending flickering strobes of light down the corridor. In between defensive moves, the Angelicum launched her own strikes, with the punches, blocks, and counterpunches blending into a furious blur between Simmons and the Malak. Simmons proved just as adept at fending off the Malak's offense, the barest glisten on his skin bearing testament that it was anything but effortless.

The Malak's instruction to stand down had not deterred Molon and Voide from advancing, but John was comforted that at least Mel had chosen to stay back. Regaining and losing Elena in the blink of an eye, and now the possibility of losing Twitch was enough of a cost today. He couldn't contemplate losing Mel too.

Voide reached into a pocket on her right sleeve and pulled out a tiny disk. She tossed it at Simmons, and it clung to his back where it struck. Simmons paid no notice, concentrating fully on his stalemate with the Malak. Voide tapped the control module on her wrist and grinned ferociously, baring her own elongated fangs as Simmons began to twitch and spasm violently for a few seconds before falling to the floor.

In the brief moments of Simmons's standing seizure, the Malak landed half a dozen lightning-fast strikes to the interrogator's head and torso, adding overkill to whatever Voide had done to bring down the GalSec interrogator.

"What was that?" John asked, his eyes fixed with wonder on *Star Wolf*'s security chief.

"A LAMP," Voide answered. "Localized Activatable Magnetic Pulsar. It temporarily frags electronic systems, sort of a mini-EMP. Marines use them to take out powered armor suits, but I started carrying one after my first run-in with that stinking cyborg. See, Molon, I told you he was an augment."

Molon clearly wasn't listening. As soon as Simmons had dropped to the deck, Molon's attention went fully to Twitch. He sprinted over to where John was kneeling beside the wounded executive officer.

"How bad is it, Doc?" Molon asked.

"Bad," John replied. "I need to get her to *Star Wolf*'s sickbay now, Molon."

"Can you save her, John?" the captain asked, his lupine eyes glistening behind a series of rapid blinks.

"I honestly don't know."

Twenty-Eight – Flight to Furi

John turned to face their rescuer as the Angelicum operative touched her wrist communicator.

"Abbot, this is Angel. Package secure. Commence diversion. We should be aboard *Star Wolf* and clear shortly. Avoid docking sections until we are away. Confirm?"

"Angel, this is Abbot," came the reply across the comms unit. *"Message confirmed. Commencing attack run. Affirm avoidance of docking sections pending all-clear. Abbot out."*

"Who are you?" Molon snapped at the Malak, whose translucent wings shimmered gradually dimmer before fading completely.

"I'll explain later," The Angelicum replied, motioning toward the corridor Dub said led to *Star Wolf.* "For now, we need to move. John, is Twitch all right?"

"Do we know you?" John asked, for the moment the Malak's familiarity derailing any focus on her question.

"I know you," she replied. "That is enough for now. Please, can Twitch be moved?"

"She has to be," John answered.

By this time Dub had scrambled to his feet and joined them, doing his best to reach behind his bulk and rub his lower back. Mel and John looked to be the only *Star Wolf* officers who had escaped the encounter unscathed.

Molon winced slightly as he moved to pick Twitch up from where she lay. John had never seen such concern on the Lubanian's wolfish features.

"Molon, are you hurt?" John asked.

"Probably cracked a rib or two, but Twitch is more important," Molon replied.

"Be careful with her neck and head. Do the best you can to move that as little as possible until we get her to sick bay for a complete exam."

"Got you, Doc. Everyone, grab those blaster rifles and clear us a path. Dub, you know the way?"

"Aye, Cap," Dub replied with a nod.

336

"Then lead on. And blast anyone that steps between us and *Star Wolf*, no questions."

"Aye, sir," came a chorus of replies.

Even John realized he had affirmed the order and grabbed a blaster rifle, forgetting for the moment that he had almost no idea how to use one. Voide snatched it from his hands and Dub grabbed the other free blaster rifle that wasn't currently serving as Twitch's neckboard.

The Malak fell in behind them and covered the rear as they made their way toward *Star Wolf*. There was no additional interference as they made their way to the airlock where the ship was docked. That might be due to the periodic spasms that had resonated through *Revenge* every few seconds since the one calling herself Angel had given the order. Alarm klaxons sounded throughout the ship, and red flashing lights punctuated the corridor every few meters. John was no expert, but those sure felt like bombardments from one or more enemy ships attacking the PI cruiser.

John's suspicions were confirmed just as they reached the airlock and an announcement came across general comms.

"All Revenge personnel prepare for emergency depressurization in three minutes. Emergency DP protocols in effect. All personnel outfit in vac-suits and report to battle stations immediately. This is not a drill!"

Fortunately *Star Wolf* had docked with *Revenge* via an umbilical attached to the primary starboard airlock. This was at least on the same side of the ship, and only one deck away, from sickbay. With Twitch's condition, every second mattered.

"Voide," Molon barked as they entered *Star Wolf*'s airlock. "You have the conn. Get to the bridge and get us underway, and no psycho-revenge crap. Get us clear and get us into voidspace now. We'll worry about payback later."

"Aye, sir," Voide said, the grudging tone clear in her voice.

"You won't all get clear until these docking clamps are released," Angel said, standing on *Revenge*'s side of the airlock doors. "Prepare to leave, I'll stay behind and clear the clamps from this side."

"We're not leaving you," John protested.

This was the first real Angelicum he had met, and he wasn't about to leave her behind to die. Could angels really be killed? He had never thought about that before now, but wasn't interested in testing the answer on their rescuer.

"Can the heroics, sweet-face," Dub said to Angel. "Get your tiny tokus in here. I've got the clamps handled."

The Malak stepped inside *Star Wolf*'s airlock, dubiously

337

eyeing Dub. The malmorph engineer approached the panel, closed the airlock doors, and snaked the mechanical appendage containing his NID into a data port in the panel as he activated a private comms channel from the controls.

"All right my little beauties," Dub said, raising his hands as if he were about to conduct a symphony, the NID umbilical extending to accommodate his movement. "Spiderbot squad seventeen, load subroutine filename: debark. Authorization code: 'parting is such sweet sorrow'. Execute."

The sound of metal clamps releasing rang through the airlock. John saw through the viewing pane that *Star Wolf* had detached from *Revenge* and begun to drift apart from the PI cruiser. Dub, in between waves of his arms to inaudible music, touched a control and closed the outer panel as his NID interface detached and retracted. Through the airlock viewport, John watched as the external airlock access closed and secured. Dub took an exaggerated bow.

As Voide punched in the codes to open the inner airlock doors and grant them access to *Star Wolf*'s middle deck, John turned to Dub.

"Anyone ever tell you your flair for the dramatic is really annoying?" John teased.

"Only all the time," Dub grinned.

"Knock it off," Molon growled, Twitch still dangling in his arms. "Dub, get to engineering and make sure nothing goes wrong between wherever the heck we are and the voidspace jump to Furi, Tede, or whatever jump point is closest that leads anywhere the heck out of Dawnstar space."

"Aye, Cap."

"Captain Hawkins," Angel said. "If I might also go to the bridge, I can help reconfigure your transponder's FF identifier to signal our fleet that we are safely aboard, and ensure there are no mistakes while *Star Wolf* makes the exit point."

Molon glared at Angel, not looking like he was ready to completely trust her just yet.

"I already have our Friend/Foe identifiers set for Unaligned, PI friendly," Molon replied. "Given that we are in Dawnstar space, I don't think we'll be changing that."

"I know," Angel answered. "However, those are not PI or Dawnstar ships firing at *Revenge*. We need to reset your FF identifier to Unaligned, Theocracy-friendly."

"You know something, lady," Molon snarled. "I've had about enough of this 'you know us but we don't know you' routine. How about you hand over that blaster rifle to my communications chief right now before I toss you back out that

338

airlock."

"And Mel," Molon said, turning toward the comms officer. "Accompany Miss Familiarity to the bridge and you personally check the ID's of the attacking vessels and execute the FF transponder ID changes if they are indeed Theocracy ships. But if you sense any duplicity or anything off at all, then kindly blast our mysterious benefactor to atoms."

"Yes, captain," Mel acknowledged.

"Suit yourself, captain," Angel replied as she handed the blaster rifle to Mel. "But I am not your enemy."

"We'll see about that, after I attend to my XO."

They then moved through the inner airlock doors and were greeted by two *Star Wolf* security officers in combat suits, weapons at the ready.

"Stand down," Voide ordered. "All friendlies."

"Aye, Lieutenant Commander," the security officers answered, stepping aside.

Voide, Angel, Dub, and Mel ran on ahead, bypassing the starboard elevator and taking the longer route, so as not to delay Molon and John getting Twitch to sick bay. Molon and John stepped into the waiting elevator and John activated the controls. The elevator took them to the upper deck, just down the corridor from sickbay.

John rushed past Molon as they reached the wider auxiliary space just outside the elevator doors by sickbay. The larger open space could serve for recreation, storage, or medical use as needs demanded, but currently held the four extra med-beds which John had prepared earlier for the encounter with *Revenge*.

"You want her here, John?" Molon asked.

"No," John answered. "These are just beds, Molon. I need her in sickbay where all the equipment is."

He sprinted down the corridor ahead of the captain to ready a medical bed for Twitch. Molon followed him a few moments later.

"Put her down here," John said.

John grabbed a handheld cranial scanner from the equipment cabinet as Molon laid Twitch gingerly down on the waiting bed. John gave him an unceremonious shove as he began working the scanner around Twitch's head.

"What else can I do, John?" Molon asked.

"Honestly, Molon, you have a ship to run and you are in my way. Get on the comms and tell Patch and Bob to get to sickbay immediately, and then go get us out of this system. There is nothing else you can do for her here. I promise I will

339

let you know as soon as I have something to report."

"Don't you let her die, John," Molon said, a tone of warning in his voice.

"I'll do my best," John answered, shaking his head as he busily worked to remove the blaster rifle to which Twitch was bound, to replace it with a proper neck board. "You have to know, Molon, after the hit she took, she's more in God's hands than mine right now."

"Then He'd better not let her die, or He'll answer to me."

*****

Molon called for the two other corpsmen to report to sickbay, as John had asked. Part of him wanted to stand outside sickbay until he knew for sure what would happen to Twitch. John was right, though. He had a ship to run. Voide was a good officer, but giving her a retreat order that ran against every grain of her aggressive nature was a gamble. With them now floating just off the hull of a Provisional Imperium cruiser, the best thing Molon could do for Twitch was to get to the bridge and make sure the rescue effort wasn't all for naught.

He had more than a few questions about that rescue. Who was this Angelicum operative, and how did she know so stinking much about him and his crew? An extended interrogation was in her future if they all lived through this.

Molon stepped on the bridge. Angel stood beside Mel's comm station, the two of them working together at the controls. Mel was a gentle soul, but very intuitive when it came to people. Molon suspected that had more to do with her Fei physiology and her people's latent psionic potential than any developed sense of discernment. Whatever the reason, in the time she had been aboard *Star Wolf,* Mel had never failed to rightly judge someone as friend or enemy. If she trusted this Malak, he would too, at least for now.

"Voide, status?" Molon said, approaching his command chair. Voide leapt to her feet, vacating the captain's chair as she moved to take over at the security station. Molon stood in front of his chair rather than taking a seat.

"Dub's got the engines fired up and we are en route to the jump point to Furi," Voide replied. "Looks like those PI scum weren't in a hurry to get anywhere else. We're almost exactly where *Revenge* grabbed us."

"ETA at voidspace jump point?"

"Seven minutes."

Molon growled and shook his head. Seven minutes was a long time in the midst of a ship battle.

340

"And are we likely to live that long?"

He had addressed Voide, but it was Mel that responded.

"*Revenge* is a little preoccupied, Molon. She is making best speed toward the Hatacks mainworld and broadcasting distress calls to System Defense."

"What put them on the run?" Molon asked, breathing a little easier at the news they were not on the verge of being obliterated.

"Well," Voide replied, "a Theocracy battleship, two man-of-wars, a half-dozen escort corvettes and a huge battle carrier with a cloaking screen projector captured her attention. *Revenge* has a few dozen holes in her hull, but is now out of range of everything except the battleship's spinal mount."

"So," Molon growled, fighting back the rage inside him. "Why doesn't that battleship hurry up and blow that fancified scrap-heap, its double-dealing commander, and that dreck-sucking cyborg to atoms?"

"Angel tapped us into the tactical frequency," Mel replied. "The Theocracy commander, call sign Abbot, ordered the fleet to disengage and prepare to escort *Star Wolf* into voidspace. The smaller ships have already returned to the battle carrier to prep for transition."

"You are just going to let them get away?" Molon said, rounding on Angel, a snarl on his muzzle.

"I'm not going to do anything, captain," Angel answered with a sympathetic smile. "I am not in command of fleet operations."

Molon glanced around for something to throw, but there was nothing in the vicinity to grab. He settled for kicking the base of his captain's chair, which the throbbing in his foot through his boot, and the sharp pain in his side from his injured ribs, made him instantly regret.

"Well, isn't that convenient?" he spat, wincing at his pain but biting it back as best he could. "You tell this Abbot that the Deputy Director of GalSec Intelligence and a Senior Special Interrogator who also happens to be a cyborg sub-cute augment designed to fight Angelicum are aboard that vessel? Maybe that'll change his mind."

Molon half felt like slapping that condescendingly sweet smile off Angel's face as she shook her head.

"Abbot is fully aware who is aboard *Revenge*. This, however, is a rescue mission, not an attack raid."

"So call it a target of convenience," Voide interjected. "Collateral damage."

"Unfortunately, given the Provisional Imperium's

341

retaliation policy, it would be a Pyrrhic victory. The destruction of a PI cruiser in a Dawnstar-controlled border system would virtually guarantee that a strike fleet from Hececcrir would be paying a visit to the Tede system in the very near future, and exterminating every man, woman, and child living there. Is that a trade you would be willing to make, captain."

Molon bit back the "yes" that had already formed in his muzzle as he considered John's homeworld, his company, and all the doctor's friends and neighbors living on Tede.

"Fine," he snapped resentfully. "But if Twitch dies, I promise you I'll hunt that cyborg mongrel to the ends of the galaxy and the threat of destroying the entire Theocracy won't stay my hand."

"I understand, captain," Angel answered. "But given that the situation here is under control, at least for now, perhaps you and I should talk...alone."

"Mel, Voide, we all clear?"

"Yes," Voide replied and Mel nodded in agreement. "We'll be in voidspace momentarily. No enemy ships in range. The fleet is standing ready to follow us. We're situation green, captain."

"Yeah," Molon replied, turning toward Angel. "Come to think of it, I have quite a few things to say to you that might not be fit for mixed company."

Twenty-Nine – Lost and Found

John could not fight off a frown as he sat on one of the extra med-beds and read the information on the datapad he held. Patch had just handed him Twitch's latest test results. John set the datapad down on the side table and sighed as he rubbed his face with both hands.

"Come on, Doc." Patch gave John a light chuck on the arm. "You've been at this for hours. She's as stable as she is going to get. You can't operate further until she gains some strength. Grab some rack time. Bob and I will take shifts keeping an eye on her. We'll call you if anything changes."

"Rack time?" John laughed. "You've got to be kidding. I've got two extra bunks filled with refugees from Ratuen camped out in my room and a security officer taking up what little floor space is left."

"So use my rack," Patch replied. "Or sack out on one of these extra med-beds. Point is, if you go dropping off from exhaustion, you won't be any good to anyone."

John did feel as though he were minutes from dropping from exhaustion. Even the antiseptic environment of the sickbay beds looked inviting. John shook his head.

"I wish I could, but if I don't let the captain know what's what with Twitch, sleep deprivation will be the least of my worries. I've never seen anything get to him like this."

Patch nodded and glanced from John back toward the bed where Twitch lay, unconscious, convalescing. The automated med bed was busy controlling and monitoring her oxygen and the cocktail of pain medication, antibiotics, and sedatives John had cooked up.

"He and Twitch are close, for sure," Patch answered. "Back in the Scouts, they went through a lot together. If she don't pull out of this..."

"She will," John said with far more fire than he intended. The corpsman was trying to help, but if Twitch didn't pull through the captain wouldn't have to pin this on John. It was his to own. None of them would have been here if he hadn't

343

hired them to return to Ratuen. Twitch was in that bed because of him.

"Doc?" Patch said, snapping John back to reality.

"Yes?"

"I know I'm just a corpsman," Patch continued, not looking at John but dropping his gaze to the floor. "But things don't look good for the XO."

"You're right," John replied, glancing at the datapad filled with bad news as it rested on the table. "Even if she survives, she will never be the same."

Patch hesitated, toeing the foot of the side table and clutching one arm with the other across his midsection. John's stomach fluttered wondering what was on the corpsman's mind.

"What is it, corpsman?" John asked, not sure he wanted to hear the answer.

Patch took a deep breath, as if steeling himself for something, and slowly exhaled. He finally lifted his head to look John in the eyes.

"Honestly, Doc, it might be better if she didn't." Patch stared blankly at John with soft, glassy eyes.

"Didn't what?" John said, tension rising in his voice, incredulous at what he believed the corpsman was implying.

"Live, I mean," Patch said confirming John's suspicion. The corpsman turned to stare at Twitch's unconscious form, not daring to look John in the eye after making such a suggestion. John choked back the bile rising in this throat.

"That's not our call to make!" John rose suddenly to his feet. "I may not know all the military rules and regulations, but when you were an Imperial corpsman, didn't you take an oath to do no harm just like civilian doctors do?"

At John's confrontational stance, Patch rose and squared off with John. John sensed the military training in the man and considered that it might not be wise to push his indignation much farther with the combat-trained corpsman. Patch returned John's stare, but without the accompanying scowl.

"Yeah, we do, Doc," Patch answered, keeping his voice even but dropping slightly into an almost imperceptibly tensed crouch. "It's not the same oath, but close enough."

"Then how could you suggest such a thing?" John replied, using all his self-control to level his own tone, trying to deescalate the tension.

"I'm just saying," Patch answered. "Knowing what's ahead for her, I'm not sure I would consider putting her through that as doing no harm."

John couldn't believe what he was hearing. He knew not everyone shared the Faithful's regard for the sanctity of life, but the thought of euthanizing a patient wasn't something John was willing to consider, no matter how grim the diagnosis or how hard the road ahead. While he was acting chief medical officer, that wasn't going to be an option.

Just then, the sickbay doors opened, ending the discussion. *Star Wolf*'s chief engineer stuck his large head in the doorway. Given the extra beds and Dub's huge bulk, that was about all that would fit.

"Hey, Doc, how's Twitch?"

"Stable for now, Dub. But she's not out of the woods yet."

"Cap won't like that news much," Dub said, shaking his large bald pate.

"I know."

John grabbed a portable skeletal knitter. Given the damage Simmons had done to Molon back on *Revenge* the captain would likely need some medical attention of his own.

"I was just on my way to tell him. Did you need something?"

"Actually," Dub shrugged as he backed out into the corridor, clearing room for John to exit the sickbay. "I just needed to talk to you a minute, Doc. You mind if I walk with you?"

"Sure, Dub," John answered. "Patch," John said flashing a parting scowl at Patch to let him know their conversation would resume later. "Call me immediately if anything changes, okay?"

"You got it, Doc," the corpsman replied, his eyes dropping once again away from John's scorching gaze.

The sickbay door closed behind them.

"Everything okay with you and Patch?" the intuitive engineer asked.

"Fine, Dub. Just a difference of opinion"

John started to turn left toward the starboard bridge entrance, but Dub grabbed his arm.

"Cap's not on the bridge. Voide says he has been locked up in his quarters with Angel since we made voidspace."

"Okay," John said, turning the other way to head toward the captain's quarters.

"Before you head there, though," Dub said, gently placing one of his mechanically-gloved hands on John's shoulder. "I've got something for you."

John frowned. He liked the chief engineer, but it had been a long day. John's heart was already heavy with his own sense

345

of responsibility in all this. Whatever Dub had to tell him, he hoped it was not some misguided attempt to cheer him up. Between Twitch's condition and Patch's gruesome suggestion, John didn't feel very cheerful.

"I'm just not in the mood for guessing games right now, Dub. What is it?"

"No games, Doc," Dub said, flashing his twisted, malmorph smile. "Just a gift."

Dub reached into a pocket and pulled out a cube dangling on a chain. It looked exactly like Elena's datacube.

John's eyes widened, his mind scrambling to put together how the chief engineer had salvaged the cube. He'd seen Dub crush the thing to dust.

"What?" John's stuttered as he searched for the right words. "Is that...?"

"Well," Dub grinned, "kind of, sort of, in a way, but not exactly. I really did pulverize your wife's datacube back on *Revenge*. I just neglected to mention I had made a copy."

"But when? How?" John babbled.

"You remember when I had you scan the thing so I could build you a reader?"

"Yes."

"Well, I might have...kind of...scanned more than just the physical dimensions. When you told me what was on it, I have to admit I was more than a little curious."

"Were you able to decrypt the data?" John said, on the verge of hyperventilating, his mind racing with the implications of Dub's revelation. "Elena was very security conscious."

"Hah," Dub shook his head, "You call that encryption? I mean come on, Doc, I'm a mutated, freak-show genius, remember?"

John couldn't control the quick laugh that erupted at Dub's remark.

"Yeah, sorry Dub. It slipped my mind for a second."

"It happens." Dub's jovial grin faded slightly. "Decrypting it was a breeze. Understanding it after decryption was the tricky part. Bunch of medical gobbledygook; I couldn't make heads or tails of it. Still, I figured you might, or might at least know someone who could."

Dub extended the datacube necklace toward John. His hand trembled as he reached out and took it.

"Dub," John said, suddenly tensing as he realized the possible implications of this copy. "Does anyone else know?"

"Nope," the huge engineer replied shaking his large head.

"Nobody else's business, not even Cap's. I figured you had the right to do what you want with it."

John wanted to hug the huge malmorph, but had no idea how Dub might take that. Instead he chose to pat Dub on the arm. It took everything John could muster to choke back the tears threatening to fill his eyes. This research was all he had left of the Elena he had known and loved.

"Do you have a way to make another copy?" John asked.

Dub shrugged and nodded.

"I was about to wipe the copy files," Dub replied. "After I delivered this to you, anyway."

"Yes, you should do that, but make me one more copy first."

"Something wrong with this copy, Doc? I can rig up a reader in a day or so, since we are going to be in voidspace for the next four days without much demand on my time. I just replicated the original datacube since I already had the specs in the system."

"You can put the other copy on a standard mini-disc that I can work with in my room or in sickbay," John said. "It's just that I have a different idea about what I want to do with this one."

"Sure thing, Doc," Dub replied, rubbing his chin with a biomechanical glove-hand. "I'll even encrypt the data with your fingerprint, voiceprint, and DNA so only you will be able to access it."

"Great," John said as he slipped the datacube around his neck and tucked it inside his shirt. Suddenly he stopped short and snapped a look at the chief engineer. "Hey, how do you have my fingerprints, voiceprint, and DNA?"

Dub flashed a knowing grin before rolling his eyes toward the ceiling, clasping his hands behind his back, and whistling innocently.

"Um," John replied. "I guess it's best if I don't ask, huh?"

"You can ask..." the engineer turned away and headed toward the bridge.

"Dub?" John fought back tears as he called out to the malmorph engineer walking away.

"Yeah?" Dub replied, glancing back over his shoulder.

"Thanks."

"Null sweat, Doc." Dub nodded as a playful grin slid across his face, before he turned away and resumed his whistling.

*****

Molon paced the floor of his quarters. He had been talking for hours with the Angelicum agent. She had laid out in rather sketchy detail the events leading up to their meeting aboard *Revenge*. Some of it Molon knew, or at least guessed, but the depth of it all had him reeling. The frustrating part was anytime Molon approached any truly meaningful question, he had been stalled, stonewalled, or evaded entirely. His naturally sparse patience was long since expended.

The pain in his chest from the blow Simmons had given him still throbbed and did little to fuel cordiality. He would have to get John to look at the injury the first chance he got, but Molon was sure he had at least a broken rib or two. He turned toward the Angelicum agent seated on his sofa and decided to take one last push at prying something useful out of their recalcitrant rescuer.

"So you are telling me the Angelicum have had agents in the Imperium and even GalSec since the Shattering?"

"Since the Shattering?" Angel smiled knowingly. "Angelicum security agents assigned to Humaniti are called Watchmen. Watchmen have been keeping an eye on humans since long before they left Earth. You don't think GalSec is the only intelligence agency in the galaxy, do you?"

Molon's brow furrowed. At least there was no record of any lupine or canine angels. Hopefully the Angelicum had kept their interests focused on Humaniti. Still, there were the Doppelgangers, so Lubanian physiology likely hadn't made them immune to outside spying. He could understand spying on the vast, interstellar Empire of Humaniti, but Angel was saying there had been spies among the humans before there was anything worth watching.

"That's a long time to be spying on a pretty insignificant race, compared to the Angelicum Host at least."

"Insignificant?" Angel's eyes widened. "You've got it all wrong, Molon. Humaniti is anything but insignificant. They have been in the Creator's plan from the beginning."

Molon swallowed a growl forming in this throat. Here it was again. This woman was delusional.

"So now you're telling me you have met God?"

"So have you," Angel replied. "You just don't realize it."

Molon harrumphed.

"When have *I* met God?"

"Unfortunately," Angel's gazed dropped toward the deck, "I'm not at liberty to talk about that with you right now."

Molon growled in frustration, bordering on a snarl.

"Why does that answer not surprise me?"

He was done with this evasiveness. John had at least tried to address the questions, but Molon wasn't sure the doctor knew anything beyond what he'd studied from some books. Finally Molon had someone who might actually be able to answer some questions, and there was a gag order. That figured.

"Okay, then," Molon said, dropping the dead-end line of questioning and turning his inquiries toward something more solid. "Let me ask about you."

"I will answer what I can." Angel's gaze rose once again, looking straight into Molon's eyes.

"Are you trying to tell me, out of all the Angelicum operatives you guys have all over Humaniti, we were just lucky enough to bump into the one angel whose call sign is actually Angel?"

The Malak laughed lightly and smiled at him, as if Molon was a child who had just asked where clouds came from.

"Actually, my real name is Shamira, and you can call me that if you prefer. In truth, every Watchman operative who is forced by circumstances to reveal their Angelicum nature just uses the call sign Angel. This happens only when the completion of the mission calls for it,"

"Well now," Molon laughed. "That's got to get confusing after a while with so many Angels mucking about."

"Not really," Angel replied. "You have no idea how infrequently our presence is even detected. Had it not become necessary to directly intervene using my gifts in order to effect your rescue, I would never have blown my cover."

Molon folded his arms before the pain in his chest gave him reason to rethink that posture. He chose to lightly drop into a chair.

"So you never planned to go all glowing wings, then?"

"No," Angel replied. "I had hoped Simmons would trust the security team to handle the planned execution. I could have easily manipulated events to allow your escape, permitting you to overpower me and my team and preserving my cover. Unfortunately Russel's ire at the destruction of the datacube pushed him to call for Simmons to see to things personally."

"Didn't see that one coming, then? I thought your type knew everything."

"No, unfortunately. Only the Creator can see the future. Sometimes He shares that with us, but this time he did not."

"So, you saved us, we saved you. Sounds like we are about even then."

Angel shook her head and lost her soft smile.

"It is more complicated than that," she replied. "I'd been assigned to monitor Operation Firelake and Senior

349

Interrogator Simmons for a long time. Getting you all off of *Revenge* cost us far more than you realize."

"You mean losing one of your Watchmen inside GalSec?"

"More than just one," Angel explained. "We may never be able to get another agent that close to Simmons. I've served on his personal security detail for over two years now, with five more years before that, working within GalSec to earn that posting. I doubt Simmons will trust anyone around him again without frequent, full genetic scans. In fact, once they realize we have infiltrated them, every one of the Watchmen in GalSec, the upper echelons of Dawnstar, and the Provisional Imperium is now at risk of being discovered."

The impact of what Angel had said weighed on Molon. Outing a spy was one thing, but she was right. If someone as paranoid and ruthless as Simmons suspected there might be spies high up in GalSec or the Imperium, he'd push the limits of technology and legality to find any others.

"So why do it?" Molon asked, not sure if he really wanted to know the answer. "Why risk all that to save a ragtag bunch of mercs from getting prematurely spaced?"

"Orders." Angel's face grew serious.

"Orders from who?" Molon pressed, expecting a reemergence of her habit of dancing around the real questions.

"From on high."

Her eyes remained locked on Molon's, but it was clear he had wandered near gag-order territory once again.

That was the last straw. Molon stood and hurled the glass, from which he had been sipping brandy, clear across the room. It shattered into a myriad of pieces against the bulkhead. He immediately regretted it as pain lanced through his chest from the broken ribs, courtesy of Senior Interrogator Simmons. That added pain did nothing to soften his tone.

"Enough of that!" he growled at Angel through the intense throbbing in his chest. "Just give me a straight answer for once. Do you seriously expect me to believe some invisible God is giving you marching orders?"

"Captain Hawkins," Angel replied, showing no hint in her voice of matching Molon's angry escalation. "All I am at liberty to say is that senior leadership in the Angelicum Host have made it clear that *Star Wolf*, and Dr. John Salzmann, are vital to future plans."

"Whose future plans?" Molon growled.

"I am not trying to frustrate you," Angel said, shaking her head. "I simply don't know anything more. I would answer your questions if I could."

"So you admit that your orders come from your superiors in the Angelicum Host, or from the Theocracy, or from Enoch, or someone else under his command, and not personally from some invisible God!" Molon growled.

"In this case," Angel replied, "that would be a distinction without a difference."

His explosive response was preempted by the sounding of the door chime.

"Enter," Molon snapped with far more bile than he would have liked.

Whichever of his crew was coming to see him hadn't done anything to earn the consequences of his frustration with the Angelicum agent. John Salzmann entered the room.

"I'm sorry to interrupt, captain," John said.

The doctor visibly recoiled a bit after glancing at the shattered glass on the far side of the room. Doubtless he did not miss the unmistakable aroma of brandy filling the air, nor the sight of the remnants of the golden brown liquid currently drizzling down the far wall.

John looked fearful as he returned his gaze to Molon. Good. Learning when to steer clear of Molon's temper was a vital survival skill if the doctor planned to continue to serve on *Star Wolf.*

"If this is a bad time I can come back later." John's gaze flitted between Molon and Angel, looking as if he were trying to get a read on the tension filling the room.

Molon relaxed his ears to set John at ease, regretting not doing it as soon as the doctor had entered. John was not to blame for the extended and frustrating game of cat-and-mouse which Molon had been playing with the Malak agent.

"No, John, I'm sorry, please come in." Molon attempted a grin before realizing a human not used to being around Lubanians might view that as a snarl. "We were just having an invigorating philosophical discussion. How is Twitch?"

"Not good," John said with a shake of his head.

Molon's heart dropped into his stomach. He hoped John wasn't going to waltz around the truth. He'd had just about enough of that from Angel.

"Say it straight, Doc. Is she going to make it?"

Before John spoke, Molon could already read the uncertainty in the doctor's face. Molon braced himself for bad news.

"She's stable, for now at least. Her condition is critical. Like I told you before, she's in God's hands more than mine."

This was too close to the nerve Angel had just been

351

dancing on. Molon's ears flitted backward again, his eyes narrowing. The change in posture caused John to take a step backward.

"I've done what I can," John continued cautiously, "but Molon..."

John's pause sent a fear through Molon like no mission ever had. If he lost Twitch, he wasn't sure he wanted to keep doing this. She had been his partner and his friend. They had started this merc crew together. Without her, what was *Star Wolf* but an empty hull?

"But what, John?" Molon finally mustered the courage to ask. "Spill it."

"Her spinal cord is severed."

"So," Molon replied, hoping John's worry was more from him being a hermit-world physician than about the severity of Twitch's condition. "We get her to a TL15 world and have it fixed. They regenerate spinal injuries all the time on core worlds."

"Not exactly." John shook his head and swallowed hard before continuing. "Partial spinal injuries can be easily repaired. Clean spinal cord breaks can sometimes be reattached and regenerated, if treated quickly enough. Even severe damage in children has been successfully treated. But her spinal cord isn't just severed, Molon, it is shredded."

Molon took a few deep breaths despite the pain that brought. In fact the pain from his ribs was almost cathartic as it gave him something to focus on beside the much deeper pain he was fighting. He was no surgeon, but if a shredded spinal cord had the normally optimistic medic concerned...

"So what does that mean, John?" Molon asked, biting back his frustration and worry. "Pretend I'm just a dumb merc captain and not a neurosurgeon."

"It's like this," John explained. "The force Simmons exerted on Twitch when he grabbed her must have been tremendous. The cranial damage looked bad, but we can fix that easily even aboard *Star Wolf*. In fact, I have already prepped her for that surgery and as soon as she is a little stronger I can do that myself. I have also already repaired the damage to her throat.

"The real issue is, Simmons crushed two of her upper vertebrae, and the bone shards ground through her spinal cord like a shredder. At this point she may not even live through her injuries. Even if she does, I'm not sure her spine can be fixed."

Molon growled. He fought the urge to pounce on John and rip into the doctor. None of this was John's fault, but for some

352

reason Molon was furious with him.

"What do you know?" Molon snapped. "You're just some backwater sawbones. I'll get her to a competent doctor on a core world and somebody who actually knows something about modern medicine will fix her."

John shook his head. Molon sensed the doctor was hurting as bad over this as he was, but right now Molon couldn't care less.

"Be mad at me if you want to, Molon. Lion knows I deserve it. None of this would have happened if I hadn't hired you all to take me back to Ratuen. However, you need to understand something. While I might have lived and practiced medicine on a hermitworld, I was educated and did my residency on an Old Empire, pre-Shattering core world. I worked under top doctors at a cutting edge TL15 hospital in the Sarren system, Orke sector. That system to this day still has the most advanced medical facilities in the entire Theocracy.

"I also keep up with all of the most recent surgical breakthroughs. That is a requirement to maintain my surgeon's license. I recertify every year with the Interstellar Medical Board and the Theocracy Board of Humaniti Surgeons.

"I have not maintained any non-human sophont certifications, a condition I will rectify if you allow me to stay aboard *Star Wolf* as chief medical officer, but as far as human physiology is concerned, I am a fully qualified surgeon."

Molon relaxed. John had already proven his worth as a doctor. Every time this ship went out, casualties were always a possibility. He just never imagined it would ever be Twitch. She had danced through hailstorms of bullets and beams dozens of times without a scratch. Molon had more holes in him than a moon in a meteor shower, but Twitch had always been untouchable. Maybe her luck had just run out.

"I'm sorry, John," Molon said, mentally biting himself for needlessly berating the doctor. "It's just a hard pill to swallow."

"I understand," John replied, giving Molon far more grace than he deserved. "You are welcome to get a second opinion, captain. I admittedly am not a spinal specialist, but my diagnosis is not one given in ignorance. Another doctor's examination is not going to change the reality of Twitch's condition."

"So there's no hope?" Molon said, unable to hide a lingering accusation in his tone.

"I'm not saying there is no hope," John replied emphatically. "With God all things are possible. I want you to understand I will devote everything I have and use all the contacts and resources at my disposal to help her, Molon."

"Then what *are* you saying, John?"

"I'm telling you to prepare yourself. Even if we do find someone, somewhere who can repair her spinal cord, she is never going to have the reflexes she had before. She is going to have to work long and hard just to retrain her body to obey basic commands coming from her own brain. There is a lot of technology out there that can help her live out her life with some major modifications. Make no mistake, though, Twitch is never going to be the same again."

That thought ate a hole in Molon's gut. Twitch had been the most independent, driven, dependable partner he could ever have asked for. Their time in the Scouts had seen countless challenges, and more than a few times Twitch's unflinching nature had been the difference between success and failure, between life and death. It sounded like she was going to need every ounce of that determination to get through this. Molon wondered if the prospect of never regaining what she had lost would ultimately shatter Twitch's adamantine spirit.

"Thank you, John," Molon managed at last. "Was there anything else?"

"How about letting me look at those ribs?"

"It's nothing. I'll swing by sickbay later to check on Twitch. You can take a look then."

"Sorry, Molon," John argued. "Unless you are relieving me of duty as CMO, I'll take a look at them now. I brought the portable bone knitter anyway, so don't think I lugged this heavy chunk of hardware all the way here for nothing."

Molon relented and winced as he pulled off his uniform shirt, exposing his fur-covered lupine torso. John worked around his tender ribcage with the medical device he had brought with him. Molon already began to feel the throbbing pain in his side starting to ease.

"Sorry for being out of uniform," Molon said to Angel after he noticed the Malak avert her eyes respectfully. "Doctor's orders, and this human is too pig-headed to argue with."

"Aren't they all," Angel quipped, keeping her eyes fixed on the bulkhead.

"Hey, now," John replied. "Aren't angels supposed to be encouraging?"

"Not necessarily," Angel remarked, a playful tone filling her voice. "Just messengers of truth."

"Okay, boss," John said, giving Molon's chest a firm pat.

354

"All better. You can swing by and see Twitch whenever you want. Patch is with her."

"Thanks, John." Molon pulled his uniform shirt back in place noting the complete lack of pain resulting from the action.

"She isn't going to be awake anytime soon, though" John continued. "I have her pretty heavily sedated. She isn't feeling any pain from the neck down, at least, but the meds I had to give her to stabilize her for surgery are laced with sedatives and pain killers. In a real hospital I would have given her something less severe, but that's what you had on board, so I had to make do."

"I understand," Molon replied. "It is probably better I not have to talk to her until I figure out what in the galaxy I am going to say."

"I get that," John said, sadness filling his tone before looking up and shooting Molon a wavering grin. "I do have some things to discuss with Angel, that is, if you two are done with your invigorating philosophical disagreement."

"Yeah, we're done," Molon replied, shaking his head at John's comment and attempt to lighten the mood. "However, you two should carry the conversation elsewhere. I need to collect my thoughts."

"Actually, of the two things I have to discuss with her, the first one you need to know about as well."

Molon furrowed his brow, his ears perking forward. "Okay then, spill it."

John reached for something beneath his collar and pulled out a small cube dangling from a chain around his neck. Molon stared in disbelief at what appeared to be Elena Salzmann's datacube dangling from John's hand.

"Surprise, captain!" John said, adding a "ta-da".

Molon's breath caught in his throat. His eyes narrowed as he eyed the seemingly impossible existence of the cube.

"Dub destroyed Elena's datacube on *Revenge*," Molon said with a shake of his head. "We saw him."

"Yeah," John replied, "but we also saw Elena die on Ratuen. I'm thinking our eyewitness testimony isn't worth a lot right now."

Molon laughed. "Fair enough."

"Seriously, though, this is a copy Dub made after we left Tede. I had him scan the custom datacube to build a reader. It seems he went above and beyond the call of duty and scanned the contents too."

"So are you saying," Angel interrupted, "that this contains

355

Elena Salzmann's malmorphsy research?"

Molon growled as he spun to face Angel.

"That's another thing," he snapped. "How do you even know anything about that?"

"I was assigned to Simmons, remember? That research is at the heart of all this mess."

"Yeah, mess is right," John answered. "I'm keeping a copy for myself, as I intend to have the R&D guys at Salzmann Pharmaceuticals start work on a line of malmorphsy-related treatments. I'll take extra precautions not to let what we are working on leave Tede —no way I want the PI or Dawnstar back on our trail. In the meantime, though, given what both the PI and the Brothers of the Lion were planning on using this for, I wanted to put a copy in the hands of the Theocracy and the Angelicum Host so they could use it proactively to counter any possible xenocidal bioweapon."

"Your sentiments are noble, John," Angel replied as she took the datacube. "I will see this gets to Enoch and his researchers."

"Thank you, Angel," John replied. "I just could not live with myself if Elena's research was used to harm your people."

The Malak angel flashed John a sweet smile.

"You need not worry yourself further about the welfare of the Angelicum Host, or the Daemi for that matter."

"Really?" Molon replied. "You aren't worried these crazy Brothers of the Lion want to wipe the Daemi out, even if it means taking your people along for the ride?"

"There is no danger of that," Angel reassured.

"What do you mean?" Molon scowled, as he anticipated another round of mystical hokum.

"By design," Angel explained, "we are incapable of becoming ill due to any naturally-occurring disease or artificially engineered pathogen. That is just a reality of our biology."

"But you are still taking the data because...?" Molon pressed

"This research will be useful in developing vaccines for Humans as well as Fei, Lubanians, Doppelgangers, Dractauri, and the myriad of other non-human sophonts. We will work with Enoch's people to develop antigens designed to defend against any derivative bioweapons that might arise as poisoned fruits of Elena's research."

Molon's ears twitched as a disturbing thought came to him. He turned to John.

"Who else knows you have this?" Molon asked.

"Besides you two and Dub?" John answered. "Nobody."

"Keep it that way," Molon said, breathing a sigh of relief. "If GalSec gets wind a copy of this still exists, Russel and Simmons will burn a swath of destruction through the remnants of Humaniti to get their hands on it. Dub will keep this secret without doubt, but you can't tell anybody else."

"Got it," John answered.

"I mean it, John," Molon pressed. "You can't fall asleep with it on a terminal where someone might walk in. You can't discuss testing it with anyone. If you are going to keep poking away at this, you keep it away from anyone other than you, me, and Dub, no mistakes."

"I said I got it," John assured him. "I didn't have to tell you, Molon, but I figured if I was going to keep a copy on this ship, you had a right to know."

Molon nodded and gently grabbed John's upper arm, giving it a reassuring squeeze.

"I appreciate that, John. I take it from this discussion that you intend to stay aboard *Star Wolf*?"

"Until something better comes along," John answered.

"Good to know. Now," Molon pointed toward the door. "Would you two kindly get out of my quarters so someone can get some work done around here? Angel, you can use Twitch's quarters until we get to Furi. Her cabin is just across from John's. He can show you the way. From what John says she won't be out of sickbay before then anyway."

"Thank you, captain," Angel replied.

John and Angel left Molon's cabin. He locked the door behind them, sat down at his desk, and finally let the wave of sadness and frustration wash over him. No one on the crew had ever seen Molon shed a tear either from pain or emotion.

And they never would.

Lubanian tears were a private thing, disgraceful if seen by anyone, even other Lubanians. Molon had been raised by humans, but the reluctance was as much genetic as cultural. Yet here, locked in his room, overwhelmed by the grim outlook facing his closest friend, Molon cried.

Thirty – New Feelings and Old Friends

John walked side by side with the Angelicum agent eponymously dubbed "Angel". Some part of him was having trouble controlling his twitching hands and wobbling legs. He'd known all his life that both the angels and the demons in the Bible had been discovered to be two branches of an alien race which the Creator had employed since the beginning of human history as messengers, protectors, and guides to the human race. But he had never expected to be walking beside one.

Much of the history of Angels was shrouded in mystery. They had never chosen to reveal to humans whether the Creator had made them a vast star empire from the beginning, or if they had developed alongside, if a few millennia ahead of, humanity. Whatever their history, this ancient and wide-spanning race had allied with the Theocracy after the Shattering. There had not been a great deal of direct interaction between the Angelicum Host and the Empire of Humaniti, but they had always been there, spinward and coreward of the human star empire.

Some speculated these beings were eternal and could never die. Others speculated that their physical forms were mere manifestations that could be destroyed, but their spirit essence would simply reform and recreate a different physical body elsewhere. John had so many questions, but he was certain he was no more likely to get any definite answers from Angel than thousands of other humans before him.

"So, John," Angel finally said, breaking the silence. "You said there was another matter you wanted to talk to me about?"

"Yes, but first, it feels so odd to just call you Angel. Do you have an actual name you would share with me?"

"Certainly. My name is Shamira. You may address me so, if you prefer."

"Shamira, that means protector, doesn't it?"

"Yes, it does. So, you know Hebrew names, John?"

"Hebrew and Greek are required in Faithful schools. I

358

wasn't the best language student, but I knew a girl in medical school named Shamira."

"And that's why you know the meaning of my name?" John's face flushed red.

"To be honest, she was cute. Elena was jealous that Shamira was my lab partner for one class. I often teased Elena that the reason she agreed to marry me was that she couldn't stand the idea of losing out to Shamira."

Shamira giggled and gave John a smile. He was surprised how at ease he felt around her. It was almost like meeting a hero from a storybook come to life, yet there was no pretentiousness or superiority about her. She exuded a sense of peace. His mind flashed back to his odd emotional experiences around Mel and wondered if psionics played a part in his impression of Shamira.

"So, what did you want to talk to me about?" Shamira prompted when John, lost in thought, failed to continue to the reason he had wanted to talk to her.

"Oh, yeah," John said, blushing. "It was about that thing you did, back on *Revenge*."

"Which thing was that?" she asked, but the knowing look in her eyes gave John the impression she had already rifled through his thoughts and knew the answer.

"I mean when you put those guards to sleep," he replied. "How did you do that?"

"I'm a Malak," Shamira answered, "the highest racial caste of Angelicum. We all have fairly extensive psionic abilities. I simply planted the strong suggestion in their minds that they were exhausted and needed to sleep immediately."

John's brow wrinkled as he rubbed his chin.

"But it didn't work on Simmons. Why not?"

"Good question," she replied. "Simmons had augments implanted in his body. One of those apparently was psionically-shielded plating around his skull. I have been assigned to Simmons for years. I knew about his enhanced strength and a few other augments, but the psionic shielding is either something new or something he kept well hidden."

John suddenly felt as if he were standing naked before her. If she could so easily enter the minds of humans, would he even know if she entered his. What secrets could there ever be around her. Then John got an idea.

"So, can you read minds and communicate telepathically?"

"Within limits. Why do you ask?" Shamira's helpful smile faded slightly.

"I'm not trying to be nosy. I was just hoping you might

359

help with one of the people we rescued from Ratuen."

"I will help if I can, John," Shamira replied, her smile returning. "What is wrong with him?"

"He's not fully connected with our reality. I have no idea how long he was there or what they did to him, but I thought maybe you could see if the old guy is still rattling around inside that skull of his somewhere."

"I will see what I can do," Shamira replied.

"Great. He's just up around the corner here, in my quarters."

As they entered John's quarters, he noticed the security officer assigned for this shift was none other than Bobby Lee "Cowboy" McGhehey. Bobby Lee was standing with a weapon trained on the former Dawnstar guard from Ratuen, the second rescuee. The other prisoner, the old man John had brought Angel to see, still sat on his bunk and stared aimlessly at the wall.

"Trouble, Bobby Lee?" John asked.

"Nah," Cowboy said with a shake of his head. "This guy couldn't give my grandma much trouble. He woke up a few minutes ago and started asking to speak to whoever was in charge. Voide told us not to take no chances with this one, so I called it in. Guess you beat Voide here."

"I wish I had gotten here before you made that call," John said, concerned at what the volatile security chief might do once she arrived. "He's fairly stable, but if I know Voide she'll have him tossed in the brig quick as a wink."

"Don't be ridiculous, Doc," Cowboy said with a snort. "*Star Wolf* ain't got no brig."

"Where do you keep prisoners?" John asked.

"Heck, long as I been here we ain't ever had a real prisoner. Been a turncoat or two Voide spaced out an airlock. Other than that, she's just got a couple of cages built into the middle deck security stations, mostly where drunk crewmen sleep it off."

"Still," John replied, repulsed at the idea of this man being tossed into a cramped cage. "That's not a proper place for a patient."

John stepped over to the reclining former guard.

"Careful, Doc," Bobby Lee warned. "He might try somethin'."

"Unlikely. After the beating they gave him back on Ratuen, I doubt he'll be up for so much as a pillow fight anytime soon."

"You got that right," the man said to John in a voice just above a weak whisper. "Name is Stellan Brannock."

A look of recognition came into Brannock's eyes as he stared at John's face. It was quickly replaced by fear.

"I know you," the man said. "You were a prisoner on Ratuen. You and that woman. You were brought in together. You're the one who escaped and got me locked up."

"You are correct," John nodded. "I'm sorry that reclaiming my liberty caused you such inconvenience, but I had been brought there illegally, so...there we have it."

"You weren't the only prisoner," the man replied.

"What do you mean?" John asked.

Something about the man's tone suggested he wasn't talking about the old man or Elena. The man's eyes went glassy as he dropped his gaze from John's face to the floor.

"Some of us weren't in cages," the man said in a warbling voice. "But I wish you had taken me with you when you left."

What an odd thing to say. John wasn't sure how best to respond, so his normal humor reflex kicked in.

"You being an enemy guard," John said, raising an eyebrow, "you can see why that would hardly have been the captain's first thought."

The man's face grew stoic as he raised his eyes to look into John's once again.

"I might have been a guard, but I wasn't an enemy."

"You worked for Dawnstar," John replied.

"Not willingly, I didn't."

John's memory flashed back to his time on Ratuen. Pain and trauma blurred much of his memory from his time there, but he did recall one guard who had never seemed to share the sadistic pleasure of abusing the prisoners that the others did. John tried to recall if that face belonged to this man, but the faces all ran together in a stream of pain in his mind.

"Well, you weren't being locked up and beaten either," John said, choking back the memories of their ill treatment at the hands of Ratuen's torturer-in-chief. "At least not when I left the first time. So how exactly were you being held against your will?"

"Before the Shattering," Brannock explained, "I was just a regular army grunt. I was stationed at the big Imperial Army base on the mainworld in the Dehdhasop system, Hand sector, on the border of what is now the Rimward Demesne."

"That's part of the New Halberan Empire, not Dawnstar," John replied.

"Yeah, I know," Brannock answered. "After the Shattering, that system came under Phoebe Halberan's control."

"So, you were in an NHE unit under Phoebe, along

Dawnstar's rimward border?"

"Yes, sir," Brannock replied. "We got deployed on a border raid not long after the Shattering. That subsector got split in half, with a huge number of military base systems in the rimward section that came under Phoebe's control. Still, there were a couple of choice systems just across the border, one of which was the Biliimigi system.

"Biliimigi had major production facilities, a class B starbase, and an Imperial Scout base right there. It was too sweet a target so, given Phoebe's military advantage in that subsector, she decided to reallocate Biliimigi and the adjacent system which Humaniti had given to the Dractauri to settle."

"I take it things didn't go as smoothly as planned?" John asked, suddenly much more engrossed in Brannock's story than he had intended to be.

"You can say that again. I was part of the Biliimigi invasion forces, but Tubal somehow got word of the attack. He must have poured every ship and troop he had in the subsector into Biliimigi. I was in one of the first troop ships to assault the mainworld, but ninety percent of our invasion force was blown apart before we ever hit dirt. I was aboard the only lander that made it out of my transport ship before it got shredded."

"Yet somehow you lived," John said, eyeing his former guard with suspicion.

"A bunch of us did," Brannock continued. "Other transports got most of their landers launched before being captured or destroyed. I guess Tubal knew how badly he was outnumbered and outgunned along his rimward border and didn't want to waste a chance to levy new troops.

"We were given a choice to become loyal citizens of the Dawnstar Technocracy and support the Provisional Imperium, or to be executed as traitors for following the separatists."

"Tough choice," John said, rolling his eyes.

"No choice at all. Look, up until the Shattering, we were all on the same side. We were Empire soldiers. Ground pounders don't care about politics, but what they told us about Phoebe and Seth trying to circumvent the rightful succession and maybe even being responsible for Emperor Halberan's death seemed to make sense."

"And you believed that propaganda?" John snapped.

"That was so soon after the Shattering that nobody knew what was what. By the time we heard about Dawnstar's attacks on civilians and all the bad stuff Tubal and Zarsus had been into, I had already cycled through a dozen different postings. I wound up a prison guard on Ratuen for asking one too many questions."

"And what do you plan to do now?" John asked. "Assuming you are not tried and sentenced by the captain, that is."

The man swallowed hard. A desperation filled his face and made John regret being so cavalier about Brannock's possible fate.

"Look," Brannock replied. "I got no loyalty to Dawnstar. If you are leaving Dawnstar space and got a spot for an experienced soldier, I'd join a merc crew in a second. I was a decorated sergeant in the Imperial Army before the Shattering. Heck, truth be told I'd sign on as a latrine-scrubber on a garbage barque if it was headed out of Dawnstar space."

John sensed sincerity in the man's plea. He also sympathized with how helpless Ratuen could make one feel. He imagined that being outside the cage had saved the man from the physical abuse; but being stuck with a legion of sadistic torturers would be its own form of torture for a good man. But was Brannock a good man, or just a good liar? John dug deep and let his gambling instincts take over. At a card table, John could read a bluff as easily as reading a datapad. Could he read this man as well?

"I've been on the receiving end of Dawnstar's treachery," John said, flashing a suspicious look at Brannock. "Why should I believe you are not just looking for a way to get back into Dawnstar's good graces by spying on us?"

Before the man could answer, Shamira spoke.

"He is telling the truth, John, at least as far as he knows it. He believes everything he has said to you."

So much for testing his skills. Who needs intuition when you have psionics around?

"Who's the swish?" the man asked eyeing Angel, using what John surmised was some military slang for an attractive female.

"Someone you should speak to very respectfully, if you enjoy living," John answered.

Brannock suddenly found something much more interesting on the ceiling to stare at instead of Angel.

"Okay," John added, satisfied the man had taken his warning concerning Shamira. "I'll speak to the captain. He will be looking for crew replacements once we get to Furi. It's his call. In the meantime, Bobby Lee, can you take this man to the extra convalescence beds we had set up outside the lift? You can keep an eye on him there as well as here. I need my quarters back, and health-wise he's stable enough."

363

"You got it, Doc. But what if Voide comes for him?" John harrumphed.

"You tell her the chief medical officer said not to touch him, and if she has an issue with that, she can take it up with the captain."

Bobby Lee whistled and shook his head.

"Man, Doc, I know I owe you my life, but you keep askin' me to do stuff like that, you gonna get me killed anyway."

"Nah, Bobby Lee. You've already been shot this month. Surely Voide will give you a sympathy pass."

Bobby Lee laughed.

"Have you met the Lieutenant Commander, Doc?" the security officer grimaced.

"Unfortunately," John replied, giving Bobby Lee an encouraging pat on the shoulder.

As Bobby Lee helped the prisoner out of John's quarters and down the hall toward the auxiliary area med-beds, Shamira turned her attention toward the old man, still staring, bleary-eyed, at nothing in particular. Suddenly an odd look came over her face.

"What is it, Shamira?" John asked.

"I know this man," she said.

John's brow furrowed. He cocked his head as he voiced his incredulity.

"This guy has been a prisoner on Ratuen since before the Shattering. How can you possibly know him?"

"Well," Shamira replied, "it would be more accurate to say I know who he is."

"Care to enlighten me?" John said.

"This is Falcion Nichols."

John blinked as the name resonated through his memory. He squinted hard at the aged former prisoner but shook his head.

"Do you mean Abbot Falcion Nichols, former high abbot of Unified Church of the Faithful?"

"The very one."

John reeled. High Abbot Nichols had disappeared shortly after the Shattering. He hadn't been heard from since, and his body was never found. Some said he had been assassinated by agents of the Commission Against Destructive Supersition, Dawnstar's anti-faith hit squad, in preparation for their planned attacks on Enoch's territories.

"That can't be," John shook his head. "I heard CADS killed High Abbot Nichols shortly after the Shattering."

"The rumor," Shamira said, "was that CADS was behind

364

his disappearance, but that doesn't mean they killed him. They might have imprisoned him on Ratuen. Abbot Nichols had access to and personal knowledge of Enoch and many of his supporters when Enoch declared the Theocracy of the Faithful's secession from the Provisional Imperium."

John stared even more intently at the old man. He had seen holopics of High Abbot Nichols, but the bright-eyed vibrant clergyman bore little resemblance to the broken, empty, emaciated shell sitting before him. Still, there was something very familiar about his features.

"By the Lion, you are right!" John said at last. "This is High Abbot Nichols. But what in the galaxy have they done to him?"

"I don't know, but I will try to find out."

Shamira stepped over to the bed where the old man sat. Focusing deeply, she gently reached out and took the old man's hand, and stared deeply into his vacant eyes. John imagined she was watching the panorama of whatever world was playing out in the former abbot's head. The two sat motionless for minutes, locked in some invisible dance that John was not privy to.

"How's it going?" John asked, losing patience.

"It is really quite wondrous," Shamira replied, apparently undisturbed by John's interruption but still not unlocking her eyes from the abbot's. "It is like the Lion has helped him to create a beautiful refuge within his mind. He hasn't been suffering all these years, he has been with the Creator. He's not lost, he just doesn't want to leave."

Suddenly Abbot Nichols turned his eyes from the nowhere and nothing upon which they had been fixed and stared directly into Angel's. His vacuous visage softened into a kindly smile. Suddenly John could see the image of the Abbot Nichols he remembered from the holopics. The man had aged considerably, but his identity was without question.

"My beautiful child," Abbot Nichols said in a dry and crackling voice, taking Shamira's other hand in his free one and lifting them both to his lips. "Has the time truly come for me to return to my physical home?"

"Yes, Falcion, it is time."

John was taken aback by her familiarity with the former high abbot, given that she'd admitted never having met him. John had always been taught one respected one's elders and always used their proper titles. He would have gotten a beating if he had ever, during his time in Faithful school, addressed a teacher or clergy by their given name. How amazing it was at his age to still feel that lesson so strongly.

"And what is your name, my dear?" the abbot asked.

"You can call me Angel," Shamira answered.

"An angel you do appear to these old eyes. My dear child, He," Nichols said, pointing a finger toward the ceiling, "told me this time would come, you know?"

Nichols sounded as if his voice was struggling to find its normal rhythm after such a long period of idleness.

"Did He?" Shamira asked.

"Yes, sweet Angel. I know His word is true, but it had been so long. I wondered if my body would last until this day came. I felt a bit like Abram waiting for the child God promised him."

"The Lion has sustained you, Falcion," Shamira replied. "Enoch needs you now more than ever."

"Enoch? What a dear boy. Terrible thing that happened to his parents. I imagine his grief is great indeed."

"It has mellowed some over the past eight years."

The abbot's forehead furrowed deeply and his smile vanished.

"Eight years? Have I been gone that long?"

"Yes," Shamira answered. "If you would come with me, we will get you something to eat, and I can tell you all about it."

"That would be wonderful, my child." Nichols turned to John as if noticing him for the first time. "And who is this man, my dear? He is far too old to be your husband. Your father, perhaps?"

Shamira laughed and gave John a knowing wink. John suspected, if even half the rumors about the Angelicum were true, she might well be far older than himself and Nichols added together.

"No, your grace," John said, bowing his head deeply and using the proper honorific for a senior clergyman in the Faithful. "Just a friend."

Shamira took the abbot's hand and began to help him to his feet. She turned to look at John.

"If you do not mind, I will take Falcion to the mess hall for something to eat. Could you direct me? I will catch him up on everything he has missed."

John was torn. He was physically exhausted, and finally had the first chance since they last left Ratuen to have his quarters all to himself. Shamira might have rescued them on *Revenge*, and be an ally as part of the Angelicum Host, but John was fairly certain Molon would not approve of him letting a rescued hostage and an almost complete stranger have the run of the ship. He opted for a compromise.

"Come with me," John said.

Shamira walked slowly as the abbot shuffled after John. He exited his quarters and led them next door to the sickbay.

"Patch," John called out to the attending corpsman.

"Yeah, Doc?"

"Please escort our guests, agent Angel and Abbot Nichols to the mess hall, and see about getting them something to eat."

"You got it, Doc. But what about Twitch?" Patch said pointing to the convalescing XO.

"I'll stay with her," John replied.

Patch shook his head as he held up an outstretched palm.

"Doc, I already told you, you are dead on your feet. You need rest."

"I'll rest here," John replied.

He gave the corpsman a reassuring smile. Truth was, after their last discussion, John wasn't sure how at ease he was leaving Twitch in Patch's care. He doubted the corpsman was doing anything more than speculating, but John was still new on board, so he didn't dare assume he had a definite read on many of the crewmen just yet.

"I assume you have the med bed configured to alarm if any of her vitals becomes unstable?"

"I do," Patch confirmed.

"So I'll be fine."

Patch shrugged and laid the datapad he had been reviewing on the small table beside Twitch's med bed.

"If you say so, Doc. Truth is, the med bed respirator is breathing for her. There's not a lot can go wrong as long as she don't give up."

"From what I know of her," John smiled, "giving up isn't in her."

"Hu-ah!" Patch said, giving the Imperial Marine equivalent of *heck yeah*. "Given what she's facing, she's going to need every ounce of that fighting spirit."

"Yes, she will," John said, dreading the conversation he would have to have with Twitch once she was awake again. "By the way, Patch," John said, grasping for any excuse to change the subject. "The captain has given agent Angel here use of Twitch's quarters for the trip to Furi. Please show her where they are."

"Aye, sir," Patch replied.

John guessed the acknowledgement came from his position as CMO giving him some sort of equivalency of officer rank. Or maybe Patch was just being polite.

"Also," John added, "if you could do me one more favor."

"What do you need, Doc?"

"Alert the deck crew that my second roommate has been relocated to the auxiliary area med beds. They can reconfigure my room now that the impending trouble is over. Just have them leave one extra bunk in there for the abbot, if you would."

"Sure thing," Patch answered.

"Shamira," John said, turning to the Angelicum agent. If you and Abbot Nichols will go with Patch, he will get you something to eat, see you to your quarters across the hall, and show you around the ship. If you need anything once you get settled, I'll be here or in my quarters."

"Thank you, John," Shamira answered as the three of them exited the sickbay.

The room grew silent, save for the gentle pulsing of Twitch's med bed and the respirator tirelessly performing its duty. John slipped off his shoes and reclined on one of the empty med beds. The gentle pinging of Twitch's med bed provided a familiar rhythm that took him back to his residency days.

A mandatory life skill for medical residents was the ability to grab a quick nap anytime, anywhere, when circumstances allowed for it. His current posting wasn't quite the same workload as a doctor in a major hospital, but if life aboard *Star Wolf* maintained the constant level of excitement and danger the past few weeks had demonstrated, this skill would come in quite handy.

John quickly reached that hazy realm between waking and sleeping when the sound of the sickbay doors opening interrupted his journey toward unconsciousness. Giving his head a quick shake, John roused himself and looked up to see who had entered.

"Hello, John," Mel said. "How is Jane?"

"Who?" John asked.

"Commander Richardson," Mel replied.

It sounded so odd to hear Twitch's real name. Mel called crewmates she had a deeper connection with by their first names. It occurred to John that Shamira doing the same thing with Abbot Nichols might have a similar rationale. Was it a psionic connection?

He knew Fei were empathic, but his own experiences with Mel suggested her abilities went beyond that. Shamira had admitted her own psionic abilities. Perhaps there was something deeply intimate about touching another person's mind or feelings that gave rise to a certain level of familiarity. John found Mel calling him by his given name comforting somehow.

"She's stable for now," John answered. "She's got a tough road and some tough decisions ahead, though."

"We all do," Mel replied, giving him a soft smile. "Now that you know Elena is alive, what will you do?"

John's stomach tightened. So much was going on and he had been so focused on doing everything he could for Twitch that he had not taken a spare moment to process the whirlwind of feelings he had about Elena. He wasn't sure this was a conversation he wanted to have with Mel of all people. Still, he couldn't leave her question unanswered.

"Elena is dead," John said through clenched teeth.

He realized his fists had also clenched. He had inadvertently met Mel's inquiry with far more bitterness than he intended.

Even Mel's kind, powder-blue face contorted slightly at the bile in John's tone. He instantly regretted letting that side of him show, especially to her.

"It must be hard to discover someone you knew and loved is not who you thought they were."

"You have no idea," John said, biting his lip hard to hold back the tsunami of emotions threatening to overwhelm him.

"I have some idea."

Mel lowered her head and slumped her shoulders. Her eyes, for a moment, drifted off as if reliving some distant memory John wasn't sure he wanted to share. Someone had hurt her deeply. Thinking about that unknown someone, John's jaw clenched so tight he thought his teeth might break.

Seeing her like this set John's chest ablaze as he labored to breathe. He had left *Revenge* uninjured, but agony riddled his body nonetheless; the raw wound Elena had left in him burning with the salt of bitterness toward whoever would cause such pain to a creature as gentle as Mel. He had only known her for a few weeks, but the connection, the desire to protect her, was something he could not shut out.

"I'm sorry," John said, wincing at his insensitivity and self-absorption. "I shouldn't be dumping my frustrations on you. I am just very tired and have not had a lot of time to process everything just yet."

"I will let you rest," Mel said, her sweet smile returning a darker flush to her cyan skin.

John ached to touch her. He reached out, longing to take her hand and let whatever the effect she had on him take control, but she had already turned to leave. John dropped his hand back into his lap, his eyes watching her walk away.

"If you ever need to talk," she added, glancing back on her way out the door. "You know where to find me."

"Thanks, Mel," he replied, and she was gone.

John sighed and rubbed his face hard with both hands. Worry for Twitch, disillusionment toward Elena, and Lion-knows-what-he-felt for Mel whirled inside him threatening to tear him apart from the inside. He would need time and a lot of prayer to sort through everything. But right now, what he needed most was sleep. He hit the controls on the med bed he had appropriated, dimming the lights as he let exhaustion drag him willingly across the threshold into unconsciousness.

Thirty-One – Hey, Abbot

Molon stared at his long-time friend. Her frail form lying in the med bed barely resembled the vibrant, determined woman who had been his partner for most of his career in the Imperial Scouts. He was only minimally aware of John and Bob, the tailless Lubanian corpsman, standing by awaiting his order.

He swallowed hard, trying to get what felt like a ball of sandpaper out of his throat. He reached a fur-covered hand out to take ahold of Twitch's. She felt so cold, so limp. The med bed had been tapped into her chest muscles and diaphragm. Electric feeds had taken over the job of her brain and nerve function and were now sending signals to the muscles controlling her breathing.

With no need for breathing tubes other than the slender oxygen line looped over her ears and the tiny nozzles feeding into her nostrils, Twitch's face was so familiar to Molon. Their years as partners had etched every line, every feature into his mind. She was so pale now, though. The usually sharp, vivacious woman he knew had been replaced by this sallow replica. Was his friend even still in there at all?

"Whenever you are ready, captain," Bob prompted.

Molon nodded. Bob inserted a small, vacuum-sealed test tube into the med bed's medication dispenser unit and closed the lid. He punched a couple of the buttons, and the readout showed the contents of the tube being injected into Twitch via the med bed's intravenous interface.

Twitch's eyelashes fluttered briefly. She smacked her lips and slowly opened her eyes. As those eyes blinked and blinked, trying to focus on Molon, the slightest grin graced her parched lips.

"You throw one helluva party, Molon," Twitch quipped, her weak voice struggling to regain its former strength.

Molon blinked back the moisture he felt welling in his lupine eyes. His whiskers twitched and his muzzle wrinkled slightly before he could force it into a wolfish grin.

371

"I knew we should have cut you off sooner," he replied. "Never could hold your liquor. You should see what you did to *Star Wolf*'s paint job."

"Friends don't let friends fly drunk," Twitch replied. "But hey, whatever Doc's got me on, this is way better than booze. I can't feel a thing."

Molon couldn't maintain his grin. He squeezed Twitch's limp hand hard. Some part of him expected her to yank it away and chide him for playing rough. She didn't. Her hand was just as cold and limp as it had been before Bob had given her the stimulant to wake her up.

Twitch's smile also faded.

"You've got that hangdog look, Molon. What's going on? Did the doc refuse to give me a collie nose job while I was unconscious? You've been threatening for years."

"I wouldn't dare," Molon replied.

"So spill it then," Twitch replied, her brow furrowing. "Will I ever play the violin again?"

"You couldn't play the violin before," Molon said with a shake of his head.

"So that'd be a no, then."

Molon tried to smile. If Twitch could be flippant at a time like this, surely he could smile for her sake. But she didn't know what he knew. He just couldn't force the somber mood from his face.

"Come on, Lobo," Twitch said, her face showing she knew something was very wrong. "I'm a big girl. Give me what you got."

Molon flinched at hearing his call sign. Rarely did anyone ever use it, and Twitch was one of the few that could get away with it unscathed. When she called him Lobo, it meant all joking aside she was angling for straight talk. The moment of truth had arrived.

"It's bad, partner," Molon replied.

"How bad?"

Molon scrambled for the words. He glanced to John, standing by Twitch's bed checking her vitals on the med bed readout. Fortunately, Molon's awkward silence had gotten John's attention.

"I'm sorry, commander," John replied. His answer failed to draw Twitch's gaze away from Molon. "You suffered a severe injury to your upper vertebrae. Your spinal cord is severed in multiple places. Currently you are paralyzed below the shoulders. While treatment options are limited, there are a number of technological advances that can restore some basic

372

functionality. I assure you, I will spare no expense to get you the best biomechanical assistance tech in the Theocracy."

"So," Twitch replied, finally shifting her gaze to John. "I guess this is going to take more than a bandage and a pint of Imperial Gin to fix, huh Doc?"

John gave her a tight-lipped, forced smile.

"I've been researching this for our whole trip to Furi. To the best of my knowledge, commander, there is no fixing this. As I said, I can use my medical connections to get you the best technology to begin restoring some mechanically-assisted functionality, but you won't ever be the same as you were."

Apart from the rhythmic pings of the med bed readouts, silence dominated the room. Twitch had locked her eyes on some fixed point on the ceiling. Molon still gripped her flaccid hand. John looked like he would rather be anywhere else in the galaxy but this sickbay. Finally, after what seemed to Molon like an eternity, Twitch's gaze, now filled with fire, locked back onto Molon.

"And you let me wake up?" she said, a smoldering edge to her voice matching the ire in her eyes.

"What?" Molon asked, caught off guard by her question.

"I could have had a genuine blaze-of-glory exit," Twitch continued, "and you brought me back for this? You selfish cur! How could you do this to me?"

"It wasn't his call," John interjected before Molon could reply. "I'm chief medical officer. I brought you back."

Twitch's fiery gaze turned on John.

"You can't wipe your own backside without Molon's leave. He's the captain on this ship. It was always his call, no matter what you think. He was just too scared to make it. Well I'll make it. Put me in an airlock and have Monkey rig a remote and put it between my teeth. I'll finish things myself."

Molon felt like he had been shot in the chest. He knew Twitch was processing her situation. Rage was a natural reaction. Being the target of it, especially from his best friend, wasn't fun though. Molon shook his head

"Not going to happen, Twitch. We'll get through this."

"Fantastic!" Twitch snapped. "So when will you be severing your spine? We'll make a great pair."

"Look," Molon said, ignoring her jibe. "John has some connections on Furi. It's a TL13 world. No doubt there will be some gadgets we can pick up there to get you moving about again."

"And then what? You sell *Star Wolf* and play nursemaid the rest of my life?"

"No, then we head spinward. John says the Sarren system, Orke sector is a TL15 world with the best docs in the Theocracy. I'm not ditching you, partner. We're in this together."

Twitch's face twisted into a teeth-bared grimace.

"Get...out!" she ordered, flushing a deep crimson.

"Twitch," Molon pleaded.

"Seriously, Lobo," she said, her voice dropping into her normal, matter-of-fact tone. "Get out and leave me alone. You too, John. Bob is here if I need anything, but right now I just need you two to leave me alone."

"Fine," Molon answered. "Be mad at me if you have to, but I'm not giving up on you. We will find a way."

No answer came. Molon motioned for John to follow him and he turned to leave sickbay.

Once they were out in the corridor on the way to the bridge, John reached out a hand to stop Molon.

"She's upset," John said. "She is in denial and it will take some time for her to accept her situation. I've brought patients through things like this before. Give her time."

"I know her better than anyone, John. Being a pilot is all she's ever known. She was gifted. There aren't a handful of pilots in all of Humaniti like Twitch. It's not just what she does, it's who she is. How does one accept no longer being who you are anymore?"

"Time, patience, and prayer, Molon."

"Time I've got," Molon replied, shaking his head. "You might have to pony up the other two, Doc."

"Gladly."

The preparations for exiting voidspace were already underway when Molon and John entered the bridge. Angel was there as well, working alongside Mel to punch in the access codes which would stand down Furi's gravatic mines that secured the voidspace gate from Hatacks.

They transitioned into the Furi system with Furi's main sequence yellow dwarf star in full view and its secondary orange dwarf sun glimmering far off in the distance. Furi's main world hovered like a bright turquoise marble. Nearly ninety percent water, the population of the small chain of islands comprising the world's land masses numbered only sixty-thousand. It was this world's amazing oceans that had brought it so much wealth, thanks to the number of rare minerals which were found in abundance in those blue-green waters.

There were ten inhabited bodies in the Furi system, but

374

this mainworld was the anchor. Its orbital highport was one of the most advanced in this sector, with a fully equipped Theocracy consulate station that housed diplomats from the other Humaniti factions.

Behind them, the huge Theocracy battleship, *Revelation*, along with a fleet of smaller vessels accompanying it, dropped out of voidspace and into the Furi system. Communication had been impossible during the transition through voidspace, but Mel's console lit up with a hail as soon as the Theocracy assault fleet entered the system.

"Put it on screen, Mel," Molon said.

A wizened officer bearing admiral's bars on his collar appeared on the screen.

"Captain Hawkins, I am Admiral Wentzler, commanding officer of the *TBS Revelation*. I see you made it safely."

"Thanks to your timely arrival we were given that chance, admiral," Molon replied, "and the entry codes provided by your Angelicum operative. We are grateful."

"You're welcome, captain. Glad to be of service. I assume you have taken good care of our Angelicum ally?"

Angel stepped toward the captain's chair so she would come into view of the communications camera.

"I'm here, James. I have been well cared for."

"Good to hear, Angel. Captain, if you would be so kind as to bring your vessel to dock at Furi's highport, I would like to meet with you and your command officers in person. As would someone else who has taken a deep interest in you and your crew."

Someone else? Molon had been in and out of Theocracy space the last few months. He had also been resupplying at Furi when he had got the mission for John's rescue. As far as he could recall, however, there had been no cause or opportunity for anyone to take an interest in him or his ship. *Star Wolf* was merely one of dozens of freelance vessels that passed through Furi every week.

"Well, admiral," Molon said with a sigh, "unfortunately my command officers will be unavailable. My XO was badly injured during our escape from *Revenge* and my chief medical officer has a number of things to check on for her while we have access to Furi's TL13 medical facilities. My chief engineer has his hands full with repairs and provisioning. My security chief has to cover for my XO's duties for the time being, so I am afraid I am the only one free to attend."

"I understand, captain," Wentzler replied, his smile undaunted by Molon's partial refusal. "However, I would urge

375

you to at least bring your CMO with you. I will radio ahead and have Furi Research Hospital's chief of surgery clear his calendar and take an STS as soon as possible to the highport to meet with us. We will put all of Furi's medical resources at Dr. Salzmann's disposal to aid your XO, but we need to talk first."

Molon bit back the snappish response forming in his mouth. How did so many people he had never met know so much about what was going on aboard his ship? This was the first time he had ever spoken to Wentzler, yet this man knew John was acting as *Star Wolf's* CMO. Was his ship just rife with spies or was there something else going on? Still, he was in no position to press the matter at the moment.

"As you wish, admiral. Where should we meet? Furi's highport is one of the biggest I have seen. Given your cryptic reference to your mystery associate, one of the local pubs probably won't suffice for this meeting?"

Wentzler laughed and gave the comm camera at his end a knowing wink.

"Very intuitive, captain. We will meet at the inter-faction embassy complex. Angel, if you would direct the captain and the doctor to Abbot's private sanctuary, we can talk there."

"Yes, James. And by your leave, I have another guest that I am sure Abbot will be very pleased to see again."

The wizened admiral's left eyebrow raised and he leaned closer to the camera.

"Really? Who might that be?"

The Malak agent smiled sweetly.

"You will see. Believe me, it will be a joyful reunion."

"Fair enough," Wentzler said, nodding to Angel before turning his gaze toward Molon. "I look forward to meeting you face to face, Captain Hawkins. We will see you soon. Wentzler out."

The comm link dropped to be replaced by the blank screen-wall of the bridge once again. Molon scratched the fur on the side of his neck as he turned to face Angel and John.

"Well, you two," Molon said, his muzzle wrinkling into a half snarl. "I suppose your surprise guest is former High Abbot Nichols?"

"Of course," Angel replied. "Who else?"

"And I also suppose you have no intention of telling me who this 'Abbot' is Wentzler mentioned before we are face to face?"

"I'm sorry, Molon," Angel answered. "That information is not mine to share."

Molon was getting a little tired of feeling like the least

376

informed person on his own ship.

"Very well, then. Grab the geezer and meet me at the starboard primary airlock middle deck."

Molon turned to the helmsman's station currently manned by Lt. JG Zach Zarizzo.

"Z-Man, put us into an open docking bay starboard primary. Mel will get clearance from highport control for an available bay. And son, don't scratch the paint."

"Aye sir. Gentle as a lamb."

Molon turned to head for the elevator, wondering if he had exhausted his quota of unpleasant surprises for the month, or if this Abbot was going to be the grand finale. As if the situation with Twitch wasn't enough to worry about, now he had to meet some mystery guest. At least in Theocracy space, dealing with Theocracy military leaders, getting double-crossed wasn't a major concern. No way he'd walk into a blind alley like this on a PI or Dawnstar station, but at least with these knee-benders, whatever surprises were ahead were unlikely to be lethal ones.

Thirty-Two – On Your Marque

Molon twiddled his fingers and tapped the ground with his foot as he gazed around the personal retreat of the mysteriously dubbed Abbot. While more than adequate in size to accommodate a large delegation if necessary, the austerity of the furnishings and decorations were more reminiscent of a remote monastery than someone rating a private sanctuary within an inter-factional embassy complex.

Molon, John, Angel, and former High Abbot Nichols sat in hard chairs around a large conference table. Strewn about the room were a few other smaller tables and chairs, all of which looked equally devoid of comfort, save for a pair of leather, thickly cushioned reading chairs along the far wall next to a huge bookcase filled with actual paper volumes. Molon had seen holovids of paper books, but it had been centuries since digital media replaced physical printing. A collection of physically printed books this size would be more valuable than the entire Furi highport if they were actual historical relics and not fabricated replicas.

The impressive personal library notwithstanding, Molon highly doubted that, whoever Abbot was, he would be the current high abbot of the Unified Church of the Faithful, Zestri Mariz. Molon had seen more than a few holovids of Mariz: the man's flamboyant, expensively attired persona was responsible, to a large degree, for Molon's current skepticism toward the leading of the Faithful. That guy was a showman with far more flash than faith about him. He reminded Molon much more of a used ship dealer than a clergyman. There was no way this spartan sanctuary belonged to him.

John, Angel, and Falcion Nichols sat calmly and patiently, chatting about some matter of theology or other, while Molon was making a concerted effort to ignore them. Enduring their philosophical pondering would only serve to make this wait even longer than it already was.

Molon was not blessed with a great deal of patience on the best of days. He understood that docking a huge battleship,

378

and making whatever arrangements needed to be made following the incursion into Dawnstar space to affect *Star Wolf*'s rescue, would doubtless take some time. It was just hard to sit here like ticketholders waiting for a live show to start when Twitch was lying paralyzed and fuming in *Star Wolf*'s sick bay. On top of that, he had a thousand things to oversee himself, especially with taking on more crew and outfitting for their next trek to the Sarren system for whatever hope there might be in getting Twitch put back together again.

Before he had worked himself into a deeper lather over the delays, the doors opposite where they were sitting opened. In walked Admiral Wentzler. Molon did a double-take at who was with him. It was Prince Enoch Halberan, son of the former emperor, and leader of the Theocracy of the Faithful. Molon caught his jaw before it hit the floor and quickly composed himself. He noticed John's shock matched his own as the doctor sat unmoving, staring at Enoch.

Angel and Abbot Nichols, however, seemed utterly unfazed. Abbot Nichols, exhibiting a spryness belying his years of hard captivity on Ratuen, nearly flew across the room and threw his arms around Prince Halberan.

"Enoch, my dearest boy," Nichols said, tears welling in his eyes. "I never thought I would lay these old eyes on your shining face again this side of heaven."

Enoch's own eyes overflowed with tears as he embraced the elderly cleric. He lifted the old man off the ground in an embrace as the prince struggled to choke back his emotions and find his voice again.

"Falcion...But how?" Enoch asked. "We thought you dead at the hands of CADS agents. Where have you been?"

Enoch set the aged abbot back on his feet and the old man took the prince's hands in his own.

"That, my boy," Nichols replied, "is a long and painful story for another time. Know that the Lion would not let those Razers take my life until I had fulfilled His purpose. But now, you have much to attend to with my rescuers. We have all the time in the galaxy to catch up. I plan to stay with you if you will permit it. The Lion has given me much that you need to hear."

"Yes, of course you will stay with me," Enoch answered. "It is true that I have things to attend to, but I haven't seen you in nearly eight years. We have so much to discuss. I need your wisdom now more than ever."

"They need you as well," Nichols answered, shaking his head and dropping Enoch's hands as he motioned toward Molon and John. "The guiding of the Spirit has shown me that you will need them too before all is done with this infernal Shattering. If you will trust me, my dear boy, I will take a rest and enjoy the lovely tea your staff has provided while you attend to matters of state. After they have been taken care of, you and I will have time to catch up."

Without waiting for an answer, Abbot Nichols returned to the table where they all had been sitting, picked up his cup of tea, and tottered off to one of two comfortably-padded reading chairs on the far side of the sanctuary. He set his cup down on a small table between the chairs and began perusing the large bookshelf along the wall on that side of the room.

Enoch wiped his eyes, swallowed hard, and turned to face Molon.

"I cannot express my gratitude for what you have done in returning Falcion to us, Captain Hawkins. He was my mentor as I sought my own theological training, and a dear friend to me after my parents were killed. Often I have longed for his counsel once again, and against all odds you have returned him to me. This is a debt I can never repay."

Before Molon could answer, John appeared at his side and replied to Prince Halberan's gratitude.

"Your grace, it was the Lion's guiding hand that led us to Abbot Nichols. In truth, we might never have recognized him or been able to bring him out of his catatonic state were it not for Shamira."

John motioned toward Angel, who joined the standing circle. Both Wentzler and Enoch nodded to the Angelicum agent.

"James," Angel said, nodding toward Admiral Wentzler before turning and nodding at Prince Enoch Halberan, "Abbot, or I suppose at least while we are here I can call you Enoch, it is good to see you both again. It has been a long time."

Enoch smiled.

"Your work within GalSec has been invaluable, agent Angel," Enoch replied. "When we received your communique a few months back that GalSec had commandeered a PI cruiser and sent Simmons and Russel here to Orenc sector, I knew that was something I needed to be closer to personally. We left for Furi as soon as we got your message, hoping to be closer to hand once their exact plans were revealed. Thankfully it took Simmons and Russel longer to get to Orenc from Corialis than it took us from Haven."

"While I am of course glad to see you again," Angel replied, "I must say personally endangering yourself on the assault force into Hatacks was an unnecessary risk. Surely your

Angelicum advisors cautioned against such recklessness?"

"Yes, they did," Enoch acknowledged with a nod, "and I proceeded to ignore them. I had such a strong leading from the Spirit that these events were a critical turning point in this war, I wasn't about to sit back on Haven and wait weeks to hear how it turned out."

"In all fairness," Admiral Wentzler interjected, "I reminded him he could wait safely here on Furi and know in a few days how it all turned out. But he didn't pay me any more heed than he did his Angelicum advisors. When the prince gets his mind set on something, there's not a lot in the galaxy that will change it."

Molon had grown tired of being a spectator to this conversation. He was eager to get on with his own work and free John to manage what accommodations here he could for Twitch. He was flattered to have the chance to meet with Prince Enoch Halberan in person, but it was time to move this meeting forward and get back to *Star Wolf.*

"I suppose now I understand all the secrecy behind the call sign Abbot," Molon said. "Broadcasting that Prince Enoch Halberan is gallivanting around the galaxy on a battleship instead of safely sequestered somewhere would prove too tempting a target if the wrong ears got wind of it."

"I suppose you are right," Enoch replied. "Still, as much as I value the advice of my counselors, I must ultimately follow the guidance of the Spirit. The Father guides and directs the Lion, but it is the job of the Spirit to direct the hearts of men."

Molon shook his head. He'd had enough of this Faithful talk from Angel and John the past few days. He bit back a sarcastic response and chose discretion instead.

"If you say so, your grace. Unfortunately I'm afraid I have no frame of reference from which to relate."

Enoch smiled at Molon. It was not a condescending smile, but rather the prince exuded a genuine warmth and gentleness that put Molon's heart at ease. It was a different feeling compared to the mind-games he had felt from Mel on occasion. This was not manipulative, but a genuine sense of peace that calmed Molon's inner fire and gave him a feeling that everything would be all right.

"I fully understand, Captain Hawkins. That is precisely why the Father and the Lion have put Dr. Salzmann in your path. It was no accident he came into your crew, and although he may not know it yet, it is no frivolous decision he will make to stay. There are great things ahead for *Star Wolf* and her crew. This is just the beginning."

A bit of Molon's resentment returned, welling up inside him. He hated people he had never met acting like they knew everything about him and his crew. Who was Enoch Halberan to tell him things about his ship and his people that even he didn't know for certain?

"Let me guess," Molon replied. "Some mystical voice has told you all these things, but if I ask you any questions, you will tell me it is a mystery that you can't reveal. I've played enough of those games with Angel here. I have no desire to go round two with you, your grace. I'm done with everybody seeming to know more about what is going on with my ship and my crew than I do."

Enoch gave Molon a sad smile, and his voice took on a soothing tone.

"Captain Hawkins, I assure you I know little more than has already been revealed. I have no desire to withhold any information or to play any games. We are on the same side."

"Are we, your grace?" Molon snapped with far more fire than he had intended. "Then why are you all keeping secrets, and why does everyone seem to know that this human dilettante we rescued from a Dawnstar prison world will so assuredly become a long-term part of my crew? What stops me from dropping him off on Tede on our way out of this sector?"

"All I know," Enoch replied, "is that I heard from my top Angelicum advisors that a Dr. John Salzmann was going to be instrumental in affecting a turning point in the war. That might be challenging to do sitting on Tede. It was only after I got to Furi that I came to find out he had joined the crew of a mercenary ship, *Star Wolf*. As soon as I learned that, the Spirit within me stirred with a feeling that this was a momentous occurrence."

"And what makes you so sure these warm fuzzy feelings aren't just indigestion?" Molon said, with more disrespect than was warranted given the Prince's graciousness thus far.

Enoch was clearly a patient man, given that all of Molon's hot-headed baiting had not changed the prince's gentle tone.

"Abbot Nichols's words just now strongly confirmed what I already felt, that somehow you and your crew have a major role to play in the Creator's plans. Sometimes guidance from the Creator is not a single shout but a series of whispers."

Molon was conflicted. There was just something likeable about the prince, but all this spiritual talk unsettled Molon. It was like there was an exclusive club that everyone in the room except Molon was a member of. He didn't know the secret handshake. He didn't know the password. And they were all sharing secrets amongst themselves that he wasn't privy to.

"So what else have these whispers clued you in to that I ought to know?" Molon asked.

"Beyond what I have already shared, captain," Enoch replied, "I don't have any greater knowledge than you do. But I do have an offer, if you are interested."

Molon's brow furrowed and his ears twitched forward. "What kind of offer?"

"Well, Angel shared with us that you have lost your freelance merchant contract with the Provisional Imperium."

Molon felt his blood began to boil. His lip pulled back over his canines and his body tensed. This set the admiral to reach toward his sidearm, but the prince motioned for him to stand down. Enoch remained unperturbed at Molon's escalated tension.

"Now wait one minute. I've been with Miss Shinybright here," Molon snarled, pointing a finger at Angel, "since we dropped out of voidspace, save for whatever time she and John had when they ran to fetch your elderly abbot friend. When exactly did she have time to report about my contract status with the PI?"

Enoch's cheeks flushed red and he cleared his throat.

"I'm sorry, captain," he said, opening his hands apologetically in front of him. "I forgot that Angel is probably the first Malak Angelicum you have encountered."

"She's the first any-kind of Angelicum I've ever seen apart from holovids and story-books. What's that got to do with anything?"

"Yes," Enoch continued. "Well, you see the Malak caste of Angelicum have rather advanced psionic abilities. I'm afraid she has been communicating with James and myself since we arrived in the room. I realize, now, that was rude to do without first informing you. It is just something I have grown accustomed to with my Angelicum advisors. My apologies."

"Great," Molon snarled, shaking his head but releasing his tensed posture. "So you three have been carrying on a sidebar this whole time. No wonder everyone seems to know more than I do about what is going on."

"Captain," Angel interjected, "I was merely bringing James and Enoch up to speed regarding the events on board *Revenge*. I also apologize for not doing it openly, but I know you are in a hurry to conclude this meeting and get back to helping your executive officer, so I thought only to save time."

Molon spun on Angel.

"So you are snooping around in my noggin too?" Molon

growled, pointing his finger and taking a step toward Angel. "Nobody invited you into my head, sister, so keep your mind games out of my skull."

Angel frowned.

"I'm sorry, Molon. It is a natural reflex for me. I automatically pick up the most basic surface thoughts unless I deliberately focus on going deeper, but I can no sooner turn that off than you can will your eyes to stop seeing or your ears to stop hearing. I only got your sense of urgency about Commander Richardson's condition because it has been so strongly on your mind since we arrived. I intended no offense."

Molon's ears relaxed as he gazed at the deck and shuffled his feet. There was a lot for him to get used to here. Other than whatever Mel was capable of, Molon had never, at least to his knowledge, been around psionic individuals before. It was unsettling, but he knew these people weren't enemies.

"Look, maybe I'm more on edge than I need to be," he admitted, relaxing his posture and removing the snarl from his muzzle. "I am worried about Twitch but it's unsettling when people you have never met already know everything about you. I play things pretty close to the vest, and being this wide open makes me feel like someone shaved all my fur. Anyway, I'd like to hear your offer, your grace."

Enoch nodded and the others seemed to relax as well. An exuberance filled Enoch as he began to explain his proposal.

"As I was saying, captain, with your PI independent operator's license suspended, or soon to be, you are only going to be legally allowed to take Theocracy merchant contracts. Given what has happened to you at the hands of Dawnstar and the Provisional Imperium, and given that many of the worlds near where you are heading are in and around the Occupied Worlds currently held by Alpha Pack on behalf of the New Halberan Empire, I thought you might like a little more freedom to operate."

"What do you mean by that, your grace?" Molon asked.

"That's simple," Enoch explained. "I am prepared to offer you a Letter of Marque on behalf of the Theocracy of the Faithful, making you a sanctioned privateer vessel. This would allow you to carry out both commercial and military actions with full protections under the Humaniti Articles of Warfare, the same as afforded any military vessel. I realize this doesn't quite replace your diminished financial opportunities with the Provisional Imperium, but it may give you a little more latitude in going where you need to, as you seek the best help for your executive officer. We are on the right side of this conflict,

384

captain. I think you know that or you wouldn't be here. I'm only offering the chance to be as involved in this war as you choose to be."

Molon was speechless. This was the very thing he had hoped after he had headed spinward and realized the corruption in the Provisional Imperium and the ruthlessness of the New Halberan Empire allies, Alpha Pack. He hadn't really thought through how he planned to join forces to serve Enoch Halberan, but now the opportunity he needed was being handed to him. There had to be a catch.

"And what exactly do you want from *Star Wolf* in return, your grace? I admit this sounds tempting, but life has taught me that when things come too easily there is always a hidden cost."

"Not this time, captain," Enoch said. "As I said, this Letter of Marque will give you what protections I can, but you may continue to come and go, do or not do whatever you please. If I get any clearer direction from the Spirit or from my Angelicum advisors, I will let you know, but you will be under no compunction to do anything other than what you will."

Freedom to pursue his goals, to choose his targets and missions, to operate by his conscience rather than blindly following orders as a military vessel would have to; was this possible? Prince Halberan seemed sincere. If there was a hidden hook somewhere, Molon couldn't see it.

"Fine, then," Molon replied. "You have a reputation as a man of your word, Prince Halberan, so I will take you at that. I gratefully accept your Letter of Marque."

Enoch beamed a robust smile and clapped Molon on the shoulder. The admiral lost his last hint of tension at Molon's earlier outburst and was also grinning broadly.

"Excellent," Prince Enoch answered as he turned toward the admiral. "James, will you see to it that the Letter of Marque gets transmitted before they leave Furi?"

"Yes, your grace," answered Admiral Wetzler.

There was a knock at the door.

"Enter," Enoch called out.

A man in an expensive and well-tailored business suit entered. His neatly groomed salt-and-pepper hair, clean shaven appearance, and upright demeanor indicated this visitor was someone of importance.

"Ah, Dr. Merriam," Enoch greeted the new arrival. "I'm glad you could make it."

The doctor flashed a mild frown.

"I wasn't given the impression there was a choice, your

385

grace. May I understand what is so urgent that I drop everything to fly to the highport at a moment's notice? I had a number of critical meetings set for this afternoon."

"Yes, well, your calendar has been cleared," Enoch replied, apparently unconcerned by the doctor's irritation at the sudden summons. "I already have my staff working with yours to reschedule your meetings. Allow me to introduce Captain Molon Hawkins, our newest privateer captain, and his chief medical officer Dr. John Salzmann."

"Any relation to Salzmann Pharma?" Merriam inquired, his irritation fading as he raised an eyebrow.

"One and the same," John answered, his face flushing slightly. This elicited a full smile from Dr. Merriam.

"You guys have a revolutionary anti-radiation medication, but your stock has been stagnant for a while. Was thinking of dumping it, unless you might clue me that you are prepping for another breakthrough sometime soon?"

"Well, insider trading info and all that, you know," John answered, "but I have an idea for a few things going into the works. No promises when the results may come, though. Might be worth sticking around for the ride."

"Hmm, interesting," Merriam rubbed his chin. "But I doubt the Prince of the Theocracy introduced us to swap stock tips, doctor. I have a suspicion my urgent summons has to do with you?"

"Yes," John replied, nodding. "I have a serious C5-C6 injury to our executive officer, and I need to know the best mechanical assistance tech you have at your disposal. I will need to get her fitted and set up as soon as possible."

Dr. Merriam's eyes narrowed.

"You looking to do a reattach-regen? We have a few surgeons who have done that, but it depends on a lot of factors."

"No," John replied, with shake of his head and a frown on his face. "Unfortunately the injuries are far too serious. The spinal cord has been severed in multiple places."

"Ah, I see," Dr. Merriam replied, his own grim visage matching John's. "A TL15 world might be able to do something, but even then it's a long shot."

"We are headed for Sarren to see what they think," John said. "I did my residency there. For now I just need to get her as much basic functionality and mobility as possible."

Merriam flashed another brief frown at Prince Enoch.

"Well, it doesn't take the Surgeon General of the Furi system to handle your request, but if you will come with me I

386

will put you with my top cybernetic assistance people, who will grease the wheels to get your crewmate sorted right away. I assume you are docked at the highport?"

"Yes, our ship isn't fitted for ground landing."

"No problem. I have a fully equipped medical shuttle on standby at the highport at all times. If you will come with me, we can get moving on that right away."

John looked to Molon with a raised eyebrow.

"Yes, John, go with Dr. Merriam and do what you can with Twitch. I'll wrap things up here and see about crew replacements. I imagine we will be two or three days at least before we're ready to get underway. Will that be enough time?"

"Yes, it should," replied Dr. Merriam. "If we can go now to the docking bay and move your patient to the medical shuttle, I will call ahead to have the cyber-prosthesis lab prepare to see us right away."

"Thank you, Dr. Merriam," John replied. "Molon, I will go straight to a terminal and release the payment voucher in Theocreds for the return mission to Ratuen as promised. I am also extending a letter of credit to *Star Wolf* for an additional two million Theocreds for any repair, outfitting, upgrading, or rearming expenses you need."

Molon took a deep breath. John was a generous soul, but Molon didn't like owing anyone. As much as he could use the advance to see to proper repairs, refitting, and hiring new crew, he couldn't accept this.

"John, I appreciate it, but I told you, what went down was part of the risk of being a merc. Pay off the contract amount, we're owed that, but I can't take an advance. We have no work on the horizon and I have no idea when I could pay that back."

John smiled and winked at Molon.

"Don't worry about it, captain. We will settle anything against the LOC over time, since the decision on whether or not I am staying aboard has apparently already been made."

Molon laughed. His medics were great, but he had to admit having a genuine trained surgeon on board, especially one with John's compassion, would be a welcome addition. That was doubly true now with what lay in Twitch's future.

"I appreciate that, John."

"It is the least I can do. If I am going to be flying about in this crate for the foreseeable future, I want to make sure you don't have to hold it together with glue and prayers."

Molon laughed and patted John on the arm. He liked Doc, even with all the baggage that came from toting a religious hermit-worlder around with the crew. Drs. Merriam and

Salzmann said their goodbyes to Prince Halberan and exited.

"As for crewing up and refitting," Admiral Wentzler said to Molon, "there is a Spacers' Club in the highport. Quite a few experienced spacers and marines in between billets hang out there looking to pick up a berth on a passing ship. However, if you are looking for a broader choice among less eager-beaver possibilities, I'd look elsewhere."

Molon was intrigued. Sometimes the spacer bars featured mostly people who had been involuntarily cut from other billets. One could find a diamond or two in the rough there, but filling out all the holes in *Star Wolf*'s roster would take more than the pick of the litter at the local Spacers' Club.

"Where would you suggest I look, admiral?"

A wily grin crept across the face of the seasoned commander. He cocked his head slightly to the side as he answered Molon's inquiry.

"You might take an STS down to the moon colony of Zaros, third moon of Furi's only gas giant. There's a dive bar there called the *Last Call* where seedier mercs and other undesirables with a wide range of skills hang out...no offense intended."

"None taken," Molon replied.

Molon had never known a military commander to be overly impressed with merc hangouts such as the one the admiral had just described. Those places were usually filled with the dregs of society; social misfits with authority issues. The better ones had trouble following authority. The worse ones had the authorities following them.

"Let me ask you, Admiral," Molon said with a grin, "If you were outfitting your ship and plugging holes for about twenty-five percent of your crew spots, spacers and marines, would you head for the *Last Call*?"

Wentzler laughed out loud and shook his head.

"Not on your life. I run a military ship, and I need the spit-and-shine, order-following, rule-book-quoters that make a military vessel run like it was jacked into my brain."

"But—

"But," the admiral continued, interrupting Molon before he could complete his objection. "If you and I swapped captain's chairs, and I was headed for the trouble you are, I wouldn't stop long enough to sniff the air in the Spacers' Club on my way to the *Last Call*."

Molon nodded. The admiral was giving sound advice. Scratching the whiskers on his chin, Molon pondered the admiral's recommendation.

388

"Interesting advice."

"Look, captain," Wentzler explained. "I saw from your service record you were a Scout. Some of the best military personnel around serve on my ship, but half wouldn't know to wipe their behind without an officer to tell them when and how. Independent thinking and insubordination are court martialing offenses aboard a space navy vessel."

"So I've heard," Molon replied.

"But you know as well as I do," the admiral continued, "in the Scouts, and even more so on merc ships, independent thinking and sometimes even insubordination are survival skills."

"Ain't that the truth," Molon said with a laugh.

This salty old admiral had a rare blend of intelligence and wisdom. Molon couldn't count the number of times he and Twitch had bent orders way out of shape, if not broken them entirely, to get the job done. Many were the times they threw the book out the window and followed their gut. That instinct had saved their lives and made whatever trouble or administrative reprimand they got in return no deterrent at all.

"If you are going anywhere near the Occupied Worlds," Wentzler continued, "you are going to need people who can think on their feet."

"People like I will find at the *Last Call* on Zaros?"

"Exactly! That's my two credits' worth of advice, captain, for whatever it is worth."

"I appreciate it, admiral. I believe I will look at getting our hardware replenished here at the highport, but will indeed head to Zaros for our personnel replacements."

Angel, who had been standing by with the prince throughout this exchange, cleared her throat to speak.

"I would offer one exception to that plan, Molon," Angel interjected. "If I may?"

Apparently whatever Angel was about to share was not part of the silent conversation she had ongoing with the admiral and Prince Halberan, as both of them turned a quizzical look in her direction.

"What exception is that?" Molon prompted.

"With your permission, I would like to join the crew of *Star Wolf*."

Molon's ears flattened and his brow furrowed. Was this the hook into his ship and his business he had missed before? It seemed unlikely. Apparently Prince Halberan and Admiral Wentzler were equally shocked by her request.

"You want to what?" Admiral Wentzler asked.

389

"They are short one pilot," Angel explained. "I not only have an excellent rating on frigate class ships and a Class A pilot's license, but I also happen to be a trained undercover agent, which may come in quite handy if they are heading for the Occupied Worlds."

"I daresay," Angel continued, turning toward Molon, "you will be hard pressed to find a more qualified replacement crewman elsewhere, even on Zaros."

Prince Enoch Halberan stammered as he tried to collect his thoughts.

"B-b-but you have not cleared this with the Angelicum Host. Don't you need to debrief with them on your last mission, and receive your new orders? You are a member of the Watchmen, aren't you?"

Angel smiled sweetly at the prince.

"I am. My mission was to infiltrate GalSec and stay as close to Senior Interrogator Simmons as possible while gathering intel on project Firelake. I have done this. My report was forwarded as soon as we hit this system."

"Don't you need to wait for new orders?" Wentzler asked, his face showing he was not sold on the idea of Angel whizzing off to Lion knows where on a privateer vessel.

"Unnecessary, James. Now that my presence has been exposed, I am unable to continue my primary assignment. Given the strong leadings of the importance *Star Wolf* will play in Theocracy affairs going forward, I am following the guiding of the Spirit in making this request. After all, what better place for a Watchman than on a vessel prophesied to change the course of history?"

Molon saw her logic, but having an Angelicum on board would carry its own set of complications. Aside from everything else, Mel's shenanigans were nothing compared to the havoc this full-fledged telepath might wreak.

"Are you sure?" Enoch asked. "What will your superiors say about this?"

"I have complete peace about it," Angel replied, "yet will certainly take leave should the Spirit lead elsewhere in the future. The Watchmen are not hierarchical, Enoch: we follow the leading of our one true commander."

"So just like that," Molon said, his brow furrowing. "You are leaving everything behind and coming with us? That makes no sense. You have no idea who I am, where we're going, or even what the pay is for the position. Why would you just offer to join my crew on a whim?"

"I assure you it is not a whim," Angel answered. "I actually

390

made this decision the moment we left *Revenge*. It was just not appropriate to discuss it with you until now."

"And as captain of *Star Wolf*, don't I get any say in this?"

"Of course! You can always refuse to accept my offer of service." Angel smiled sweetly. "But you won't."

Molon shook his head and thought to himself:

When you are caught in a current you can't fight, it's best to just turn and swim downstream.

"You know," he said to Angel, "with what you did to pull the former high abbot out of his catatonia, maybe I can use you after all. Twitch may not be able to pilot anymore, but unless she proves completely unfit for duty, I have no intention of relieving her as XO. Doc say she is going to need someone to help her even if he finds the cyber-gizmos to restore a lot of her functionality. Are you willing to room with Twitch and help me keep an eye on her mental state?"

Angel's smile faded.

"Are you asking me to spy in your executive officer's mind, captain?"

"No, I'm saying you told me you can't help but listen. So I'm just asking you to listen and let me know if you see any danger signs. Beyond that, be a nursemaid when she needs one and a pilot when I need one. You okay with that?"

"Aye, captain, I am," Angel replied.

"Well then, welcome aboard, Angel."

Molon turned to Prince Halberan and Admiral Wentzler.

"I am glad to have met you, your grace, admiral, but if you will excuse me. As we travel I will be sure to keep you informed if I come across anything the Theocracy should be aware of."

"Your efforts will be greatly appreciated, captain," Prince Halberan said.

Molon and Angel left the sanctuary and headed towards *Star Wolf* to finish their business at the highport. There was a great deal to do on Furi, not to mention preparing an STS for the trip to Zaros and the *Last Call* Bar.

Thirty-Three – Last Call

They had been in the Furi system three days. Top-notch starport facilities and senior shipwrights assigned by Prince Halberan had, under Dub's watchful eye, completed repairs and refits in record time. *Star Wolf* was fully fit and ready to head spinward as soon as Molon and the senior officers hired the replacements. Thanks to Dub rigging up a remote camera, monitor, and transmitter, Molon had even convinced Twitch to play a role in selecting crewmates.

Twitch hadn't been happy at the suggestion, preferring to sulk and brood over all the technological toys Dub and John were adapting to her physiology. Thankfully Molon knew which buttons to push to trigger Twitch's stubborn streak. He used her own comments about being able to spot traitors and rogues to convince her she was a necessary part of selecting new crew.

Voide was also using her human-camouflage tech and colored contacts for this recruitment drive. No sense stirring up the locals with a Prophane's presence in their local watering hole.

Besides the odd-and-ends assortment in front of him, plus a couple of choice recruits he had managed to pull out of the Spacers' Club, there were three others officially seeking to join *Star Wolf*'s ranks. First was Dr. John "Doc" Salzmann who had been their de facto chief medical officer since his rescue. Second was Stellan "Pounder" Brannock, the former Empire Army soldier turned unwilling Dawnstar Security guard whom they had liberated from Ratuen. Finally there was the enigmatic Malak agent, Shamira, with the call sign "Angel". All that was left was to sort through the motley crew of applicants at the *Last Call* and they would be on their way spinward.

They had a recruitment table set up inside the *Last Call* with Molon in the center, Voide on his right, and Mel on his left. The monitor and camera rig for Dub and Twitch, joining remotely from *Star Wolf*, took up the table space between Molon and Mel.

392

Two days before, they had posted notices around the bar that a merc vessel would be hiring spacers and marines for various positions. They were to submit their service and skills records and show up today for interviews.

There was a line out the door and halfway around the building, of dubious looking rabble, shifty characters who could have passed for the usual suspects in any police lineup. Molon was second-guessing the admiral's advice. Too late now. They were here, and *Star Wolf* needed replacements, so he would try to pick the best of the bunch.

The applicants here at the *Last Call*, however, looked like as rag-tag a bunch of recruits as he had ever seen, and he had seen some dregs. He had checked their submitted service and skills records. Those that weren't heavily redacted showed most to be experienced soldiers, engineers, spacers, scientists, commandos, and communicators with a vast range of experience. Their one common denominator, the one element that likely landed most of them here rather than serving in a military berth somewhere, was an aversion to following orders.

Almost to a person, this collection of sophonts had write-ups, disciplinary actions, and a stack of demerits high enough to post a sniper on to go along with their list of skills and accomplishments. They would be a challenge to command, but *Star Wolf* had more than its fair share of ex-military shining stars. Where Molon was headed, they were going to get more than a little dirty, and a crew who wasn't afraid of a little mud-wallowing might be the difference between life and death.

However, the first few candidates were quickly dismissed. Most were local gang-bangers or thugs looking for a way to get paid to do what they were inclined to do anyway: fight.

Next in line stepped up a man who looked to be in his mid-forties with just-below-shoulder-length, dark brown hair tied back into a pony tail. He was wearing a tattered denim jacket, and had several days of stubble on his face. The only thing that set this man apart from the rabble Molon had just dismissed was a high tech-level laser pistol strapped low on his thigh. A slight bulge under the man's jacket suggested a second weapon.

"Name and preferred call sign?" Molon asked.

"Sivio Rayce," the man replied. "And I go by 'WW' when I need something other than a name."

Molon and the rest of the senior officers punched up his name on their datapads, which contained all the submitted service and skill records for the applicants. The file was so heavily redacted as to give little more information than the man had just told him, other than the fact he had been with GalSec until about four years ago and had declined to provide any information on what he had been doing since.

"So what's the 'WW' stand for?" Molon asked.

The man adopted a greasy smile and shrugged.

"Eh, you know, Wild and Wooly, World Wide, whatever you want it to mean, man."

"I'll take him!" Voide interjected, emphatically.

"Thanks, chica," Rayce said, beaming a smile at Voide.

Before Molon could inquire how she could make such a quick assessment from an almost totally redacted service record, Twitch interjected through the remote monitor.

"*Wet Works,*" Twitch remarked.

Rayce's eyes widened at the sound of Twitch's voice. He glanced around as if trying to locate the source.

"What?" asked Molon?

"*That's what the 'WW' stands for,*" Twitch replied. "*He's an assassin, Molon.*"

"How do you figure?" Molon asked.

Before Twitch could respond, Rayce stopped looking around and fixed his gaze on Molon as he let out a sigh.

"So you hear that voice too, man?" Rayce said, wiping the back of his hand across his brow. "Whew, I thought it was just in my head."

Molon's eyes narrowed at Rayce's strange behavior. It was true the monitors that allowed Molon, Voide, and Mel to see Twitch and Dub were facing away from the applicants, but the camera mounted atop the monitor was obvious, so Rayce's reaction was very odd.

"Anyway," Molon said, putting aside Rayce's behavior for the moment. "How did you reach that conclusion, Twitch?"

"*Easy,*" Twitch replied. "*The service record devoid of any meaningful details, plus a blank for the last four years. Add that to our sociopathic security chief's eagerness to recruit him, plus the quick-draw rig on his sidearm, it all adds up.*"

Molon looked at Voide who appeared as if she was ready to leap through the monitor and tear into Twitch.

"That right?" Molon asked Voide.

"It was my guess," Voide confirmed. "If we are going toward the Occupied Worlds, I am going to need some security people who can drop the military spit and polish. If we are going to survive, it won't be by stand up fights. I'll need guys like this for things our soldier-boys can't or won't do."

"I'm sorry, Voide," Molon said, shaking his head. "We are mercs, not assassins. We have no clue what this guy did, or

394

why GalSec ousted him. An assassin is one thing, an assassin who GalSec doesn't even want, that's a gamble I don't want to take."

"Hey, man," Rayce interjected. "If you wanna know why I'm not a spook anymore, just ask. I got nothing to hide."

"Your service record says otherwise," Molon replied.

Rayce spread a wide grin and nodded slowly. Molon wondered if the man was on some kind of mind-altering drugs or something. He seemed way too relaxed for such a tense conversation.

"That's a good one, man," Rayce replied. "You got me there. Well, dig this; GalSec cut me loose because I refused a mission."

"What kind of mission?" Molon pressed.

"The gnarly kind. Suits wanted me to take out a dude's family; a wife and three kids, man. The main target wasn't even going to be home; some kind of psychological move to convince this guy to start cooperating or something. I wasn't down with that. Real targets I figure got it coming one way or another, but wife and kids ain't done nothing. So I walked, man."

"You walked?" Voide asked, her eyes widening. "I was with GalSec also, and I wasn't aware they just let trained operatives just walk away."

"Yeah," Rayce continued, smiling and nodding. "They weren't too happy, but hey, they taught me how to disappear, so what did they expect?"

"And what about the last four years," Molon asked. "What exactly were you doing?"

"Gotta make a living, man. I was running the shadows. Been a shade taking private gigs where I could find them."

"So how did you end up in a merc bar on a Theocracy world? Not exactly the best place to pick up shadow runs."

Rayce giggled as if laughing at a joke only voiced inside his own head.

"Yeah, man, my last run was a pretty major job against Dawnstar. NHE patron company with holdings in the Theocracy hired me and a team to swipe some key augment designs; cutting edge stuff. Dawnstar was steamed, so I asked for my payment in Theocreds. Figured I'd chill for a while waiting for opportunities. I was staying on the mainworld at the Furi Imperial Island Resort, lounging on the beach, when the bartender here messaged me about your posting. With all the heat from the PI and Dawnstar, spinward sounded like a good direction to go."

Molon was considering his response when Twitch

interjected through the monitor screen.

"*Too pat. I'm not buying it.*"

Rayce's smile faded as he glanced around again. "That's not very nice, disembodied voice lady. I'm being straight. Got no reason to lie, man."

"I believe him," Voide said.

"*You would,*" Twitch snapped.

"Ladies, please," Molon said, motioning his hands up as if to keep the two apart. Not like Twitch was coming through the monitor screen or vice versa anyway. "Mel, care to weigh in here?"

Mel nodded and looked at Sivio Rayce. She held out one of her slender, powder-blue hands, palm upright.

"Sir, would you take my hand please?"

"Sure, blue-chica. I'd love to," Rayce replied.

Without any hint of hesitation Rayce reached out to place his hand in Mel's. After only a few seconds, Mel jerked her hand back quickly as if she had been bitten by a snake.

"What is it, Mel?" Molon asked.

"Something's wrong," she answered.

Molon's hand casually dropped to his automag and quietly extracted it from its holster. He leveled it at Sivio Rayce below the table, watching the man out of the corner of his eye as he faced Mel.

"What is wrong?"

"Darkness," Mel replied, sounding a bit dazed as though she had just awakened from a dream.

"I would expect an assassin's mind to be dark, Mel. Was there anything in particular."

"I don't know," she replied, snapping out of her stupor to focus intently on her conversation with Molon. "I couldn't sense anything. No emotion. No deception. No desire. Only darkness."

Molon's ears flattened as he clicked the safety on his automag to the off position and readied his finger to fire.

"What does that mean?"

"It means I do not know if he is lying or telling the truth. I've never had that happen with a living being. I've only seen tactile holograms, robots, or very powerful psionics completely mask themselves from detection."

Rayce seemed utterly unaffected by the raised tension. He just kept that broad smile, nodded his head again, and tapped his temple with the forefinger of his gun hand, clearly not reaching for his weapon.

"Oh, blue-chica must be one of those mind-readers. Yeah,

396

that don't work on me. GalSec didn't want anyone forcing me to tell all their business. So they fixed up my noggin real good."

Molon mulled over the strange individual. An assassin with a redacted record who had disappeared for the last four years and suddenly wanted to join his crew was... off. Even stranger was the man's spacy demeanor. Molon could not believe that a top-notch GalSec hit man could be such a basket case. It had to be an act, but to what end?

"I'm sorry, Mr. Rayce," Molon said, looking Rayce in the eye and shaking his head. "There are too many variables. This just ain't sitting right with me. Twitch, you claim to be able to spot a plant. What's your call?"

"Honestly, between the pain meds and having to operate through a screen, I wouldn't trust my judgment right now. But if this guy has been on Furi longer than a few days, it's unlikely he is a plant."

Molon could hear the distraction and sadness in his XO's voice, even through the remote uplink. He knew Twitch was trying to focus and do her job, but everything she was facing with her paralysis had to be hard to push out of the way. Molon would have to walk the line between pressure and responsibility until Twitch had a chance to find her new normal.

"Yo, mysterious lady voice," Rayce interjected, gazing around as if speaking to the air. "I've been catching waves and taking in the suns for two weeks now."

"Dub, can you check that out with the hotel records?" Molon said, addressing the microphone in the remote setup which connected them with Dub and Twitch back on *Star Wolf.*

"Hacked in as soon as he mentioned the hotel, Cap," Dub replied. *"His photo is showing him as a guest registered under the name T.C. Head."*

Rayce once again looked a little dazed and was looking around for the person to go with Dub's voice.

"Whoa, now a bodyless dude voice," Rayce said as he focused his eyes on Molon once again. "Tell me you are hearing that too, man."

"Dub, how long has he been there?" Molon asked, ignoring Rayce's nonsense for the moment.

"Fifteen days paying with an anonymous, numbered debit account card that has been refilled twice with enough Theocreds to cover the room as well as room service charges and surfboard rentals."

"Yeah, ghostly dude voice," Rayce replied. "Imperial Island has some seriously awesome waves, man."

"I still don't like it," Molon grumbled.

"Look, Molon," Voide said in a low whisper, pulling Molon's ear close to her mouth. "Put him on my security team, and I'll take responsibility for him."

"You want this guy on your team?" Molon whispered back. "He looks like he is one or two brain cells away from a talking monkey. No way this wasteoid has been running the shadows for four years. More likely he's been in a drug den slowly killing his brain."

"I don't believe he is half the burnout he is pretending to be," Voide replied. "Sometimes deep cover agents don't know when to stop working a cover. Doubtless he figures GalSec isn't going to be looking for some brain-fried beach bum on a Theocracy world. I ran his current image against his GalSec service record photo through my facial recognition app. Didn't even trigger a possible partial. This guy is good."

Molon sat back up straight in his chair.

"Looks like your lucky day, Rayce. You have a billet on our security team if you want it. Since your rank, and everything else, is redacted, you'll start as a base security officer with the effective shipboard rank of a marine private. You okay with that?

Rayce was grinning broadly.

"Sure thing, man. Rank is just a system of oppression anyway. I don't wanna be bossing nobody around. You won't regret it, chica. You'll see."

"I already regret it," Voide replied. "And the name's Voide, not chica. See the sergeant over there and grab a chair until we are done."

Rayce looked over to the table where Sergeant Jackson "Banger" Padenesa was handling all the record keeping for the potential hires.

"Chilly," Rayce answered. "Hey, you guys buying the drinks?"

A silence and stern looks from Molon and Voide was their only reply.

"Okay, man, I'll cover my own tab. Jeesh, not a very good way to welcome a new guy."

Rayce staggered his way over to the bar and took a stool and began regaling the bartender with tales of monster waves and skimpy swimsuits.

Over the next hour they picked up a couple more unremarkable grunts. Voide had by far the most billets to fill as the boarding action, plus their previous encounters, had hit her marines the hardest. These guys were decently skilled, and

398

Molon wasn't worried about disciplinary issues with Voide in charge of them.

The next unusual individual seemed to be more machine than man. He had externally augmented arms, legs, and what seemed to be an external metal carapace around his torso covered lightly by a woven poncho. His right eye and ear were a single unit of cybernetic replacements connected by a sheet of steel that wrapped around his cheek on that side. The man was large, even slightly taller than Molon, and all the weight of all that hardware sent shivers through the floor when he walked. His wrinkled, bald head and thick neck were the only obviously biological parts of him left.

"Name and preferred call sign?" Molon asked, eyeing the individual warily.

"Sergei Orov," the man answered with a thick accent. "call sign Verks."

"Verks?" Molon asked. "What is that supposed to be?"

"No," Orov said shaking his head. "W-E-R-X. Like short for clock-vorks but spelled cooler. Vas smart-alek Major give me this name after my refit."

Molon punched Orov's name into the datapad.

Error: Record Not Found

"Ah, Cybertrooper," Molon said, staring at Orov. "We seem to be missing your service record. Why is that?"

"Saw line. Asked. Said ship vas hiring. Got in line. Can provide service records if needed, but don't have vit me."

"Ah, I see," Molon replied, noting the plate that held his service time rank held the barely-visible remnant of a first lieutenant's bar. "So, lieutenant, let me guess. Barton Rebellion?"

Orov's face went even more stony. He didn't answer but gave a slight nod.

"Empire or rebels?" Molon pressed.

Orov let out a deep sigh and scowled. He shook his head as he folded his large, cybernetic arms across his metallic chest.

"This matters now? Rebels gone. Empire gone. I'm just old Cybertrooper looking to find honest verk."

"So rebels, then," Molon snarked and saw Orov's face flush a bit as he tensed and his scowl deepened.

Molon knew provoking a Cybertrooper was not exactly the height of wisdom, but he figured that between himself and Voide, they could handle Orov if it came to that. Provocation was actually the best way to test for cyberpsychosis. Most suffering from the condition had very little self-control. They were like the human id cut loose. Most external augments

399

didn't exhibit cyberpsychosis nearly as frequently as those with extensive sub-cutaneous augmentation. Still it would be better to find out here than when locked in a space ship with a Cybertrooper gone off the rails.

"Vas like this," Orov explained, in a calm and level tone. "Barton colonies vanted independence. Empire said no. Empire von argument. End of story. Ancient history. So you need soldiers or vat?

Molon was satisfied. Orov seems a tough old bird, but sane enough. The Barton Rebellion was almost thirty years ago. Even at Orov's age, which Molon guessed was maybe late fifties, early sixties, these Cybertroopers were some of the best soldiers around. Their augments kept them from suffering some of the effects of aging that normal soldiers would have to deal with. As long as his parts were maintained and his mind stayed sharp, a Cybertrooper like Orov could hold his own against any other soldier.

"Okay, trooper. See the sergeant over there," Molon said, pointing to Banger's table. "He has a comms link set up to our ship's database and the planetary records. If you were part of the Barton Rebellion, he should be able to pull up your service record. Let him know if you have anything else to add. Provided there are no red flags, we could use an experienced combat officer."

"Thank you, captain," Orov said as he snapped to attention and issued a salute.

"No need for all that formality, lieutenant. For now, you will take your orders from Master Gunny Tibbs, but once you've been vetted, you will be given a billet in line with your rank and experience. You good with that?"

"Just happy to be verking again, captain."

With that, Orov lumbered over to where Banger was processing the applicants. When Orov moved, it felt like the whole bar shook.

"Dub?" Molon said into the remote link microphone.

"*Yeah, Cap?*"

"You think *Star Wolf*'s decking is up to the wear and tear a Cybertrooper is going to be putting on her? Guy has to be pushing two hundred kilos easy."

Dub laughed.

"*I'm over one-seventy myself, Cap. He's big, but he ain't no wider than me. Might have to reinforce his bunk, and he'll probably take two seats on an STS, but we'll work it out.*"

"And you can keep his parts in working order?"

"*Heck yeah. When I was apprenticing I used to build*

Cybertrooper models. Those guys were my heroes."

"Well try not to drool all over my shiny new marine," Voide quipped. "He might rust."

Half a dozen sub-par rejects later, a dark-haired man in his mid-twenties stepped up. He was not like most of the rest of the dregs. This guy was decked out in the latest street-armor outfit, a hodge-podge of style and functionality. He had a pulse blaster on his right hip, an automag on his left fitted for a cross-draw, and a needler pistol fitted in a shoulder holster. Molon noted all these weapons had the nub of a smart-weapon interface built into their grips.

"Expecting trouble?" Molon said as the man stepped up to the application table.

"Always," the man replied.

"Name and preferred call sign?" Molon said, noting out of the corner of his eye Voide was accessing something below the table; probably a weapon of her own just in case.

"Rafael Fuentes, but people call me Dex."

Molon punched up the name on his datapad but found not a military service record but a civilian *curriculum vitae* and a list of references. Fuentes had half a dozen computer and sensors certifications, a doctoral degree in starship sensor operations, and oddly enough a perfect marksmanship certificate from a gun club on Furi's mainworld.

"You lost, son? This ain't computer club tryouts. We're hiring mercenaries."

The man smiled, not at all rattled by Molon's sarcasm.

"That's my life," Fuentes replied. "Dex stands for cyberdecks," he said extending his right hand and showing a palm-mounted datajack that looked different from Twitch's or Dub's.

"*Wow,*" Dub replied through the uplink. "*That looks like a Novacorp C2700 CID/NID tactile port. That's top of the line hardware there, kid. How'd you afford a toy like that?*"

Fuentes beamed and nodded.

"Good eye," he said holding the interface up closer to the camera. "I definitely burned a half dozen paydays on this baby, but worth every credit."

"If you bought that and those toys you are loaded down with using just six paydays, I take it you aren't a desk jockey," Molon said. "Shade?"

Fuentes nodded.

"Yessir. Decker, mecher, and marksman extraordinaire."

"Well, if you are that good," Voide said, "then why would you take a massive pay cut and join a merc crew? Who is after

401

you?"

The fur on the back of Molon's neck stood up and his ears twitched forward. Voide was right. Top-notch shades could write their own ticket working as shadow runners for megacorps. Most mercs lived payday to payday, not knowing if there was going to be any pay at all. Something didn't add up.

"Last run went all bonzo. Corp snuck a mole onto the team. I was decked in remotely and barely jacked out before some of the meanest black ICE I've ever seen punched my ticket."

"And your team?" Molon asked.

"As far as I know the rest of the team got slagged. None showed at the rendezvous spot, no comms in three weeks to our check-in line. They're gone, and Zephyr Technologies knows a shade decker got away. Right now any ship moving away from PI space is a good place for me to be."

"*Zephyr Tech?*" Dub replied. "*Thought they were a biofoods company. What'd they have worth pillaging, nuclear carrots?*"

Fuentes looked around and lowered his voice.

"Let's just say their R&D division is working on more than ways to boost food's nutritional effects on the body."

Molon had heard enough. Shades were the scum of the earth to the megacorps, but to common people they were like the legendary Robin Hood, taking up the fight against the powers that controlled everyone's lives. In truth, most were just thugs hired by one oppressive corporation to raid another, but most shades had a strong sense of loyalty to a team. Once bonded, they didn't break faith easily. Molon had a few former shades on the team, and they were shorthanded on the bridge.

"I need a replacement sensors officer. You're more than qualified. You will get an honorary rank as ensign, as bridge crew must be officers, but don't go getting any ideas. You ain't in charge of nobody, so don't get heady with the rank. Crew is full of hard-core soldiers that earned their bars and stripes, so don't give them a reason to frag you. We clear?"

"As crystal," Fuentes replied.

"Good. See the sergeant over there and he'll get you sorted. Welcome aboard."

Fuentes nodded and walked away.

"So we're babysitting deckheads now?" Voide grumbled.

"He's got great skills we need, and he is clearly no stranger to combat. If he's been running the shadows, he's gotten the chance to shoot at more than gun range targets. He'll be fine."

"He has a naïve confidence," Mel added. "He will need

guidance, Molon."

"He'll be on Hoot's team. They speak the same lingo and Hoot is not much older. They'll be fine."

The next interesting candidate was a man in his early forties with a receding hairline and a well-developed paunch around his middle. Not much taller than Mel, the man's slightly skewed eyes, large nose, and somewhat nasal voice pattern were an unusual mix.

"Name and preferred call sign?"

"Retired Lieutenant JG Dassous Ajam, formerly of the Imperial Navy. Call sign is Ace. I'm a pilot."

Molon pulled up Ajam's impressive service record.

"Lots of shiny bits here," Molon said noting the medals Ajam's record showed he had earned. "Career man. In at eighteen, put in your twenty, then retired. What have you been up to for the last few years?"

"Enjoying my retirement. Traveling, sight-seeing, you know, living the life."

"More like eating the life," Voide quipped, noting the man's rotund middle.

"Ah yes," Ajam laughed, rubbing his stomach. "Let's just say I haven't been as diligent keeping up my service time PT. But then again, pilots burn a lot of chair time, so I would be lying if I said I was ever in tip-top shape, even while I served."

Molon did note the only smudge on the man's records were the note on every physical evaluation that he needed to lose weight. As far as dings on the record went, that was one Molon could live with, and with Twitch out, even with Angel they were short on pilots. Twitch's second pilot, Lieutenant Lawrence 'Angel' Mallory had been killed in *Revenge's* boarding action, and they were already down a pilot after one had been killed while defending a grounded STS on previous mission. Twitch and Z-Man had been it, with Warbird being able to help in a pinch.

"What brings you out of retirement, then?" Molon asked. "And signing on with a merc crew no less. Surely the academy would love to have a decorated officer come back to teach the new recruits."

"Truth be told, captain, I'm bored out of my skull. If I tried flying a desk, I'd lose my mind. I miss being out there; being at the helm."

Molon nodded.

There was a pause, and then Ajam cleared his throat again. "Let me ask you, captain," he said, eyeing where Rayce was sitting at the bar. "Did that strange fellow over there sign on with your crew as well?"

"What's that to you?" Molon asked, laying his datapad on the table as he wondered at Ajam's odd question.

"It's just that I have seen him around the beach. I'm not sure he is right...in the head I mean."

Molon smiled.

"Don't worry about him, my security chief here will make sure to keep an eye on him."

The man smiled and nodded as he pointed to his service record on Molon's datapad.

"I'm a top pilot, captain. Help me do what I love to do again."

"Fair enough, Ace. Check in with the sergeant."

A few other applicants stood out and were hired, but Molon was growing tired as the line wound down. The final applicant for the day was easily the most unexpected, Cybertroopers, shades, and brain-fried assassins notwithstanding.

A huge Dractauri approached the recruitment table. Dractauri were interstellar nomads. They were reptilian with four solid legs beneath the main part of their body but a forward torso that bent upward, like the earthly centaur legends. The scaly torso held high a fearsome-looking lizard head and large, human-like arms and hands covered in scales. At the end of each three-fingered and one-opposable thumbed hand were wicked-looking black claws, still sharply pointed but filed down for improved manual dexterity.

The Dractauri wore no clothes to speak of, but did have several utility belts and harnesses hooked around to carry tools, weapons, and anything else they needed. While there was a long knife sheathed at one side, the Dractauri carried no other obvious weapons. Instead, he looked more like a walking tool chest.

Dractauri could not speak Galactic Common. Their vocal chords couldn't form most of the sounds, so typically they wore collars with a translator module attached. The module would render their own sub-sonic speech into audible Galactic Common while sub-sonically translating other languages back to them.

"Name and preferred call sign?" Molon asked.

"*My name is unpronounceable to you, and the closest transliteration is devoid of beauty. The humans I have encountered have called me 'Draco'. I believe they intended it as a pejorative. However, it is not displeasing when translated to my own language, so I will accept this moniker.*"

404

Molon stifled a smile at the response. Dinos, Dracos, Sauros, were all slurs referencing Dractauri. They were interstellar gypsies most believed had fled across the Stygian Rift far rimward and tailward from Humaniti space.

"I take it you have no service record?" Molon asked.

"*My people have no use for such trivia. I am what you would call an engineer. That is sufficient.*"

"And how did you wind up at a Humaniti merc bar looking to join a crew? I thought Dractauri only flew on Dractauri ships?"

"*Our ship was badly damaged by pirates. We escaped to Furi, but the water-world was unsuitable for us. The Furian government directed us to Irnedag, whose mainworld is a desert world more suitable to our physiology. Our ship was gone, so the crew decided to settle there. I am not a settler. I am an engineer.*"

"Dub, can *Star Wolf* accommodate a Dractauri?"

"*Should be no issue, Cap. If he can tell me what he needs, we can rig something up.*"

Before Molon could answer, Draco replied.

"*I require nothing unusual. I sleep standing, so a corner of a shuttle bay or cargo area would be sufficient. Most engineering sections are dehumidified, so that will be fine. I have a portable heating device mounted on my person, so your temperature settings also should not adversely affect my person. So may I nest with you?*"

That last comment Molon took in stride. Sometimes idioms or cultural sayings, translated literally, didn't always come out smoothly in Galactic Common, but he expected Draco was only talking about joining the crew, not cohabiting.

"Welcome to the nest, Draco," Molon said, eliciting a fearsome-looking toothy smile from the Dractauri. "See the sergeant over there and he will find some way to fill out your forms. You will report to Chief Dubronski, my chief engineer."

"*I quiver with anticipation,*" Draco replied. Molon wondered if sarcasm existed for the Dractauri.

And just like that, they were done. There were still a few open billets, but they had a few more stops at quality worlds before they flew into the danger of the Occupied Worlds. Molon expected to have a full crew complement before he took the ship into danger. He only wondered if that crew would find a way to include Twitch. Doc and Dub were working hard to come up with a solution, but the rest was up to her.

An hour or so later, with their gear packed up, the chosen recruits had been led to the docking pad where *Star Wolf*'s cargo STS was parked. As Banger and a couple of other marines loaded the last of their gear and supplies into the STS, Molon addressed the new additions to the crew.

"Listen up," Molon barked in a commanding tone as he walked up and down the line of new recruits. "You came looking for work and have been selected for service aboard the unaligned mercenary destroyer *Star Wolf*. If you wanted a safe, stable, milk-and-bread runner, this ain't your ship.

"*Star Wolf,* after a stop or two along the way, is heading to the Occupied Worlds. I aim to take this ship directly into the conflict to assist the cause of the Theocracy. Anybody not looking for danger in your next billet, feel free to step off now and I wish you well. Anybody that stays and boards this STS is voting with their feet to become a part of this crew and to be willing to pull their weight against any trouble that finds us."

None of those lined up so much as twitched nervously, much less stepped out of line. That was a good sign.

"This is my ship," Molon continued. "You will follow my orders and the orders of my command officers. You will respect the chain of command inasmuch as you are under orders. Should the situation arise where you are not able to receive orders from a superior, you will be expected to use your judgment and experience to carry out the mission to the best of your ability."

That brought a cacophony of responses from hu-ahs, to amens, to emphatic nods.

"*Star Wolf* is not just a job," Molon continued. "It is a family. You fight for your family the way you would fight for yourselves. Expect the same in return. As a member of this family, you give your all. If a time comes when you no longer wish to be a part of this family, let me know and we will put you ashore at the first possible port-of-call. Until then, do your job, earn your keep, and you will have a home aboard *Star Wolf* as long as you like. Any questions?"

Not a single sound came from the line of recruits. None stepped away either, so Molon took their silence as assent.

"Very well. Step aboard the STS, and Lieutenant Sarum, call sign 'Mel', will have your billet agreements for you to sign as well as your rack assignments. Welcome to *Star Wolf*."

*****

As Molon piloted the STS back toward *Star Wolf* waiting in orbit around Zaros, John slipped into the copilot's seat. He had been on Zaros picking up a few more components from a medical warehouse there while the rest of the command crew had been hiring new recruits.

406

"So then," John said. "I have the cybernetic prosthetics and mobility chair all set for Twitch, and Dub has some nifty ideas about how to utilize her CID to do even more. I found the biomechanical interfaces he asked me to pick up on Zaros, so that's about all we can do until we get to Sarren and see what is available there. She's no longer looking to toss herself out an airlock anymore, at least as far as I can tell, though I daresay she is a long way from fully adjusting."

"It will take time, John," Molon replied. "Thank you for all you have done. Do you really think the folks on Sarren will be able to do more?"

John scratched his head, but the look on his face was not the doctor's usual cheerful optimism.

"I made full use of Dr. Merriam's library while we were planetside on Furi main world. There have been some pretty stunning recent advances. Honestly though, Molon, I won't know for sure until we get there and I can talk to their chief of cybernetic surgery."

"So you're saying she is going to need to be like our new Cybertrooper, or worse yet like Simmons?"

"Not necessarily. I haven't ruled out a surgical solution completely just yet. It is hard to say to what degree until the top spinal surgeons at Sarren examine her for themselves. Even if they are able to restore some permanent functionality, she won't ever be the person she was again. She is going to have to get used to that at some point. Hopefully Angel can help her adjust."

Molon rubbed the back of his head as he let the STS's autopilot controls take over. Twitch might have gotten over her despondency, but Molon wasn't sure if she would ever get over her anger at him for not letting her die on *Revenge*.

"I don't know, Doc. Twitch is one of the strongest people I have ever met, but she has a long way to go. You and I have to be ready. She's got a lot of anger that needs to go somewhere, and we are likely to get the brunt of it."

"I expect as much," John said, nodding. "Given her situation and your desire to keep her as XO, are you sure it is wise to head to the Occupied Worlds after we leave Sarren? Maybe some of those milk-and-bread runs might be a better choice until she gets used to things."

Molon shook his head emphatically.

"Doc, I appreciate your concern, but I've known Twitch most of my adult life. If there is one thing she needs, it is feeling needed. The best thing I can do for her is get her somewhere she will be too busy surviving to mope about what she can't do."

"I guess that's it then," John said.

"Yep, Doc. We head for Sarren. After you wrap up with whatever those fine folks can do for Twitch, then we are off to the Occupied Worlds."

"Looking for trouble, I imagine?"

"Yep, if we're going to get Twitch back, I'm aimin' to pick a fight."

Glossary of Technology and Terms

Anti-gravity systems—Anti-gravity systems are generally vehicle mounted and allow ground transportation to function as gravatic hovercraft. STS-capable craft use anti-gravity systems for initial liftoff. These, in combination with thrusters or other more conventional propulsion systems, work together to achieve flight. Anti-gravity ground vehicles lack the vertical propulsion systems of STS craft and are generally not sealed to withstand the vacuum of space or pressure differentials that STS craft are built for. Dawnstar among others have toyed with the idea of self-contained STS suits, similar to the old diving bell suits for early deep sea exploration, but the inability to carry enough power for both flight and any meaningful offense/defense have made this line of research and development largely impractical.

Battle Carriers—these large, skeletal structures are little more than giant voidspace drives. They have docking bays large enough to transport several smaller ships, such as destroyers, pocket carriers, and pocket battleships, through voidspace to a deployment location. They allow for combat ships to be built less expensively and with more space for crew, fighters, or armaments by foregoing internal bulky VS drives and instead depending on battle carriers to transport them to other star systems.

Battle dress—Battle dress is fully powered, military-grade combat armor. There is a small, self-contained power system in the suit that drives not only the computerized and scanning functions, but can also be used to power heavier energy weapons without bulky external power packs. It is bulkier than combat armor, so not quite as well suited for boarding actions aboard smaller ships. This armor really shines on planetary missions as it not only offers a full array of environmental and hostile-atmospheric conditions but offers the best protection against a broad spectrum of weaponry as well. Due to its

409

slightly more bulky dimensions, boarding parties will generally intersperse no more than 20% of personnel in battle dress, with the remainder protected by unpowered combat armor. The tradeoffs for the bulk, however, are much greater physical strength due to the powered servos built into the suit. Battle dress is the pinnacle of personal defense armor.

Brightworlder—Slang term for someone who grew up on a high-light world, possibly with multiple main stars in the system or otherwise highly proximate to their system's star. Their vision tends to require higher concentrations of light to function and is often completely blinded in lower-light environments, requiring light-enhancing optics or other technical aids to function in low-light environments.

Combat armor—Unpowered military-grade vac-suits reinforced with armor to be highly resistant to physical and energy weapons. They are also shielded from radiation and provide a range of protection for different environmental conditions. They contain a full six-hours of independent life support. Combat armor is agile and only slightly bulkier than normal clothing. It is much more flexible than lower TL vac-suits and allows mobility around even the tighter corridors of smaller ships.

Coreward—A galactic "direction" indicating space located closer to the galactic core than one's current position. Space is three-dimensional, but on a galactic scale, space as we know it in our little section of our little arm of our little spiral galaxy is relatively flat. The Milky Way is a rotating disc that is itself in motion throughout the universe. There is no such thing as fixed points of reference. Normal terrestrial directions are meaningless in space, so galactic directions are used in order to indicate direction relative to one's current position.

Cybertrooper—A soldier who has undergone major external augmentation. Almost all Cybertroopers were in some way related to the Barton Rebellion.

Darkworlder—Slang term for someone who has lived for a considerable time on a low-light world. Their vision is likely to be adapted to lower light, and they may even require light-restricting goggles to function in normal or high-light environments.

Denseworlder—Slang term for someone who has lived a considerable time on a high-gravity world. If they are indigenous to a high-gravity world, their physiology is often much shorter and stockier than normal, with them exhibiting much greater physical strength in lower gravity environments.

ECM—Electronic counter-measures. Electronic jamming devices designed to proactively interfere with the targeting systems for ship's weapons and/or missiles.

GalSec—Galactic Security Force. This was the intelligence arm of the Old Empire that was inherited by Zarsus and the Provisional Imperium. While they technically reported to the Emperor, they were historically run with a considerable degree of independence under command of the Overdirector of Galactic Security. The OGS has been even less inclined to take orders or report more than basic data to High Archon Zarsus since the Shattering. It is almost an independent shadow organization with access to Imperium ships and data but run largely as a separate quasi-military intelligence organization with its own goals and ends.

Gravatic stabilizers—An adaptive technology based around the principles of anti-gravity systems. These are ship-mounted systems designed to regulate gravity aboard ship, even during intense maneuvering and variable gravity conditions near large planetary bodies or stars. These, combined with inertial dampeners, are what allow crews of ships to function during space battles or exploration of varying interstellar conditions. They serve to help "normalize" gravity and inertia aboard ship. Extreme maneuvering or external conditions, such as those within the gravity well of a black hole or hypergiant star might overload the compensation abilities of these systems.

Lightworlder—Slang term used to describe someone who has lived a considerable time on a low gravity world. Generally their physique is unaccustomed to standard gravity, and depending on how far below standard gravity their world is, may even require mechanical accommodation to function in higher gravity.

Pocket Carrier/Battleship—All carriers and battleships are classed as capital ships, but smaller versions, commonly called pocket ships, are small enough to be transported in a voidspace-capable battle carrier. The use of battle carriers allows pocket carriers, destroyers, and pocket battleships to forego the tonnage and internal space required for VS drives in favor of extra armaments, crew space, or fighter capacity. Pocket ships generally serve as system defense boats that can be deployed further out if needed, with the assistance of a

411

battle carrier.

Proximity jump—A maneuver where a voidspace-capable ship uses unmapped rabbit hole voidspace entry points to quickly close and launch a sneak attack on another ship. This deprives the attacked ship of the time to prepare, depressurize the hull, or utilize other defensive measures before attacks are launched against them. This requires extensive knowledge of rabbit holes within a system, as well as monitoring beacons directly in front of rabbit holes that can communicate with ships preparing to transition but still in voidspace. The Prophane in particular have been known to utilize this tactic to ambush enemy patrols. Their affinity with voidspace allows them to do this even in systems they have not previous entered, and apparently without the need for pre-set monitoring beacons.

Rimward—A galactic "direction" indicating space located closer to the galactic rim or edge than one's current position. Space is three-dimensional, but on a galactic scale, space as we know it in our little section of our little arm of our little spiral galaxy is relatively flat. (See Coreward, above.) The Milky Way is a rotating disc that is itself in motion throughout the universe. There is no such thing as fixed points of reference. Normal terrestrial directions are meaningless in space, so galactic directions are used in order to indicate direction relative to one's current position.

Ronin—A top freelance soldier for hire with no military, corporate, or team affiliations. A true lone wolf. Generally these are ex-military or former GalSec enforcers, but can be former gang members as well. They are frequently enhanced with cybernetics designed to improve combat or infiltration abilities. There are no mediocre ronin, as mercs without some type of team or backup don't last long enough to make a reputation. Ronin are the best of the best in the mercenary trade, and are feared and respected even by military commanders and top corporate security.

SEC-COM—Military term for "secure communication". SEC-COMs can take the form of heavily encoded electronic messages, secured courier delivered communiques, or even personal messages sent via emissaries or spies, all according to the particular needs of the situation.

Shade Mercs—Freelance mercenary teams that operate outside military, security, or gang structures. They are self-contained soldier-of-fortune teams and generally consist of members with a widely variable skill set, equipping them to complete a wide range of infiltration, espionage, or security assignments. Generally shade mercs focus on jobs for corporations, usually on core worlds, although some shade merc teams have retained a more deliberately military bent. Unlike merc ships or merc crews, shade mercs tend to be based on a single world, or at least within a single core system as opposed to the unaligned merc crews who have their own ships and who focus more on smuggling or interstellar assignments.

Shadows—Leaders of shade merc teams. Shadows are usually former military officers or security heads who have far-reaching connections to the corporate or mercenary world. Shadows are what make the difference between effective shade merc teams and regular hired muscle. They are strategic planners and excel at finding and organizing individuals of widely varied skill sets into effective mercenary units.

Shattering—Once all of Humaniti existed in a single, massive star empire. There had been a legacy of cooperation and expansion for centuries. Emperor Zariah Halberan and Empress Rhia Sagum-Halberan had four children, fraternal quadruplets, three sons and one daughter. Tradition dictated that a chosen Halberan heir was given control of a large part of the Empire to govern for the four years prior to their coronation and appointment as heir-apparent. This was to demonstrate they were fit and able to take over the throne of the Empire of Humaniti. Since Zariah had four potential heirs, he decided to give each of his children a different segment of the Empire to govern. After their testing period, he would evaluate each and choose an heir.

On the night this was to happen, Zariah and Rhia were assassinated before naming an heir. It was unclear who was behind the assassination, and suspicion was raised against each of the four potential heirs. Per legal precedent, High Archon Zarsus, Commander in Chief of the Empire military, enacted marshal law and established the Provisional Imperium until the guilty party could be determined and a suitable successor named. Extended delays in the investigation protracted Zarsus' control, and each of the Halberan children returned to their respective governing seats for the section of the Empire they had managed.

Once it was clear that Zarsus had no intention of surrendering the throne, the Empire was split into factions following each of

413

the four heirs, plus the tailward core of the Provisional Imperium that remained under Zarsus. Tubal aligned the area under his control with Zarsus, in hopes of currying favor and being named the rightful heir to the Halberan throne. Seth and Phoebe, their sections of the empire sharing a large border, aligned and put their support behind Seth as the rightful heir.

Enoch, an ordained priest of the Lion of Judah, and leader of the religious movement called the Faithful, seceded from the Provisional Imperium and established the region under his control as a religious protectorate for all members of the Faithful. Enoch has expressed no desire to seek his father's throne, but was drawn into the conflict as a consequence of incessant attacks by Tubal and Zarsus, as well as the Provisional Imperium's alignment with Humaniti's ancient enemy, the Daemi.

This division of the Empire of Humaniti is consequently referred to as the Shattering. The Shattering took place eight years prior to the events detailed in *Star Wolf*.

Sophont—From the Greek σοφός (sophos) meaning "wise". Sophont is any sentient being with intellect and self-awareness equal to or exceeding humankind's.

Spinal Mount—A large weapon whose core runs along the "spine" of a ship. In essence, the ship is literally built around the weapon. Spinal mounts take up tremendous real estate within ships and use a great deal of power, thus they are generally only found on large, capital-class warships. No commercial vessels, within the realm of Humaniti at least, may be legally equipped with spinal mount weapons. They are military grade only. Spinal mount weapons may be very large lasers, plasma cannons, meson guns, neural weapons, or even solid projectile weapons, though this last category would be extremely rare, due both to the space needed and to the danger of storing a large quantity of explosive ordinance on board a space-going vessel.

Spinward—A galactic "direction" indicating space located in the same direction as the galaxy is spinning relative to one's current position. Space is three-dimensional, but on a galactic scale, space as we know it in our little section of our little arm of our little spiral galaxy is relatively flat. The Milky Way is a rotating disc that is itself in motion throughout the universe. There is no such thing as fixed points of reference. Normal terrestrial directions are meaningless in space, so galactic directions are used in order to indicate direction relative to one's current position.

STS—Surface to Space capable craft. A general term used to describe all small craft designed to land on planets but which also have the ability to enter near-orbit. All shuttlecraft designed to go from non-atmosphere-capable ships to the surface fall into this category. They can be any size from single-passenger shuttles all the way up to large cargo/personnel transports. They are generally unarmed or very lightly armed ships and are considered non-combatants. This is the general feature that distinguishes them from combat craft, such as fighters or gunships, which may also have surface-to-space capabilities.

SysSec—Short for System Security. Most star systems with worlds of any import will have some ships devoted to system defense. These are similar to U.S. Coast Guard vessels or Merchant Marines of 21st century Earth. They can be associated with the military of that faction if a military base is housed in the system, but are usually civilian paramilitary forces. Quite often these ships are decently armed but are not equipped with Voidspace Drives, so they are not capable of FTL travel. This restricts them to operation within a single star system unless they have the aid of a battle carrier.

Tailward—A galactic "direction" indicating space located in the direction opposite the galactic spin relative to one's current position. Space is three-dimensional, but on a galactic scale, space as we know it in our little section of our little arm of our little spiral galaxy is relatively flat. The Milky Way is a rotating disc that is itself in motion throughout the universe. There is no such thing as fixed points of reference. Normal terrestrial directions are meaningless in space, so galactic directions are used in order to indicate direction relative to one's current position. (See also Coreward, Spinward, and Rimward, above)

TL—Technology level. Before the Shattering, many systems benefitted from interstellar trade and featured high technology levels even in non-core systems. Since the Shattering, however, interstellar trade has severely diminished and each system's TL will only be as high as they can sustain without relying on interstellar trade. This severely reduces the TL of all but key core systems with either abundant in-system resources and production capabilities or stable trade with other core systems. Every device has a TL level associated with it. The TL denotes the general TL level a world must be able to sustain in order to produce those devices. TLs run on a scale from 1-15, with 21st century Earth being around TL8.

Vac-suit—Lower tech vacuum suits are bulky, Jules Verne-like inventions. At TL7 and above, they become much more resistant to damage and much lighter and less cumbersome. The common general issue vac-suits aboard most commercial ships are TL6-8, while those aboard fighting ships are TL8-10. TL10 suits are well protected as well as having HUD units in the helmets. Above TL10, suits that are not already integreated with combat armor can be refined either for increased durability and functionality, or made much lighter and maneuverable. At TL13, the vac-suits are no more cumbersome than regular clothing and can even have disguise capabilities, most frequently as normal clothing. This enables executives or political leaders to have the appearance of casual ease while maintaining a constant state of readiness in the event of boarding or hostile actions.

VDEs—Voidspace disruption emitters. These are ship-mounted devices that scramble the frequencies used to open voidspace jump portals. When used in relatively close proximity to a particular portal, it will prevent ships using voidspace jump drives from opening the portals and entering or exiting voidspace. VDEs can be mounted on fighters, but draw a lot of power, thus preventing any other energy-type weapons or defenses on such small craft. They are much more commonly used on 50+ ton craft. Due to their extreme tech level, post-Shattering there are very few factions that are still able to produce or maintain VDEs. Dawnstar, the Angelicum, and the Daemi are the only factions in the known part of the galaxy who have them in any large supply, though any faction may have at least a handful of ships equipped with VDEs spread among their entire fleet.

Afterword

Part of the challenge of writing a Christian Speculative Fiction book is that often people see an inherent conflict within the term itself. Speculative Fiction is about exploring the realm of possibilities, and within the sub-genre of Science Fiction, this means wrestling with the realities of science as far as it applies. From a Christian perspective, some see this as dangerous ground upon which to tread, fraught with the dangers of writing something that countermands or contradicts God's word in Scripture.

Being a Christian, however, is viewed by non-Christian readers of Speculative Fiction, especially Science Fiction, as somehow contrary to the genre. They do not believe a Christian author can possibly let themselves explore the full realm of possibilities while boxing themselves in with some narrow, dogmatic view of the universe.

I hope, having read Star Wolf, you now see that a middle-ground is indeed possible. While this novel is a far cry from what could be considered hard Science Fiction, I hope I have treated science as fairly as possible where it ran this side of the edge of speculation. Even where I exceeded the bounds of current scientific and technological discovery, I did strive to maintain speculative laws of physics and to design a system that is at least internally consistent. Where I did deal with things like medical situations and lower technology, I sought the advice of experts in their fields to ground my fiction in fact as far as possible.

On the spiritual side, while I realize some people will always find things to take issue with, I do believe I kept my speculation within the borders of the gray area. I am not aware of anything within Star Wolf that directly contradicts explicit Scripture, but there is quite a bit that pushes the limits of human tradition and interpretation. It is important for Christian readers to realize, I am not teaching doctrine here, I am writing a Speculative Fiction novel that, as far as I am aware, is still honoring to my Christian faith and the word of God.

I hope everyone found this novel to be a happy middle ground that can be enjoyed by both Christians and non-Christians alike. I make no apologies for the spiritual content within the book, but I also feel I kept it situation-relevant, where germane to the characters or setting at hand. I feel I fairly represented both believers and non-believers in the story, and made no attempt to demonize one more than the other. Star Wolf certainly has unbelieving bad-guys, but more than one of the main characters in the story are not really believers. I also represent some believers who have clearly taken their interpretation of acting upon their faith far beyond the boundaries of Scripture, and are called to task on that fact. In short, my intent with Star Wolf, as with all my novels, is to make it approachable, accessible, and enjoyable regardless of one's worldview.

Beyond this point in the afterword, I will share a bit more about the underpinnings of the author's own worldview. In other books I have shared pieces of my personal journey to faith, so I won't rehash that here, but I do not want to end this afterword without at least giving the opportunity for deeper understanding of my worldview for those interested. If you are not interested and consequently choose to skip the remainder of the afterword, be reassured that you will miss out on nothing story-related . I do hope, however, that if you have read this far, you will see it through and explore with me some of the aspects and reasons behind my worldview.

Now, I hope that if you have read this far in the Afterword, it is because God may have you searching for truth in your own life. I have deeply researched the historicity, the archeological evidence, and the truth claims of the Bible for many years and found the more I learn, the more reasonable and solid my faith has become. There are many resources along these lines, so I won't do a disservice to the field of apologetics by trying to do a *Cliff's Notes* version in an Afterword, but I do want to share a few basic truths with those seeking and open to hearing what the Bible has to say.

1)   We are all sinners (Romans 3:10; 3:23). That is hard to hear, but the fact is there are two kinds of people in the world, perfect people and sinners. If you aren't one, you are the other. If you truly believe you are the former, there isn't much else to discuss. Most people, however, are honest enough to admit they have lied, they have not always honored their father and mother, they have lusted, they have coveted, they have hated someone. Any of these things puts you firmly in the category of sinner.

2)   We cannot remove our own sin. God in the Bible says the wages of sin is death. If, like many of the other world religions teach, we could counterbalance or work off our own

sin by praying, giving alms, making pilgrimages, doing good deeds, meditation, or whatever, then God lied in the Bible and Jesus died for nothing. In Matthew 26:39-44 Jesus prayed three times asking if there were any other way, and yet still He went to the cross and died. If there could have been any way apart from Jesus that man could be saved, Jesus would not have died upon the cross (Acts 4:12).

3)   We will stand before God and be judged one day (Hebrews 9:27). God created us and He has the right to judge His creation. He takes no pleasure in the death of sinful man but truly desires that all may come to repentance and faith (Ezekiel 33:11). To that end, God has made a way for our sin to be forgiven and for us to be restored to righteousness.

4)   Jesus is that way (John 14:6). Jesus says "I am the way, the truth and the life; no one comes to the Father but through Me." Some have called this narrow-minded, arrogant or elitist, but if we open our hearts and minds to the truth, God was not obligated to make *any* way for man to be saved. He did so because He loved the world and mankind (John 3:16) and wanted us to have a hope. Does a drowning man look at the person throwing them a rope from a lifeboat and say, "Don't you have another way? That is very narrow-minded for you to only have one rope for me to choose from. I prefer a life preserver or life jacket instead." How silly would that be? No, a drowning person would grab onto that rope and hold on for all they were worth and be very grateful to the person who had tossed it to them. Yet this is exactly what society has conditioned us to do in response to the gospel. We sneer at the rope and criticize the boat captain who has thrown it to us.

If you are seeking truth, then the one true truth that exists is Jesus. A way has been made by a loving God for you to be saved from judgment and wrath. All that is needed is for you to recognize and repent (turn away from) your sin and put your faith in Jesus Christ. Grab onto that rope and hold on for all you are worth. You can do that by saying a prayer wherever you are, asking that God forgive your sins and draw you to Himself.

If you have done, or are willing to do that, you have taken the first step. The road does not end there, however. Profession of faith in Christ is not a "get out of hell free" card. There is nothing in the Bible that mirrors the false teaching of "easy believism." Faith in Christ means living your life for Him. Three times in John chapter 14, Jesus equates loving Him with obedience. So how do you know what to obey? You need discipleship. You need to find a Bible-believing church in your area and get plugged into not only Sunday services, but Bible study classes as well. Every day you eat food to nourish your body; in the same way, set some time aside every day to spend in prayer and in God's word to nourish your spirit.

You may have questions still. As you read and study you may have things come up that you don't understand. Your first resource should be your local pastor or teacher at the church you attend. If you don't find the answers there, I might suggest a few websites that might help. These are excellent resources for Christian apologetics and questions about the Christian life.

1)   www.carm.org This is the website of the Christian Apologetics & Research Ministry. It is an excellent site to find many answers to a broad range of questions.

2)   www.reasonablefaith.org This is the website of Dr. William Lane Craig, noted Christian apologist and speaker.

3)   Beyond those websites, if you have specific questions about the gospel or Christianity and cannot find the answers with either your local clergy or the above sites, you can contact me with questions at haoxiaoxi@gmx.com. Please be aware, I am opening this email up to my readership as a resource and help. I will not argue or debate questions I feel are aimed in that direction, but will gladly do whatever I can to help sincere enquiries concerning biblical truth. There are numerous debate boards on Facebook and elsewhere for those looking for that, but this email address is for sincere seekers of truth who have earnestly sought answers elsewhere and yet have been unable to find those answers. I cannot promise to be able to answer every question, but coming from the background of a skeptic and having researched truth claims and studied apologetics for several years, I hope that I can be a resource to anyone sincerely seeking faith or struggling for answers. Your patience with my response times is appreciated, as I have a number of responsibilities on my plate, but ministering to seeking souls is a high priority.

Finally, for those who do not have specific faith-based questions but would like to send fan-mail, questions, comments, feedback, etc. specifically regarding any of my books themselves, those types of responses can be sent to chadashchronicles@gmail.com. If there are things sent here requiring a response, please be patient and know I will do my best to respond. I also have an author page up on Facebook at:

https://www.facebook.com/DavidGlennJohnson, so feel free to drop by and like my page, and keep your eyes out for new projects and new releases.

By His grace,

David G. Johnson

For those seeking works from other Christian Independent Authors, join the Christian Indie Authors Readers Group on Facebook: https://www.facebook.com/groups/291215317668431/

Made in the USA
Lexington, KY
27 October 2017